10/13

THE ONE-EYED MAN

The Imager Portfolio

Imager
Imager's Challenge
Imager's Intrigue
Scholar
Princeps
Imager's Battalion
Antiagon Fire
Regis Regis (forthcoming)

The Corean Chronicles

Legacies
Darknesses
Scepters
Alector's Choice
Cadmian's Choice
Soarer's Choice
The Lord-Protector's Daughter
Lady-Protector

The Saga of Recluce

The Magic of Recluce
The Towers of the Sunset
The Magic Engineer
The Order War
The Death of Chaos
Fall of Angels
The Chaos Balance
The White Order
Colors of Chaos
Magi'i of Cyador
Scion of Cyador
Wellspring of Chaos
Ordermaster
Natural Ordermage
Mage-Guard of Hamor
Arms-Commander
Heirs of Cyador (forthcoming)

The Spellsong Cycle

The Soprano Sorceress
The Spellsong War
Darksong Rising
The Shadow Sorceress
Shadowsinger

The Ecolitan Matter

Empire & Ecolitan (comprising *The Ecolitan Operation* and *The Ecologic Secession*)
Ecolitan Prime (comprising *The Ecologic Envoy* and *The Ecolitan Enigma*)
The Forever Hero (comprising *Dawn for a Distant Earth*, *The Silent Warrior*, and *In Endless Twilight*)

Timegods' World (comprising *Timediver's Dawn* and *The Timegod*)

The Ghost Books

Of Tangible Ghosts
The Ghost of the Revelator
Ghost of the White Nights
Ghost of Columbia (comprising *Of Tangible Ghosts* and *The Ghost of the Revelator*)

The Hammer of Darkness
The Green Progression
The Parafaith War
Adiamante
Gravity Dreams
Octagonal Raven
Archform: Beauty
The Ethos Effect
Flash
The Eternity Artifact
The Elysium Commission
Viewpoints Critical
Haze
Empress of Eternity

L. E. MODESITT, JR.

THE ONE-EYED MAN

A Fugue, with Winds and Accompaniment

A TOM DOHERTY ASSOCIATES BOOK

NEW YORK

THE ONE-EYED MAN: A FUGUE, WITH WINDS AND ACCOMPANIMENT

Copyright © 2013 by L. E. Modesitt, Jr.

"New World Blues" copyright © 2012 by L. E. Modesitt, Jr.

A Tor Book
Published by Tom Doherty Associates, LLC
175 Fifth Avenue
New York, NY 10010

www.tor-forge.com

Tor® is a registered trademark of Tom Doherty Associates, LLC.

Library of Congress Cataloging-in-Publication Data

Modesitt, L. E., Jr., 1943–
   The one-eyed man : a fugue, with winds and accompaniment /
L. E. Modesitt, Jr.—First Edition.
        p. cm.
   "A Tom Doherty Associates book."
   ISBN 978-0-7653-3544-9 (hardcover)
   ISBN 978-1-4668-2235-1 (e-book)
   1. Imaginary wars and battles—Fiction.   2. Imagery (Psychology)—Fiction.
3. Science fiction.   I. Title.
   PS3563.O264 O53 2013
   813'.54—dc23

                                                          2013022128

Tor books may be purchased for educational, business, or promotional use. For information on bulk purchases, please contact Macmillan Corporate and Premium Sales Department at 1-800-221-7945, extension 5442, or write specialmarkets@macmillan.com.

First Edition: September 2013

Printed in the United States of America

0 9 8 7 6 5 4 3 2 1

For David Hartwell, without whom this book would not exist

There are none so blind as those who will not see.

THE
ONE-EYED
MAN

1

Court procedures on Bachman were old-fashioned, requiring all parties be present. So there I was, after two hours of evidence and testimony, on one side of the courtroom, standing beside my advocate, Jared Hainsun, before the judge's bench, and on the other side was Chelesina, with her advocate. Chelesina didn't look in my direction. That didn't surprise me. For the three years before she left, she'd barely looked at me even when she'd been looking at me. That didn't bother me so much as the way she'd set me up after she'd split . . . so that the only option was no fault.

The judge looked at me. I could have sworn that the quick glance she gave me was almost pitying. I didn't need that. Then she cleared her throat and spoke. "In the proceeding for dissolution of permanent civil union between the party of the first part, Chelesina Fhavour, and the party of the second part, Paulo Verano, the Court of Civil Matters, of the Unity of the Ceylesian Arm, located in the city of Smithsen, world of Bachman, does hereby decree that said civil union is hereby dissolved."

She barely paused before going on. "In the matter of property allocation, the net worth of the assets of both parties has been assessed at five point eight million duhlars. The settlement to the party of the first part, Chelesina Fhavour, is four point one million duhlars, of which three million has been placed in an irrevocable trust for the daughter of the union, Leysa Fhavour, said trust to be administered by the Bank of Smithsen until Leysa Fhavour reaches legal civil and political maturity . . ."

At least, Chelesina can't easily get her hands on that.

". . . Civil penalties for breach of union are one point five million duhlars, to be split between you, as mandated under the laws of the Unity. The remainder of all assets is allocated to the party of the second part, Paulo Verano.

"The court will revisit the situation of both partners in one year and reserves the right to make further adjustments in asset placement. That is all."

All?

I looked at Jared.

He shook his head and murmured, "They let you keep the conapt."

And two hundred thousand duhlars. "But . . . she left me."

"No fault," he reminded me.

Three million for Leysa, when she hadn't spoken to me in two years. When she had only a year left at the university? When her boyfriend's father was the one for whom Chelesina had left me?

So . . . out of some six million duhlars, I had two hundred thousand left . . . and a small conapt in Mychela. And a consulting business that the Civil Court could suck duhlars from for another two or possibly three years? All because I went to bed with someone besides Chelesina a year after she'd left me?

Jared must have been reading my mind . . . or face, because as we turned to leave the courtroom, he said quietly, "Equal no fault doesn't weigh things."

"I know that. I do have a problem with most of my assets going to an ungrateful daughter who won't speak to me even after I've paid all the bills for years."

"That's Unity policy. Permanent civil unions are supposed to protect the children. If the civil union is dissolved, the Court allocates enough assets to ensure that the child or children are adequately protected and able to continue in roughly the same lifestyle as before the dissolution."

"Which punishes me for making sure she was educated and raised with all advantages," I pointed out. "It doesn't punish Chelesina."

"It can't. Her design firm went bankrupt."

I had my doubts about the honesty of that bankruptcy, but Jared would just have told me what I already knew.

There wasn't a thing I could do about it.

2

Spring was the garden of my sky, thought one,
Where there we loved in joy and saw no sun.

"Daisies are the perkiest flowers, don't you think?" Ilsabet looked to the wall and to Alsabet, framed in the wallscreen. "Petals of sun and light, centers of ink."

"If they don't get caught in the wind," replied Alsabet. "Then they're just scattered petals."

"The skytubes let them be, as any can see."

Alsabet was silent, as if waiting for a prompt.

"I know," Ilsabet finally declared, "because it's so."

"How do you know?"

"I just do. But I won't tell you. You'd tell *them* now, but you don't know how." With that, Ilsabet's hand came down in a cutting motion, and the wallscreen blanked. After a moment she smiled. "I know you're still there, but it makes me feel things are fair." Her voice changed slightly. "I'm going outside. Matron says I can go and bide. I wish there were a storm today, but they've all gone away. So the door will open for me. It only closes when I want to see. I learned to know that about doors a long time ago."

Her grayed braids swung girlishly behind her as she danced out through the door that had irised open at her approach. Once outside, her wide gray eyes lifted to behold the twisted purple tubes that festooned the sky to the south. Far to the south. Too far.

3

For the next few days, I didn't do much of anything, except wind up the handful of contracts I had and step up my exercise. Over the past few months, I hadn't been as assiduous as I should have been in looking for new clients, but it's hard to think about ecology, especially unified ecology, when you'll have to subcontract "experts" in order to provide the expected range of credentials and then pay their fees. Especially when you're worried about getting fleeced and when you suspect anything left after your expenses will go to your former spouse. I hadn't even considered that so much would go to Leysa. Needless to say, she'd never contacted me, either by comm or link . . . or even by an old-fashioned written note.

The netlink chimed . . . and I frowned. I thought I'd turned off the sonics. Still . . .

After a moment I called out, "Display." The system showed the message. Simple enough. It just said, "After everything, you might look into this." The name at the bottom was that of Jared.

What he suggested I look into was a consulting contract proposal offered by the Unity's Systems Survey Service. I read the proposal twice. It looked like the standard wide-spectrum ecologic overview contract, but there were two aspects that were anything but standard. One was the specification that the survey had to be done by a principal, or a principal and direct employees—no subcontracting essentially. The second odd aspect was that the contract amount ranges were staggering for a survey contract. Together, that meant the survey had to be not only off-planet, but most likely out-system, very out-system.

Out-system meant elapsed relative travel-time . . . and that might not be all bad.

I thought about dithering, but I didn't. Instead, I sent a reply with credentials and vita.

I had a response in less than a standard hour, offering an appointment in person later in the day, or one on twoday of the next week or threeday of the following week. The in-person requirement for an initial interview was definitely unusual. Since I wasn't doing anything but stewing in my own juices, and since the interview was in the Smithsen Unity Centre, less than half a stan away by tube, I opted for the afternoon interview. Then, I had to hurry to get cleaned up and on my way.

I actually arrived at the Unity Centre with enough time to spare, and was promptly handed a directional wand to lead me to my destination—and told that any significant deviation could result in my being stunned and removed from the Centre. I followed the wand dutifully and found myself in a small windowless anteroom with three vacant chairs and an empty console. Before I could sit down, the door to the right of the console opened, and an angular figure in the green and gray of the Ministry of Environment stood there. Since he wore a belt stunner, I doubted he was going to be the one interviewing me. At least, I hoped not.

"Dr. Verano?"

"The same."

"If you'd come this way, please."

The Ministry guard guided me down a corridor to a corner office, one with windows and a small desk, behind which sat a man wearing a dark gray jacket and a formal pleated shirt, rather than the gray-blue single-suits of the Systems Survey Service, indicating he was either a classified specialist or a political appointee. That, and the facts that there was no console in the office and that a small gray-domed link-blocker sat on the polished surface of the desk, suggested the proposal to which I'd responded was anything but ordinary. He gestured to the pair of chairs in front of the desk and offered an honest warm smile, but all good politicians or covert types master that early on or they don't remain in their positions, one way or the other.

"We were very pleased that you showed an interest in the Survey proposal, Dr. Verano. Your credentials are just what we're looking for, and you have a spotless professional reputation, and the doctorate with honors from Reagan is . . . most useful."

I wondered about the inclusion of the word "professional." Was he one of the Deniers, the right wingers of the Values Party? Or was he just being careful, because the second speaker was a Denier, and the SoMod majority was nano-thin? "I'm glad that you found them so. I am curious, though. Why were you so quick to reply?" I had to ask. Most proposals from the Unity government took months before they were resolved even, I suspected, "unusual" ones.

"Ah . . . yes. That. There's a matter . . . of timing."

"Out-system transport timing?"

"Precisely. The system in question has but one scheduled direct ley-liner a year, and it departs in three weeks."

And sending a special ship would raise questions—and costs—that no one wishes to entertain. "Can you tell me more about the survey I'm to conduct?"

"It's a follow-up to gather information to determine whether the ecological situation on the planet requires continuation of the Systems Survey Service presence, or whether that presence should be expanded or reduced . . . or possibly eliminated."

"Given that we're talking one ley-liner a year, this has to be a system at the end of the Arm. That's a lot of real travel-time."

"And you wonder why we even bother?" The man who had not introduced himself, and likely would not, laughed. "Because the planet is Stittara."

That, unfortunately, made sense.

"I see you understand."

"Not completely." I did understand that the Unity Arm government didn't want to abandon Stittara, not given the anagathics that had been developed from Stittaran sources, and what they had done in boosting resistance to the Redflux. On the other hand, the costs of maintaining outposts were high—and there had always been the question of whether and to what degree the indigenous skytubes might be intelligent, or even sentient. The Deniers, the anything but loyal opposition, and several minority parties questioned the need for far-flung outposts, while the Purity

Party wanted all connections to "alien" systems severed, notwithstanding the fact that almost all systems were alien to some degree. "Funding, sky-tubes, anagathic multis threatening the uniqueness of Stittara, the threat of takeover from the Cloud Combine?"

"Any of those could certainly be issues, but the contract only requires delivery of an updated ecological overview of conditions on Stittara."

I managed not to laugh. Whatever report I made wouldn't even reach the government for over 150 years. What the unnamed functionary was telling me was that the Unity Arm government was under pressure and that they had to come up with a series of concrete actions to defuse the larger issue raised by the opposition parties.

"We had thought you might find the contract fit in with your personal goals," he added.

Had Jared told someone what had happened? It wasn't out of the range of possibilities, given that his aunt was a well-placed senior SoMod delegate. I was getting the definite feeling that the SoMod majority in the assembly had barely held in the face of systems-wide concern that private entities might either be destroying something unique on Stittara or, conversely, because of Denier concerns that the government was wasting trillions of duhlars in research subsidies and tax credits on research that either benefited the wealthy or was pointless. The contract certainly wouldn't be described that way, and there likely wouldn't be much media attention, but if I accepted the contract, I would become a small bit of SoMod political insurance, among other steps of which I knew little, only that they had to exist, to allow the first speaker to claim, if and when necessary, that steps had been taken. So I'd be highly paid, lose all contacts with my past life, and no one would even know how the problem might be resolved, or if it would be, but the first speaker could claim it had been addressed, at least to the best of anyone's ability.

"It might," I admitted.

After that, it was merely a matter of negotiation, and not much at that, because I knew they could make my life even more difficult than it was, and also, that taking the contract would mean Chelesina couldn't do much more to me. In fact, the relativistic time dilation of some seventy-three years one-way was looking better and better. With any luck, Chelesina would have doddered into seniority and forgotten me, or at least found some other ram to fleece, by the time I returned to anywhere in the

Arm. Why the Unity accepted my proposal so quickly I had no idea, except there probably wasn't anyone else with my experience in ecological interactions who was desperate or crazy enough to want the assignment . . . and they wanted political cover quickly.

The up-front bonus, while not huge, combined with what I'd get from the sale of the conapt and the few hundred thousand I had left, would create enough to purchase a dilation annuity, hopefully compounded substantially. That might actually amount to something when I returned, and I'd still be physically young enough to enjoy and appreciate it. If everything went to hell, and that was always a possibility, at least I'd be away from the worst of the collapse.

And who knew, the Stittara assignment might actually be interesting.

4

I made it away from Smithsen before my contract became public . . . but not away from Bachman. Well, not out of orbit. The *Persephonya* was about to break orbit when I got a message from Jared, with a linknet clip of a sweet-faced woman talking about the last-moment efforts of the So-Mods to influence the elections with a series of expensive cosmetic and very political actions. Mine wasn't the first listed, but it was far from the last, and the bottom line was that the SoMods were spending millions if not billions of duhlars on useless surveys and assessments whose results wouldn't be seen for decades, if not generations . . . if at all. And, of course, they had to provide a return bond as well, in the event that something catastrophic had occurred on Stittara, either physically or politically. I didn't worry about the physical catastrophes. Planets were pretty stable as a whole, and it took hundreds of millions of years to see any basic changes. Political changes were another matter, but, again, given Stittara's low population, the reliance on Arm technology, even if filtered by time, and the distance from Bachman, it was unlikely I'd be declared persona non grata upon arrival. If that did happen, I'd still get return passage and my bonus . . . and that wasn't bad.

The media summary on my assignment was simple: Stittara is the source of anagathics that have more than doubled the life spans of Arm citizens. Why spend millions to reassess what's already known.

The Ministry of Environment view I'd been given earlier was somewhat different: Do an environmental assessment to make sure no one is altering the environment on Stittara, because the research of that environment has created and continues to create products that affect billions of lives . . . and supports billions of duhlars in research, investment, and healthcare products.

Jared also sent a confirmation that he'd filed the documentation and the taxes on the proportion of my contract advance that I was transferring with me to Stittara. I'd learned from some of the old-timers that no matter where you thought you were going to go, it wasn't a good idea to go somewhere, especially somewhere multiples of light-years away, without enough assets to last a while—or to give you the chance of a new start. I hardly planned on that, but it's always better to learn easily from others' experience than the hard way by making the same mistakes yourself.

I sent back a query asking about anyone I should watch out for, and his response was, as usual, less helpful than it could have been.

"Not until you debark on Stittara." That meant he didn't know or wouldn't say, neither of which was useful. Or that nothing would happen onboard the *Persephonya,* which I'd already figured out.

I sent him a simple "Thanks!"

I didn't expect a reply, but there was always a chance. In the meantime, I left my links open and went to explore the ley-liner . . . or what of it was open to "standard" passengers, which equated to "second-class" passengers, all that the Survey Service was paying for. Personally, I could see that standard meant second-class, and that was what I had expected, and the way in which I regarded all of us in "standard accommodations." At least, I didn't have to go under life-suspension. That was true steerage, with the added risk of long-term complications, which was why the Survey Service could justify the cost of standard passage for a consultant.

Besides the cubicle termed a stateroom, there wasn't much to explore—an exercise room, too small to be called a gym; the salon, with tables for snacks and talking and cards or other noninteractives; the dining room; and, lastly, the observation gallery, which I knew would be closed off once we entered translation space. At that moment, though, the gallery was where most of the passengers, all twenty-odd of those of us in second class, were located.

From there, through the wide armaglass ports, Bachman hung in the sky like a huge sapphire globe smudged with clouds, poised against the sparkling sweep of the Arm. I got there just in time to see the umbilical from the orbit station retract—Orbit Station Four, to be precise, the smallest of the five. Several of the men standing at the back of the gallery looked slightly green. Ultra-low grav will do that to some people.

At first, the *Persephonya*'s movement was scarcely perceptible.

By the time we were moving out-system, I sat down in the salon, by myself. Once the ship was away from a planet, the view of the stars and the Arm didn't change, not to the naked eye, anyway. An attractive black-haired woman in a tailored shipsuit that showed off her figure, just enough, settled into the chair and table beside mine. She had to be older, not that I or anyone else could tell by her appearance or her figure, but because her features were finely chiseled in the way that never happens with young women, and her dark eyes had seen at least some of life without shielding.

"You've seen the Arm from out-planet before, haven't you?" she asked in a way that really wasn't a question.

"A few times. I'm Paulo Verano, by the way." That wasn't giving a thing away.

"Aimee Vanslo. What business takes you to Stittara?"

"A consulting assignment. What about you?"

"Family business. I'm the one the others can do without for now." She laughed humorlessly. "Besides, it's the only way I'll end up younger than my children, and I do want to see them after they've realized that they don't know everything they think they do."

"And you're effectively single," I replied, smiling politely, and adding, "and you don't play on my side."

Her second laugh was far more genuine. "You have seen more than the Arm. You obviously are widowed or dissolved."

"Not single by choice?" I countered.

She shook her head. "You're not a beauty boy, and you're obviously in-telligent, and the only ones who would pay for you to travel to Stittara are the Arm government or one of three multis. They wouldn't send a perma-nent singleton. No loyalties."

"Very perceptive. Do you want my analysis of you?"

"No. You may keep it to yourself. My partner was killed in a freak ac-cident three years ago. The children are all grown, but young enough to think they know everything. My ties lie in the family business." She shrugged. "I like intelligent conversation without complication. Unless I miss my guess, you'll do nicely."

I smiled. "So will you."

"I know."

We both laughed.

"What are you comfortable telling me about your business?" I asked.

"Only that it's in biologics."

"And it's very big," I suggested.

"It's only a family business."

She wasn't going to say. "And your expertise?"

"Management and development. I'll talk about theory and what I've observed anywhere outside the biologics field. And you?"

"Ecologic and environmental consulting, and I'll talk about anything except my current assignment."

"Which has to be on Unity business."

"Anything but my current assignment." If she could limit, so could I . . . and I should.

She nodded. "What do you think about the fiscal posture of the Arm Assembly?"

"Mass-wise and energy deficient, so to speak."

At that point a steward arrived. Aimee ordered a white-ice, or whatever the vintage was that the staff was providing as such, and I had an amber lager.

If she happened to be what she offered herself as, she was unlikely to be one of those who I needed to watch out for . . . but who was to say she was exactly what she said she was? And what sort of family business could afford to send someone as far as Stittara, unless it was truly huge? In which case, why was she traveling standard class?

I doubted I'd be getting any answers soon, but talking with her was likely to be interesting, and if I listened more than I talked, which was often hard for me, I might learn more than a few things I didn't know.

5

Aboard any trans-ship, time passes slowly, unless you're in life-suspension, and the trip on the *Persephonya* was no exception, especially given that it would take more than a week to get far enough out-system that the ship could even enter trans-space. While I certainly spent a fair amount of time with Aimee, there were others in whom I had some interest, if only because their presence aboard the ship seemed in one way or another anomalous. One of them was Roberto Gybl, clearly of dark hispano heritage, and likely of an equally wealthy background from his manner-isms . . . unless, of course, he was playing a role. But, in some ways, we all were.

He'd immediately insisted, "Call me Rob, please." That tended to con-firm the wealth, since all too many of those with enormous assets went out of their way not to be standoffish, but those who played roles would know that as well.

My response had been, "Paulo Verano, and it is Paulo." I'd said it dryly enough that he'd actually smiled.

Gybl was one of those men whose original genes would have left them bald after thirty bio-years. Biologics have stopped that, but his natural thick black hair looked anything but natural. He probably would have liked to have adopted the skinner look, except that the skinners were all cyborg-enhanced, and Gybl definitely wasn't their type.

On the fourth day, we were back in the salon—late morning, ship-time, essentially waiting for a midday meal that would be filling, decent, and hardly inspiring—after I'd spent a good standard hour exercising in one corner of the so-called gym, and trying to brush up my Juchai, and another cooling off before I took what passed for a shower.

Gybl was a permanent singleton and professional freelance documentarian. He claimed to be headed to Stittara to see if he could gain access to the forerunner digs. "There's never been much published or on the links about them, and one of the multis actually has grandfathered exclusive rights to one site. It's hundreds of millions of years old, if what I've been able to ferret out is halfway correct."

"Who would be interested in something like that?"

"That sort of personal docu-trip never goes out of style. I know. I'm still getting residuals on a docu-visit to a piece of space-junk that no one ever identified—except that it was too young to be forerunner and too old to be human or Farhkan . . . and too strange to be Ansaran . . ."

Too strange to be Ansaran? I had a hard time conceiving of that . . . unless it was some forgotten form of human space art . . . an artform that had died out thousands of years earlier when people had gotten over the idea of spending hundreds of thousands or millions of duhlars to see something they couldn't even identify with.

". . . I've even got residuals on a piece I did looking into the original sewers of Smithsen."

"You came out here without any guarantee of access to the site?"

"The rights are held by the Stittaran subsidiary. I'd grow old before the papers went out and came back. Besides"—Gybl laughed—"it doesn't matter. If they grant me access, that's one documentary. If they don't, it's another . . . and they wouldn't like the second one very much, and if something happens to me, that's a third, already in the hands of my advocate, and they'll like that even less."

"You've thought it all out."

"Oh . . . they'll let me do it. Done this more times than I can count. They get good PR for letting me say how odd and mysterious what they've discovered happens to be, and I go away, and we're both happy." He paused. "But you've always got to have backup. That's the problem you technical consultants face. No backup. What do you do if you don't get the information or the access that you need? Or if it's the wrong information?"

I smiled. "Usually . . . if they try to give me the wrong information, that provides all the assurance I need to get the right information." I took a sip of the lager, more of a prop than a necessity.

Gybl sipped his seltzer, then nodded. "Suppose we're alike in that respect. You've been talking with Aimee Vanslo. What do you think of her?"

"Intelligent, extraordinarily well informed, and not the sort I'd really want to cross."

"I got that impression. She didn't exactly want to talk to me."

I almost laughed, but managed to nod. Gybl clearly hadn't looked beyond Aimee's firm femininity, but most singletons, of either gender or sexual proclivity, tended to believe that no one in whom they were interested could resist their charms, at least for conversation.

"Oh . . . there's Lars. I need a word with him, if you don't mind." With a quick smile, Gybl was gone.

I'd met Lars earlier. Short, muscular, and trim, he was the very model of a multi junior middle manager, with always a pleasant smile and a charming laugh. His wife, Larissa—and that was her given name—at least seemed to be the type to be a permanent civil union partner, the feminine and supportive type. She'd even taken his last name, and that didn't happen often. She wasn't with him at the moment, most likely in the gym, working to keep her own figure trim, since from what I'd seen, she spent two to three standard hours a day there. Lars had made no secret of the fact that he'd been sent to update the Eterna facilities on Stittara—along with a cargo of tech patterns. That was the sort of pre-retirement assignment the multis gave middle managers. The time-dilation allowed elapsed time to swell their retirement assets while they were still being paid, and by the time they returned, if they did, they were effectively isolated from the current power structure.

As I watched the two of them, I wondered what other angle Gybl was playing . . . and what Lars had in mind for Gybl.

Sitting at the table nearest me was an older man, not so much in appearance as in manner, the type for whom politeness and courtesy have been a way of life, and who have discovered that courtesy is often viewed as a manifestation of weakness. Men such as those, and it is usually men, because women tend to be more practical, either end up politely tough and cynical or politely world-weary. Torgan Brad looked as though he embodied both.

"For which administrative colossus are you traveling to Stittara?" I had asked him cheerfully when I'd met him the first time.

"The Ministry of Technology and Transportation," he'd replied.

"Advice on transport systems or contracts?"

"Does it have to be either?" he countered with a smile.

"Of course not, but it's likely, given that technical advice or information and money are usually the greatest concern bureaucracies have with their far-flung constituencies, while power and position are the greatest concerns at headquarters."

He had laughed in a mannered way. "We'll see when it's all over, Doctor. Isn't that always the case?"

We'd had a dozen short conversations, after that, and I'd never gotten further, using either bluntness or subtlety. Still . . .

"What pressing issue awaits you on Stittara?" I asked. "Ox-carts or wind-ferries? Or a long and painful audit?"

"Doctor . . . you are pressing. That can be most depressing."

"Of course. We ecologists are insatiably curious, and we're the practitioners of the secondmost dismal science. We have to press because no one wants to listen."

"And when you press, they listen less."

He had a point, and we both knew it.

"Wind-ferries, it is, then," I said cheerfully.

He laughed and turned away.

"Do you mind if I join you, Ser Doctor Verano?" Constantia Dewers eased into the chair that Gybl had vacated before I could say a word. Her silver hair was the product of age, if far more healthy than had once been the case for someone approaching her second century bio-time. Given the likelihood she'd traveled extensively, I wasn't about to guess in what past century she'd actually been born.

"Of course, your presence is always welcome." I smiled and meant it, not that I totally trusted anyone her age or someone effectively slumming, since she was a first-class passenger.

"You still wonder why I come down here, don't you? It's very simple. There are more interesting people in the second-class salon. In fact, there are more people. Half the first-class staterooms might as well be empty on this voyage, for all that I've seen of their occupants."

"You're most interesting. I'm certain there are others—"

She waved off my perfunctory protests with a gracefully dismissive gesture. "I can't very well converse with myself. I'd always know what to say, and that becomes exceedingly boring rather quickly. You often have something fresh to offer, and more insightfully than one might expect from someone of your age."

"And you deliver the backhanded compliment—or the encouraging putdown—in such a charming fashion." I said that lightly enough that she actually smiled.

"You are so kind to a woman of my age," came the reply. "You might even remind me of my grandsons and the way I wished they'd been, but then, if you'd been one, you'd likely have ended up as they did."

"And how was that?"

"Splendidly successful . . . and quite boring." She beckoned to the steward. "A dry bond, and do use the Excelsior and not the Jennings."

"Yes, lady."

"Boredom is the ultimate sin?" I asked.

"The inevitable outcome of overwhelming ambition, great ability, and extreme caution."

"Then you were not extraordinarily cautious, just prudent?"

"Not even always prudent. Prudence can also be dull, without even the dubious approbation granted to boredom."

"Then your tie to Stittara is Eterna?" I asked with a smile.

"Oh . . . you'd like me to confess. When you're my age, you have to confess nothing, and it's far too late for regrets." She accepted almost languidly the crystalline flute from the steward, who had responded to her request far more swiftly than to any of mine.

"By the time anyone has realized the need for regrets it's usually too late."

"Obviously spoken from experience, if the wrong kind of experience."

"Is any kind of experience wrong if you survive it and learn from it?"

"If you learn the wrong lesson, it's worse than no experience." Constantia took a sip from the fluted crystalline.

"Misguided learning being worse than naiveté?"

"Naiveté is merely a euphemism for pretended innocence, used by and for those who fear the honesty of ignorance."

"So what, do you judge, was the incorrect lesson I learned from whatever it was?"

"Men usually learn the wrong lessons from women, because most women prefer men not know women, but only an image of them. But then, all of us prefer others to admire our images rather than our reality." She took another sip of the bond, whatever that drink was. "I'm vain enough to appreciate others admiring my image and old enough to know that's what it is."

During that conversation, and several others, I never did learn why she was headed to Stittara, nor who she truly might be, since I doubted her real name was Constantia Dewers. But talking to her was never dull, if always challenging.

6

The crew members did eat with the passengers, that is, the captain dined with the first-class passengers, and the senior pilot, or once in a while the second pilot, ate with those of us in the *Persephonya*'s "standard" accommodations, at a two-sided table that was more than a semicircle and less than a full circle and that could have seated thirty, fifteen on each side of the presiding officer. With diners on each side of the pilot, no one was truly out of earshot of the pilot. The senior pilot was Sandrina Zoas, a thin-faced redhead with a firmly husky voice who was perfectly charming and managed to convey as little as possible in a warm and cheerful manner.

Two days after we entered trans-space, the second pilot replaced the senior pilot at the evening meal. He didn't look that much older than Leysa, in bio-years, anyway. At that thought, I realized that, in all probability, my ungrateful daughter was now older, in bio-years, than I was. Somehow, that didn't give me much satisfaction. It just depressed me, although I couldn't say why, and I definitely didn't want to explore those feelings at the moment.

Like the senior pilot, Aelanzo was gracious, in between carefully spaced bites on the platter in front of him.

Larissa asked what it was like to look at trans-space from the bridge.

He just smiled. "We don't look out that way. The lights and patterns move so fast they're a dark gray. If we traveled more slowly, they'd just give anyone a headache. In the early days, when the ships weren't as fast and before pilots relied on screens, they gave some pilots epileptic seizures."

"Don't you worry we might hit something?"

Beyond Larissa, one of the passengers who talked almost not at all—Torgan Brad—winced.

I wondered why, since that hadn't been a problem for decades, if not centuries.

"That's why we have to get clear of systems. We plot courses on low-matter trajectories, and the trans-fields bend around small amounts of matter."

"What's a small amount of matter?"

"Most planets."

"Do you just travel back and forth from Bachman to Stittara?"

"No. Every ley-liner has a multiple-stop flight plan. Our next port after Stittara will be Hayek . . ."

"How long have you been with Ceylesian Transport?" asked Lars, pre-empting his wife's next question.

"Eleven years. Bio-years."

He looked younger than he was. Maybe CT picked them for that.

"How many years of training?"

"Only six months. I spent a tour as a Unity Alliance courier pilot."

A hotshot military courier pilot. No wonder he only needed six months' training, and like all of them, he used the official title of Unity Alliance, rather than Space Service, the old name that almost everyone else used.

"That must have been exciting."

Second Pilot Aelanzo smiled. "I really can't talk about that."

On the other side of the table, Torgan Brad gave the smallest nod.

In the momentary silence that followed, I asked, "Do pilots have collateral duties when they're not piloting?"

Lars and Larissa looked at me as if I'd been wearing an emergency evac suit. Aimee smiled politely.

"Yes, we do. I'm the purser, and the senior pilot is also the navigator. Every crew member on board has several duties."

At that point, the two stewards began to remove the main course and to serve dessert, a variation on a Reaganian Crème.

Later, before Aelanzo excused himself, I waited until Rob Gybl finished asking him a question about the frequency of singularity-interrupted trips—the answer was less than one in a thousand transits, none with fatalities in the last two hundred years—then moved in.

"Do you see many passengers time and time again? I mean, for example, are there people onboard that have traveled with you before?"

"I've seen two that I recall since I've been with Ceylesian. No one in several years. Now . . . if you would excuse me . . ."

"Thank you . . . I just wondered."

I still wondered at the specificity of his answer. He hadn't seen any out of our current passengers, but that didn't mean that someone onboard wasn't traveling often between Bachman and Stittara.

At that, I almost shook my head. Even if someone were concerned about me and my assignment, it was far more likely that the ship just carried a message to someone in the Survey Service on Stittara . . . or to an already placed intelligence type there. That made far more sense. Besides, given the time-delay between my departure and the soonest my report could possibly return, why would anyone bother?

Except . . . if no one cared, why had someone created the proposal and sent me?

Maybe it was just personal ego, but I had trouble believing that the System Survey Service would spend millions of duhlars on a throwaway political gesture.

Then . . . we all want to believe what we do is important. I tried to tell myself that was all my concerns were based on, most likely because it had been all too clear that Chelesina had thought very little of me. Nor had Leysa.

Still . . . I did shake my head, but after I left the dining chamber.

"Shaking your head at the pilot's efforts at diplomacy, Dr. Verano?"

I looked over to see Rikard Spek standing by the archway into the salon. We hadn't really met, but I'd picked up his name in passing and gathered he had a scientific background. "Not at his diplomacy, Dr. Spek. Not at that. Would you care to join me to while away some time?" I gestured toward the salon.

"Why not?" Spek offered a good-natured, almost lazy smile. He was a big man, a good fifteen centimeters taller than I, and broad across the shoulders.

We were among the first into the salon and took the corner table that offered the best view of the wallscreen that displayed a series of vistas of the Arm from various locales in Unity space. They'd been striking for the first week or so. I settled into the chair at an angle to the wallscreen. Spek took the other one. He didn't even glance at the screen, either.

"Why are you headed to Stittara?" I asked. "Research?"

"More of an application of that research."

"Can you tell me the general nature of that application?"

He grinned and shook his head.

"So, are you like all the other science types aboard, involved in bio-logics?"

"I wouldn't be able to pick out protozoa from a giant bacterium." He laughed. "My background is high-energy physics. Leave it at that."

"You from Bachman?"

He nodded, then looked to the steward. "The usual."

"Pale lager," I added.

"Very good, sers."

"What about you?" Spek asked.

"Smithsen."

"I understand you're an ecological consultant. You must be very good."

"Well . . . good enough for someone to pay to send me out . . . but that goes even more for you."

He shook his head. "Very little new in my field in years. It was time to look at things from a different angle. Haven't you noticed that the pace of scientific development has slowed?"

"It started slowing right after the dawn of the space age back on ancient Terra," I pointed out. "All the easier problems were solved, and the costs of research on each new generation of challenges increased geometrically."

"In a way, I envy you, Paulo. You can use the same tools on a different ecology and make new and fascinating discoveries. The building blocks of the universe don't change no matter where you are."

I had to think about that for a moment. But, in a general sense, he was right. Each ecology was different, while, in general, the universe stayed the same. Still . . . "But isn't each system, each nebula, each stellar unity somewhat different? The arrangement of bodies around a sun or suns? How is that different? You use tools, and we use tools, and few of those tools are based on startlingly new principles . . ."

"How about the fact that none of our tools are based on such startlingly new principles?" His laugh was genial enough, if with a certain resignation behind it. "From what I've read about your field, there's more variety on any one planet with a developed ecology than there is in the mass/energy/dark matter structure of an entire galaxy."

I shrugged. "I can't address that. I don't know your field . . . but there are quite a few worlds with astoundingly simple ecologies that never developed beyond a basic stage. Complex ecologies are comparatively infrequent, and intelligent life is still statistically exceedingly rare."

"Whose rarity is overcompensated for by its proclivity to expand everywhere," he pointed out sardonically.

I laughed and waited for the steward to set my lager on the table before I took a small swallow. Whatever Spek was drinking was pale pink and looked fruity, but I wasn't about to ask. "Where did you do your grad work?"

"The Institute. Where else is there on Bachman?"

I wasn't about to comment on the fact that a great percentage of science types on Bachman came from elsewhere, a fact attributed to the heavy hand of the Deniers on pure scientific studies.

"What about you?" he returned.

I grinned. "Solara as an undergrad. Institute for the doctorate."

"Are the girls at Solara . . ." he ventured.

"Only a very few," I replied. And I'd had the misfortune or stupidity to marry one of them, even if it had been years later. "The rest are like undergrads anywhere. Believe me . . . that's better."

"I don't know," he said, again offering that genial lazy smile. "There are some myths worth believing in, especially regarding women."

"Perhaps." I still had my doubts about that. "But there are myths about everything worth believing in . . . like the idea that we'll be able to discover the actual source of life . . . or the universe."

"You think those are myths?"

"Right now, they're myths. For as long as we've been in space, no one still can prove where the universe came from. What if we're not capable of discovering that?"

"Then"—he nodded—"you're right. It's better to have myths."

I hadn't said that, and I wasn't certain I even agreed, but I nodded and took another swallow of lager.

7

The *Persephonya* left trans-space just before the evening meal, while I was sitting in the chamber that passed for the standard-class lounge talking to a young couple, a good twenty years younger than I was, bio-age, of course. Both were techies. She was a biologist. He was a biochemist, and both had been hired by Syntex, one of the original biologics multis on Stittara.

For a moment or so, I didn't realize that we'd left trans-space, only that I'd felt disoriented for a moment, until the captain announced, "The ship is now in norm-space and proceeding to Stittara. Our estimated time of system transit will be four days."

Considering the fact that it had taken eight days to get far enough from Bachman to enter trans-space, four didn't seem all that bad.

That gave me four more days to see if I could discover who might have been sent with me, for whatever purpose that might be. I doubted that I'd find out any more in four days than in the three weeks of personally experienced time that the trip had already taken, but it couldn't hurt to keep my eyes and ears open. Even if I could determine who was watching me, assuming anyone was, what exactly could I do onboard ship? I'd been doing the only thing I could, and that was to step up my practice on the old Juchai martial arts routines, those that I hadn't practiced with or against anyone in years. At the same time, I consoled myself by asking what they could do without getting caught.

I couldn't really believe that anyone cared to watch me, but the strangeness of how my contract had occurred left me suspicious. More likely, even if someone had been co-opted, they were just information couriers who would relay information about me to others groundside on Stittara, who would then decide to act, or not to, in one fashion or another. In fact, I wouldn't have been surprised to find that several individuals might have been used for that purpose, all reporting to different local entities, all of which had differing agendas and priorities.

At the same time, I had to say that I wondered about Torgan Brad, if not for that reason. He was pleasant enough, in his world-weary monosyllabic way, but he didn't fit any category or reason for a Ministry employee or contractor being sent to Stittara . . . or any outland world. He was too old to be a bureaucratic émigré and too polite and tactful to be a troubleshooter of the standard sort, and any other sort was likely to be dangerous.

So I smiled politely at Holly Peppard and said, "Did you feel it?"

"That dizzy-like feeling? Was that what it feels like to leave transspace?"

"That's the mild feeling." The few other times I'd left trans-space had been years ago, before I'd met Chelesina the second time and married her, and the trips had only been a few light-years. The disorientation had been far more severe, and I wondered if it had to do with the proximity of more gravity wells.

Georg Golitely frowned. "You'd think that after all the thousands of years of trans-space travel someone could have figured out how to eliminate that altogether."

"In the early days," I offered, "ships were twisted apart at times. Mild disorientation represents great progress."

"Still . . ." He shook his head. "They ought to be able to do something."

Georg was a scientific type who felt there was a technical answer for everything. I liked his wife better, and not merely because she was a woman, although I had to admit that was part of it. I've always liked women. Too bad I'd exercised such poor judgment when it counted.

"Do you have any idea what you'll be doing at Syntex?" I'd asked before, but he'd had three of what passed for pale ales, and he might not remember my question.

"They never told me. Never told Holly, either. Oh . . . it has to be something to do with the biochemistry of grasses on the nanetic level—or something similar."

"That was what his thesis was on," added Holly brightly.

"And what about you?"

"Lichens. They're fascinating . . ."

As she went on to tell me about lichens—with an occasional prompting question from me—I realized I'd never heard much about grasses in connection with Stittara, except as being the basis of the ecosystem, since trees and other large arboreal flora and fauna were comparatively rare. Oh, there were certainly studies about the grasses, but most of the data and studies were on the comparatively ground-hugging foliage, largely in mountainous regions, and the fact that both reptilian and marsupial analogues had never evolved into large herbivores or carnivores. I'd already noted that in my background work, with questions as to why and what the relationships were . . . and the fact that those issues didn't appear at all in the material filed with the Systems Survey Service in Bachman . . . or presumably anywhere else off Stittara.

When Holly finished with the lichens, I did ask, "What's the nutrient load for Stittaran grasses and lichens?"

"I don't know. There's nothing on that. Why do you ask?"

"There aren't any large fauna. There doesn't seem to be any evolutionary record of any."

"You're wondering if that's because . . ."

I nodded.

She pursed her lips. "That's an interesting idea, but there's also the possibility that there are other factors . . . atmospheric factors . . ."

"The skytubes?" I asked. Because the skytubes were far more sinuous in their movements than the waterspouts and tornadoes on water worlds, many had speculated if they had an organic basis, or might have a low-level intelligence. Most scientists felt that anything else was unlikely because an atmospheric-based organism had to be so dispersed to remain airborne that even low-level intelligence was impossible. I tended to agree, but the question would doubtless come up. Of course, were the skytubes intelligent, the Unity would have had to turn Stittara over to them, but centuries of observation had shown nothing along that line.

"And the winds."

"Not to mention that there's not been much work done on the bio-chemical basis of the ecosystems," added Georg.

"Well . . . none's appeared off Stittara," I pointed out.

The couple exchanged glances, as if I'd brought up the unthinkable, that good scientific research had either been ignored or suppressed.

"It has happened," I said gently. "The multis usually aren't that interested in pursuing science that doesn't lead to profit."

"Paulo," interrupted another feminine voice, "are you attempting to corrupt these idealistic young people?"

I looked up at Aimee Vanslo. "Would you join us?"

"I would, but the grande dame should be here in a moment to escort me to dine with those too refined to mingle here."

"The grande dame?" I knew who she meant, but I wanted to hear what Aimee might say.

"Constantia Dewers, in her present incarnation." With a bright smile meant to be false, she nodded and moved on.

Holly and Georg looked slightly bewildered, and that was probably for the best.

"What else can you tell me about what grasses might be like on Stittara?" I prompted.

In the end, I discovered that, overall, I knew more than they did, but that was fine. They were young, and they'd learn.

8

The administrative director scanned the screen, then looked up. "The Unity's finally sent an investigator."

"An investigator?"

"Don't be silly. Even the densest of Arm politicians wouldn't announce it that way. He's one of the top ecologists on Bachman. Possibly the best of the independents, according to Vergenya. His name is Paulo Verano."

"A true ecologist sent from Bachman? Sounds like an oxymoron to me."

"There are some. Not all are throwbacks to the Deniers. He was sent by a SoMod government."

"The SoMods are back in power?"

"They have been for the last few elections, but barely, she says."

"Is that why he's coming here? Because he's actually supposed to do something? Or because he's caused trouble for the Deniers, and they want him out-system? A SoMod concession to the Deniers? Or a plant by Vergenya's superiors."

"More mundane than that. The first speaker is fending the Deniers off. He needs to claim he's done something to keep a very slim majority. He needed someone with absolutely no political connections or ties. Verano has none. He's never even worked for a known Denier-linked outfit. Most of his assets went to an ex, with a multi-year readjustment. He needed the bonus, and he was available."

"Poor bastard. Didn't want to see everything taken."

"Maybe he was the bastard. It does happen that way."

"Anything's possible. No pre-contract?"

"He may have been so involved in his work that he never saw it coming." She laughed softly, ironically. "Or he's the type who believes in true love. Or he upset her so badly that the only place he's safe is off-system and years into her future."

"Either way, that's trouble."

"But for whom?" She walked toward the office door. "The multis here know where we stand. No one in the Arm who cares about the ecological consequences will even be holding office, if they're still alive, when he or his report arrives back on Bachman. Even if he does find out something, and that's highly unlikely for an offworlder—what could he do?"

"There's always something to discover."

"Precisely. And I'll need to leave to pick him up from the dropport in a few stans."

"So soon? Usually you get messages earlier than that, when the ships are a day or so out, if not farther." The man frowned.

"This was a sealed comm, not through an intermediary. Those are always the last sent because they're the responsibility of some junior officer who has too much to do and who figures that something sent years before couldn't be that urgent. Vergenya had no one to spare. Besides the apparent political impartiality, that's another reason why they had to send Verano, rather than a Survey Service assessor."

"That suggests . . ."

"It does indeed, unless it's actually an honest contract."

"That might pose even more problems."

"We'll have to wait and see." She stood. "I'll need to make arrangements. He'll likely have equipment of some sort. It might even include updates and new tech that we could use. As a contractor, he's obliged to share that with us."

"At our expense."

"It's more than worth it, and you know it."

"I suppose so. What does he look like?"

"Vergenya sent his bio and image, just in case."

"None of the multis would go that far, would they? Not those upstanding conglomerated legal entities that want nothing on Stittara to change?"

"Your biases are showing."

"And yours aren't?"

"I imagine he's like every other consultant. Vaguely good-looking and competent. A shade taller than average, I'd judge. You can see for yourself. I've allowed you access to it."

"Most kind of you."

"Practical . . . as you know."

The man frowned as the door closed behind her.

9

Not quite four days later, the *Persephonya* locked to the umbilical of Stittara's lone and small orbit control station. I didn't rush, although I did pack all my gear. The local orbit station personnel would take some time to process everyone, although it was largely a formality for most travelers, since Ceylesian Transport vetted passengers thoroughly before they embarked. The one aspect of clearance that wasn't a formality was a check to determine if any passengers had been past visitors to Stittara or former residents. It was scarcely unknown for those deemed undesirable, either for political, criminal, or civil reasons, to leave a world before their misdeeds were uncovered and use trans-space travel to try to escape their past and then eventually return to their home world. Sometimes, it worked, especially if there had been a significant change in government—or a revolution. Then, that also worked against travelers who had been "desirable" under previous governments . . . and who found themselves considerably less so under a "nouveau regime."

In all the time coming in-system, I'd continued to talk to the other passengers in standard accommodations, and even to the grande dame Constantia Dewers, when she deigned to visit the "standard" salon. Both Rob Gybl and I were convinced her shipboard name was totally pseudonymous. Aimee Vanslo wouldn't commit, one way or the other, and said it was Constantia's business, not ours. Of course, I didn't learn much about Aimee's dining with the grande dame, either, except Aimee did reveal that she had noted one of the bracelets "Constantia" wore was An-saran in origin, and had doubtless been anything but a bracelet, given differences in anatomy . . . and dated back at least several hundred mil-lennia.

On one level, that indicated either great wealth, or a gift from someone with great wealth, but the fact that she was traveling first class meant she wasn't exactly impoverished. What it also indicated was that Aimee knew Ansaran artifacts . . . and wanted me to know that she knew them.

The other thing I did once we linked to orbit control was arrange for the transfer of my ship-carried funds to Stittaran Planetary. I knew I'd take a loss on the time-conversion, because there was no interest com-pounding for personal funds in transit, but I didn't like the idea of not having more than expense funds. The expense funds had been taken care of separately, in an escrow account under my name, and were there for me to draw on. I knew, because I'd checked.

Clearance on the orbit stations varied little from station to station, and before long I was standing in line in a gray composite chamber with the other standard-class passengers, waiting for a multipoint DNA sampling, scan, and comparison. The interior of the few stations I'd visited was gray, and others had relayed the same experience. That made perfect sense, for a number of reasons, but mainly because gray aged better and was less offensive to most people than any other color. The fact that it was also depressing hadn't seemed to have mattered throughout history, human history, anyway. Most human stations were indeed gray, although I'd heard that the Farhkans preferred a dull red, and some scientists insisted that the forerunner culture had a disproportionate number of violet walls. But then, maybe whatever coloration the forerunners had preferred had simply faded or shifted over eons, given that the color was part of the structure, rather than additive.

I stood behind Rob Gybl, who snorted gently. "It's the same thing everywhere. Hurry up and wait while they look for people who made a mistake and want to come home."

"That's a mistake in itself," I replied. "Time changes everything. The river's different each time you step into it."

"Too philosophical for me," he replied dryly. After several minutes, and two passengers in front of us being scanned—the couple headed to work for Syntex—he added, "Seems to me that every place isn't that much different from any other, once you get beyond the furniture."

"People are the same pretty much everywhere, but the patterns differ," I pointed out.

"No. They just repeat, shuffled into different configurations."

Before I could reply to that, he was first in line, and the pleasant-faced woman in a gray singlesuit, the shade of which somehow clashed with the gray of the composite walls, motioned for him to step into the scanner box. After less than a minute, she waved him on, and it was my turn.

I tendered my Unity ID, and she slipped it into the scanner.

"Paulo Verano?"

"That's me."

"Purpose for visiting Stittara?"

"Consulting assignment for the Systems Survey Service. It should be on file."

Her eyes flicked to the screen. Then what felt like jabs of air sampled my bare skin in random places. "Put your right hand on the scanner."

I did. Perhaps forty seconds passed.

"You're clear, Ser Verano. Next . . ."

As I stepped out of the scanner, I could see that Lars Lenstren was next, followed by his wife. Of course, he'd go first . . . and she'd let him.

The corridor beyond the scanning room led to the drop shuttle, and there I was pointed to the cocoon next to Sinjon Reksba, who I'd barely talked to onboard.

He immediately offered a smile too broad for his narrow face. "Paulo . . . we had so little chance to talk during the trip. How did you like the *Persephonya?*"

"I've only made a few trans-space trips, none but this recently. How could I compare? What do you think?"

"The *Persephonya* is hardly the finest vessel of those proffered by Ceylesian Transport. Ah, but her name is singularly appropriate, traveling always in the darkness trying to make her way into the light and never being able to remain there for long. The accommodations are adequate, the crew and staff generally accommodating, and to a destination such as Stittara, I doubt we could do any better . . . or any worse."

"You never did say why you were coming here."

"Nor did you, as I recall."

"I'm a consulting ecologist on a contract assignment." I suspected all Stittara would know in hours after the drop shuttle landed. "You?"

"The proverbial black sheep . . . ram, really. Or prodigal son, if you will. It appears as though I've inherited the family lands. I suppose it's more accurate to say that I'll be taking them over from the trust that's administering them in my absence, assuming that there's anything left to administer. There is something to be said about returning to one's roots. What that might be, or whether it's even a good idea, is another thing altogether. I take it that you've never been on Stittara before?"

"No. Until I was briefed, the only thing I knew was that it was the largest source of anagathics for the Arm and that it has skytubes that people still argue over as to whether they're intelligent."

"Intelligence is overrated by any species that has it, and that's provable by the fact that all intelligent species are outlived by a factor of a hundred to one, if not a thousand to one, by nonintelligent species, who don't have the brains or perversity to destroy themselves or their environments."

"You're originally from Stittara," I pressed gently. "Do you think the skytubes are semi-intelligent?"

"How could they be, up in the air like that? Brains are dense, in both senses of the word. Even if there were the possibility, and that's been proven otherwise, I believe, how can any species evaluate another, except by its own criteria, and who would ever want to be evaluated by human criteria? Do you, really?" countered Reksba. "Hades, I've never thought of myself as judgmental, but I wouldn't want me judging me, not impartially, anyway. Nice and competent as you might be, Paulo, it'd even be a risk to have you judge me . . . and as for most of the ladies on the *Persephonya* . . . no, thank you."

"You don't like the ladies?"

"I love 'em all, and lust even more, but the only time they're sentimental is over small helpless creatures and occasionally their own children, but only before puberty. Men can be sentimental, now and again, but it's usually over the wrong things, like women . . . or daughters."

I managed not to wince. I hadn't seen the last word coming, and it made me wonder exactly how much Sinjon Reksba knew about me. "Not sons?"

"Hades! Every man ever had a son knows the son wants to do him one better. Hard to be sentimental about that, and it's not good for the boy, either."

"You ever had any sons?"

"Not a one. Not any daughters, either. Being a son was enough to cure me. Might have to change that now." He looked toward the blank wall of the drop shuttle. "Be nice if they had ports or viewscreens, but this is Stittara."

That did tell me he'd done more than his fair share of traveling . . . under varied circumstances.

After that, it was only a few minutes before the last passengers were cocooned, and the shuttle dropped away from Stittara orbit control.

10

When the hatchway opened on the drop shuttle I filed out after most of the others, and right in front of Sinjon Reksba. Stittara turned out to be a purple-gray world, just as all the briefing materials indicated, but mere words and screen and link presentations aren't the same as the reality. Not for me, anyway. As for why that purple-gray was so intense, rather than dull, I couldn't have said. Oh, I could have presented reason after reason, and they'd all make perfect sense, beginning with the translucent always-airborne microorganisms that absorbed certain frequencies of visible light. The meteorologists have their measurements, their analyses that confirm those reasons. For them, that solved the problem. For me, it didn't. An old, old physicist once told me that labeling anything had nothing to do with solving a problem. Neither does explaining how something works. As far as I was concerned, the meteorologists had just analyzed and labeled the planet's atmosphere, and let it go. There were reasons for letting it go, and I suspected that what lay behind those reasons might be why I was there.

Well . . . not exactly. They were why the Unity's ecological arm, the Systems Survey Service, had posted that freelance consulting assignment that I'd jumped at just to get away from Bachman and Chelesina, except it had been dangled right in front of me, and I'd jumped at the bait like every other consultant who thought a proposal had been written exactly for his or her experience and abilities. And I was fairly certain this one had. What galled me the most was the feeling that I was part of a multimillion-duhlar political throwaway vote-getting gambit . . . that the experience that the Survey Service was paying for was only midlevel camouflage and that the results of my assessment would change nothing. Except . . . I'd known that the assignment wouldn't likely change much. Every consultant knows that ninety percent of what they do is to either give cover to doing nothing or to support a decision already made. In the case of Stittara, it was more than clear which was most likely.

Now . . . I was wondering just how good an idea it had been to take the contract, given that I was stepping off an antique half-winged/half-lifting body shuttle, carrying a modest duffel, in addition to the two crates in the shuttle's cargo bay. I'd had a look at the planet from the viewers on the orbit control station, and while the atmosphere looked hazy, I had been able to make out the outline of the continents and the comparatively narrow oceans that separated them. From space Stittara hadn't looked all that different, just another water world, with less water than many, except the veil of stars that was the Arm was far narrower, and the blackness on each side much wider . . . and there had been a shading of purple, but the view from outside the atmosphere had given no idea of the intensity of that purple-gray . . . or the fact that the sun was not a circle hanging in the sky. Rather the microorganisms in the upper troposphere diffused— and diminished—its illumination so that almost a quadrant of the sky was intensely luminous. Part of that was because Stittara's sun was an F class, but Stittara wasn't as far away as it should have been to be in the habitable zone because the atmosphere reflected more heat than did that of most T-type worlds.

Once I was down the ramp and clear of the shuttle I looked around, past the faded low greenish gray stone structure at the edge of permacrete tarmac to the west, looking around to see who from the local Survey Service was there to meet me. I couldn't pick out anyone in particular from the thirty or so individuals standing near the blockhouse-like dropport terminal, but I did see a pair of men in what appeared to be security singlesuits, along with a woman, greeting Aimee Vanslo, while a single functionary met Holly and Georg. The others before me had merged into the small crowd.

Once I looked away from the passengers and their greeters, the next thing I noticed was the grass, brownish purple-green, that seemed to cover everything, leaving no bare ground or rocks. The next was that there were no trees, not anywhere I looked, and the clumps of bushes that I did see were domelike and barely a meter tall. Nor were there any sharp shapes or jagged peaks, even of the hills or mountains in the distance. All that presented a landscape with an almost surreal and streamlined appearance, and in colors that would have seemed dull, monochromatic, had it not been for the intensity of those colors themselves.

Then . . . there was the sky, or what was in it. Stittara didn't have clouds. Well . . . not clouds in the way anyone from a standard water world would consider them. What struck me immediately was the complexity and the intricacy of the skytubes, that and the intensity of their purple-gray, a shade that didn't stay exactly the same in one place for more than moments. Yet I couldn't actually see the shift in color and intensity, but that might have been because the skytubes I saw were far to the southwest.

I kept walking, my eyes on the sky because all the briefing cubes in the world couldn't have conveyed that vibrancy . . . and yet, as I looked at the skytubes, they were somehow both intense . . . and just plain dull purple tinged with gray. The sky was a lighter gray, tinged with purple, also intense, just not so intense as the skytubes themselves.

"Gets you somehow, doesn't it?"

I looked away from the skytubes to see walking toward me a pleasant-faced woman of indeterminate age, not that I expected anyone on Stittara to show obvious age, given that it was essentially the source of cosmetic and physiological anagathics for the Unity. She smiled, obviously waiting for me, since she wore the gray-blue singlesuit of Systems Survey, if one in a style long since abandoned on Bachman, conservative as it was compared to styles on Eduardo or elsewhere in the center of the Unity.

"Aloris Raasn," she added.

"Paulo Verano. I'm the—"

"—the ecological assessor sent by the Unity, more precisely under the direction of the Assembly's oversight subcommittee," Aloris finished for me.

That an oversight committee had been involved didn't surprise me, but that I hadn't been told and that she had told me that she'd clearly received a beamed message from the *Persephonya*, which had reached her more swiftly than I had, for all that it had traveled with me, there being nothing faster for practical interstellar communication transmission than a ley-liner. Even so, she'd had to have acted quickly. "What do you do with the Survey?"

"I'm the assistant meteorologist and the administrative director." A smile slightly more than polite crossed her lips. "I have a groundcar. A Survey Services van, actually. We'll have to wait for your equipment."

"Don't we have to pick it up?" I gestured toward the blockhouse port building.

"It's easier for everyone if they deliver it to the van. I told Tadao you'd likely have some equipment."

"Two crates and a few templates." More than a few, since I'd brought as many as I could beg, borrow, or steal.

"Not exclusive single use, I hope."

I shook my head. "You're welcome to all of them, so long as I have access to the first prods on any I might need for my work. Where do we go from here?"

"To the Survey compound. You'll be staying in the guest quarters."

"The first in how many years?"

"They're used often by Survey personnel from the out-continents. You are the first off-planet visitor in several decades."

That wasn't exactly surprising. I would have bet that I was the first in longer than that.

There wasn't any ground debriefing, nor any entry formalities and procedures. All those had been taken care of on the orbit station. That made sense, because there was only one ley-liner a year from Bachman. Perhaps another handful from elsewhere in the Arm ported at Stittara, bringing either bored trusters on tours to see the oddities of the galaxy or industrial science types arriving—or departing—from the handfuls of projects scattered around the globe that had been established to study and to attempt to replicate the internal structure and properties of the various natural anagathics in the local flora.

We walked past the single long and low stone blockhouse set back from the shuttle strip toward a large flat expanse of permacrete, on which were arrayed a variety of vehicles, mostly ground types of some sort. There were two flitters, both with fuselages finished with the smooth dark gray that suggested years of usage and more than a few refinishings and repairs. The Survey Service van was finished in a yellow that had doubtless been brilliant and designed to stand out against the gray of the sky and the purple-gray of the skytubes. Now, it was just yellow.

"What do you expect to find here on Stittara, Ser Verano?" She opened the rear of the van, and I put my duffel in on one side, leaving more than enough room for my small crates. "Or not to find, as the case may be?"

"Paulo, please." I smiled. "I don't *expect* to find anything. I'm here to determine whether there are environmental and ecological impacts arising from the various projects that have been established to further develop the immunological and anti-aging boosters gleaned from the local organisms . . . and, of course, those studying the skytubes."

"There's little of that these days."

"Oh?"

"It's proved futile and fatal too often. You can see that in the Survey records."

That was interesting. Of course, neither of us had to mention the fact that Stittara likely would have long-since been abandoned without the intermittent flow of data and bio-discoveries. Those discoveries were another reason why I was standing there, since no one really wanted to abandon Stittara, for whatever reason, and my presence, at the very least, would buy enough time for a fickle electorate to forget and move on to the next sensational political revelation. My greatest danger was that I actually might find something that would change everything.

"If they were having such an impact, don't you think we would have reported it?" Aloris's voice was calm, but that didn't disguise the edge behind it. "And who might care when you return in over a hundred and fifty years?"

"The Environmental Ministry might. It has lasted more than a while." And I'd care, just out of professional pride, which might be all I had left by then.

"Ah, yes. The Ministry." She smiled. "Tadao will be here in a few minutes with your equipment."

I glanced to the west, where the skytubes were barely visible in the distance.

Aloris said nothing while we waited, and I didn't feel like making small talk. That's always been a problem for me. Chelesina complained that I was always pontificating or boring people with details. Somehow I never cared much for debating the latest linkpopper's hair shades or private life that was really scripted for public consumption.

Before long an open ground lorry appeared, moving first to one of the flitters, where a uniformed patroller and another man in a silver-gray singlesuit waited while the loader transferred three cases, all covered in quantum-locked film, to the flitter.

"The latest microprint specs," said Aloris.

That made sense. With molecular assemblers—microprinters—given an energy source and raw materials—tech transfer and updating was simply a matter of information. And since every ley-liner carried backup printers, if an out-system world had suffered some form of catastrophe, rebuilding was certainly possible, not that I was aware it had ever been necessary.

After the microprint templating specs had been off-loaded, the flitter lifted almost immediately and headed westward. What did strike me as odd was that the craft stayed low, no more than a hundred meters above the ground. Yet the sky was clear. Were the skytubes actually aware and sensitive to aircraft? The old reports I'd read had speculated on that, but had come to no conclusions. I hoped that the Stittaran Survey office had more recent and conclusive data, but that remained to be seen.

After a few minutes, the stocky young man with serious dark eyes guided the ground lorry over to the van. "Professor Doctor Verano?"

I nodded.

He extended a hand tablet. "Please authenticate receipt of your crates. Receipt does not invalidate any claims for damage, but you must make such claims before the *Persephonya* breaks orbit."

"When will that be?"

He grinned. "Not for another two months. The systems have to be recalibrated."

That only took a week or so. The rest of the wait time was to accommodate those who only needed a few weeks before departing.

Then he swung down and lowered the lorry's drop gate until it was level with the rear of the Survey van. In quick movements, he slid both crates into the van.

"Our thanks, Tadao." Aloris nodded.

"Summer calm, and my best to Raasn," he replied.

I assumed that he referred to some relative of hers, but since I didn't know the relationship nomenclature on Stittara, I just mentally filed the comment.

"Summer calm?" I asked as the lorry glided back toward the single structure serving the dropport. "Are the skytubes or the local winds less violent in the summer?"

"Not really. The early colonists thought so. By the time they found out, the expression had stuck, and now it's as much ironic as custom."

"By the way, what is the local season here?"

"Spring. The seasons don't vary much here. There's almost no axial tilt."

"And there's life here?" My question was rhetorically sardonic, designed to provoke a reaction.

"Stittara wasn't always this calm, the geologists say." She turned and walked to the driver's side of the van.

I walked to the other door, opened it, and slid into the seat. I actually had to manually fasten the safety straps. When I looked over, after fumbling them on, and nodded to Aloris, she pressed a stud on the flat surface before her and then put both hands on a steering wheel. I didn't say a word as she guided the van from the parking area onto a narrow permacrete highway. I hadn't expected a planetary or even a local VCS, but it was still a slight jolt to ride in a wheeled conveyance traveling a highway at high speed that was actually controlled by a person and not a system. I knew it wouldn't be the last surprise I should have anticipated and didn't.

"What have you found most intriguing about meteorology here on Stittara?" I asked as an opening question.

"That it's comparatively predictable and seldom intriguing."

"Even with the skytubes?"

"They seem to coexist with the weather. There's no data and no documentation on any instances where they could have changed or influenced meteorological conditions. You could make a rough analogy that they're an airborne cross between plankton and jellyfish. Ocean jellyfish merely ride the currents. They don't create them."

More than a stan passed as the van continued westward, and as Aloris Raasn expanded on her theory. During that time, we passed exactly two other vehicles, and I saw not a single structure once we left the dropport. Nor did I see any trees, only gently rolling hills covered with the thick low grass with its undershades of brown and purple, and low bushes of various types, whose leaves held close to the same shades as the grass. I'd read about the ecology and studied the reports, with the notations that only the mountains held any flora or fauna of significant height, but there's always a difference between reading and experiencing.

Finally, Aloris pulled off the highway and guided the van along a narrow way, over a rise, and down a slope into a wide grassy vale that held an array of hundreds, if not thousands, of structures, all but a few less than ten yards on a side, and none of them more than a story in height, if that. While there was a clear plan to the community, what it was escaped me, because all the streets were the same narrow width and all curved. There wasn't a straight stretch of permacrete anywhere, not from what I could tell, and not a single one of the tiny structures had any sharp corners, not even gently smoothed right-angled ones.

"Welcome to Passova."

"This is civilization, then?"

"There's more here than meets the eye, as you must know."

My eyes didn't see more, which confirmed that there was a lot underground, given that supposedly close to a hundred thousand people lived in Passova, the administrative center for the geographic area centered on the dropport.

The only indication of the nature of the structure into which she guided the van was the Service logo beside the vehicle doorway. Once the door had closed, and we had driven down the ramp behind it and into a vehicle bay, she seemed slightly less tense, but I wasn't certain why, unless she didn't care for driving a van more than a stan each way to the dropport.

"Why is the dropport so far from Passova?" I asked as I unstrapped and opened the door.

"It's located midway between Passova, several research communities, and eight other towns. It's also in the area with the best weather—and the greatest visibility."

"Have the skytubes ever destroyed a drop shuttle?"

"Once. That was over two hundred years ago. That's another reason why the dropport is where it is."

"And why everything on the surface is aerodynamically smooth and why important installations are underground?"

"It makes sense. You can leave your duffel in the van for now. You can meet some of the others, but the executive director won't be back until late tonight, and then we'll get your equipment transferred to the vacant lab space and your personal gear to the guest quarters."

I followed Aloris Raasn down the ramps to the open receiving area on the main level, lit by piped light. The diffused atmospheric light was close to T-standard, but far from identical. There another Survey member stood. He could have been her brother, or regendered clone. He probably wasn't either.

"Ecologist Verano, this is Meteorogist Raasn Defaux."

I managed not to gape. I'd obviously been wrong, in more ways than one. "I'm pleased to meet you."

"And surprised. You shouldn't be. It's in the Charter. Without imprint cloning, Stittara couldn't maintain critical expertise."

"He's also a far better meteorologist than I," added Aloris.

That might be true, but it was irrelevant. What was relevant was that Raasn was effectively her twin brother. Even if I reviewed the Stittaran Charter, I'd find that such a provision existed, and Raasn knew it, which was why he'd offered the statement, I suspected.

"Raasn and Demotte will take care of your gear while I show you the guest quarters," said Aloris smoothly. "This way, if you will."

I followed her to the end of the open area through what was clearly a pressure-seal door and out into a corridor a good six meters wide and three high, effectively an underground highway, emphasized by the fact that Aloris immediately moved to the right side of the tunnel corridor. Given that the top of the corridor had to be at least two meters below ground level, I had to ask, "Why the pressure-seal doors?"

"At times the storms can be so violent that there's a significant pressure drop in the center. If there's a break in any aboveground structure, the pressure differentials could wreak havoc with the equipment."

That made sense. I didn't think it was a complete answer, either, since wreaking havoc with equipment suggested even worse impacts on those operating the equipment.

We walked past another open pressure-seal door.

"Those are the quarters for some local Survey staff. The visiting quarters are accessed through the next door."

After walking another hundred yards, and being passed by a silent small conveyance I would have called a tunnel lorry, we reached that door, also equipped with pressure seals. Beyond the door, the much narrower corridor sloped gently upward until we came to a simple iris-door. Aloris palmed it, and it opened. "You can add your print to the setting before you leave the next time."

I nodded, following her into a foyer of sorts, with a narrow closet. Beyond the foyer was a modest-sized receiving chamber.

"Receiving chamber, dining, kitchen, and spare bedroom and bath down here, sleeping quarters, study, and bath/fresher on the upper level."

"Are all the quarters like that?"

"No. We've just discovered that outworlders feel confined without an outside view."

"You don't need it?"

She shook her head. "Most of us prefer the lower levels. Dermotte from maintenance should have your personal gear here shortly. If you'll enter your prints on the door, that will confirm your biometrics and cancel other access. Then I'll show you your spaces in the Survey complex."

I did just that, a little chilled, but not totally surprised that she had my biometrics. Then I followed her on what was likely to be a comparatively long walk through endless tunnels.

11

"What do you think?" Aloris asked. "First impressions."

"He's a man who thinks he's simple. He's not. The gray singlesuit trimmed in black is a pretty good indicator. He's also trim and muscular. He probably works out a lot, but never where anyone notices. I'll bet everything he brought is conservative and tasteful." Raasn smiled. "Tell me what you think. You spent several hours with him."

"He mostly asked questions and listened. He sees things without making you aware that he does."

"He made you aware."

"Only because I was watching for it."

"That alone says that he needs to be watched. He's the kind that Zeglar will underestimate. Even Venessa will."

"You know how—"

"I understand, but we have to work with who and what we have."

"That means less obvious observation," she replied. "Check him out with a van, and let him go where and when he wants as he wishes. When Rahn gets back tomorrow, I'll tell him that's the norm for consultants sent by the Ministry at the direction of an oversight committee."

"Since that is the norm."

"Rahn wouldn't know it. He's a political appointee. Because he got Willisen elected to the Council."

"He's been here over three years."

"And what has he learned?"

Raasn shrugged. "More than you think, but it won't hurt to tell him that it's the norm so that he can tell the Council just that."

"You're right, but I'd be surprised if Verano goes anywhere immediately. He did ask for the chief ecologist in the Survey."

"What did you tell him?"

"The truth. That we don't have one, but that Benart Albrot at Field Two is the closest approximation to that."

"Was that . . . ?"

"He'll find out about Albrot sooner or later. Verano will distrust anything we push on him. He strikes me as very methodical. He'll review the records first. Then he'll make visits to the multis and field stations." She pursed her lips, if momentarily. "Once he has that information, he'll come back to those of us in headquarters and ask more questions."

"That approach won't hurt us. No one will be able to claim that he was rushed into anything." He paused. "You don't think he intends to hurry through his work and try to leave on the *Persephonya,* do you?"

"What difference does it make? If that were to happen, and we both know how likely that is, he and his report would still reach Bachman more than a hundred and forty-six years after he departed, a lot more since the ley-liners don't take straight return trips. He stays five or six months and digs in, or even a full year, and it's a hundred and forty-seven years, and he'll get back earlier. That's if he even wants to return. It's not as though he has a lot to return to."

"He can't claim that bonus unless he returns . . . unless he brought some of it, or the equivalent, with him. That might be worth checking. Indirectly, of course. It might bear on our options."

"It might indeed."

"You won't co-opt him, Aloris dear. We might not need to do anything, but he's not the type to fall for wiles, feminine or otherwise."

"He did once."

"I think he's the kind that only gets burned one time . . . on anything."

"We'll see."

Raasn nodded.

"You'll take care of that . . . looking into accounts?"

"You already know about his expenses, don't you?"

"We can't touch them. He's got a year's per diem, keyed only to him, with Stittaran Planetary. Anything happens to him, it reverts to the Survey on Bachman. They really don't care, except that it's a way to discourage local stations from creative local fund-raising."

"Finding out about private accounts will take a few days."

"We've got more than enough time." She cleared her screen. "What do you think he'll do if he finds something? Given that he's methodical, like you?"

"He'll likely want to verify it, but that's not the only question."

"No, but Edo and Grantham and the other multi directors will be even more methodical. I worry about Edo. There's something going on there. Have you checked out the passenger lists yet?"

"They won't be made public until threeday."

"You have sources . . ."

"There's no point in wasting them on that."

She laughed, softly. "You're right . . . but let me know."

"Don't I always?"

12

I began the next morning, locally oneday, although it had actually been threeday onboard the *Persephonya* when we took the drop shuttle, by waking early, running through my standard exercises and Juchai workout, and eating lightly. After all the time I'd spent working out alone on the trip, I wondered if Passova had gyms or private workout equipment for lease or rent . . . but that could wait.

Then I met once more with Aloris, who, in her capacity as administrative director, gave me a work space, actually a small personal office, as well as clearance and codes for the Survey Service research and reports databases . . . and the observation that I only had access through the console in the office—or through other Survey consoles. There was no access through outside links.

"Why not?"

"It's not necessary, and it simplifies and strengthens security. Most Survey personnel live close to Survey installations." She offered an ironic smile. "That wouldn't work in Smithsen or on Bachman, but it does here."

I had to wonder why security was such a concern on Stittara, but I didn't ask, making a mental note to revisit that issue later.

"Now . . . you need to meet Rahn Zeglar," announced Aloris. "He's the executive director of the Systems Survey Service here on Stittara."

"Appointed by the Planetary Council?" I asked blandly, looking for a reaction.

"The executive directors of all Unity Ministry planetary entities on Stittara are appointed by the Planetary Council."

I knew that was standard, but from what I'd read and heard some executive directors were sinecure figureheads and others were truly in control. I already had my suspicions, but meeting with Zeglar would give me more to go on.

"After that, we'll stop by and you can meet Jorl Algeld. He's the operations director."

"Operations director?" That sounded more like a multi or military title.

"He's the one who coordinates the research, studies, and operations of the individual media branches . . . And enforcement, of course. Each media branch is headed by an assistant director."

That made sense, in a way, I supposed, although I had my doubts.

"Shall we go?" asked Aloris, although it wasn't really a question.

I followed her past the administrative area and through another set of pressure doors, then along a short hallway to yet another set of doors, white pseudowood, teak, I thought, as I opened one and gestured for her to enter. Beyond the doors was an anteroom holding a black shiny console desk, behind which sat a most attractive and petite black-haired young woman with a pleasant face and a pleasing smile.

Her gray eyes didn't smile as much as her mouth as she said, "He's expecting you and Dr. Verano, Director."

"Thank you, Venessa," replied Aloris, leading the way through another set of double white teak doors.

Zeglar's office was large—especially for a city such as Passova, where every square meter had to be excavated and reinforced—stretching some ten meters from the double entry doors to the scenic wallscreen above the white pseudo-teak credenza behind the matching desk. The wooden armchairs and the wide desk swivel were upholstered in a bluish purple, the same shade as the thick carpet that was bordered in a light golden green. I'd seen bureaucratically tasteless before, but I had the feeling I was beholding a new low. The wallscreen shifted from a scene of endless brownish green-purple grass to one of low hills covered with grass and foliage of a near identical shade.

Zeglar was a tallish man, taller than me, anyway, with blond hair, blue eyes, and skin that was either genetically or artificially colored like amber honey. He stepped forward and extended a muscularly beefy hand. "Dr. Verano, welcome to Stittara and the Survey Service." His voice was warm, pleasant, and well modulated, and his attention was focused totally on me.

That combination told me that he was a politician through and through. I inclined my head politely. "Thank you. I'm glad to be here and to meet you. Director Raasn here has been most helpful, and it appears as though you have a most professional Survey Service here on Stittara."

"I'm glad to hear that. We'd certainly like to think so."

"I'm sure you do."

"What can I personally do for you?" The warm smile was directed at me and no one else.

"I think you've done everything you need to do by letting me work with the professionals here in the Survey. If I need more, I'll certainly let you know."

"Well . . . don't hesitate to stop by if you need anything."

"I certainly won't."

After a few more generally meaningless pleasantries, Aloris and I took our leave and departed, nodding politely to Venessa on the way out.

Once we were beyond the doors, I did ask, for reasons of my own, "Did Venessa come with Executive Director Zeglar?"

Aloris barely managed to keep a straight face. "The executive director chooses his or her own personal aide. The Planetary Council believes it should be that way."

"I can see why."

We walked back through the short corridor, then took a door to a ramp down a level. Then headed back along a corridor that seemed to match the one leading to Zeglar's office, except when we went through the pressure doors, rather than double doors, the corridor continued, with offices on each side. We stopped at the first one, slightly larger than my cubicle and about the size of Aloris's office.

A short bulldog of a man turned his swivel and bounded to his feet. "You must be Dr. Verano. Jorl Algeld." He extended a hand and shook mine firmly. "I read the articles that came with the announcement of your assignment. The water overviews I thought were very perceptive."

"Thank you."

"Be interested to see what you think of our aquatic eco-relations once you look at them."

"I'll likely be looking at many interrelations." That was safe enough.

"I'd appreciate it if you'd let me know when you're ready to talk to any of our assistant directors of media or field personnel. Might be able to make sure you get to the right people."

"I'll do that. I'd thought to study the background reports and research before doing any visits or interviews. There's no point in wasting people's time over issues that have already been reported and analyzed."

"Thought you might do something like that. Your reports are organized . . . methodical. I can see why the Survey Service on Bachman sent you. Is there anything you need from me right now?"

"Probably not for a few days." *Or longer.*

"Well . . . let me know."

"I will, thank you."

Since Aloris had been effectively ignored and I had been dismissed, I nodded to her, and we left.

Algeld was back in front of his screen before we were even out of his spaces.

As we headed back to the upper level, I said, "He seems rather energetic."

"He's always been that way."

"He came up through the water media?"

"He was the assistant director for water."

I just nodded.

When we got back to my spaces, I turned to Aloris. "Thank you for introducing me to the executive director and the operations director. I do appreciate it."

"It was my pleasure." A hint of a smile almost escaped her professional expression.

After Aloris left, I personalized the data interface in my "laboratory spaces" so that I could easily direct-access all the local Systems Survey files to which I'd been granted access. The next thing I did was access the personnel directory. I'd been surprised when Aloris had told me that the Stittaran Survey Service didn't have a chief ecologist. When I finished going through the directory I understood why . . . and it also, in a way, gave yet another reason why the contract proposal had been offered and why I'd been sent. The entire Survey Service on Stittara was organized by environmental media—essentially by continental water resources, air, geology, oceanography, and solar impacts. There was no integration, and in a way, that made a strange kind of sense because the laws and regulations were also set out by media.

After shaking my head at the bureaucratic structure, I began to read, painstakingly, all the data and reports gathered on the grass/lichen sym-bionts, although technically they weren't exactly symbionts, that had engendered the anagathic boom. I wasn't really particularly interested in that, because the anagathic multis had been investigated time and time again, and I suspected that aspect of my assignment had just been thrown in as even more political cover for the charge to look into the ecological impacts that hadn't been so thoroughly addressed, such as the airborne microorganisms that—presumably—comprised the skytubes. That the microorganisms did was, of course, a presumption based on indirect evi-dence, since the reports indicated no one had yet survived an attempt to take a sample. Not a direct sample, at least. There had been analysis of organic material shed from the tubes, which revealed both similarities and significant differences between the free-floating microorganisms and the skytubes, assuming, of course, that the shed detritus actually repre-sented some integral aspect of the skytubes and wasn't merely a waste product—which was my suspicion as well as that of a number of other researchers.

Even so, a quick reading of just the summaries of the anagathic reports took until midafternoon, and my conclusions tended to be similar to those of scores of other researchers. The properties of the pharmaceuticals produced by the local "grass" that covered almost every surface that wasn't actively cultivated, or inside the hill and mountain forests, or on solid rock, appeared limited to certain tissues, and were most effective in those with close contact with free oxygen/air. In short, every compound, formulation, and derivative created by Syntex, Eterna, ABP, and a few smaller entities extended the life span of human skin cells, the strength and durability of human hair, as well as the exposed collagenous parts of the human body, such as fingernails and toenails. Given the time-dilation, and the costs, of course, the anagathic multis produced their derivative products in the Arm, close to the billions of women who sought—and received—the expensive creams, salves, and the like that gave them close to flawless skin for as long as the rest of their bodies endured.

But, of course, since human skin was also effectively the largest human organ, having good skin had translated directly into extended life spans, also possibly because of the impact on human keratin, found in various forms in critical internal organs, although the effect was less pronounced when it involved internal organs. The formulations also effectively eliminated an entire range of carcinomas as well. Because the multis had never been satisfied with limiting themselves, they had gone on to develop formulations targeted at other areas of the body. All that the various Arm regulators had determined was that such formulations did no harm and that they basically still only affected the various forms of human keratin.

After the initial boom and bust, and the winnowing out of less-capitalized anagathic multis, what remained on Stittara were the research installations that continued to pursue efforts to find the ultimate bio-rejuve substance that could create either cellular immortality for other organs or for the entire organism. More than five hundred years of research had only yielded modest improvement on previous formulations . . . so far.

Three days later, I'd completed a quick run-through on all the files dealing with the anagathic aspects of my contract, necessary for two reasons. First, if I did run across adverse ecological impacts from those multis, I'd need that background. Second, I had no doubt that every file I accessed was being reported to Aloris—or Raasn or someone in the local Survey—and I wanted no complaints that I had slighted anything. Then, after taking some time out at Aloris's insistence to get a complete familiarization with the Survey vans, I started in on my assignment, to determine if current monitoring was effective and if anyone was altering the environment in ways that weren't being detected by current monitoring.

At the same time, especially after seeing them, I couldn't help but wonder about the skytubes. How old were they? While they formed intermittently, like a tornado, there were always tubes in the sky. Was that only the visible manifestation of something more? How could anyone tell, exactly? They'd been a feature of Stittara from the first explorations nearly a thousand years earlier, and the flora and fauna suggested that the intermittent and violent storms that scoured the surface of the planet had been in existence for at least tens of millions of years.

Almost immediately, in looking at the files containing historical data, I ran across a reference to geoscanning, and what had to be a reference to forerunner remnants, if remnants buried hundreds of meters below the current surface of Stittara.

I went to find Aloris. She was engaged in some sort of administrivia, but looked up with a smile. "What is it, Paulo?"

"The geo-records indicate the possibility of, or the remnants of, forerunner culture . . ."

"Oh . . . those. They definitely are."

"Then why isn't there any mention of that?"

"There is. All that information is in the Archaeological History section."

"Could you make that available as well?"

"Certainly." She smiled. "You are being thorough."

"Thank you. For what I've been assigned"—*and paid*—"I need to be quite thorough. I should have guessed, but thinking about archaeological history hadn't crossed my mind in dealing with an alleged current ecological problem."

"Alleged? You *are* being careful."

"No. Merely professional. My first task is to determine if there is such a problem, and then, if there is, whether any recent actions caused it." I offered a half grin. "Who knows? Perhaps those forerunners had a similar problem."

"I doubt archaeological history will tell you that." She arched her eyebrows. "As I recall, those traces date back hundreds of millions of years."

"Well . . . thank you, anyway."

So I dug into the archaeological archives and discovered—for myself, since it was clear the findings had been sent to Bachman more than two centuries earlier—that at least a hundred million years earlier there had been a number of forerunner cities on Stittara. All but one of the clearly identifiable remains had been located, with difficulty, under or near lava traps, and had been identified as belonging to the civilization classified as the Builder (A) culture. There was no certain way of telling how long the ruins had been abandoned before geological processes took over and buried them, not after that many eons. The one site that had not been located under or near a lava trap was, interestingly enough, the site to which Syntex had the rights of access. I went back to the "clearly identifiable" wording, and found an interesting qualifier in the notes buried at the end of the file: "more than fifty other far smaller anomalies of a similar composition have tentatively been located at the same geo-strata, but initial probes indicate that further investigation is unwarranted at this time." What, if anything, that meant I'd like to find out, but at the moment, I didn't have a reason within my contract to go around asking about that. Not directly, anyway, but perhaps . . .

So I went back to the comparatively more recent environmental and ecological reports and discovered pages and pages of data, meticulously classified, and well-written analyses and findings. I spent all the rest of the day reading and studying them . . . and had a headache by the time I finished and leaned back in the chair in my small personal "laboratory spaces," well away from those of anyone else.

Finally, I took a moment to think things over. Essentially, my assignment covered four phases. First, I had to determine whether the multis, the municipalities and installations, or any other entities were creating violations of environmental standards. The next question was whether any were, even within the parameters of those standards, altering the environment in a way that made significant changes or threatened it. Then I'd have to determine whether the outland settlements and practices had that sort of effect. And there was the remaining question of whether the skytubes were an organic entity or entities threatened by human activities on Stittara.

In theory, I could rush through my evaluation . . . and finish in less than a month . . . and still return to Bachman on the *Persephonya*, returning some 146 years after I'd left, and only three months or so older.

Then I stopped and laughed. The *Persephonya* wasn't headed back to Bachman anyway. I'd get back sooner by staying longer for a direct return ley-liner, assuming there was one.

Was there more than a month's worth of material to evaluate?

I doubted that the Survey files would take more than another few days to comb through, but I'd still have to visit each of the outlying multis and then the Survey's research installations . . . and how long doing that would take I didn't know, but it would take weeks at the very least to do that part of the contract justice, and there was no telling where that might lead. All that didn't even include a survey of the impact of the outlying settlements and areas of cultivation, although the files I'd scanned hadn't made much reference to them, nor had my contract. Still, I wanted to do it right, if only for my own personal pride.

13

Dark summer gardens of my sky, thought two,
land grubbers twisted sky soul from the true.

"Come to me, whether sky is clear, or free, or you are near," chanted Ilsabet, walking swiftly up the gentle slope.

"Don't talk nonsense," said the one Ilsabet called Matron, "or I'll have to insist that you come back inside, where it's always safe."

"I never talk nonsense through," replied Ilsabet. "It's only no sense to you who cannot do, and cannot call those who'll bring again the Fall."

"Nonsense is as nonsense speaks," said the Matron, her voice condescendingly soft, her hand close to the stunner at her waist.

"As you wish and say," said Ilsabet. "I'll be good today." After a pause, she added, "It's always safe outside for me. You'd see, if you'd let me be." She danced across the thick carpet of brown-purple-gray-green grass at the top of the low ridge, not looking back, her eyes to the west and south.

The Matron did not answer, only glancing nervously to the south, then back to the door in the small and low section of the building aboveground.

A light breeze rippled the white cloth of Ilsabet's blouse, a wind neither hot nor cold.

"From the south please come, and let this charade be done . . ." Those words were chanted barely in a murmur before the bright blank expression returned to her face.

14

Fiveday morning, I sipped tea—or what passed for it—up in the study. I saw no one outside, even after it got lighter—not that there would ever be a true sunrise—no one at all. As I thought about it, I hadn't seen anyone outside any time that I'd actually looked, but I hadn't looked that much. Then I dressed and made my way past the concealed pressure doors at the top of the ramp, and walked down to the main level, then out into the tunnel way, and to the Survey Service and my "official" office, where I went back to my detailed and increasingly boring study of the local Systems Survey records and reports.

It was a very long day, with a quick break for a meal prepared by the synthesizer in my quarters. I did arrange with Dermotte for him to make template copies of some monitoring equipment and a new analyzer design, for distribution to the Stittaran Survey Service. In late afternoon, as I was massaging my forehead and about to stop pushing my way through more and more documents, there was a rap on the open door to my spaces. I turned my head and saw Aloris standing there.

"Good afternoon," I offered.

"The same to you. I haven't wanted to bother you. You've been working rather hard, and I thought you might like to join several of us for dinner tonight at Ojolian's." Her smile was more than professional and less than flirtatious, and that was fine with me.

"I'd be delighted." And I was. Eating alone in a strange city, if that was what Passova was, on a strange world gets old quite quickly. Besides, who knew what I might discover . . . even by what no one talked about. "What time, if I might ask?"

"Around seven."

"I'll be there. Thank you."

"We'll look forward to seeing you." With that, she slipped away.

She'd left me largely to my own devices for four days, except for politely occasionally asking if I needed anything and insisting I get checked out on how to operate the Survey van . . . and now I was getting a dinner invitation?

It couldn't hurt.

That left me a good hour before I had to get cleaned up for the evening. So I took a deep breath and went back to reading another series of responses to Survey Service proposals, most of which dated back hundreds of years and had never even gotten to the study stage, about possible investigations of the skytubes. What still amazed me, after all the years as an ecologist, was how much administrivia led to absolutely nothing. Almost as amazing was how often good data and studies were ignored once they'd been completed.

I didn't have a chance to read in detail the last three studies, ones that looked to be among the most promising, but I did skim them and make quick notes so that I could go over them in more detail.

At seven I walked into Ojolian's, what I would have called a bistro back on Bachman, and I'd had to take one of the tunneltrams or trains, since it was on the far northeastern side of Passova. Even with a link, I'd had to ask the system for directions once, but that was probably because I was used to orienting myself with an open sky around me, something that the tunnels and even Ojolian's made not the faintest attempt to reproduce in any sort of fashion.

Ojolian's looked to be a cross between an ancient Anglo pub, with dark pseudo-oak walls and partitions and an equally antique Frankish bistro with spindly-looking chairs and glass-topped iron-rimmed tables. The light came from wall sconces from a period or culture I didn't recognize . . . and could have been Ansaran or Farhkan, for all I knew. The floor was of square tiles, alternating black and white.

When I approached the table where Aloris and the others sat, she gestured to a young man, accompanied by another young-looking person.

"This is my son. Haraan, this is Paulo Verano, the noted ecologist I told you about."

"I'm pleased to meet you," said the young man. "And this is my partner, Amarios."

"I'm also pleased to meet you," said Amarios.

With that low husky voice and silky hair of midlength, androgynous looks and figure, Amarios could have been female or male, or either attempting to be the other. I wasn't about to guess. "It's good to meet you both."

Both Haraan and Amarios looked young—and so far as I knew Stittara had no rejuve technology or biologic systems beyond those available in the rest of the Arm. Yet . . . if Aloris could have children, why had she also, even earlier, permitted or agreed to degendered cloning? Was the birthrate that low? Haraan barely showed any resemblance to Aloris—or to Raasn Defaux—except in the eyes and in general build, yet my eyes flicked from one to the other, because there was . . . something.

"You know Raasn," added Aloris, gesturing, "and that is Darlian across from him. No, she's not in the Survey. She's a private advocate."

I turned and inclined my head to her. "Domestic, commercial . . . or both?"

"Both," replied the woman with short-cut blond hair. "Stittara's too small for that kind of specialization." Her voice was firm, just short of being hard. In the comparative dimness of the bistro, I had no idea what color her eyes were.

"Commercial infringement one day, and domestic unity and property disputes the next?" I returned lightly.

"More likely water rights one day, and domestic disturbance hearings the next."

I nodded and settled into the sole empty chair, between Aloris and Darlian, and directly across from Amarios.

"To keep things clear in my mind," I said, looking at Amarios, "what do you do, if I might ask?"

"I'm a singer."

"This is one of her few nights off," interjected Haraan.

"Just because there was a power surge that fried half the systems in Invireo . . . about three stans ago." Amarios shook her head. "Aelston kept saying he'd have it fixed. It didn't happen. It never does."

"Does it happen often?"

"Two or three times a year."

"That seems like a lot." But then, I reflected, Stittara's year was four hundred and twenty days. On the other hand, all the power sources and lines were underground.

"You're thinking that's too many, aren't you?" asked Raasn, an amused expression on his face.

"I was . . ." I stopped because a server, an elflike young woman—I thought—had appeared, with a tray of crystal-like beakers and goblets, placing one of whichever before everyone but me.

"What would you like to drink, ser?"

"Pale lager or whatever comes closest?"

"We have Spendrift and Yelos. We're out of Zantos."

"Whichever is less bitter."

"Spendrift."

"That will be fine." I turned to Raasn. "There's obviously something I don't know. What is it?"

"There's always a fairly strong magnetic field with the storms. They can put stress on the power grids and components, and if the stress doesn't immediately cause failures . . ."

"It does later . . . and unpredictably," I suggested. *But a power surge and not just a failure? When there haven't been any storms?* Maybe I just didn't know enough about Stittara and especially its infrastructure. That was understandable after not quite a week planetside.

Raasn nodded.

"So what systems failed at Invireo?" I asked Amarios. "Or was it just the combination of too many black boxes?"

She smiled. "Doesn't every club anywhere have a system that's been added to and modified so many times no one's quite sure what goes where . . . until everything goes wrong?"

"I've known some clubs like that," I admitted, even if I'd only known them because they were the kinds of places Chelesina and Leysa liked.

"Are you in the Survey?" I asked Haraan.

"I fear not. My talents don't lie in that direction. I'm the entertainment coordinator and director for Passova Comm. I'll be especially busy for the next few months, scanning, rating, and the like . . ."

"Oh . . . the downloads from the *Persephonya?*"

"That's right. They always need editing and localization, the ones that aren't period pieces of some sort."

"Haraan is one of the best at that," added Amarios.

"Then there's the problem of pricing and distribution, and no matter what I do, some staffer for some member of the Council is always complaining."

"The Council pays for the acquisition and shipping?"

"They wanted to make certain that no local media linkster had monopoly access. It's by bid, but no media combine can obtain more than thirty percent."

"Why thirty percent?"

Haraan chuckled. "Given the amount of material that comes in at one time, that seems to be the right number to assure that no one can buy enough of the more obviously popular content."

"There are always shows, dramas, concerts that weren't that popular on Bachman, but do better here than they did there," added Amarios.

"Do you send back local entertainment?"

"Some," replied Haraan, "but we only net about a quarter of what it costs us. And the Unity government actually subsidizes us. We get what we get at a fifty percent discount. The rationale is maintenance of cultural homogeneity."

Those, frankly, were factors I'd never even considered. So I just nodded.

"Enough of what I do," said Haraan with a self-deprecating laugh. "My mother says that you're one of the top ecologists in the Unity. How did you ever decide to be an ecologist?"

"It happened. I couldn't explain everything that went into it, but what kept me interested is that ecology is the organic equivalent of fractals, if you will."

Amarios offered a husky soft laugh. "That sounds like entertainment."

"Music is most ordered and not fractal," said Aloris, not quite primly.

"Mother is also an oboist in the Passova Symphony."

They still had community or civic symphonies on Stittara? The only symphony orchestras on Bachman were those maintained by a few entertainment multis. They generally catered to older and wealthier eccentrics. "Oh . . . how long have you been playing with them?" I asked Aloris.

She laughed. "Long enough to know better."

"She's really quite good," insisted Haraan.

"She is," added Amarios.

"But why do you equate ecology with fractals?" asked Haraan.

"Because the same uniqueness persists no matter how far down you go in size and how far up . . . well . . . until you get to the point where intelligent species start destroying the interrelations." At that point I caught a quick glance between Aloris and Raasn.

"Surely you don't mean us?" asked Raasn ironically.

"Perhaps I should have said pseudo-intelligent species."

Everyone laughed.

At that point, the server returned with my lager and asked, "Are you ready to order?"

I had to grab for the menufilm and scan it while Aloris began. Thankfully, or perhaps she gestured, the server went around the table the other way, and by the time the others had ordered, I'd decided. "I'll have the torna salad, and the beefalo crepe with pommefrit and vegetables." The beefalo was likely either synth or tank, but that didn't matter to me.

"That's actually pretty good," said Haraan after the server left. "I'd recommend against the calamari in the future. Perforated sonic foam is tastier and more tender."

I winced at that.

Amarios gave a brief but amused smile.

"What do you sing?" I asked.

"It depends on which set. The early set, that's mostly old and slow, ballads and an upbeat art song or two . . ."

She had to have searched long and hard for any upbeat art songs, I suspected, but maybe they weren't art songs at all.

". . . and the second set is usually old pop, twenty years back, maybe more . . . the third set is the edgy stuff . . . and the late set is pretty much whatever people request. There are some songs I won't do . . . just claim I can't do it. Aelston backs me up on that."

"Once he turned the system into a deafening squeal every time one asshole tried to demand 'Bareback,'" added Haraan with a grin.

"How many nights a week do you do that?"

"Five . . . twoday through sixday. The club's closed on sevenday. On oneday, the music's all playback from earlier shows." She shrugged in a way that was feminine, and not at all androgynous . . . but I still wasn't certain.

"You never said what your initial specialty in ecology was," said Haraan.

"Water. Fresh water, sources and interactions, chemistry and biologics . . . regulations . . . pollution of all sorts, including sonic and nanetic . . ." It was my turn to shrug. "That led to everything else, because you really can't separate out the components of a planetary ecosystem, not without horrible mistakes and even worse political, technical, and developmental decisions and regulations . . ." I talked for a good ten minutes nonstop, until Haraan's and Amarios's eyes began to glaze over—but not Raasn's, I noticed.

After that, the conversation got lighter—how could it have not?—and I had a good meal and conversation that wasn't too taxing . . . even if I still wondered about Haraan, his partner, and his mother. I also noted that no one said a word about my assignment or the Survey Service.

Hell! I worried about them all, even the advocate who'd said almost nothing.

15

Early on sixday morning, after I'd exercised and eaten in my quarters, I did see someone outside, for the first time. She was close to a half kay away, her back to me, and she was looking south, toward the distant sky-tubes. She wore a white blouse and stood in the middle of an expanse of the grass, grass that was somehow brown and green infused with purple. One hand gathered part of a purple gray skirt, the kind that no one donned except for formal balls, if then, and certainly not for everyday wear, and the other held a flower, a single stalk with white petals. I couldn't identify it, not surprisingly, because on Bachman, few flowers had survived the Terran mutebees designed for food crops and little else, since the founders hadn't been exactly all that interested in what they termed frills, a shortcoming the Arm was still paying for.

Then she skipped lightly up the treeless slope, and white petals dropped off the flower stalk. At the top of the slope, she stopped again. After a time, another woman, one with a weapon at the wide belt around her waist, approached and said a few words to the woman in the anachronistic long skirt.

The woman in the white blouse turned and walked down the slope, almost like a dejected child, although she was clearly older than that.

The image of her, looking toward the giant but distant skytubes in the southwest, remained in my thoughts even after I went down to the Survey System spaces and my temporary office there. As was typical for a government organization, sixday wasn't a workday, but I saw a few people in passing as I made my way to my space and console.

For the first stan or so of my continuing perusal of the Systems Survey records, I went over the three studies that had looked intriguing . . . and came away somewhat disappointed, in part because of the fact that all the evidence and factual presentations were observational, rather than experimental. What was intriguing was the notation that no attempt at penetrating a skytube had ever been successful, and would likely not be unless attempted with a hardened military type penetrator—which the study authors recommended against "for obvious reasons." Those reasons were never presented, but there was a short section that had been deleted—two hundred years earlier. What was odd was that the deletion was noted. I doubt I would have noticed otherwise, even with the awkward transition to the next section, the one that noted that Stittara had no high-flying birds, that all avian species were small, and used burrow nests.

I was still puzzling over that when I began reviewing the documentation submitted by the various research multis—both those that had come and gone and those that remained. For some reason, my thoughts drifted back to the woman in the antique garb, but I finally pushed the image aside and concentrated on the voluminous files.

After several stans more of heavy reading, I decided to walk through the tunnel ways over to one of the "local" eating establishments. I'd no more than stepped into the tunnel than Aloris appeared, with a shorter brunette.

"Paulo . . . are you going to lunch? Would you like to join us?"

"I would."

"This is my friend Zerlyna, Zerlyna Eblion. We were catching up on some data systems changes while no one was around. We're headed to Carlo's. It's not bad, and it's quick."

Zerlyna offered a warm smile, almost too warm, I thought, before I replied, "That's fine with me."

Carlo's was down a narrower pedestrian tunnel, what might have been called a side street or a lane, less than a hundred yards away. Unlike Ojolian's, it was brightly lit, with shimmering off-white plastreen tables, covered with red oilcloth. We ended up beside a fountain set in the middle of perhaps fifteen tables. The antique-looking fountain was a representation of a circular tower, leaning at an angle. Clearly, that was deliberate, but why that might be escaped me.

"What do you suggest?" I asked, leaving it up to the two as to who might answer.

"I like the risotto funghi," offered Zerlyna

"If you're in the mood for something solid," added Aloris, "you might try the kalzone."

"What are you having?"

"Mixed antipasto." She paused. "Both the house red and white wines are good."

In the end, I settled on a kalzone, and the limpid lager that the server immediately brought was nowhere near as good as that at Ojolian's, which had been barely passable. I realized, belatedly, that Aloris had been offering a veiled warning about the lager. I'd have to keep that mannerism in mind.

As we sipped our various beverages, Zerlyna looked across the circular table and asked, "Are you finding everything accessible?"

"Very much so." *So far as I know.*

"That's Zerlyna's doing," explained Aloris. "She's the data manager . . . and the one who compiles all the annual budget reports to the Planetary Council."

"Then you're the one who could tell me what occupies most of the Survey's effort here."

"That comes under operations. It's keeping the outies under control."

I hadn't the faintest idea what she meant. "Outies? I haven't seen anything on that. Why is that such a big problem?"

"All those entries are under Outland Operations." Zerlyna paused.

"That's not under an assistant media director?"

"No. Outland Operations are enforcement, and it's directly under Jorl." She paused, just for an instant. "I'm sure you've noticed how close Stittara is to T-norm, despite the anomalies. The official population is maybe four million. Half of those are outies."

Four million struck me as an incredibly low population figure for a world that had been first occupied a thousand years earlier, but that would be easy enough to check. "Meaning they don't live in places like Passova?"

"That's right. Their birthrate is higher, too, and where they can crop or herd is limited under the Unity protocols. If we let them cultivate or grow anywhere they wanted, with the storms and winds we have, we'd have ecological disaster in less than two generations. Most of our enforcement personnel are detailed to keep tabs on them, and most of the people who are in rehab or work custody are outies."

"For ecological and environmental violations," added Aloris, in case I didn't see the obvious.

"Speaking of outies," I commented dryly, "I saw someone outside early this morning."

Aloris frowned. "I can't imagine who that might be."

"White blouse, long skirt, the kind no one wears anymore." *Except in the more conservative communities on Bachman.* But I wasn't going to get into that.

The two exchanged a knowing glance.

"Oh . . . that's Ilsabet . . ." offered Aloris.

Zerlyna nodded. "Had to be."

I nodded, wondering how the two immediately knew from my sketchy description who the woman was. "Local character?"

"You might say so. She's been around as long as anyone can remember."

"She didn't seem that old." *Especially since even the best combinations of anagathics and genes generally reach their limits around two hundred.*

"They say she's close to four hundred."

I looked at Aloris. She seemed serious. "How can that be?"

"No one knows," replied Zerlyna. "Her behavior mimics senile dementia, but there's no sign of that in her system. When they found her, all she could do was recite nursery rhymes or something like them. Every medical tech and doctor have studied the test results, and every so often someone comes up with another set of tests. Biologically and physiological speaking, so far as anyone can tell, she's a perfectly normal female of forty to fifty standard years, except for the gray hair, but she never ages, and there's nothing in her system to explain it."

"Nothing that hasn't been observed in other people," added Aloris.

"And what is in people's systems here that isn't in mine, for example?"

"Various local micro and nano compounds and organisms. Some are likely natural anagathics," explained Zerlyna.

I thought I caught the hint of a frown from Aloris, but that vanished as the server reappeared with our meals. The kalzone was filling and spicy, but I did appreciate the small side portion of truffled risotto that accompanied it.

After several mouthfuls, I asked, "Is this Ilsabet one of those outies?"

"No. She was, according to the records, attached to a research station that was largely destroyed and then abandoned—after whatever it was happened to it and her."

"Why was it abandoned, and what happened to her?"

"Because, somehow, a skytube ripped open an exposed upper level and sucked everyone and everything out, down to the lowest level. Everything that wasn't part of the structure, that is. She was found wandering around outside afterward. She doesn't remember what happened. After that, the multi involved closed operations on Stittara. I don't remember the name, but it's in the records."

In one sense, I could see why neither of them knew the details, given how long since those events had occurred. In another sense, it seemed to me that someone should have pursued what had happened and why, and that there should have been records in Systems Survey Service headquarters. "And that was it?"

"Pretty much. There were investigations. One lasted for years, but they didn't lead to anything, and the storm's magnetic field wiped all the data from the systems."

"It was that powerful?"

"They're the most powerful recorded on any T-type world."

That was hard to believe, but that wasn't something Aloris would have lied about. It was too easy to check, but it was another fact that hadn't shown up in my briefing materials, which were turning out to be rather selective. I had to wonder if they'd been edited by a staffer who'd swallowed the Denier line.

"Has Ilsabet been reported to the Unity?" From my research on Bachman, I was fairly certain that there were no open references to this Ilsabet or such an event. That meant that they'd likely been deleted or remained classified. And since part of my assignment dealt with the skytubes, that was more than a little interesting. Of course, it might not have been a Denier plot—I was skeptical of great conspiracies and those who believed in them—but not of something as simple and nefarious as the multis getting the references removed or classified so that nothing interfered with the profits and demand for continuing anagathic products. That, unfortunately, suggested just how impulsive I'd been to take the contract.

"The destruction was certainly reported, and the reports on Ilsabet go back over three centuries. I assume someone on Bachman has read them by now."

"How did this all happen?"

"It's all in the records," said Zerlyna. "Just keyword Ilsabet."

I didn't ask any more questions while I finished the kalzone and the risotto, and the lager, out of necessity.

With the slightest hint of a smile, Aloris looked at me and asked, "You're going back to work, aren't you?"

I nodded.

"I know you're on contract," Aloris went on, "but sixday afternoon isn't a work time."

I managed a grin. "So far as I know, none of sixday is."

"Since it's not," Aloris added with a smile, "we're going shopping. Don't work too hard."

"It's not that hard when you're having fun."

They both shook their heads.

Then Aloris picked up the tab, over my protests, although I didn't protest too much, and the two of them left.

Once I returned to my spaces, I keyed in Ilsabet. The summary entry was short.

> *Ilsabet [presumed to be Elisabetta Vonacht, based on survivor accounts. Early records destroyed in storm of 651 . . .] . . . woman of approximate chronological age of 40 standard years, with the exception of prematurely gray hair, no apparent physiological aging during extended periods of observation. Mental age of 8+, but advanced mathematical capabilities, not of savant profile.*

The pages of detail that followed, along with the references to physiological and psychological studies and more studies, ran to more pages/words than I wanted to count or read. I did skim through them, but nothing ever changed, as if the woman had been frozen in metabolic time, so to speak. I didn't know how that was possible, and neither, apparently, did any of the doctors and researchers who'd examined her over the centuries.

No one knew quite what to do with her, because there was always the possibility that someone might unravel the puzzle and potential she represented.

But there was one question I had—why hadn't she been removed from Stittara?

To find out that took another hour of digging, which was probably wasted, since she certainly didn't bear directly on my assignment, but I was intrigued. The answer to the question was simple. She was a ward of the people of Stittara, and the Planetary Council had refused to allow her to travel off-planet. Given the precedent set by the Assemblage Genocide, that was that. Ilsabet wasn't going anywhere. Researchers could visit her, test her, whatever, but not remove her from Stittara.

Yet . . . If, *if* that profile was correct, Ilsabet, or Elisabetta, since the early records used both, was not only more than four hundred years old, but more than five hundred, since the station had been obliterated 474 years earlier. Yet she moved like a girl, apparently thought like an eight-year-old, and could handle mathematical problems with the best of graduate doctorates—provided the problems were presented in formulaic format.

The more I studied the files on Ilsabet, the more I knew I was missing something, but at the same time I hadn't been assigned to handle missing and seemingly impossibly long-lived women, and I did tend to be task-driven. Of course, that also might be another reason why Chelesina had left . . . but I wasn't going to look too deeply into that. Not at the moment.

What I did begin to investigate was the material the Survey had on the storm that Ilsabet had survived . . . and it was indeed some storm. The estimated wind velocity, and it was estimated, because no instruments survived, exceeded eight hundred klicks.

I read that again. *Exceeded eight hundred klicks.* From what I recalled, the highest wind velocity ever recorded on a T-type planet was somewhere around five hundred klicks. That had to be a typographical error or an incorrect estimation of wind speeds. I wondered what else was inaccurate in the report, but continued to read.

The residual energy and magnetic distortions suggested that the magnetic field associated with the storm was immeasurably larger than the planetary magnetic field.

I had to stop again. That didn't make sense. The magnetic fields associated with storms on most T-type worlds were low, usually creating variances from the planetary magnetic field of not more than ten to twenty percent, and those with high variance were associated with tight and intense storms, such as tornadoes, rather than tropical cyclones or hurricanes.

Still . . . the skytubes did look like tornadoes . . .

I shook my head.

Still . . .

I put those files on hold and searched out recent storm reports, those made with current instruments and containing multiple inputs and measurements. I read the most recent report, and then the one before that, and the one prior to that . . . until I'd found myself back almost twenty years, with a stunned feeling and a tightness in my guts.

For several moments I sat back in the standard Survey swivel. Not only were the storm numbers for the storm associated with Ilsabet unprecedented on an inhabited T-type world, the measurements associated with the "average" storms, although far less impressive, were as well. And I'd run across nothing mentioning them in any of the background material made available to me on Bachman.

Then I recalled that Aloris hadn't mentioned what multi had operated the station that had been destroyed, and I went back and checked. It was Pentura—one of the largest and oldest of the fusactor producers and operators in the Arm.

Fusactor producer? What the frig had they been doing on Stittara . . . and why? And why had they abandoned operations?

There was certainly no way for me to find that out, not when they'd closed up operations 470 years earlier.

Then I recalled Zerlyna's offhand comment about anomalies. I'd already checked into that. Stittara was slightly smaller than T-type, but the gravity was close to the same because the core was slightly larger. It was farther from its sun, but the sun was larger and hotter than the "standard" K, but the unique nature of the Stittaran atmosphere and the greater distance tended to cancel out the effect of the greater solar energy. The only anomaly I could see was that the core was larger and hotter, but the planet was older and less seismically active than predicted—except there were vast lava traps created less than two hundred million years ago. The seismic reports suggested that Stittara was a planet where plate tectonics operated more gradually, punctuated by occasional "excessive" readjustments.

I couldn't help but hope that such readjustments came with some advance warning.

All in all, the more I found out, the less I liked it . . . and I hadn't even ventured out of the local Systems Survey Service offices in Passova.

16

As on almost all Unity system planets, sevenday wasn't a workday, unless, of course, you were in food service or entertainment or a few other occupations. I wasn't including places like Salem, where nothing happened on sevenday, except endless worship and religious studies, something that continued to amaze me, given that no one had ever found proof of a deity in all the time humans had possessed interstellar travel. But since it's impossible to prove a negative, and since faith provides comfort, I understood, intellectually, the appeal.

While I had work to do, I didn't rush to get started, but let myself have the luxury of sleeping in before working out, and then sipping morning tea while scanning the local news. The stories were the same as those in Smithsen, if with far fewer killings. In fact, the newslinks reported none. For a moment I wondered about that, then nodded.

There wouldn't be many because the population was so low, and I had checked, and it was officially 4,102,155 people, with the notation that there could be a three percent error due to "uncertainties in the outland population census." Because all the cities on Stittara were comparatively modern and underground, every public space was monitored. Homes wouldn't be, and it was likely most violent deaths were either the result of bad tempers, excessive stimulants, or domestic violence.

Still, there were the food poisonings at an unlicensed café in Boito, wherever that was; the boy whose legs were crushed by a tunnel lorry malfunction; a dozen outlanders sentenced to some sort of work program for illegal cultivation, presumably some of the outies mentioned by Zerlyna; crop and environmental damage from a storm on Conduo at an unlicensed agricultural plot—doubtless one of those that Aloris or Zerlyna had mentioned—and the results of the regional scholastic korfball competition, whatever that happened to be. As I watched, I kept glancing at the sky, which seemed darker, yet without clouds, but I didn't see a single skytube, and I had no idea whether that was good or bad, although the darkness seemed closer when I looked out from the upper-level study windows just before leaving.

When I entered the Systems Survey Service spaces, they were dark, and I had to turn on the lights as I went, unsurprisingly. Since I still hadn't finished plowing through all the background documentation on the skytubes, I set aside my curiosity about Ilsabet and concentrated on what I felt, at least for the moment, should be one of the initial focal points of my assessment and evaluation.

Around midday, I took a break and left the Survey offices. I walked through the tunnel ways, finding myself after a time in what almost seemed an arcade, except on both sides were all sorts of small shops, bistros, and cafés, and most of the eating establishments had plenty of patrons. From the noise level, most of them seemed to be having a good time. Near the middle of the arcade, there was one entrance that was closed. Over the archway was the name INVIREO. While it was hard to infer much from merely an entry, the shimmering midnight-blue floor tile, outlined in a dark gold, and the maroon wall tiles, as well as the fact that there were no suggestive holo displays, or even concealed projectors, from what I could determine, suggested that it was neither a sleazy dump nor a club so exclusive that I'd likely be turned away.

Then again, I still might be turned away, simply because I wasn't the target audience, although, from what Amarios had said, there were different audiences at different times of the evening.

"Yeah . . . it's a shame Aelston's such a straight," came a voice from a table at an open café to my right. "Never open on sevenday. Still the best live music in this part of Passova. You ever hear Amarios?"

I turned and shook my head at the all too happy young man holding a beaker of something that was purplish. "Met but not heard."

"Man . . . you're the lucky one . . . She's something . . . you should hear her . . ."

"Let the poor guy find out for himself, Pons." Those words came from a most attractive blonde seated beside the happy drinker.

Her eyes met mine, and I could sense . . . interest. That definitely confused me, but I managed a pleasant smile and nodded to the pair, then turned.

"She'll find out about him . . . she should . . ." Those words from the blonde, and the feeling that her eyes rested on me gave me a clear sense of disorientation.

I kept walking.

Farther along there was another open café, this one with an awning, not that any such was necessary, and I noticed a family sitting on one side, a couple with a daughter, perhaps four. Two couples stood beyond the railing. Both of the women outside the café were talking to the mother, but their eyes were on the child.

". . . darling . . ."

". . . so fortunate . . . such a dear . . ."

I could see that the girl was an attractive child, and well dressed, although a few flecks of powdered sugar had streaked her pink blouse, and I eased around the group, thinking that I really hadn't seen that many children. But then, that was scarcely surprising, since my walk along the arcade or tunnel boulevard was really the first time I'd been anywhere that I'd have been likely to have seen a child.

Perhaps a quarter kay farther along, to the west, according to my link, I passed another club, with the name Exotia . . . and it was open, with a beefy hawker/bouncer standing outside.

"See it all! Hear it . . . you won't believe your eyes . . ."

What my eyes had to do with believing or hearing was another question, and I nodded and walked by. He didn't even try a second time. It could be that my black-trimmed gray singlesuit proclaimed me far too much a straight, if straight even meant what I thought it did on Stittara. But then, I've never been one who enjoyed extravagance for the sake of extravagance, unlike Chelesina. Nor was I an exhibitionist. If I had been a performer, I'd probably have opted for conservatively bright vests or jackets over a tastefully sparkling dark singlesuit.

Eventually, even in walking boots, my feet began to get sore, and after consulting my link, I found a tunnel transport that took me back to within a quarter kay of the Survey offices.

Once at my console, I went back to researching, but the first research I did was a search of names—the ones of the passengers with whom I'd talked on the *Persephonya*. I'd waited almost a week to run the search for several reasons, one being that local sources and media wouldn't pick up on new arrivals immediately, and second, I didn't want the search to jump out at Aloris and Raasn—or Zerlyna—whoever was doubtless logging and tracking my data requests and console operations.

Needless to say, my results were rather sparse. There was a listing of all inbound passengers on the *Persephonya,* or rather all those who had come planetside, and I saved that for future reference. There was also a Planetary Council notice granting residence and permanent employment status to a number of people, including Georg and Holly by Syntex, and Rikard Spek by RDAEX, and temporary residence and employment to others, including me and Rob Gybl. That suggested that Gybl's trip to Stittara was not so spur of the moment or whimsical as he'd tried to portray, but more thought out. Other multis or institutions sponsoring people were ABP, Eterna, Valior, and, interestingly, the local office of the Unity's Ministry of Technology, with their new or transferred employee or officer—Torgan Brad—but with no other information. Conditional residence was granted to Julea Sorensyn, for lack of a sponsor. In short, she'd arrived without a sponsor, but had enough assets of some sort, or personal contacts, to be allowed to remain on good behavior, and without being put in detention. There was a listing of twenty passengers who had come under life-suspension, none of whom were linked to government or multis. But there was no mention of Aimee Vanslo or Constantia Dewers, only a note to the effect that four passengers were exempt from public notice requirements as per regulations. Those with power and position usually manage it somehow, if often not quite so obviously.

I was about to close that file when I noted something. For each person granted permanent employment status, the sponsoring organization had been noted, and for Georg and Holly, that was Syntex. I'd known that from talking to them, and from the notice, but what I'd almost overlooked was the phrase following their sponsor Syntex—"a subsidiary of VLE, Bachman."

I'd heard of VLE, vaguely, an Arm multi of significance, but not among the largest, meaning a market capitalization of hundreds of billions of duhlars, rather than more than a trillion. VLE? Possibly Vanslo Enterprises? I'd have to see. It might just be a stretch or coincidence . . . or not.

There were no references in any local link or linkpubs to anyone on the passenger list. So, with that taken care of, I went back to reading the last of the more recent reports and skytube observations, not that they were all that recent.

17

The autumn skies spun their storm knots, thought three,
In time-tied eons before you and me.

Ilsabet walked toward the armaglass window, standing there for a time, before turning away from it and the pressure door to the outside.

"You can go outside," observed Alsabet from the wallscreen.

"I don't want to. It's not the thing to do."

"You always want to."

"Today is different and ill," declared Ilsabet. "I'll stay in and do what I will."

"Don't you feel well?"

"I feel fine. The decision's mine."

"Can you tell me why today is ill and different?" pressed the wallscreen image, the tone of voice subtly changed.

"No, you can't make me. It's different and there for you to see."

"Well . . . suit yourself. I won't unlock the door or send for Clyann."

"Matron will do what she will. That's for better or ill."

"You're not making sense again."

Ilsabet ignored the hint of exasperation behind the pleasant voice from the screen. She took a last glance through the armaglass window to the south, trying not to close her eyes. Then she turned and walked back to her chamber. She did not respond to the voice or the image of Alsabet in the screen.

18

By oneday night I'd finally managed to get through the Systems Survey records that seemed to bear on my assignment. I rewarded myself with a solid dinner at Ojolian's, by myself. I didn't see anyone I knew, but that meant nothing. After a second lager, which I took my time if not enjoying at least drinking, I took the tunneltram back, then walked the remaining distance to my quarters and got a decent night's sleep.

Twoday morning started as had the other mornings, and although I kept an eye out for Ilsabet, or Elisabetta, while I cooled down from my workout and sipped my morning tea, I didn't see her. I checked several times before I left the guest quarters and walked to the laboratory. When I stepped through the pressure-seal door into the Survey spaces, I saw Raasn Defaux and Dermotte hurrying away, both moving almost stiffly. I couldn't help but think of the difference between Raasn and Rahn Zeglar, one angular and almost stiff, but very bright, and the other warm, friendly, and graceful, probably politically cunning, but devoid of any real depth.

The laboratory seemed empty, in that I didn't see anyone else, but that had happened on several occasions. As I settled into my chair, trying to consider how I'd approach the field aspect of my investigation, the part I usually enjoyed, I realized I could feel what I could only describe as a tingling, a feeling that slowly intensified.

Abruptly alarms sounded from everywhere, and from hidden speakers came the announcement: "Storm warning! All pressure doors are sealing. All nonessential power will be secured in one minute. All personnel remain in secure areas. Storm warning!"

Before the power was cut, I accessed the system and tried to call up an outside view, only to get a message on the screen: *All direct vid-feed outlets are now shuttered. Close all applications to avoid information loss.*

Shuttered? For a storm? When almost everything was underground and the few aboveground windows were of armaglass?

As the announcement repeated itself, I closed down the console, finishing just as all the lights cut off, leaving only one small emergency lamp on the ceiling of my space. At the same time the tingling continued to build until it was close to painful.

More than two hours passed before the power was restored, and the pressure-seal doors opened. The viewers were unshuttered, and everything outside looked just as it had the day before. I didn't even see any gouges in the grass, and that told me just how tough it was.

Then I accessed what data I could get from the system on outside atmospherics. The first was wind velocity—in excess of 550 klicks. I sat there and reviewed the storm, or rather what data had been gathered that revealed what I had not been able to see directly, or even in real time through the console. The atmospheric pressure varied tremendously, at one point dropping some forty percent below ambient norm.

The wind velocity of standard hurricanes on most water planets seldom exceeded three hundred klicks, and such velocities didn't last more than half a standard hour in most cases. The outside wind velocity remained above five hundred klicks for close to three stans, and the tingling continued even longer. All that definitely explained, in technical as well as emotional terms, why Passova, and everything else on Stittara, was essentially underground.

At that point, Aloris arrived and peered into my spaces. "What did you think of our little storm?"

"Little? Or is that sardonicism?"

"We've seen storms that have lasted five hours. One even shattered shutters and armaglass ports."

"I do see why you build the way you do."

"You ready for a late lunch?"

I discovered I was when I joined Dermotte, Zerlyna, and Aloris at another place I hadn't visited—Rancho Rustico—that claimed to feature the most authentic T-beef anywhere, authentic presumably referring to the closeness of the steak on my platter to what used to come only from horned bovines.

I also discovered that no one even mentioned the storm after the first few moments, when Dermotte said, "That was a quick one."

"It's been a good half year since a skytube storm came over Passova," replied Aloris.

I couldn't help but ask, "Did the name come from the fact that storms pass over the area?"

Zerlyna nodded. "The original name was just Baseuno. According to the stories, the location was picked because so few storms hit here."

"It turned out to be wrong, eventually," added Aloris. "Over the past four centuries or so, we've had a significantly higher percentage of storms than the other towns and cities. Not outstandingly larger, but significant. Those things do even out over time."

She was probably right about that, and I nodded, then addressed the T-beef sandwich, which tasted authentic. By the time I'd taken a bite, the conversation had turned to Planetary Council elections.

"Cloras Dulac would raise conapt taxes by ten percent, and that'd just be the beginning. We need larger assessments on the outies. They take a disproportionate percentage of planetary government spending," Zerlyna declared.

"They claim that doesn't take into account that the Unity subsidized building Passova and that they have to provide their own services . . ."

I just listened.

When I returned to my spaces, I tried to push away my thoughts of the storm, for the moment, although I wanted to look more into the dynamics behind such violent localized weather, because I needed to get on with my specific assignment. But I did take a moment to use the console to determine where the Planetary Council met . . . and discovered that there was a government enclave north of Passova proper, accessed by a separate tunnel, under which was, of course, a tunneltram.

Then I got back to work. After having read all the data submissions in the local Survey files, it was clear enough that I wasn't going to find answers there, and it was time to visit the various "research" installations.

I needed to talk to and gain access, if I could, to the environmental documentation of each of the multis with operations on Stittara. All of them, except one, were involved in biologics or anagathics in some fashion or another. The one that wasn't happened to be RDAEX. When I'd run across Rikard Spek on the *Persephonya,* I'd been intrigued and puzzled as to why a physicist, or someone with that kind of background, was being sent to Stittara. Then when I discovered he'd been sponsored by RDAEX, I was especially puzzled.

RDAEX was a space-based resource extraction and refining operation. Why would a resource extraction concern with subsidiaries in most Arm systems even be interested in Stittara? It was the only habitable planet in the system, with a population so low that it would be centuries, if ever, before it would need off-planet resource augmentation. And why had a space/vacuum mining concern built a planetside research facility on Stittara, rather than elsewhere in the system? The most obvious conclusion was that RDAEX was interested in some aspect of the planetary-based skytubes. Given that, and given that one of the earlier reports had noted that nothing short of military weaponry was likely to penetrate a skytube, the arrival of Spek, a specialist in high-energy physics, was more than a little disturbing. And, for that matter, so was the arrival of one Torgan Brad, and his assignment to the Ministry of Technology and Transport. I had my doubts as to whether that was coincidence, but then . . . at times life was indeed stranger than any holodrama.

I would certainly approach RDAEX on the grounds that to do a thorough assessment of the ecological situation on Stittara, I needed input from all the multis on the planet. None of them, unfortunately, were in any way compelled to provide such information, but I doubted that any of them would attempt an outright refusal, especially since I was in fact a temporary employee of the Systems Survey Service conducting Survey business. I suspected that any refusal would consist of either not providing data or providing only limited data on the grounds that more data would reveal proprietary technology, knowledge, or research not relevant to an ecological survey.

Even so, I'd have to contact each one . . . and see what happened.

19

Threeday morning, I looked for Ilsabet, but did not see her before I left my quarters for my Survey office. As I turned to depart, I paused. There was something . . . something I'd seen . . . that hadn't been quite right, but I couldn't remember what it was, only that it wasn't her, not exactly. But I couldn't remember, and I needed to get on with what I feared would be time-consuming efforts to obtain interviews with the appropriate people at the various Stittaran multis.

Once I was at my console, I called up a series of maps of Stittara, continent by continent, looking at both topographical and then geologic versions and then what passed for an ecological version, finally overlaying each with the map showing communities, facilities, and highways, such as they were. Perhaps I was stalling, just a little, but before I started making contacts I wanted a better "feel" for Stittara.

After I checked the map locations of all the multis, one thing became very clear. RDAEX was an outlier in more than one way. All the other multi headquarters were within roughly 150 kays of Passova on Conuno, although several had outlying facilities on Conduo or Contrio. RDAEX had one location, and that was in the middle of Contrio, the smallest of the three major continents, and that location was at the foot of a mountain range called the Triad.

Before I made any arrangements or commitments, I decided that I'd best discuss transport with Aloris, and I didn't want to do that on a link.

I missed too many subtleties that way. I walked back through the laboratory spaces to the administrative section, but she wasn't there. Dermotte was in the corridor outside.

"Have you seen Aloris?"

"She said she'd be back soon. That was . . . well, about a quarter stan ago now, ser. She didn't say where she was going."

"Thank you."

Since she wasn't in her spaces, and I didn't want to reach her through her personal link, not immediately anyway, I asked him, "Do you know anything about RDAEX?"

"No, ser. Not really. I've got a cousin that works there. He says they've got a right nice place, all the things we've got here in Passova. Just not so many of them. They take good care of their folks."

"What does your cousin do there?"

"Oh . . . he's a maintenance tech . . . he says he can't talk much about it, except that it's some sort of drilling project . . ."

Drilling project . . . from a deep-space research multi? "That's different. All the other multis are into biologicals."

"So they say, ser."

"Have you ever thought about working somewhere else?"

"Me, ser? No, ser. I've enjoyed working at the Survey. Good folks, all of them."

"How long has your family been here on Stittara?"

"From the beginning I guess. I wouldn't know. I leave the genealogy to my sister." Dermotte looked up. "Here comes Dr. Raasn."

"Thank you, Dermotte." I turned to watch Aloris striding toward me with a firmness of expression that suggested she was less than pleased about something, although her expression softened, if only slightly, when she caught sight of me.

"I was looking for you."

"I'm here. Come in." She gestured toward her spaces.

I followed.

"What do you need?" she asked, not seating herself.

"I think I have enough background on what the Survey has done and accumulated in data so that I won't be totally lost in meeting with environmental people and their superiors at the various multis. There is, however, one possible problem . . ."

"It wouldn't be the location of RDAEX, would it?" She actually offered what could only be called an impish smile.

"It would indeed. How does one arrange transport?"

"You can fly on the scheduled flitter to Contrio. Your contract covers local transport. It flies out on oneday, threeday, and fiveday, and back on the even numbered days." She paused, then added, "It takes seven hours. RDAEX also operates its own shuttle service."

"And if I'm polite and charming, that might be offered? Especially since it's likely to be better."

"RDAEX tries to be very accommodating, Paulo. We've never had any difficulties with them . . . unlike others."

I understood both messages in her statement. "I will endeavor to be polite and charming and to convey my interest in being as open and as fair as possible."

"I'm certain that will be appreciated." She bent over her console and keyed in something. After she straightened, she added, "I've forwarded the direct link to Belk Edo's office to your console. His staff is usually very helpful."

"Thank you . . . again. Might I impose for other contact suggestions?"

"Indeed you might. I'll go through my lists and send them to you shortly."

"Thank you," I repeated.

"My pleasure." Her tone was pleasant, and more than purely professional, with an undertone of amusement.

I paused. "You didn't look very happy marching back here to your office."

"I wasn't. The Planetary Council is asking for an audit for the services we provided last year."

"It's an election year, then?"

"You understand that. Why don't most people?"

"Because they don't think in those terms. Any government restricts some freedoms. People don't like restrictions. Ambitious politicians exploit those dislikes. The comparatively honest ones pick semilegitimate grievances. The less honest ones don't bother with legitimacy; they just pick the things that make most people the maddest. Usually what makes people maddest are those things they don't understand that get in the way of what they want to do. Few people understand the environment. So the

Systems Survey Service is always a political target. That's why I'm here. You know it, and I know it."

Some of the anger dropped away, and a ruefully amused smile appeared. "I wish I could turn what you just said into a public linkspot."

"It wouldn't work. I'm just another techie-lobbyist hired to make the Survey look good. That's what those who don't like the Survey would say. Those who do would be angry that I wasn't attacking the politicians directly."

"You're as cynical as Raasn."

I was probably more so; I'd seen more. I didn't admit it. "Cynicism is often the last refuge of the idealist." That wasn't original, either. It came from some early space-age writer whose name I'd forgotten.

"I wouldn't think you'd claim to be an idealist." Her eyes had a wicked twinkle, something I wouldn't have expected.

"Just a pragmatist, ma'am. Just a pragmatist."

She did laugh, if only for a moment.

I nodded and turned. On the way back to my spaces, I just hoped I wasn't walking into more than I bargained for. Then I almost laughed. Since when had any assignment I'd ever had not been more than I'd anticipated in one way or another?

Belatedly, as I sat down in the swivel that had been templated so recently it still smelled of resin, I realized that I'd best get on with contacting Belk Edo's office since RDAEX was a third of the way around Stittara, and it was already late afternoon there. I did do a quick check to see exactly who Edo was. He turned out to be the chief operating officer, in short, the highest placed RDAEX official on Stittara.

I took a deep breath and completed the link.

A very professional-looking young man, every hair perfectly in place, wearing a light blue singlesuit that complemented his fair and totally unblemished complexion, answered the link. "Executive Edo's office."

"Yes . . . I'm Dr. Paulo Verano, on assignment from the Systems Survey Service on Bachman. I'm at the Stittaran offices of the Survey in Passova conducting an ecological overview of Stittara, as directed by an Arm government oversight committee. I was hoping to have a few minutes with Executive Edo and whoever serves as the chief environmental director or ecologist for RDAEX on Stittara . . ." I smiled politely.

"Yes, ser. If you could hold for just a moment."

"I will, thank you."

The screen blanked, to be replaced with a stellar view, obviously shot outside a planetary atmosphere. I didn't recognize it. Nor did I recognize the semiclassical music that had been chosen as neither a stimulant nor a soporific.

In less than three minutes, the smiling visage of the receptionist or aide reappeared. "Executive Edo would be happy to meet with you next twoday. Our shuttle will be leaving from the Passova dropport at six hundred hours on twoday, and that will allow you to meet with Ser Edo at sixteen hundred hours that afternoon. Local weather permitting."

"Thank you very much. Is there anything I should bring?"

"You'll be here for at least one night, ser, depending on Dr. Ermitag's schedule. Our guest quarters are at your disposal, Doctor. Our shuttle will be traveling to Passova on both fourday and fiveday."

"Thank you very much."

"Good day, ser."

As I leaned back in the resin-scented swivel, I realized that the entire communication with RDAEX had taken less than ten minutes . . . and had left me vaguely unsettled. Was it because it had been handled so smoothly that I felt like I'd been processed like a product?

That suggested that I needed to prepare for those meetings with great care.

In less than half a stan, Aloris's contact list had appeared, and I spent the next hour checking her contacts against the public directories, where names were listed, and against submissions to the Survey Service, before I began to call the various multis, starting with Eterna.

By just before noon, I had appointments at Eterna for fourday, and a tentative appointment on fiveday, subject to confirmation, with Dyart, one of the small multis.

At that moment Zerlyna peered into my spaces. "Are you up for lunch?"

"Absolutely!" And I was, both because I was hungry and because I wanted to hear what she might have to say.

I let her lead the way through the maze of tunnel ways into a place I couldn't have found on my own—but would again if I liked it, because I had my link note the route and the location.

The small sign on the outside read "Bellisimo." There were less than twenty tables not quite crammed into a space that allowed a table against the wall on each side and a narrow aisle down the middle. The ceiling, thankfully, was high, and the walls a light and clean off-white decorated with pictures of ancient ruins, some of which were from Old Earth, and some that had to be alien ruins, including three deserted deep-space cities. What ruins had to do with the name of the café I had no idea.

"It's a bit eclectic," said Zerlyna as we sat down.

"I got that impression." I also had the sense that the space had once been an underground lane or alley at one time. "What's good here?"

"Almost anything. That's why I like it. Not expensive and not a place where you have to worry about what to order. Except the ouzo. It burns like hydraulic fluid and tastes like template resin."

I was thinking about pointing out how many types of template resins there were when she added, "Whatever the worst tasting resin might be." She offered that warm smile that was almost inviting.

"That's enough for me to avoid the ouzo." I settled for a five-cheese ravioli, the local salad, and a lager, feeling that combination was as eclectic as the café.

The lager and her red wine arrived almost immediately, and Zerlyna let me have several swallows of the lager, good but not great, before she said anything. "You've been spending all your time here in headquarters."

"That's about to change. I'm working to meet with ecological personnel at all of the Stittaran multis."

"And then what?"

If that wasn't a leading question and suggestion all rolled into one, I'd never seen such. "Then I thought it would be a good time to meet with some of the Survey field personnel. Do you have any suggestions?"

"I'm sure Aloris must have mentioned Benart Albrot at Field Two . . ."

"That name did come up. Whom else would you suggest?"

"Reeki Liam might have a different perspective. She heads the bio-survey teams out of Field One." Zerlyna sipped her wine, which looked to be a shade more like a blackish maroon, before adding, "You might also want to visit some of the better managed outie communities."

"I wouldn't have the faintest idea which qualify as 'better managed,'" I pointed out. "Could you help with that?"

"I could, but you might want to talk to Geneil Paak in GeoSurv."

"Is she here in headquarters?"

Zerlyna nodded. "Down on level two. In the depths."

At that moment my salad and ravioli and her calamari sandwich and truffled fried onions arrived. The salad was acceptable, the ravioli good, perhaps better than that, as were the onions. "Have you ever met an advocate named Darlian . . . ?"

"Oh . . . Raasn's friend. I've talked to her a few times."

"I wouldn't have thought that there'd be that much demand for advocates here in Passova."

Zerlyna laughed. "Where every square centimeter of space is valuable? Where martial arts contests have to be noncontact because the rate of injuries and fatalities was astronomically high before they were? Where the average permanent civil union lasts ten years, if that? Where politeness and manners are a societal necessity . . . and are underlain with venom? Where paranoia is a survival trait?"

I had to say I hadn't noticed what she was suggesting. Was that because I was an outsider, and much of it wasn't targeted in my direction? Or was she exaggerating and the overly paranoid one? I'd only talked to her twice . . . and she didn't strike me that way . . . but . . .

"And why everyone in an office has his or her own private spaces?" I frowned. "The outside windows in the Survey guest quarters . . . do they serve a dual purpose?"

Zerlyna smiled. "Yes."

"They have more space, but no one says anything because most people wouldn't want to live that exposed to the skytube storms?"

"You have three times the space of most people in Passova, if not more. Having your quarters where most people would feel uncomfortable helps."

I took another bite of ravioli, then of salad, nodding at her to see if she'd say more.

"I'm exaggerating a little, but Darlian and the other advocates have plenty of clients."

"You said she was Raasn's friend."

"They're more than friends, likely lovers, but both are too analytical to keep company too closely for any length of time."

That did make sense, sadly.

"Did Aloris ever have a partner?"

"She did. He was a contractor from Adlayd who thought he'd stay. He didn't. He took a ley-liner all the way out of the Arm. He couldn't deal with her relationship with Raasn. That was when Haraan was one."

"The brother-sister thing that isn't quite that? Or more than that?"

Zerlyna nodded. "What about you?"

"Permanent union dissolved. She and our daughter got most every-thing. Seemed like a good time for me to take an out-system contract."

"The farther away from Bachman, the better?"

"Something like that. What about you? Your status?"

"Permanent union for seventeen years. Two daughters." There was a slight emphasis on the word "two."

"Can I ask about your partner?"

"You can ask. He'd prefer I say little about him. I respect that pref-erence."

"So will I."

She laughed and for an instant her eyes met mine. They were golden green. "It's clear you're a consultant and not an investigator."

"The only thing I know how to investigate is ecological interactions, and probably not all of those. Can you tell me anything interesting that the Survey's discovered along those lines that might not be in the files?"

"It's all in the records, whether it makes sense or not."

That was how I left that, by asking her, "Would you mind telling me about life in Passova?"

"It's like life in any other small city, but there's not that much greenery except in the arboretum and the gardens . . . more cafés, restaurants, and clubs, I'd judge . . ."

I mostly listened.

When I got back to my spaces, there was still no response or confirma-tion from Dyart . . . and I needed to keep making contacts and, along the way, try to figure out exactly what game Zerlyna was playing . . . and why.

20

"Zerlyna had lunch with Verano. Alone." Aloris stood outside the door to the conapt.

"She didn't tell you that, I take it?" Raasn glanced down the tunnel whose narrowness identified the area as one of the older in Passova.

"You're being polite. No. She wouldn't. She's up to something, and it's not just Verano's obvious outworld appeal. What do you think it is this time?"

"It's too early to say, but it's likely designed to give her full director status. She wants Verano to find something that will show how her recommendations have been ignored and led to a problem that can only be remedied by giving the head of data systems equal power with the administrative director and the operations director. That way she can play you and Jorl to get what she wants."

"Is Venessa behind this?" asked Aloris.

"I doubt she's behind it. It would suit her purposes, though, and she wouldn't have to do anything."

"Sometimes, it just amazes me how blind Zeglar is to her machinations. It took Verano one look and about a sentence to figure it out."

"And he's not the most discerning when it comes to women? Is that what you meant?" Raasn offered a crooked smile. "You're misreading Verano. He's the kind who's very astute at reading most women—just not the one he loves."

"Or lusts after?" Aloris's voice turned slightly acid.

"For him, those are likely the same. You might keep that in mind."

"I'm not interested. Once was more than enough."

"That wasn't what I meant, and you know it. Give him time. Zerlyna isn't available so far as Verano's concerned. He won't pursue the unavailable, for many reasons . . ."

"So he'll see what she has in mind?"

"I'd be surprised if he already doesn't suspect that her motives are less than completely altruistic. Remember, you told me that he was the one who made the off-color allusion to Venessa and Zeglar immediately after meeting them."

"I don't know . . ."

"Time is on our side," Raasn said.

"Only when you consider the Unity government. The Planetary Council is another matter altogether." Aloris pursed her lips tightly. "Especially Morghan and her bitch Melarez."

"Then we need to find a way to use Verano . . . put the Council in a position where they can't oppose him."

"They might just try to remove him, then."

"That wouldn't hurt, especially if he caught them at it." Raasn smiled.

"You honestly think he could get the multis to back us against the Council?"

"No. He doesn't have to. All he has to do is to have them pressure the Council not to interfere with the way the Survey operates."

"I don't see that happening."

"Zerlyna thinks he can do something. You might try to see why."

Aloris frowned. "You know what I think . . ."

"Yes, I do. Get over it. Verano's a gentleman."

"I thought Gaeller was one."

"I didn't. Remember that."

"Thank you so much for reminding me."

Raasn smiled. "You're welcome. Someone has to." He nodded, then turned and headed down the pedestrian tunnel way.

21

Just before I was leaving my Survey office on threeday evening, I received a link from a professional-looking woman at Dyart, confirming my appointment with Pavlo Vanek, for fiveday at 1300. When I reached my "official" console on fourday morning, I was still waiting for responses from Syntex, Valior, GenArt, and ABP. I walked out at nine hundred hours to head up to the vehicle garage and take possession of a Survey van to drive some fifty-three kays to the northwest, and I was still waiting.

After loading the van with a case of equipment, and a second case that held various printer templates, it wasn't without a certain amount of trepidation that I eased the van up the long ramp and out into the surprisingly bright purple-gray light of Stittara, given that I didn't have that much experience in personal physical control of a vehicle massing more than a metric ton. Even so, within a quarter stan of leaving the Survey, I was on my way, speeding westward on the permacrete strip that served as a highway, still bemused at the thought of having personal control of a vehicle at high speed, something unheard of on Bachman or any truly civilized world with any degree of population. Given that I drove almost another quarter stan before I saw another vehicle, a large lorry that shook the van as it passed me, I could see why Stittara didn't think a planetary or even a local vehicle control system was necessary—and why an onboard vehicle guidance module was unnecessary.

What skytubes there were seemed to be located far to the north, the first time I'd seen them there, and the sky overhead seemed a brighter, if still purpled, pale gray. The permacrete road ran almost due west in a straight line, although the display indicated that in some forty kays I'd take a turn onto another road and head northwest. With the exception of rocky outcroppings here and there, all with rounded contours, the ground was totally covered by the same brown-green-purple grass I'd seen everywhere else, and the few bushes were the same domelike types I'd seen at the dropport. Again, I saw not a single tree, no animals of any size, and no people at all, except in the occasional vehicle that passed me coming from the opposite direction.

That gave me time to think more about what I might say when I talked to people at Eterna. Long, long before, the multi had made a splash on Bachman with its anagathic skin preparations of the same name, and was one of the oldest multis on Stittara, one of the reasons why I'd decided to start my "visits" with the Eterna research facility, located northwest of Passova. The reports I'd read on the facility indicated that it was almost totally self-contained, with no emissions to the atmosphere except . . . atmosphere . . . and absolutely chemically pure water released at a temperature some ten degrees higher than its intake temperature. But the effluent—if pure water could be called an effluent in the traditional sense—was carefully reinjected to an aquifer at multiple points and showed no adverse effects.

I had been slightly surprised that I'd been granted an appointment with Jeromi Grantham, the Eterna facility director, but the fact that I'd been granted time with both Grantham and Edo suggested that my presence wasn't totally a formality to them, or perhaps that it was a necessary formality. How those visits went might likely tell me how the multi officials regarded my assignment, but then, they might not, given just how talented some of the multi officials I'd met in the past had been.

The odds were very long that Eterna had even minor adverse environmental impacts, but determining even such negatives were part of what I had to do, and the faster I could dispose of the negatives, the sooner I could concentrate on the other aspects of the assessment. Of course, by going to RDAEX comparatively early on, I was breaking my own policies, but what were a few inconsistencies? Better those than foolish consistencies.

Almost two standard hours later, I was stopped in front of a closed vehicle door in a low gray structure, in a space identified as the visitors' receiving area of the Eterna complex, a much smaller version of Passova, with scattered small structures peering out of the ground spread across an area about a kay on a side and suggesting a fairly large structure or set of structures stretching beneath the service.

I used the van's comm and pulsed the local system.

"Survey van, request reason for entry."

"This is Paulo Verano, on Survey business, appointment with Jeromi Grantham."

"Wait one." The wording and the clipped tone suggested a military background, either local or Arm military, but that was a guess on my part.

After several minutes I got a response.

"Straight through the entry and down the ramp to the first left. Park the van in one of the visitor spots. Then go through the pressure door to the right."

Whoever it was didn't sound pleased, but some people were like that.

I followed instructions, although there were three empty parking spaces, and made my way into the foyer beyond the pressure door, empty of all equipment and furnishings, where a smiling figure in a pale green and gold singlesuit stood waiting.

"Paulo Verano," I offered, extending the infocard with the government authorization, the one for which Aloris had never asked, unsurprisingly, since she and the local Survey had already known what I looked like and had received my biometrics.

"Jeromi Grantham." He took the card and passed a pen scanner over it, then returned it to me, almost as if the authentication were a necessary formality. He gestured. "This way."

I followed him through another pressure door and past a guard in a dull green singlesuit with the style of a security uniform, who took us both in, scanned a display, then returned to whatever else he was doing.

Grantham passed two closed doorways, then stepped through a set of double doors that opened into an anteroom with a single desk console, behind which sat a woman who looked to be my age, if not older, although I could only tell that by the experience in her eyes. "My assistant, Anna DeVerr."

"Pleased to meet you." I inclined my head.

"If you need me again, Anna will know how to reach me."

Grantham led the way into an office smaller and more modest than the one occupied by the executive director of the Stittaran Survey Service. The console desk behind which Grantham seated himself actually showed some wear. I took the seat directly across the desk from him and waited.

"We expected you sooner. You've been on Stittara over a standard week."

"I didn't expect you to be the one to meet me."

"Why not? You wanted to see me, and it would have wasted someone else's time to meet you and then walk you to see me. Why did you wait to start contacting local multis?"

The fact that he knew that, or even assumed it from my timing on contacting Eterna, was interesting. "I thought it might be best to review all your reports to the local Systems Survey before I visited you. That way I wouldn't be asking for information you'd already supplied."

Grantham laughed. "It's easy enough to tell that you're an outside investigator. Survey investigators would never consider that."

"I am what I am." Grantham's response told me that he'd either received a briefing transmission carried on the *Persephonya* or that he'd come to Stittara from elsewhere, if not both. "How long have you been here on Stittara with Eterna?"

His brow wrinkled slightly for a moment. "Ten years local."

"From Bachman?"

"Randtwo, actually."

I nodded. Randtwo was the most conservative world in the Unity after Bachman, and the home planet for Eterna. That it was the headquarters for Eterna wasn't surprising. Conservatives always opted for things like wealth, personal beauty, and simple answers.

"What are you looking for?" Grantham asked directly and openly.

"Information as to the impact your operations have on the ecology here on Stittara, both directly and indirectly, in all environmental media."

"And you don't think our reports provide that information? That is their purpose, you of all people should know."

"It's likely that they do . . . if what they report is accurate, and the odds are that your reports are accurate. But"—I paused—"it's very clear from the nature of my assignment that both the Ministry of Environment on Bachman and the Systems Survey Service headquarters there believe that there are impacts that may not be reported . . . by someone. My job is to determine if such impacts are occurring, and if so, who is responsible. It may be that there are no such unreported impacts, but if they do, my job is to determine who or what is responsible."

"What if such impacts have been reported, at least locally?"

"That is one reason why I've spent so much time studying the reports made to the local Survey. So far as I can determine, the final annual reports do not contain data or observations that indicate adverse environmental impacts. One of the things I hope to do, with your assistance, is to assure that what I have studied in the Survey files matches what you and others have submitted." I smiled politely.

Grantham nodded. "You don't trust anyone, do you?"

"I neither trust nor distrust. I don't know. I'm here to find out."

He offered a sardonic smile. "I can't argue with that approach. All our records are open to you. They wouldn't be on Randtwo or Bachman, but we're a research facility, and we don't have to worry about profit margins, marketing strategies, or actual product development."

"I'm most interested in your sampling techniques and anything that deals with interaction with the local ecology."

"That's what we'd expect from a Systems Survey investigator. I had Ripley Weavar pull together a guide to those files for you. She's our expert on alien biology," he said with a laugh, "except, after generations here, we don't really regard it as alien."

"From your reports to the Survey, the local biology would seem rather alien."

"Some is, and some isn't. It's all carbon-based, of course, but you really should talk to Ripley about that." Grantham rose.

In minutes I'd been escorted through two open pressure doors and down a short corridor to a space about the size of my guest quarters' bedroom.

There, Grantham gestured to the woman who had risen from behind a small console. "Ripley, this is Paulo Verano, the Systems Survey ecologist and investigator sent here." Then he turned to me. "Ripley can answer your questions far better than I, and doubtless much more quickly." With that, he was slipping out the door.

Ripley Weavar was as tall as I was, with short black hair, a slightly oblong face, and a no-nonsense manner about her. "You don't look like a Survey ecologist."

"I'm not. I'm an independent consultant on assignment."

"You've still been foisted off on us." Her voice was quiet. Not soft, just quiet.

Not only were her words judgmental, but the way she studied me, if just for an instant, was more like I were an alien, an animal, or a piece of meat . . . if not all three.

"And on every other research installation on Stittara," I said mildly.

"The only real research installations are our two and the one RDAEX established 150 odd years ago. Well . . . maybe Syntex. They keep things very quiet."

RDAEX was established here only a 150 years ago? "What about the others?"

"Pallias closed up shop two years ago. But they hadn't produced a new insight in a century, not since they developed a spin-off based on the chemistry of the wiggler worms that are part of the lichen grass biological cycle. Dyart . . . they claim they're close to something with the volents . . ."

I'd read about the volents—the term being a cross between a vole and a rodent—small four-legged hairballs that lived off various insectoids that otherwise might overwhelm the spore-seed reproductive capabilities of the lichen/grass.

"On top of that?" She shook her head. "ABP . . . who knows what they're doing? They send sealed crates back to Bachman on every ship, and they get significant duhlar credit transfers, and no one looks too closely because every transfer from out-system helps keep things going . . . Gen-Art . . . they're still twiddling with that proprietary nail additive, and I doubt they'll ever go beyond that."

"What else about Syntex?"

"You mean . . . their investigation of the forerunner site? They've been at that for five centuries, looking for some clue to the technology . . . as if they'd find it on-planet anywhere after more than two hundred million years when there's been no trace in any of the deep-space finds. Vacuum preserves things far better than a geologically active planet."

"Geologically active . . . that's another thing . . ." I waited.

"Oh . . . you mean the fact that the core is as molten as it is?"

"Compared to other T-type worlds, you have to admit that it's an anomaly for a planet this old."

"In a vast universe," she said, "there will always be outliers."

That may have been, but outliers always made me suspicious, usually of the data, rather than the object being studied or analyzed, but there was far too much data on Stittara for it to be younger than what the other data, besides core activity, revealed.

I smiled, waiting.

"Where do you want to start?" she finally asked.

"I'd like to begin by reviewing your copies of your annual submissions to the local Survey."

"Haven't you already read them?"

"I've read what's in the Survey files," I said blandly.

She just barely blinked, but I could tell that surprised her. "Then I'd like a tour of all the points where you measure influent and effluent— after I reclaim some equipment from the van. I also would like to see your analysis on ambient air—outside, received inside, treated, and discharged."

"You may have better measuring accuracy than we do."

"That's possible. I'll make the templates of my equipment available to you. Call it a value exchange."

"At what cost?" Her voice was wary.

"No cost, except whatever it costs you to copy them and produce the equipment." That wouldn't be cheap, even for a research multi, but it would be easier and cheaper than if they had to license the templates from the Planetary Council or its agents. "Oh, and I have template release documentation from both the Unity and the Ministry of Environment. So you won't have to pay licensure fees."

She didn't bother to conceal her surprise, although it was only a moment before she asked, "Are you going to want to visit the Conduo facility as well?"

"I may have to," I pointed out. "We'll see." I couldn't see not doing so, but I'd learned it was unwise to make firm commitments without as much information as possible. "We can work that out."

She nodded. "Any other questions before you get your equipment and start your tour?"

"What sort of environmental impact do you think the outies have?"

She snorted. "It can't be good. The Survey's enforcement people are always shutting down something they're doing. Half the public works projects in Passova, Dualle, and Trieste have been built by outies under work detention. A few outie troublemakers have suffered accidents on those projects as well." She shook her head. "Can't say I blame the enforcement types."

"Have you ever had any occasion to measure something they might have affected?"

"That's not something that we're required to report."

"I know. You're not responsible. But . . . if there is an outie impact . . . any measurements or observations . . . well . . . if it turned out all the multis were doing what they were supposed to . . ."

Ripley's smile was almost enigmatic. Almost. "There aren't any outie communities or licensure areas near us here. There's one near our Conduo facility. If there are any records . . . they'd be there."

That made sense, in a way, but I wasn't about to question that. Not yet.

"Are you ready to start looking at reports?"

"No." I laughed. "But that's where I have to start."

22

Fourday had been long . . . very long, and I hadn't gotten back to Passova until close to eight that evening, or twenty hundred hours. As I'd suspected, I'd found absolutely nothing out of order or even suspicious at Eterna. Their reports appeared identical to what the Survey had on file—I'd copied those into my link so I could compare. My somewhat better sampling gear had measured things to more decimal points, but really hadn't shown any deviation from what Eterna was reporting.

I did find one interesting thing. Eterna didn't scrub the ambient air coming through their intakes. They just screened the air drawn into the facility for potential chemical contaminants, then scrubbed it of all potential chemical pollutants before releasing effluent air, but left any airborne biologicals largely untouched.

The other unusual aspect of matters was more disconcerting than interesting, if I happened to be reading things right. For all her apparent initial hostility, I'd felt that Ripley Weavar had been looking at me when she thought I wasn't noticing, and I didn't think that was just because I'd supplied the sampling and analytical equipment templates, although she did seem appreciative. That was disconcerting because I'd known for years that while I wasn't ugly, and might even have been termed decent-looking, I wasn't the type of man on whom women's eyes lingered. Even Chelesina hadn't doted on my appearance. But feeling that kind of scrutiny again, and even the muted reactions from both Aloris and Zerlyna . . .

and those of the young woman in the café on sevenday . . . all that defi-nitely left me disconcerted.

There were far too many things that weren't adding up . . . and I had no way of determining, yet, which unusual aspects of Stittara were just native to the world and disconcerting to an outsider and which might bear on my contract assignment. And the only way to find out what was which was to plow ahead, keep my eyes open, and try to keep my back covered.

For an ecological assessment? Except I should have realized that anything for which I'd been paid as much as I had wouldn't be simple. Then again, getting clear of Chelesina was worth it.

Fiveday morning I was in my Survey office early, loading the Survey's copies of the Dyart reports into my link. After that, I thought about mak-ing follow-up calls to Valior, ABP, and Syntex, but decided to wait on that until oneday. It wasn't as though I could do anything about meeting them immediately.

Then I did some more background research of a general nature on Stit-tara itself, looking at the location of the various cities and communities, about which I could see nothing that stood out. After that, I looked at the population figures, beyond the current levels, all the way back to the beginning. Population growth had averaged roughly one percent per year for the first five hundred years, and then had begun to decline, if slowly. At present, it was just slightly above replacement value. That was particu-larly interesting. While I was an ecologist, not an economist or a sociolo-gist, those figures weren't anything like the way most human populations grew. In fact . . .

I didn't want to even voice that suspicion before I did a bit more re-search and recollection, but by a stan later, I was convinced. The human population was more like that of an invader species moving into an estab-lished ecosystem and reaching what might be called the ecological carry-ing capacity. But I wasn't aware of any other system where that had happened, not with a human population. There were systems that would-be colonists had abandoned, and colonies that had died out, but one like what the Stittaran population figures suggested?

What also bothered me about such a conclusion was that there weren't any large predators, and there hadn't been virulent small ones, either, such as killer viruses or bacteria. I'd checked mortality rates, and they were abnormally low, as were birth rates. Could that be just because so much of the population was in underground cities? Other artificial habitats, such as deep-space stations and military posts on airless worlds, generally had negative population growth, requiring immigrants.

That was where I had to leave my calculations and speculations because I had to go check out the Survey van I'd reserved for the trip to Dyart . . . and I needed to load my equipment.

Almost three-quarters of a standard hour later, I was on the permacrete highway headed south. Dyart was the closest of the multis to Passova, a mere thirty kays due south, but the drive took somewhat longer because the road was narrower and toward the end I had to guide the van around some rather large and almost crude-looking lorries. I didn't have to wonder where they were headed for long, because there was an even narrower way that forked off to the southwest about a kay before I got to the turnoff for Dyart. I saw two more of the purplish-gray lorries headed farther southwest on that road.

I pulled up to the entrance door to Dyart with only ten minutes to spare. Unlike at Eterna, before I could pulse or try a contact, the doors recessed, one to each side, and I drove down the ramp, following the "Visitor" arrows down two levels.

When I got out of the van, a young woman wearing a dark maroon singlesuit with pale green piping stood just outside the pressure door leading into Dyart from the visitor parking. "Dr. Verano?"

"The same." I had my Survey ID ready, but she barely looked at it.

"This way, ser, if you please."

I followed her brisk steps into the facility and up a ramp to the level above the visitor parking and through another pressure door into a receiving area. Since the console desk there was empty, I suspected she served as receptionist, security, and escort. Some fifty meters along the narrow corridor, she opened a door. "Ser Vanek's office, Doctor."

"Thank you." I stepped inside, and she closed the door behind me.

Pavlo Vanek stood from behind a set of screens, nodded solemnly, and gestured toward the single chair facing his console. He was half a head shorter than I was, probably five kilos heavier, and no broader across the shoulders. The entire office wasn't all that much bigger than my temporary office at the Stittaran Survey Service.

"Paulo Verano. Thank you for taking the time to see me."

"I don't know that we had much choice." His voice was slightly hoarse, or raspy, and he reseated himself as I took the chair. "I was wondering if you'd been held up."

"I didn't realize it would take as long as it did," I said.

"Oh . . . the outie lorries. There are usually more of them on fiveday," replied Vanek.

"What were they carrying? I'm assuming they were returning from Passova."

"Most are. They carry luxury goods, land-grown produce usually, sometimes furniture crafted from trees felled in their upland woodlots."

"Do they supply that much to Passova or the other towns or cities?"

He shook his head. "Some. They do it for duhlars to buy equipment. They consume most of what they grow. What they send to Passova and other cities or installations might be called frills, things not really needed." He leaned forward. "What do you require of us?"

"There's not much on Dyart in the Survey files beyond the environmental reports, and a page that says you provide unique biologic templates, based on studies of the volent."

Vanek nodded.

I waited.

"That's exactly what we do, except it's not based on just the volent. We've moved away from that, although the volents provided the clues. We research every bit of flora that could be called herbal and analyze them, replicate them, and then determine how they might be useful in enhancing various beauty aids."

"I have to ask. How much of that is placebo effect?"

He shook his head. "That's not our business. We supply the replicas and templates to firms all across the Arm. Along with a complete analysis and evaluation. What they do with them is their determination."

"You must be on some sort of continuing retainer then."

"It's something like that, but you'd have to talk to the comptroller about that. I'm the environmental manager and compliance officer."

That was a quiet reminder for me to get down to the official reasons for my visit. So I smiled. "As you may or may not have heard, I've been sent to Stittara by the Ministry of Environment at the behest of a Unity oversight committee . . ." I went on and gave him the entire spiel, mainly because he looked like he needed it, and because I wanted to see his reaction, and partly because he was acting like an officious asshole. But I offered it very politely and courteously.

When I finished, all he did was nod and say, "That was what I heard. What do you need from me and from Dyart?"

I refrained from sighing and told him.

In a few minutes he took me to a console where I spent a little more than a stan going over reports. Then I linked him, and we returned to the van where I recovered my equipment case. I didn't offer him or Dyart any equipment templates.

Then I spent the next three stans going through the same routine as I had at Eterna, except there were far fewer measurements and samples to take. Dyart was really only a multi by courtesy, it seemed to me. I left Dyart at five-thirty, and since there were no outie lorries on the road, I was back in Passova by six. Still, by the time I had turned in the van to the transport pool and made my way back to the Survey Service, most everyone was gone, except for Dermotte, and he was headed out as I was entering my small spaces. I had to wonder if he'd been detailed to wait for me.

"Have a good weekend, ser."

"Thank you. You, too."

I stowed my cases in the locker and sat down at the console. There were no messages from any of the multis I hadn't yet heard from. Somehow, that didn't surprise me. I put it on standby and left, deciding that I'd go to my quarters and then head out for something to eat at Rancho Rustico, since I hadn't been there except once.

After washing up and putting on a clean singlesuit—black with gray trim, rather than the other way around—I made my way back into the tunnel maze, noting again that the Stittarans never changed the light levels in their tunnel ways, whether it was morning, noon, or night. I would have thought that they would, but obviously they didn't.

There was actually a waiting list at Rancho Rustico, something I hadn't thought about, but that made sense, given that it was a fiveday evening. There was what they called a lounge, where one could get a drink and wait, and I did, settling myself at a small raised table. The table was of distressed wood framed in what looked to be wrought iron and wasn't. I would have preferred a quiet table along the wall, but the tiny high table with two stools was the only vacant one, empty because a couple had just left.

The table to my right held two women, engaged in an intense but quiet conversation, one holding a beaker of something pale orange in a death grip. To my left was another couple who looked to be younger than I. The man was about my size, but wore a skintight royal-blue front-pleated formal shirt and tight white trousers. She was a redhead with her hair drawn back and pale slightly freckled skin, wearing a tailored forest-green single-suit with a pale green vest.

She looked in my direction, pausing for an instant and smiling. I offered a pleasant smile in return before turning to the server. "Pale lager, the least bitter that you have."

"Yes, ser. That would be Zantos."

"Fine."

I glanced toward the restaurant area, hoping it wouldn't be that long before I could be seated and order.

"Your Zantos, ser. You're waiting for a table for dinner?"

"I am."

"I'll put that on your tab."

"Thank you." As she moved away, I tried the Zantos. I had to admit that it was the best lager I'd tasted so far on Stittara. I took several sips, trying not to gulp it down simply because I was hungry.

When I set down the lager glass and looked to my left, the redhead was smiling at me again. I had to admit she was good-looking, but she was with the young man who seemed to think that having muscles was unusual rather than a normal mammalian trait. I smiled briefly and looked back toward the bar.

"You!"

I couldn't help but turn at the vehemence behind that single word. "I beg your pardon?"

"Yes . . . I meant you." The young man was clearly angry. "Don't need any hot straights like you coming on like I wasn't even here."

I hadn't the faintest idea what he meant, except that it had to do with the look his woman friend had given me, and he was the kind you couldn't back off from without encouraging them. But the last thing I wanted was to get into a fight, especially after what Zerlyna had suggested about the anger and paranoia under the polite surface.

"I honestly have no idea what you're talking about."

"Sure you don't." He turned on the stool as if getting ready to stand.

At that moment a tall and muscular man in a dark gray singlesuit appeared, as if from nowhere. He looked at me. "I believe your table is ready, ser."

As he said that, a petite woman appeared and beckoned to me.

I looked at the security type and nodded. "Thank you." Then I slipped off the high stool and followed the hostess.

I only heard the first few words from the security type. "That was unnecessary . . . might be more comfortable elsewhere . . ."

I didn't immediately glance back, but did so when we turned into the restaurant area. Both the table where I'd been sitting and the one where the couple had been were empty. I still couldn't say what had set off the stud in tights. I'd exchanged two glances with the redhead. She'd looked interested, but I certainly hadn't encouraged her, and I'd had no intention of doing so. While I'd recalled what Zerlyna had said, apparently people were even touchier than she'd suggested and I'd need to be even more careful, it appeared.

Still . . . I was looking forward to having a good steak . . . and I intended to make sure I didn't look directly at any attractive women.

23

Sixday morning, I woke a bit later, exercised, lingered over tea, and watched Ilsabet dance over the grass on the low ridge south of my quarters. As before, she was accompanied by a woman guard or security officer in a singlesuit the same shade of gray as that worn by the security type who'd intervened at the bar the night before. That had to be coincidence because the one at Rancho Rustico had offered a table and a hostess had been ready to escort me. I didn't see any skytubes, and Ilsabet was still outside, with her guard, who was looking at everything but Ilsabet, clearly conveying that she was protecting Ilsabet and not confining her—or that her principal function was protection.

Because I couldn't link to my Survey Service console, I made my way to the office, leaving a trail of lights from the tunnel-way doors to my space. Once there, I sat down and cross-checked the records on Dyart. As had been the case with Eterna, all the reports matched and provided absolutely nothing new or anything that might have pointed the way to some ecological problem or oversight.

The next thing I did was look into the information on the outie settlements. There were listings for established and approved settlements, as well as maps and even directions to each of them. I quickly found the one near Dyart, called South Centre. It was listed as the first open land cultivation center on Stittara. After reading through the entire summary file on the others, more than five hundred, I found a notation at the end.

"Other outland settlements may exist, but information on any settlements not approved by the Unity's Systems Survey Service and the Planetary Council of Stittara is enforcement privileged."

Enforcement privileged? I had the feeling that meant such settlements existed at their peril.

It took me some doing, and some tricks I'd learned years before, but I finally got into the Stittaran Survey's enforcement records. I'd hoped to find some statistics, but if they existed, they were buried somewhere. Oh, there was a long listing of enforcement proceedings and the justiciary result of each, but I wasn't in the mood to try to add up all the names involved, not over even the last twenty years, except to note that there were hundreds, possibly thousands, and most of them had been sentenced to "work release" under the supervision of the enforcement director of the Systems Survey Service on Stittara. That meant Jorl Algeld, or his predecessor, from what I could tell.

While that might not exactly square with sentencing guidelines on Bachman, the proceedings had apparently been open, since I'd heard two cases on the linknews. Also when people talked openly about problems, usually, but not always, I reminded myself, that meant that they were seldom the worst kind of abuses. After noting the access points and copying some of the records, I left the enforcement records and sat back, thinking.

Based on what I'd learned—or not learned—at Dyart and Eterna, I had the feeling that any ecological or environmental problems that might exist wouldn't be showing up in any of the official records. They usually didn't. Anything that fell within the scope of laws and regulations was usually worked out. It often took years, hundreds of millions in fees to consultants and advocates, and often a great deal of political effort, but some resolution was reached.

The more I'd searched, the more I was convinced that there just wasn't much information on the skytubes . . . and that whatever existed, beyond the basics, had been destroyed, hidden off-system and off-link, or carefully never been pursued—possibly all three. I could even think of a motive for that. Stittara existed to make duhlars for the anagathic multis and to keep the most affluent citizens of the Unity young and beautiful-looking for as long as possible. Anything that threatened those two purposes would be stopped, one way or another.

That also meant, so long as I discovered nothing and did nothing beyond going through the motions, I was more or less safe—maybe. My
calculation was based on what I'd observed on Bachman. Murders of
people carrying out government business upset the politicians. But murders
more than 73 light-years and 150 years later might not.

I took a deep breath.

What next?

I shook my head. I was tired of statistics, records, and reports. I'd also
been on Stittara almost two weeks, and I hadn't seen anything that looked
like a tree, not even a bonsai or a potted tree. I frowned. Come to think
of it, I hadn't even seen a live flower. I wasn't sure I'd even seen an artificial one. Were there gardens anywhere?

I tried a search and discovered that Passova had both an arboretum
and a public garden, just one of each. The arboretum was on the far west
side of Passova and the public garden on the far east. After a moment I
turned off my console and stood, then made my way out of the Survey
Service offices, turning off the lights as I left. I walked about three blocks
and then took a ramp down four levels to the tunneltram.

The trams were spotless and cramped, basically silver-gray composite
shells with darker gray bench seats on each side running the length of
each car, with barely enough space for one person to walk between those
sitting on the seats. Fortunately, they were seldom crowded, although
there was no charge to use them. I wondered if they'd been designed to be
not terribly comfortable just so they wouldn't be overused.

I was the only one to get out at the stop nearest the arboretum. Following my link directions, I did have to walk down three more levels. The
tunnels were narrower than those around the Survey offices and on the
east side of Passova, suggesting that the area to the west was older—or
that the deeper levels had narrower tunnels for structural reasons. While
the walls were smooth and clean, they had more of a feeling of age, and I
didn't see nearly as many people around, even after walking almost a half
kay farther west before nearing the arboretum. Those I did see quickly
and carefully looked away, especially the few older men . . . which I found
disconcerting.

An open space, something like a small underground square, roughly
fifty meters on a side, fronted the entrance. As I walked toward it, I could
see a handful of people, several with small children, standing before the

linkiosks with lettering above—"Admission: ten duhlars." That didn't bother me, and once I reached the linkiosk, I used my link to transfer the funds. In turn, the linkiosk pulsed the admit code to my link, and I walked toward the pressure doors.

Once through them, I got my first surprise.

On the other side was a second pressure door that led to a boxlike structure. Beside the second door was a guard, an older man in a brown singlesuit with an insignia of a tree in green upon each shoulder. He wore a stunner as well, the first I'd seen in a while in public—except for the one worn by the woman guarding Ilsabet.

I just stood there for a moment.

"Please step into the decon chamber, ser. Let it cycle. Proceed when the arrow turns green." He sounded as though he'd repeated those words thousands of times. He probably had.

I followed his directions and stepped into the decon chamber, where I was subjected to a brisk breeze and likely several forms of decontamination. But decontamination to enter a T-type arboretum? The arrow next to the pressure door on the far side turned green, and I stepped out into another open space with a fourth set of pressure doors in the wall presumably separating me from the arboretum.

Ahead of me, a woman bent over to talk to a child.

"All the doors are to protect the trees. They're like all the other pressure doors. There are just more of them."

That apparently reassured the boy, and the two walked toward the last doors. I followed them, but not too closely. Beyond the doors, there was a wide stone terrace, and beyond that, everything opened up. The arboretum was huge . . . a good two kays in length . . . and close to a kay in width, and the ceiling, if the arched overhead some fifty meters above qualified as a ceiling, radiated the yellowish light of a G-class sun. That stunned me, and I realized, belatedly, that the light in Passova and all the installations replicated the ambient light of Stittara. That made sense, but I just hadn't really noticed it—until now. What I also realized was that the light in the arboretum wasn't brighter—just . . . yellower.

There was a stretch of grass beyond the terrace and two pathways, one from the right end of the terrace and one from the left. I took the left one, simply because the two women with children took the right one. Just at the edge of the terrace was a sign.

STAY ON THE PATH!
VIOLATORS WILL FACE CHARGES
AND WORK RELEASE PENALTIES.

That was very clear. I resolved to stay firmly on the path. That shouldn't have been hard to do because on each side of the synthstone path was a pseudostone wall slightly above knee height.

Beyond the stretch of grass, I passed through a grove of terrestrial-type oaks, and then some maples, some with dark red leaves, a variety I hadn't seen. Through an opening between the maples, I thought I saw the straight trunk of a linden. As I walked, keeping on the path, as requested by the signs, I noted that there were guards in brown singlesuits stationed at various points along the path. I also noted a slight breeze that seemed to flow toward me, or down the pathway. It took me longer than it should have to realize that was because there was directed barrier airflow and that the pathway was designed as a return airflow. That flow wasn't to protect the viewers, and that meant it was designed to keep the viewers from contaminating the arboretum. *But what sort of contamination from people could harm trees?*

Offhand, I didn't have an answer. So I stopped by the next guard.

"Pardon me, but I've noticed that the airflow and the pathways are designed to separate viewers from the trees. Why is that?"

"Lignin borer grubs. They're tiny, but they're everywhere outside the arboretum."

On the surface, that didn't make sense. All vascular plants—all T-type vascular plants—contained some lignin within the cell walls.

The guard must have read my expression, before I could ask, he went on. "I don't know all the details. Something about the greater the concentration of lignin cells in a plant, the more attractive the plant is to the borers, and big trees are like a beacon. The grubs don't like T-type light either."

"What about local plants?"

"The biologists say most of them have some natural repellent, unless the plant is weakened."

"Thank you." Another peculiarity of Stittara to check out.

He just nodded, and I continued on for several hundred yards, where there was a larger circular area where people could stop and look at a birch grove. At first, at a distance, I'd thought they might be aspens, but realized that was unlikely, given that aspens didn't do well in low-altitude high-atmospheric pressure conditions.

I just looked at the birches for a time, not sure even what I was thinking, then was about to go when I realized that a dark-haired woman and a boy about five were standing less than two meters away.

She was blotting her eyes and cheeks, then looked at me, almost guiltily. "I'm sorry. I miss the trees . . . even after all these years . . ."

"You don't have to apologize," I said gently. "I take it you're not originally from Stittara?"

"From Bachman." She took a filmy tissue and blotted her eyes again. Then she sniffed.

I wondered why she'd come, but I didn't ask, just tried to look sympathetic, hoping she'd say.

"My husband . . . he had a choice . . . a transfer to the Technology Ministry field office . . ."

"Or a reduction in force?"

She nodded, then asked, "How did you know?"

"I'm from Bachman. I'm a consultant on a field assignment. I understand what happens when the politicians let public opinion override good decision-making"

"Why did you come here, of all places?"

"Money," I replied wryly, "and a costly dissolution." I shouldn't have said that, but her openness had disarmed me . . . after all the days of careful monitoring of what I said—another reminder that I'd never have made it in a field requiring covert operations.

"I'm sorry . . ."

"That's all right. She left me before it all happened."

"Mommy . . ." The five-year-old tugged at her singlesuit. "Can we go now? You said we wouldn't stay too long."

I smiled. "You'd better listen to your friend there."

"I suppose I should. Thank you for listening."

"I'm glad I was here to listen."

She smiled, tentatively, then took her son and headed back down the pathway.

Even with the tears, she'd been attractive, but I felt sorry for her, not anything else. I was already beginning to see how hard living on Stittara could be for someone from an open world.

After that, I took my time, pausing, looking at trees, recognizing many, but having to link with the arboretum information system to identify others, such as a catalpa, a sycamore, and a bristlecone pine, identified as the oldest individual tree in the arboretum. There was also a note that several T-type trees, such as giant redwoods and sequoias, could not be accommodated because of their height. All in all, it was a respectable collection, and I spent over two stans making my way all the way around the facility.

As I was standing on the terrace, about to make my way back out through the elaborate pressure-door system, I heard a child, a boy, I thought, talking. I turned, slightly, not enough that the woman could think I was trying to make eye contact, although she was alone with the child.

"Mommy . . . why don't we have trees like this outside?"

"They won't grow there, dear."

"Why not?"

"They just won't."

"That's sad . . ."

I didn't know that it was sad, but the environmental separation technology and precautions were rather elaborate, even as a prevention for a borer grub or the like, especially given that the outies were clearly growing some variety of T-type crops, and the cities and installations were synthesizing and tank-growing similar foodstuff. That raised another question, one that I could certainly ask without raising alarms . . . if I didn't find an answer in the Survey files and records.

Given that it was already past midafternoon, I decided to visit the public garden on sevenday. What else was I going to do?

24

Much as I wanted to sleep in on sevenday morning, I found I couldn't because too many questions were swirling around in my mind. After readying myself for the day, I did go to my office and look up the lignin borer grub. The arboretum guard's explanation had been greatly oversimplified. The grubs were a larval stage of a lichen beetle that attacked the roots of the local lichen/grass symbionts, except they were only marginally successful because the anagathic precursors in grass functioned as a grubicide, so to speak, so there was a low beetle population in the natural Stittaran ecosystem under normal conditions. The grubs also required a long larval period and didn't do nearly so well with smaller vascular plants with a faster life cycle, such as decorative angiosperms, i.e., flowers. I wondered if trees that had floral displays, like dogwoods or magnolias or tulip trees, might have been more resistant to the grubs . . . but the information I could find didn't address that.

I also ended up doing a series of searches on pests affecting outland cultivation. I didn't find anything. Then I wondered about native trees, or their equivalent, and spent some time on that, discovering that there were a few hundred native species, none of them particularly impressive in height or in numbers, and virtually all of them were located in either rugged or mountainous terrain. They all were analogous to T-type gymnosperms, although there were some minor differences. I didn't find anything that would have disproved congruent evolution, but I didn't expect anything like that because, the theorists to the contrary, so far humans hadn't found any complex life forms that weren't essentially carbon-based.

As in any research, one thing led to another, and it was already early afternoon when I decided I'd been digging in files and records for all too long, and made my way out of the Survey offices. I wasn't all that hungry and decided on an early dinner after I'd inspected the public garden.

Once again, I boarded a tunneltram, this one headed to the eastern side of Passova, and less than half full. After I got off, I had to consult my link again because the tunnel directions didn't make much sense. I didn't have to go down any levels, but stayed on the tram level and walked a good half kay almost due south. All the walking through tunnels and from tram stops to my various destinations did suggest one reason why I'd hadn't seen any generously overproportioned residents of Stittara. I supposed that some of the more affluent residents might have small tunnel vehicles, but I certainly hadn't seen any.

From the open underground space outside the public garden, it appeared similar to the arboretum, and the admission charge was the same. Even though it was a sevenday, when fewer people were working, I only saw three other people at the linkiosks as I walked up. Once I went through the first pressure doors I could tell there were definite differences. There were no decontamination spaces, just another set of pressure doors leading into the garden.

The terrace just inside the garden was similar to that at the arboretum, but in addition to the signs forbidding visitors to leave the walk, there was another very large sign.

POSSIBLE ALLERGENS
ENTER THE GARDEN
AT YOUR OWN RISK

I glanced around and noticed several people walking toward me, apparently ready to leave the garden, who were wearing masks across their nose and mouth. Almost in reaction, I found myself taking in a deep breath. To me, the air felt more alive than it did in the tunnels or in my quarters, but I could see tears oozing from the eyes of one woman who hurried past me and out of the public garden.

For a moment I studied the garden, roughly half the size of the arboretum. While there were low walled walks leading through the garden,
there were far more walks and fewer guards, and there were no obvious
indications of a differential air barrier system. Then I took the path that
headed to the far right, simply because it was empty. The first flower bed
had been tilled, but contained no plants. There were no signs and no link
notices explaining why.

The second bed held a sort of bushy creeping vine called Oragrape. I'd
never heard of it. The third held an array of irises, but they'd apparently
stopped blooming and were turning brownish because it was past their
season . . . or because the lignin grubs had gotten to them. But the thorny
roses in the next bed were tiny, with a pervasive gentle scent so sweet I
just stood there enjoying it for a time.

Somewhere amid the flowers, I came across a plant with white petals
called a daisy. It looked familiar, and yet I couldn't recall ever seeing one.
Then I remembered that the flowers looked similar to the one on a single
stem that I'd seen Ilsabet carrying. A daisy. I tried to fix the image and
the name in my memory because I didn't want to record it in my link.

I kept walking and looking at flowers, many of which I'd never seen
and which had to have come from outside the Arm. Some that I recognized were sweet Williams and sour Anns, morning glories, sunflowers,
black-eyed Susans, violets of several varieties. There were only a few roses
after the wild thorny kinds, and several of those were clearly ill, but that
made sense because they were woodier and perennials. The lower and
greener varieties seemed to do better, unsurprisingly.

In the end, I hurried past the last score of flower beds, and it was late
enough in the afternoon that I was almost alone when I left, except for
several women, clearly older and to the point where anagathics were no
longer much help. Two of them wore anti-allergen masks as well. At least,
that's what I assumed they were.

Once I got off the return tunneltram, before heading back to my own
quarters, I stopped at Carlo's to see if it happened to be open. It was, and
less than half the white plastreen tables were occupied. The hostess motioned, and I got a table against a wall, well away from the fountain. I
looked around, but I didn't see any greenery, and no flowers, not even
artificial ones. Some of the reason for the lack of floral decoration might
have been that Stittara had been colonized from Bachman, but there

were certainly some flowers on Bachman. I knew, from having been politely chastised for not occasionally presenting them to Chelesina on what
she thought were appropriate occasions when we had first been married. I
had learned, though, and that was why I was somewhat aware of floral
necessities, except they didn't seem to be anything close to necessities on
Stittara.

The server was a woman, not young enough just to have finished her
education, whatever it might have been, but also likely not to have been
more than ten years older than that. Her glossy black hair was cut moderately short, just below the ears. She had a welcoming smile when she asked,
"Would you like something to drink before you order?"

"Yes, please. A glass of the house white." I hadn't forgotten my experience with the lager the last time I'd been at Carlo's.

"You've been here before, haven't you? With the two from the Survey
Service, weren't you?"

"I was. You didn't serve us, though, did you?"

She smiled and shook her head. "Clenton did."

"What do you recommend this afternoon?"

"Well . . . it is evening . . . and the evening special is lasagna. It's good."

I grinned. "Now that you've done your duty, what would you suggest?"

"The fowl piccata is really good."

"Then I'll have it, with a green salad of some sort."

"I can do that for you." She smiled again, and her eyes met mine, if but
for an instant. Then she was gone.

I was glad of that, because I'd been getting too many looks I was afraid
I recognized, and I had no idea why. Oh . . . I knew some of the reasons
why women were attracted to men who did not have overwhelming talent
or charisma, and all of them amounted to some sort of power. The problem was that I didn't have anything remotely connected to either wealth
or power. I was decent looking and had some assets. I wasn't in a position
of power, bureaucratic, political, or otherwise.

The other aspect of those looks was that those who were doing the
looking were almost random. At least, I couldn't figure out anything they
had in common.

The fowl piccata was indeed excellent, and the service even more so.

Tips were customary on Stittara, and I left a generous one.

My server looked at it, then offered a smile somehow both pleased and sad, then said, "Thank you so much." She smiled once more. "If you come again, you can ask for me. I'm Giselle."

"I'm certain I'll be back, Giselle."

That brought forth another smile, and another intense look. I returned the smile, inclined my head, then rose and left the café.

After leaving Carlo's I walked back to my quarters. I didn't see a single sign of greenery, especially no flowers. Not a single plant.

25

I'd only been in my space a few minutes on oneday morning when Aloris peered in and said, "You're here early. How was your weekend? Or did you spend all of it here working?"

"Of course. I slaved straight through, then hurried to my quarters, cleaned up and returned, without food, water, or other nourishment . . ." I offered a grin. "No. I did some work, but I also toured the arboretum and the public garden."

"The arboretum is interesting . . . in a way . . ."

"What do you mean by 'interesting'?"

"It's amazing that they've been able to keep it in such good condition for so long."

"Because of the lignin borer grubs? Or something else?"

"Unmodified T-type vascular plants don't do well here. The borers aren't the only potential parasite. Many of the beetle species are more analogous to T-type termites, and they regard most T-type plants as preferable to the local variety, but they tend to gorge and die because of what's essentially a glucose imbalance or overdose. By then, it's usually too late for the plant or tree. I'm sure you've discovered that."

"Actually, I didn't come across the imbalance. I did find some references to the fact that only short-lived and fast-growing varieties of T-type plants do well, and I noticed there weren't many woody flowering plants in the garden. There's not much on the modifications."

"That's not my area, but the outies have found or forced crosses that seem to thrive and that we can digest. They're not much interested in decorative plants, for obvious reasons. If you want to know more, you might want to talk to Dylen Mallon about it. He's in research."

"Thank you. How was your weekend?"

"Quiet, and that's how I like it." She softened the terseness of her words with a smile, fleeting though it was.

"I can appreciate that."

She nodded and slipped away.

Should I try to contact Syntex, ABP, and Valior once more . . . or give them until later in the day? I decided to wait a little longer, although patience had never been one of my strongest traits.

As I pondered over what Aloris had said, what I couldn't figure out was how crops got pollinated if there weren't any flowers native to Stittara, because there hadn't been enough time for native pollinators to adapt to imported food crops. A quick search revealed that the local sawfly had adapted and that the outies had early on imported digger bees, and the combination seemed to work. Who was I to argue with that, even if I did have questions?

Her offhand reference to Dylen Mallon in "research" raised yet another question. How many subdivisions of the Stittaran Survey Service were there, especially those unique to Stittara? I tried a search for "research," and found it quickly, located as a subdivision of Enforcement under Jorl Algeld. What the main directory didn't tell me was how people fit in the organization structure. Oh, there was a complete directory of people, alphabetically listed, and there were the main branches of the Survey Service, with the media divisions below that. Period.

I needed to know more, and Zerlyna was the logical one to give me access, or at least as logical as Aloris, and Zerlyna seemed a bit friendlier. Before I went to see her, though, I studied my assignment contract closely to see if it said what I thought it did. It did, or at least close enough.

So I got up and headed to find her.

"You're here early, Paulo," Zerlyna said, before I said a word when I stepped into her spaces. "You must want something."

"I do. How do I get the background on the environmental specialties of Survey Service personnel? The directory is too sketchy."

"By demonstrating need to know. Why do you need to know?"

It was a good thing I'd thought that out. "So that I can report whether there are enough technically qualified personnel covering each environmental medium with the qualifications to evaluate and assess potential problems."

"Isn't that a stretch from an ecological survey?"

"I thought you might ask that question. I sent my assignment parameters and authorities to you. I highlighted one section. And, technically, my contract is described as an assessment and investigation."

A faint smile of amusement crossed her lips before she turned to her console. After several minutes, she looked up. "That definitely gives you the authority to ask for almost anything you want. Could I ask why?"

"Every question leads to another question, and being able to search for those I need directly would be helpful. So would having the entire structure of expertise available."

Zerlyna didn't quite conceal her frown, but rather than protest, she turned back to the console, her fingers flashing across and into the projected data matrix. Personally, I preferred the more linear flat displays, but to each his or her own. Finally, she turned. "You now have access to everything but pending enforcement actions. No one has direct access to those, except on a case by case basis."

"I seriously doubt I'll be needing those." *And you hope you never will . . . because if you do, that will only be the start of your troubles.* I smiled. "There's one other thing. I toured the arboretum on sixday and the public garden yesterday." I paused to see what her response might be.

"I haven't been there in years. I've heard that the garden has gotten run-down."

"It doesn't seem as well kept as the arboretum, but there was one other thing. There was a sign posted, warning of allergens, and some of those visiting were wearing masks."

"That sign's been there as long as I can remember." Zerlyna paused. "Sometimes I got a stuffy nose when my mother took me, but she didn't make me wear a mask."

"Have you been since she took you?"

She offered an embarrassed smile. "No. The garden never appealed to me."

"You never took your own children?"

"They weren't interested. They liked outings in the hills better."

That surprised me. "I didn't realize people did that."

"Some do. The hills, especially the rugged areas, are pretty safe, even when there are storms around."

"You don't walk out there?"

"You can rent camping vans."

"Do you have any flowers or plants at home?"

Zerlyna looked surprised at the question, or perhaps at the change of subject. "No . . . I can't say that I do. I tried a miniature violet when I was a teener. I had to throw it out. I sneezed any time I was around it for long."

"Do you have other allergies?"

Zerlyna shook her head. "Why do you ask?"

"I just wondered. I saw all the people with masks, and I haven't seen that much greenery anywhere." In fact, I couldn't recall seeing any T-type greenery in Passova except in the arboretum and the public garden . . . with one exception.

"Part of that is the light, I suppose."

"Plants don't do as well under Stittaran light, and the city replicates it?" That didn't make sense, but that was the implication of her reply.

"It's one factor."

I nodded.

"For whatever reason, Paulo, I don't think we're flower people here. What's the purpose of growing decorative plants that don't flower?"

"Especially if they make you sneeze."

"That's true."

"And if you're a very practical people?" I asked gently.

"Too practical, perhaps, but Stittara does have a way of weeding out the impractical."

Stittara or Stittarans? I didn't voice that question. I inclined my head. "Thank you. I hope I don't have to bother you more."

"It's not a bother. You're trying to do your work, and we need to give you the tools to do so."

"I appreciate it." With what I trusted was a friendly smile, I turned and headed back to my spaces. I didn't even have a chance to sit down and start my personnel research when my screen offered a gentle chime and then flashed, "Incoming message from K. Guffrey, Syntex."

"Accept."

A youngish-looking male with hair longer than I thought either attractive or appropriate appeared on the screen. "Dr. Verano . . . Khredron Guffrey from Syntex, returning your inquiry. You had asked for an appointment with our head environmental officer. Dr. Tharon has been somewhat tied up, but he will be available this coming fourday or fiveday and hoped that one of those days would work for you."

"I have all fiveday available."

The young man glanced to the side, then back to the screen and me. "Dr. Tharon would prefer ten hundred . . ."

"That would be fine with me."

"Then we'll see you at ten hundred on fiveday." Khredron Guffrey smiled brightly before his image vanished from my screen.

I immediately initiated a linknet search. There wasn't much on a Tharon at Syntex, only a few references to a Dr. Bryse Tharon, with degrees from the Stittaran Unity University in north Passova. He apparently had a daughter who was a star korfball player. That was it. I could see that privacy and personal information were more highly regarded on Stittara, at least so far as the linknet was concerned. Or was it that in a world of a comparatively few million people, individuals weren't screaming in every way possible for others to notice them? Or was there some other reason?

I pushed those questions aside. They definitely weren't in the scope of my assignment, an assignment that I felt was expanding with each new aspect of Stittara that I uncovered. Because my next meeting was with RDAEX, I went back over their submissions, focusing on the sections that dealt with ongoing projects. Most of the multis spelled out their purposes in general terms. Syntex declared that it was investigating the Stittaran biosphere to develop further improvements in anagathic pharmaceuticals and cosmetics. Dyart's avowed purpose was just what I'd been told—extensive and continuing research on Stittaran flora to determine potential commercial use in the fields of pharmaceuticals and beauty aids. The other multis had comparatively similar purposes, except for RDAEX.

RDAEX listed one objective—the investigation of self-organizing microorganic structures under variable atmospheric conditions. As if all microorganisms weren't self-organizing and all atmospheres weren't variable. But what did that purpose have to do with a space-based power and resource multi?

26

To get to the dropport by 0600 hours on twoday meant rising no later than 0430, dressing and eating, and then meeting Dermotte, who had to drive me there, because, given Stittara's weather and the limited number of Survey vehicles—and the few underground parking spaces at the dropport—Aloris didn't want any vehicles left there. I didn't stagger to the Survey vehicle spaces, but I felt as though I wasn't at my best, especially carrying the case with my equipment in one hand and a kit bag with clothes and personal items in the other. Dermotte took it from me and stowed it with ease, then closed the back of the van.

I climbed into the front passenger seat and fastened the safety harness. "Sorry to get you up so early, Dermotte."

"Not a problem, ser. One of the things I get paid for. At least once a week someone's heading somewhere." He eased the van up the ramp and out into the purple darkness before sunrise, although it was more like before the eastern sky lightened.

"Oh . . . where do they go?"

"Conduo or Contrio. Mostly, the enforcement folks. Dealing with the outies, you know. That never stops."

"I've heard some people say that, but no one really says why. Do they steal? Or is it just because they're different?"

"They're different, all right." Dermotte shook his head. "They even smell different."

"Why is that, do you think?"

"Wouldn't know, sir. Might be because they live on the surface more."

"Do they have dwellings in the open?"

"Nope. They're not that dumb. They dig down, not so far as the towns and cities. Been told every outie family has their own hole."

"Could it be what they eat?"

"Might be. They don't like synth or tank foods."

"Where are these outie settlements? I tried to find maps of them . . ."

"Might find locations in enforcement, sir. Director Raasn says there are too many that are too small to map them, except for the largest."

Except for the largest? I hadn't found mention of any on the maps of Stittara, but maybe the maps didn't distinguish between underground cities and outie settlements. Every mention of the outies suggested in some way or another that there were far more of them than anyone in Passova wanted to acknowledge. That raised an interesting possibility. I'd been given the assignment for doing an ecological assessment with the belief that the underlying question was whether the multis were interfering with the ecological balance . . . but the more I heard about the outies, I couldn't help but think they might be the problem. Human agriculture changed planetary ecologies far more than most industry, and seldom was that ever acknowledged. The classic case was that of Old Earth, where agriculture totally changed the cyclical pattern of global warming and cooling, and kept doing so even while politicians and industrials fought over industrial emissions practices and policies.

Could something like that be happening on Stittara?

I wanted to take a deep breath. I'd barely started, and I wasn't feeling in over my head. I was beginning to feel as though I were at the bottom of the ocean.

For the rest of the drive from Passova, I offered leading questions to Dermotte, although I didn't really learn much more, but it did pass the time, because for most of the way, the purpled darkness was so pervasive, especially with neither stars nor moons in the sky, that there was little to see beyond the beams of the headlights, which revealed only the permacrete highway and its shoulders. The lowlight panel display had a wider range, but still didn't show anything except grass and low bushes.

By the time we neared the dropport, the eastern sky was lightening, and I could make out the outline of the single low building—and one shape on the permacrete strip. Dermotte drove me right up to that shape—a lifting body bearing the insignia of a lightning bolt superimposed on a stylized solar system on the rear of the fuselage.

"Here we are, ser."

I'd expected a long-distance flitter, rather than a magfield suborbital lifter, but the young man who'd confirmed the arrangements had clearly said "shuttle." It made sense, in a way, given Stittara's strong magnetic field, but the initial cost of a magfield shuttle dwarfed that of even the largest flitters, and the maintenance costs were anything but insignificant.

I hurried out of the van, but Dermotte was even faster and had the back open as I reached it, handing me my gear, beginning with the equipment case. "Here you go, sir."

"Thank you." Then I turned and walked toward the shuttle.

A crewman in a dark green singlesuit appeared as I neared the extended ramp. He held a scanner. "If you wouldn't mind, ser." His words weren't a question.

I set the case and the bag on the bottom of the ramp and stepped back while he scanned both.

Then he turned the scanner on me, waited a moment, and said, "You can board now, ser."

I nodded, picked up my gear, and walked up the ramp and through the hatch, taking a quick look around to see what I was supposed to do with the case and the kit bag.

"The baggage lockers are aft, at the back of the cabin." The voice came from a woman almost my size, clearly in fighting trim, and wearing a black security suit, with a belt stunner and a few other items I didn't recognize. From her voice, equipage, and posture, I had no doubts that she could have turned me into raw meat without using any of that equipment. She stood beside a luxurious padded acceleration cradle that seemed unnecessary, one of ten in the cabin, five on each side, with a wide aisle between them.

"Thank you." I eased past her and the first two cradles to the rear of the cabin and slipped the equipment case into one locker, the kit bag into another, and closed both, then walked forward, stopping short of the woman.

"What do you think of our shuttle, Dr. Verano?"

"I was initially a bit surprised."

"Good. I'm Kali Artema."

"You're obviously security."

She smiled, an expression with the amused arrogance of a large feline predator. "You might say that. I'm the assistant director of security for RDAEX. I had to meet with the Stittaran director of security yesterday, and it wasn't feasible to return last night. So we could offer you transport."

"I'm very grateful. I'd prefer not to take long flitter trips."

"No one in her right mind would." She stepped toward the forward bulkhead and gestured toward the cradle away from the hatch. "Just the two of us on this trip."

I wasn't about to refuse that invitation and eased into the cradle. Artema must have signaled somehow, because the crewman hurried up the ramp, and it closed behind him. He disappeared through the door in the cabin's forward bulkhead, and Artema took the forward cradle next to the now-closed hatch.

I had the feeling Artema wasn't a Stittaran native. Even in the comparatively short time I'd been planetside, I was beginning to sense a difference between those born on Stittara and those who had immigrated or been transferred by multis. And her parents, assuming they'd named her, had a very nasty sense of humor. I wasn't about to guess at her gender preferences.

"Is RDAEX the only multi on Stittara using magfield shuttles?"

"Yes."

"Why is that? I'd think some could afford them."

She laughed softly. It wasn't a gentle sound. "The ones that could use them don't want to pay what it costs."

"False economy?"

"That's not for me to say. Security is my concern, and a magfield shuttle is far safer on Stittara than a flitter."

"Because of the storms and skytubes?"

She didn't answer immediately because someone announced, "Secure for liftoff."

I straightened in the cradle and looked for whatever it took to activate the restraints.

"The red square on the armrest."

I pressed it and waited. In instants, I was fully cradled and restrained, not that it was likely necessary, since I understood magfield drives didn't require terribly high initial acceleration.

The shuttle seemed to lift, and I got a sense of gentle movement. Then I was pressed firmly but inexorably against the cradle. The pressure continued for a good fifteen minutes, before slacking off, at which time my guts protested the sudden weightlessness. I swallowed hard, and they subsided.

"I hadn't expected quite so sudden an acceleration," I said.

"Stittara has a strong magnetic field. That allows greater acceleration and a quicker trip."

"Where are you from originally?"

"Teppera."

That figured, in one way, although I wondered why a woman from one of the systems only loosely allied to the Unity would be employed by an Arm multi.

"Technology transfer," Artema replied to my unspoken question. "We serve ten-year contracts in return for local licensure privileges."

"I take it that the question I didn't have a chance to pose is asked all the time?"

"No. Most don't even know where Teppera is. It was the look on your face."

The look on your face? That told me she was linked to all the shuttle surveillance systems . . . and that she was likely at least slightly cyborged, with psych profile recog background.

Artema laughed again.

"I'm glad you find me amusing, Director."

"Assistant director."

"You're director in everything but name."

"You understand some . . . matters. That's why I'm enjoying having your company."

"Because I know a bit more than most?"

"You know a great deal more than most, and if the Stittarans understood what you know, Doctor, you might have a hard time returning to Bachman."

Or anywhere else, from the way you said that. "Unfortunately, I don't know as much as you think I do."

"Then you'd best discover it before they discover you can."

"Knowing that about me, you're going to let me come to RDAEX and depart?"

"RDAEX has no problems with your visit. I don't either."

"You just like to watch the more intelligent male rodents struggle through the more complex mazes. Especially political and bureaucratic ones."

"You could put it that way, but . . . give yourself more credit."

Our conversation, such as it happened to be, was cut short.

"Stand by for deceleration."

Smoothly, but quickly, the cradles swiveled so that we were looking at the rear of the cabin, and once more I was pressed deeply into the cradle, although the deceleration didn't seem to last quite so long as the acceleration had, but I could sense we were still airborne.

"No low-level sonic disruptions?" I asked.

"Not here on Contrio. It doesn't matter so much over Conuno."

"To RDAEX or to the Planetary Council?"

"Either."

I could feel the shuttle descending, then moving on a level, before slowing and turning, apparently air-taxiing toward wherever we would disembark. I felt the craft tilt forward just slightly, as if we were headed down a ramp.

"Underground hangar and reception area?" I asked.

"It makes more sense, don't you think?"

"It does, but why doesn't the Planetary Council do that for the drop-port at Passova?"

"Why is anything not done? They don't want to spend the duhlars to do it. They have an underground hangar for the two drop shuttles, but they're strictly for protective storage, and a few underground spaces for the well connected. Also, we seem to have far more storms here. That's why RDAEX is positioned farther underground and has almost no surface access except through heavily reinforced doors with multiple pressure seals."

"Has anyone determined why there are more storms here?"

"I wouldn't know, Doctor. That's outside my area of expertise."

When the shuttle came to a halt and settled, the cradle restraints released, but the cradles remained facing rearward.

"Feel free to reclaim your gear, Doctor."

"Thank you, Director."

She did offer a brief smile, but once I had my case and kit, the hatch was open, the ramp extended, and she gestured for me to proceed first. I nodded and headed out. I wasn't about to argue.

The first thing I noticed as I stepped out of the shuttle and onto the ramp was that the underground hangar was enormous—and that there was not only another magfield shuttle, but also a small drop shuttle, of a design that indicated a magfield-plasmajet hybrid. The hangar arrangements, and Artema's comments about sonic impacts, suggested that the RDAEX installation was even more underground than Passova itself, although that was just an initial impression. Also, the walls and overheads were a pleasant blue, not the institutional gray that pervaded Passova, while the floor surfaces were deeper and darker blue.

The same impeccably dressed and groomed young man who had made my appointments stood waiting, most likely for me, with a small open vehicle. Today, though, he wore a light gray singlesuit, but every single golden blond hair of his coiffure remained perfectly in place, and a pleasant smile was fixed on his face.

As I approached him and stopped, Kali Artema eased up beside me. "Fabio . . . this is Dr. Verano. I'd appreciate it very much if everything went smoothly."

For just an instant, the young man blanched and stiffened. If I hadn't been studying him, I wouldn't have noticed.

"Yes, Director Artema. I'll do everything I can."

Artema looked to me. "I enjoyed talking to you. If there's anything I can do, just let me know." She slipped a card into my hand, then turned and strode toward another waiting tunnel vehicle, with a gray-clad security type at the controls.

I turned to the young aide. "Paulo Verano."

"Fabio Marghina." He looked at my case and kit.

"Where do I put them?"

"Oh . . . in the back." He moved swiftly and lifted the rear bench seat.

There was barely enough space for both items, but I managed to position them so that they fit.

"We have enough time to drop your personal gear at the guest quarters."

"I may need the equipment. I'd like to keep that with me."

"Whatever you wish, ser."

The tunnel from the underground hangar to what appeared to be the main part of the installation was a good kay in length, if not longer, and as we passed through a set of open pressure doors, above which the name and logo of RDAEX were emblazoned, I asked, "Were we passing through the base, or is there a separation between the dropport and the main facility?"

"There's a separation, ser. One point six kays, I believe. The designer of the original facility was a bit of an antiquarian, I understand."

Several minutes later, when Marghina eased the tunnelcar to a stop at an archway with an eagle at the top, I couldn't help but comment. "This was designed by the same person?"

"I wouldn't know, ser." He left the vehicle as gracefully as a dancer and opened the storage compartment.

I took the kit bag and left the case. "Where next?"

"Through the archway, ser. This way."

I followed him through the eagle arch, which held concealed pressure doors, and then into a sitting area of sorts, from which three corridors diverged. We took the right corridor, and he stopped at the second door, where he handed me a placard. "That opens the door. Once inside, you can use it to set the door to open to your handprint. If you take this corridor down the other way, there's a dining room. They serve from six hundred to nine hundred in the morning and from seventeen hundred to nineteen hundred in the evening." He paused. "I'll be waiting with the tunnelcar, ser. That's if you won't be long."

"I won't be."

Marghina retreated as I opened the door and stepped inside. The "guest" quarters at RDAEX consisted of a study, bedchamber, and bath, all moderately good-sized, if Spartan. It only took me a few minutes to reset the door, clean up, and make my way back to the tunnelcar.

The trip to wherever I was meeting Executive Edo took less than three minutes, even climbing one ramp up a level. Marghina eased the tunnelcar into a space beside another archway, this one with closed pressure doors, and with the RDAEX logo on top.

"These are the executive offices."

I *thought* we were less than a half kay west of the guest quarters, but my geographic senses didn't do as well in tunnels, and I didn't check my link. I reclaimed my equipment case, although I doubted I'd need it in meeting with Edo.

Marghina offered his hand to the scanner and the door slid open. We walked less than ten meters and through a regular door into a reception area with several dark blue chairs, once more of templated Spartan design, and a console desk. He slipped into the swivel behind the console, and manipulated the projected display before announcing, "Dr. Verano is here."

I didn't hear any response, but the good Fabio nodded and said, "You can go in." He gestured to the door.

I left my equipment case beside his console and walked to the door, which irised open as I approached. The iris pattern suggested that the door was almost ancient, as did Fabio Marghina's remarks about the separation between the landing area and the main installation, and the eagle over the guest quarters entrance but . . . from what I'd heard and the records I'd perused, RDAEX had only been on Stittara slightly more than 150 years.

The door closed behind me, and I stood in a slightly vaulted chamber close to fifteen meters long and eight wide. The overhead was a stellar view, likely projected in real time, that I didn't recognize, and that meant it was unlikely to have been a view from Bachman, unless it was a polar perspective.

"What do you think of it?" The speaker was a burly man with a warm smile and bright green eyes.

"Quite spectacular." I inclined my head. "Paulo Verano. I appreciate your making the time to see me."

"Any time a Unity government oversight committee requests a survey, the least I can do is to find out what I can, and there's no better way to do that here on Stittara than to meet with you. For the record, I am Belk Edo." He turned to the second man, who had risen from one of the chairs in front of the console. "Haans, here, is our chief of environment and ecology."

"I'm pleased to meet you both."

Edo gestured to the chairs. "Little sense in standing."

I took the end chair of the three, leaving a vacant seat between me and the other man, whom I presumed to be Dr. Ermitag.

"Dr. Verano," continued Edo, "precisely why does your assignment concern RDAEX?"

"Because it concerns every possibility of adverse ecological impact on Stittara. RDAEX is operating here. So it concerns RDAEX."

"That is a rather . . . ambitious project for one ecologist, even one as distinguished as you."

"It is an interesting assignment," I replied.

"I can't imagine anything here that would be that interesting to the man who successfully eco-engineered the restructuring of the subarctic ecology of Nuarfelk on his very first assignment off Bachman."

"That was years ago," I said dryly. That Edo knew my early work was disturbing, and suggested he also had received some warning or information carried on the *Persephonya*. "But I have always liked challenges."

"Stittara's not a challenge," said Haans, a short but angular figure, even seated. "An enigma, perhaps."

"Is there a difference?" I laughed softly.

"Perhaps not," replied Edo. "What can we do for you? I do presume this visit is for more than courtesy."

"I asked to see you for courtesy and to let you know, as I've indicated, that I've been sent to conduct a survey of the ecological implications of the work you and others are conducting on the native ecology . . . and to review what in the way of environmental implications you've discovered." I paused and watched Edo nod, but went on before he could reply. "What *have* you discovered?"

"Surely you must know. We have made all our information available to the Survey."

"Or did you come out here before reviewing that?" asked Ermitag.

I smiled politely, ignoring Ermitag for the moment. When people keep telling me that I must know something, it tends to irritate me, because they're either being condescending or trying to hide something behind a façade of compliance. "Ah, yes, the investigation of self-organizing micro-organic structures under variable atmospheric conditions. That doesn't say much about your objective . . . or about the environmental implications."

"You're assuming that we have a concrete objective, Doctor."

I didn't know a multilateral that didn't require a research objective, and I doubted if he did either. I smiled. "I'm not assuming anything." I just knew that an organization like RDAEX didn't spend hundreds of billions on absolutely pure research.

Edo smiled in return. "Given your reputation, I'm certain you aren't."

"By the way, there's no mention of your drilling project in any of the reports. Could you tell me what that has to do with microorganic structures?"

"Of course. We're also investigating the response and survival of those organisms under a range of geologic and pressure conditions."

The way he'd fielded that left me feeling cold. He'd not only anticipated the question, but had rehearsed a perfectly plausible explanation. Plausible as it might superficially be, I had my doubts . . . and then some.

"I'm sure you understand," added Ermitag, "that the parameters of that research are proprietary."

Translated loosely, I'd learned about all I was going to learn, directly. "I understand absolutely, but I assume you'll be conducting me around the area of the research and any sources of emission so that I can verify that the project has no adverse environmental impacts?"

"Definitely," agreed Edo. "It's always a pleasure to deal with a professional who knows his field and what's required and what's not." He paused, just slightly. "I am curious as to why you took this assignment . . . if you'd care to enlighten me."

"Let's just say that I welcomed a professionally challenging and remunerative out-system contract at this time for intensely personal reasons."

Edo nodded again. "Unfortunately, there are times when personal circumstances do impact one's profession."

That statement did surprise me, because there was a personally ironic tone to it that suggested a certain sincerity, not that I trusted him in anything. "Unfortunately," I agreed.

"Even with the time differential involved in coming from and returning to Bachman, I don't envy you, Doctor," Edo went on. "If you find anything of significance, it will be embarrassing to whoever is in power when you return. If you don't, you'll likely face an investigation for misuse of funds, because no politician wants to admit that the government spent millions of duhlars for nothing. And, if you remain here, you've effectively become an exile."

"And that's feasible only if I discover nothing major," I finished.

"Quite so, I fear. And if you do find something . . ."

"It's better if I leave," I finished with a tone that was light and ironic, "because the Stittaran Survey couldn't afford to give me a permanent position, and none of the multis would be interested."

"You don't have any illusions, I can see."

"Better that way," added Ermitag. "Anyway, good thing we don't have any environmental disasters to hide."

"I'm glad to hear that . . . but I'll still have to go through all the tests."

"Expected that," added Ermitag.

"I am curious, though," I said after several moments of silence. "What is a deep space energy and resource multi doing on a planet like Stittara?"

"Because our being here seems so out of character with our other operations?" asked Edo. "I can't tell you how many people have raised that question . . . including our oversight board." He leaned back slightly in his swivel and steepled his fingers for a time before speaking. "One of the problems we face, one that we've always faced, is the energy cost of resource extraction and transportation. We discovered from earlier reports on Stittara that a number of the microorganisms in the upper atmosphere, well into the ionosphere, are capable of functioning across a wide range of pressures and temperatures."

I had to comment, if only because he expected it. "We've known that some viruses and bacteria have survived hundreds of thousands of years—"

"Survived, yes. Functioned, no."

I thought about the magfield shuttles.

"You have a certain look," said Edo, with an amused smile.

"The magfield shuttles . . . they're sampling vehicles as well."

Edo looked to Ermitag. "I told you he'd figure it out."

"I didn't argue with you, Belk."

"There's another question," I said. "Has anyone determined why the prevalence and intensity of storms is greater here?"

"As far as the continent's concerned," replied Ermitag, "it's not. We did discover that, for various reasons, likely topographical, the facility is located along what might be called a storm corridor."

"But that's never been fully determined?"

"That's a very different line of research and well outside our expertise," replied Ermitag with a smile.

Edo eased forward in the swivel and stood. "I thought we might continue this discussion over an early dinner, if you're agreeable, Doctor."

"That would be much appreciated." It would really be lunch for me, but I was hungry.

So Ermitag and I followed Edo down a side ramp from his office and into a small private dining area, where a circular table had been set for three, with a brilliant white linen that had a deep blue trim and the RDAEX logo worked into the cloth in the exact center of the table. The cutlery was silver, and the pale blue chargers at each place were a matching blue, with the RDAEX logo in white. A steward or server in a RDAEX blue jacket and trousers stood waiting.

Edo gestured to the table. "Any place you like."

I sat to what I thought would be his left, and it turned out that I'd guessed correctly.

"Allyn," said Edo, "I'd like the white grisio." He turned to us. "Your beverage preference, Dr. Verano?"

"Pale lager, if you have it?"

"We have Zantos, sir."

I nodded. "I'd like that, then."

"The hill red," added Ermitag.

"Haans likes the robust outie wines," said Edo.

Ermitag laughed. "I like to taste what I'm drinking, not search for a faint bouquet and wonder if I'm drinking wine at all." He turned to me. "Lager you can taste, not that pale white imitation Belk drinks."

"We do have our differences over vintages," said Edo.

"And other things," said Ermitag.

The steward reappeared, deftly setting a goblet with a clear vintage before Edo, a dark red wine before Ermitag, and a crystal beaker before me.

"Give us a few minutes," Edo murmured to him before turning and lifting his goblet. "To your safe arrival and a successful survey."

I lifted my beaker. "With thanks for your hospitality."

We all drank . . . or sipped. The Zantos was as good as I recalled it, although it had just the slightest taste of something I would have called heather, but far more pleasant, that gave it a unique edge, without being at all biting.

"Where were we . . ." offered Edo, almost musingly.

I could tell that was an affectation. He knew exactly where the conversation in his office had ended, but I just smiled. "So you're sampling the microorganisms in the upper atmosphere?"

"Into the lower reaches of near-planetary space."

I laughed.

Ermitag frowned.

Edo smiled, knowingly. "I see you understand."

"It's not planetary ecology under any Unity statute."

"Exactly. Even so, we've been careful to follow all the planetary protocols. Tomorrow, Haans will show you through everything. Do you have any questions not related to that?"

"Just curiosity. According to all the records RDAEX has been here something like a hundred and fifty years, but I've seen indications that the installation, at least in places, is much older than that . . ."

"It's quite a bit older. It was actually sealed for several hundred years when we purchased it. It had been used as an outlying research facility by another multi."

"Who was that?"

"Pentura."

"The fusactor manufacturer? The one that lost a facility to a record storm?"

"You know about that?" asked Ermitag.

"It came up in the course of my briefing at the Survey." *Let Edo chew on that.*

"When they lost their headquarters, they closed the outlying research facility. We purchased it, rather than build something from scratch, although we did have to undertake a great deal of rebuilding and modernizing. It turned out to suit us perfectly."

"It's quite impressive, from the little I've seen."

"I hope you'll feel that way when you leave."

"I'm certain I will." *If not in the way you might wish.*

After that, conversation stayed firmly on other topics, from the current entertainment trends on Bachman to recent deep-space archaeological finds, not that I knew much more than the Alliance Space Service had discovered a cache of so-far-undecipherable forerunner technology in a system slagged by what might have been an artificially created solar flare that came close to being a small nova.

It was close to eight in the evening by the time one of the RDAEX tunnelcars, driven by a security type in dark gray, dropped me off back in front of the guest quarters. I lugged the equipment case back inside and dropped into the swivel in the small study to think. I wasn't that tired, and I did need to think.

The coincidence of RDAEX buying the sealed Pentura research facility didn't exactly seem coincidental, but sometimes coincidences happened, even with multis. And . . . sometimes they didn't.

By the time I finally dropped off to sleep, it was close to midnight local, but that was only five in the evening in Passova. The problem was that I didn't want to tackle RDAEX and Haans Ermitag on six hours' sleep, seven at the most.

27

My link dragged me out of an uneasy sleep on threeday morning, and I struggled to the dining room, ate sluggishly, then returned to my quarters and finished readying myself for the day. Then I met Haans Ermitag at eight, outside the guest quarters, my equipment case in hand.

The entire day was long, intensive, and exhausting. I used almost every measuring device in my equipment case and visited at least the outside of every laboratory and local ancillary production facility within the RDAEX installation. I didn't even try to compare readings with those in the Survey Service records, but I did enter all my findings in the link, and used the planetary link to copy them to my console at the Passova survey. As Haans had predicted the night before, everything that I could see or measure seemed to fit well within Survey regulations and parameters, although I wanted to check a few things once I returned to Passova.

The drilling project—although Haans insisted it was a high-pressure biological investigation experiment—was located two kays to the north of the main RDAEX installation, accessible through a tunnel. The tunnel was, interestingly enough, as old as the original installation, although Haans insisted he had no idea for what purpose Pentura had used the isolated laboratory. My measurements showed nothing out of line in terms of ambient conditions or airborne effluents. There were no other discharges, since all liquids were fully recycled and reused.

I hadn't expected anything else from my day-long investigation, but I had thought that I might get some clues as to whether RDAEX was either skirting the rules or, as in the case of upper-level atmospheric sampling, operating totally outside the scope of existing statutes and regulations. I didn't, and I was more than a little worn-out, with a slight headache, when I walked into the guest quarters and made my way through the reception area to my rooms. I knew I'd have to hurry, as well, since it was already 1830, and the dining area closed at 1900.

With a sigh, I palmed the door and stepped inside.

"Greetings," came a low voice from the study.

I managed not to gape. Kali Artema stood there. She wasn't even wearing a security singlesuit, but black trousers, a shimmering pale gray blouse or shirt, and a short black jacket. I suspected there was still a stunner under the jacket, and possibly a few other items of that nature. I wouldn't have called her beautiful, but more a handsome woman, striking enough that she took my breath away momentarily.

"Greetings," I returned. "I see security has its advantages."

"How else was I going to arrange for you to take me to dinner? A professional dinner, Doctor."

"I wouldn't dare any other kind with you, Director."

"Kali . . . for the evening, please."

"I presume I asked on the shuttle?"

She smiled. "Where else?"

"Where would you suggest?"

"I made reservations in your name at Stellara."

"Do we need transport?"

"No. There is one better restaurant in Rikova, but Stellara is . . . more suitable, and far closer."

"Rikova?"

"That's the town name. Most people don't call it that, but the RDAEX facility is technically within the boundary of the town of Rikova. The town proper is west of here."

I managed to nod, although I never would have known—just another aspect of taking an assignment where what was obvious to a local was totally obscure to an outsider. "One more suited to a guest?"

She nodded. "I'll wait while you change and clean up."

Change? I didn't question that, although I had my doubts as to what I'd be changing into, since I'd brought only two singlesuits.

I needn't have worried. The suit I'd worn on twoday had been cleaned in my absence. Who knew what else had been done to it? So I washed and changed.

"I like the gray with the black trim," said Kali as I returned to the small study. "It makes you look distinguished."

"It also complements what you're wearing."

"I thought it might."

"Thought?" I raised my eyebrows.

She only replied with a knowing smile.

"Why me?" I asked, walking around the all too functional settee.

"Why not? You're intelligent, single, and well groomed. You keep your-self in shape, and don't flaunt it. Just as important, I've made a point of not fraternizing with coworkers."

There was something about the way she phrased that, but what it was I couldn't put a finger on. "And you can make a quiet point by having din-ner with me."

"That had crossed my mind. Shall we go?"

I wasn't about to disagree, and besides, she was clearly intelligent and attractive, and there was always the chance I might learn something . . . although no matter how careful I was, she'd likely learn more. Once we were out of my quarters, I offered my arm, and she took it, gracefully but lightly, in a way that signified propriety but neither dominance nor sub-mission.

"You will have to point the way, so to speak."

"To the left at the main entrance, then three blocks to the main down ramp, and turn right at the first level down. It's two blocks west from there."

There was no one in the main reception area or near the entrance, al-though two tunnelcars glided past us just as we entered the larger tunnel toward the ramp.

"How long have you been with RDAEX?"

"Three standard years."

"How are you finding Stittara?"

"As opposed to what? Teppera? Bachman? RDAEX or Rikova?" Her words were mild, not challenging.

"How about all of them?"

"Bachman I don't know. You'll have to enlighten me on that. Teppera is far more . . . established in its ways than many places." She paused. "I'd have to say that Stittara is far more set in its ways than I would have thought."

"Often frontier worlds or those with small populations are," I suggested. "Especially if the conditions are challenging."

"Unless those set ways are contrary to survival," she pointed out.

"That's true, but then, you have a world that no longer has a viable population . . . or none at all. That's happened more than once in history, even on Old Earth."

Before long, we arrived at Stellara. The entrance consisted of two pewter doors set in a flat wall of nonreflecting black tiles edged in pale green. I opened the right door and held it for Kali. She didn't complain. A hostess in a long pewter skirt and a black overblouse looked to me.

"Paulo Verano. I believe we have reservations."

"Yes, sir. This way."

I took in Stellara as quickly and thoroughly as I could. The overhead was a dark and starry pattern that shifted, if slowly enough that it took a moment to determine that it did. From the relative size and position of the Arm, I suspected that the projection was what would have been visible overhead, were not Stittara's atmosphere so translucently impermeable. The tables and chairs were templated to resemble ebony, and every table was set far enough apart that if one talked quietly casual eavesdropping would have been difficult. The table linens looked to be off-white, tinged with violet.

At least one and possibly two men took long looks at us as the hostess guided us to a corner table. That might have been because Kali was more stylishly dressed than most of the women, or it might have been for other reasons. Once we were seated and before the server arrived, I said, "You definitely made an impression."

"So did you."

"I have my doubts about that . . . unless it's because they know you professionally."

"There might be something to that." She smiled, an expression that was surprisingly demure.

"They're wary of you."

"Aren't you?" she asked lightly, the corners of her mouth turning up.

"Absolutely." I managed a hint of humor in that single word. "Any man with sense would be. You're extraordinarily competent, as well as attractive. That's a dangerous combination."

"Flattery yet?"

"I don't think so. I'm the one who's been flattered." I looked at the menu. The fact that it was on actual paper suggested that the fare would command serious duhlars. Browsing just the appetizers confirmed that. "What would you recommend?"

"That always depends on individual taste. I've preferred their fowl dishes, especially the ones with locally grown mushrooms and natural cheeses."

"Fowl and fungi . . . that sounds like some multis."

"I fear that is an old cliché, Paulo. Most multis are antiseptically clean."

"Ah . . . so antiseptic that nothing vital long survives there?"

The server, a tall man with a complexion so dark that he and his black jacket and trousers almost faded into the dim light, appeared at the side of the table. "Something to drink, lady, ser?"

"I'll have the Windling," said Kali.

"Zantos, please."

The server vanished as quietly as he had appeared.

"You might say that," replied Kali, "but let's not talk of business right now."

"What would you suggest?"

"Politics might be nice. In the general sense . . . on Bachman. I've never quite understood how a system with such a great income disparity among the people has lasted so long."

I laughed softly, then stopped as the server reappeared with our drinks, then asked, "Are you ready to order?"

"The fowl picattina," said Kali, "with the heather bisque first."

The server nodded and turned to me.

"I'll try the fowl marsalana," I said.

"An excellent choice, sir, especially tonight."

"I'll also try the bisque."

The server nodded and slipped away.

"Politics on Bachman?" Kali prompted.

"First," I said, lifting the beaker, crystal tinged purple, "to you with thanks." I decided not to call it her invitation, since nowhere in public was truly private.

"Thank you."

We both sipped, and I cleared my throat. "From what I've seen, the income disparity on Bachman is less of a disparity than it seems, especially if you look at it over time. Very few people or families remain in the top five percent for more than a decade or two."

"How is that when Bachman and the Unity don't have significant inheritance taxes?"

"You might call it predatory capitalism. Earned income is taxed moderately, but all physical property and everything of monetary value that is not money or not clearly defined as a publicly traded security that is held by any individual, except that received through inheritance, is subject to capital gains taxation. All other compensation is defined as earned income. The shorter the time period one holds any asset subject to capital gains, whether property or securities, the higher the tax rate. On securities held for less than a standard week, for example, the capital gains taxation is fifty percent, and no deduction for capital losses is allowed. Dividends and interest are considered earned income. Houses, conapts, or other owned quarters used as principal residences have the lowest capital gains. Properties held as rental units have higher rates, and the income generated is considered earned income."

"Doesn't that make the economy sluggish?"

"It slows things down a bit, but that's the idea. Too much money and too many assets moving too quickly have always been the fundamental cause of financial and economic bubbles and disasters. The Unity doesn't forbid quick turnovers in assets; it just recognizes that there's a high cost to them and taxes accordingly. The tax structure means that people who speculate unwisely tend to lose their assets rather quickly. Tax fraud, as is any kind of fraud, is penalized rather stiffly." I shrugged. "It's far from perfect, but it seems to work. That could be because the definitions of assets and income are set in permacrete, and creative accounting can't change them."

"I hadn't thought that there was much to admire in Bachman."

"There isn't," I replied. "Except that the finance and tax laws allow a new group of talented predators to rise every generation and to devour the previous generation, so to speak. That way we have competent predators that have to provide goods, services, or financial transactions that contribute to the Unity's coffers, because the incompetent ones can't compete. I've seen families economically destroyed in days because of a cascade of bad decisions. So we have very few generationally institutionalized wealthy families, and that gives the impression that anyone can get to the top. And anyone can—if they're brilliant, well educated, and obey the laws while behaving in ways that are legal but morally corrupt." I was, of necessity, simplifying, but not overly so.

She shook her head. "We have our problems, but I think I'd keep them if the alternative was what you describe."

At that moment the server arrived with the heather bisque. I wasn't sure what to expect from a cream soup with that title, but since Kali had ordered it, I thought it couldn't be too bad . . . and it wasn't . . . almost like a cream of mushroom with an overtone of that heathery taste I could just barely taste in the lager.

I took several spoonfuls before asking, "What do you see in the politics of the Stittaran Planetary Council?"

"If you can believe what shows on the linknews, they worry continually about the costs the outies place on the Council and the people."

"The Survey people talk about enforcement problems with the outies."

"I'm not surprised. It's all surreptitious, though. If the Council or the Survey finds an area where timber has been illegally cut or the land cultivated, it's almost impossible to discover who's truly responsible."

"So much area, so few people, and so few resources?"

Kali nodded.

"Tell me about Rikova, the part that's not RDAEX."

Over the rest of the bisque and the beginning of our entrees, she did. In the end, what it boiled down to was that Rikova, named after some ancient engineer, was essentially a multi town and a miniature of Passova.

"How do you find working for RDAEX?" I finally asked.

"You've been waiting all evening to ask that."

"No . . . just half the evening." I grinned.

"It's a job. I've trained for it, and I do it well. I'd prefer to do the same thing closer to home, but that's not possible."

I understood the "not possible" part, if in a different way. "What about family?"

"I didn't have much. Our families are small. My older sister left when I was still in school."

"Out-system?"

Kali shook her head. "Just halfway around the planet. She didn't think the way my parents did. There wasn't much else that appealed to me. So I went into security . . . and here I am."

"I don't think it was anywhere close to that simple. It never is."

She leaned forward across the table toward me and said in a low voice, "Were you this charming when your wife decided to leave you?"

Her question left me without an answer for a moment, because it confirmed that someone had made some inquiries. Kali just waited, although I thought there might have been a hint of mischief in her eyes. Finally, I replied, "I doubt it. Part of that was likely me. Part of it was likely that I was seldom given the opportunity to be charming."

"That's a shame."

"At times like this, I'd agree." I paused. "Would you like anything more? Dessert, perhaps?"

She shook her head. "I've eaten far more than I should, and I'll have to up my workouts for a week to pay for it."

"No artificial aids?"

"Genetically, they don't work the same for us."

"Everyone on Teppera?"

"Most of us, except more recent immigrants. Over time, it seems, every planet changes its people, in one way or another."

Was that why Bachman was so predatory? Certainly, the stories of the early colonization suggested it had been touch and go with the reptilian cat-lizards for close to a century, and that didn't take into account the interstellar border disputes with the Cloud Combine . . . disputes that still smoldered. "You're probably right about that. How do you think it's changed people here?"

"I couldn't describe it, but I can look and tell who's from families that have been here for generations."

"I've had that feeling."

"There's another thing . . . you might have noticed."

"Some of the women . . . you mean." I didn't want to say more. It would have sounded . . . well . . . far too presumptive.

Kali laughed, softly and not unkindly. "You are sweet. Yes. Out-system men attract and fascinate them. Or good-looking ones do. I don't know why, but I've seen it. There are two women over there who must have looked at you a dozen times."

I took a last sip of the Zantos. "I've been occupied."

"I do appreciate it, Paulo."

"So do I." I paused. "Shall we go?"

"We should. I'll be up early tomorrow."

"I won't . . . well . . . not too early. The shuttle doesn't leave until eleven-thirty. I might walk around in the morning."

After using my link to pay for the meal, I stood, then watched as she rose, with an ease more athletic than graceful, although it was both. We walked back through Stellara, where every table was still taken, and out into the main tunnel.

Once we were away from the entrance to the restaurant, I turned to Kali. "That was a most enjoyable dinner."

"It was," Kali replied, and she sounded as though she meant it.

"Now what?"

"You walk me to my quarters, and we say goodnight."

"They're close enough?"

She actually grinned. "They're in the other wing of the guest quarters. That's where those of us who are single and executive status are billeted."

Billeted? And fraternization earlier? "You're military . . ." I murmured.

"Detached duty."

"That's not widely known, but it's no secret. The multis like Tepperan military culture. And women officers are less directly confrontational. The Council likes the multi templates and information. Mutually beneficial."

"And you all return with more information than that."

"Naturally."

"And what about the Space Service?"

"They hate us. Always have."

We walked quietly, neither dawdling nor hurrying, and she took my arm, as before.

At her door, she turned, leaned toward me . . . and actually kissed me, if on the cheek, her hands running down my arms for a moment before she stepped back. "I did enjoy and appreciate it, Paulo. I know you'll have a safe trip back. After that . . . do take care."

Then she slipped inside, and the door closed.

I walked back to my quarters, trying to figure out exactly what to make of the evening. Was it all to find out something? I couldn't even determine what she sought. Was it a personal way of guarding me? From Edo or Ermitag . . . or RDAEX . . . or keeping me safe from others while under RDAEX's care? But her last words suggested that I didn't have that much to fear from RDAEX . . . at least while I was actually in Rikova.

I did open my door and enter my quarters warily, but they were empty.

As I began to take off the singlesuit, I discovered a card in my side pocket. I removed the card and studied it. It was one of Kali's cards, but it felt much stiffer, less flexible. Then I swallowed. I would have bet that it was an infocard disguised as a business card. But why?

I had a strong feeling that, when I found out, back in Passova, since I had no way of reading it at RDAEX without the contents being known immediately, I wasn't going to like what was contained in the information.

Just what sort of environmental disaster was RDAEX committing, or about to commit? And why would Kali want to give me that information? Did it contain something else entirely? Or was the card some sort of Trojan that would allow RDAEX access to Survey Service files if I used a Survey console to read it? That problem, at least, I could get around.

The others, including those I doubted I even knew about, I was sure wouldn't be that easy.

28

I didn't sleep all that late on fourday morning, but I was tired when I woke in the RDAEX guest quarters, and I spent a good half stan just watching what passed for a local newscast. Most of it was just the usual, but there was one section that definitely concerned me.

"Apparently, the Ministry of Environment on Bachman is less than pleased with the performance of the Systems Survey Service here on Stittara. At least, that's the word in the back halls of the Planetary Council. The office of Executive Director Zeglar has denied that anything unusual is going on, other than a routine environmental survey, which occurs on a time to time basis on all inhabited Unity planets."

That was it, but it meant political gaming was well under way.

Since there was little I could do about that, except be aware, I took a walk and tunneltram ride around Rikova. That only confirmed my feeling that there really wasn't that much apparent difference between RDAEX/Rikova and Passova, except in the size and scope of the structure created under the apparent surface of the planet. I met Fabio at half past ten, and he had me to the magfield shuttle hangar in less than fifteen minutes.

There were already five others on the shuttle when I arrived, two women and three men, none of whom I knew, not surprisingly. I took one of the cradles in the rear and tried to listen, but no one was talking, at least not in a voice loud enough for me to hear. I did get the impression that the five were not going as a unified group since a man and a woman had taken the first two cradles, and the next three were seated in the third and fourth row. I was in the last seat, on the side away from the younger man who'd accompanied a hard-faced woman and a man who acted like her subordinate.

There were two vans waiting in the near darkness just after dawn and well before sunrise when the shuttle landed at Passova, one the Survey Service van driven by Dermotte and the other a dark gray van into which all the RDAEX people slipped.

"I don't think I met your cousin," I told Dermotte as we loaded the case and my kit bag into the rear of the van.

"He doesn't meet many folks. How was your trip, ser?"

"Everyone was very friendly, and they seem to be meeting all the environmental standards." *Those that apply to them, anyway.*

"Jermodie says that they're very strict . . . always follow procedures to the letter."

Dermotte closed the rear of the van, and we both climbed in. The dark gray van was already leaving the dropport.

"They must be meeting with someone at the Planetary Council," Dermotte said. "That's a Council van. They're fancy inside."

"This isn't a bad-looking van."

"It's not, but I do my best to keep them all in shape."

"How many things are you responsible for keeping going?"

"The vehicles and the office equipment, mostly, and anything else Director Raasn wants me to do. That's if I have time."

"As well as driving people here and there."

"I like that."

"You like the outside?" From what I'd heard and seen, most Stittarans—those who lived in the underground cities and towns—didn't.

"I do, ser. Might be because my father was from out-system. Or so my mother said. I never knew him."

"He left Stittara?"

"No. He went somewhere on Contrio. One of the outie places that no one even knows where they are."

"That must have been hard on you."

Dermotte shook his head. "Can't be hard if you never knew what you missed. I don't even remember him. Mother's always been there."

There wasn't much I could say to that, and I didn't.

Once we returned to the Survey vehicle pool, Dermotte took my equipment case. "I'll leave it in your office, ser."

"Thank you. I'll be there in a bit." Not that I had to hurry. It was still only a few minutes past seven.

Once in my quarters, I did wash up, then looked out into the early morning to see if Ilsabet was outside, but she wasn't, most likely because it was much earlier than the other times I'd seen her. Then I headed for the Survey spaces. Some people were already there, early risers, I supposed, but the lights were on in the corridor leading to my office, as were those inside, and my equipment case was sitting beside my console.

It took me almost fifteen minutes to re-create from imperfect memory the steps necessary to do a direct transfer to my link's private storage that bypassed all recording and system storage. After that, it was less than a minute to scan Kali's card and get the information into the privacy partitioned memory of my link. What was there read like a consultant's report.

> *The deep penetration project [RDAEX Stittara R-3, mod alpha] has been represented as a means of subjecting microorganics to conditions of intense pressure and heat to determine their biological survival properties. Such tests have been conducted at every depth achieved by the high-energy, self-sealing aspects of targeted photonics . . .*

Targeted photonics? What in the frig is targeted photonics? Why not just high-energy laser probes? I vaguely recalled something about pumped photonics and the quantum implications or defects, but I had the impression that there were definite limitations to laser amplification through photonic pumping. Then again, RDAEX was a very accomplished research outfit.

> *. . . such tests have never before been conducted in penetrating the mantle of a planet with a core, particularly an outer core, that comprises such a high percentage of the planetary mass . . .*

All that was merely another affirmation of why Stittara had such a strong magnetic field.

. . . Recent data suggests an anomalous discontinuity between the inner mantle and the outer core, and more research and probes have been developed to investigate the possible reasons for that discontinuity. Special expertise has also been obtained . . .

Rikard Spek . . . perhaps?

I went back to reading . . . except there wasn't any more to read. That was it. It broke off in the middle of a sentence.

What exactly did Kali want me to know? Or was it a red herring or a false lead?

I wasn't sure whether to sigh or throw up my hands in frustration . . . or start looking for some sort of weapon. That wouldn't have helped much. I'd learned Juchai years ago, and even placed in a few tournaments, but that had been mainly to impress Chelesina, and I hadn't practiced Juchai with anyone in so long I couldn't remember when.

Still . . . the snippet of information that Kali had put on the card disturbed me, especially knowing that Rikard Spek had been hired by RDAEX—and that a new employee for the Ministry of Technology and Transport had also been sent from Bachman. That seemed unlike coincidence. Was there any more information on Spek? A biography or publication of some sort?

I began to search—and found two mentions—recently entered into the planetary links, doubtless from information carried on the *Persephonya*. Both were abstracts, followed by longer articles. The abstracts were abstruse enough, but if I understood them correctly, dealt with circumventing the quantum defects in high-energy lasers used in cutting adiamantine materials or materials hardened by extreme pressure.

That certainly fit in with the RDAEX drilling project and the material Kali had provided. What it didn't tell me was why RDAEX was both sampling microorganics that were viable effectively in space and drilling deep into Stittara.

I went back to the console and searched for Torgan Brad, but all that I found on him was the announcement of his entry to Stittara and his name and position at the Unity's Ministry of Technology and Transport on Stittara. He was listed as a special assistant, and the listing didn't place him in a specific office or branch.

There wasn't much more I could do there, and I went to work on comparing the measurements I'd taken at RDAEX to those submitted by the facility over the past several years. Two stans later, I was still comparing, when the screen flashed an alert. "Planetary Council Staff Assistant Melarez."

"Accept." I watched as an image filled the left half of the screen. Melarez was female, with short hair almost dark enough to be black, an oval face, and hazel eyes. She was old enough not to be recently out of school or training, but probably young enough not to be that close to my age.

"Dr. Verano?"

"Yes?"

"I'm Paem Melarez, staff assistant to Councilor Morghan . . . of the Stittaran Planetary Council. The councilor understands that you've been sent to Stittara to conduct an ecological survey of matters here. Is that correct?"

"Yes." It was correct, if somewhat oversimplified, but I wasn't about to get into that, not on a console where Aloris, Zerlyna, and who knew who else had access to what I said.

"We'd very much appreciate it if you would come and brief us on the scope of your study. The councilor has always been interested in ecological issues, and she is particularly concerned about potential changes in Unity law and policy and how they might impact Stittara."

"I'd be more than happy to brief you. I must caution you, though, that I know of no pending or even anticipated changes in Unity environmental policies or laws, either connected to my study or in other areas not at all connected."

"Nonetheless, Doctor, the councilor would greatly appreciate your briefing. Tomorrow, perhaps?"

"I'm afraid not. I already have appointments all day tomorrow, and since they required advance notice and travel . . ." I didn't finish that sentence on purpose. After a moment I smiled and said cheerfully, "I could do any time sixday, sevenday, or oneday . . . or later next week."

Melarez didn't look pleased, but she nodded. "Eight on oneday morning, perhaps?"

"I'd be happy to do that. Where, might I ask?"

For a moment she appeared surprised, as if I should have known. Then she smiled. "I forgot. You wouldn't know. In the Planetary Council complex, level three, room 471."

"Level three, room 471," I repeated. "I'll be there."

"We'll be looking forward to it. Until then, Doctor." With her last word, her image vanished.

That explained, or at least had something to do with, the news rumor I'd heard that morning, and it also meant I needed to pass that along. While I could have used the console to tell Aloris, I preferred to tell her in person. I was much better at reading reactions face-to-face. So I got up and headed down the corridor to her spaces.

She was at her console, and she didn't look surprised to see me.

"I thought you'd like to know," I began, *before you've had a chance to review the conversations and messages that have crossed my screen,* "that I just had a request from the Planetary Council. A staff assistant named Melarez requested I give a briefing on the scope of my study. She wanted it tomorrow. I declined because I've already scheduled matters for then, and we agreed on oneday."

"She's the one who handles environmental and energy matters for Councilor Morghan." Aloris offered a tight smile.

"From your expression, I take it that either the councilor or her assistant, if not both, are not terribly esteemed by the Survey Service here?"

"No. They're not. Morghan feels that on a world as lightly developed as Stittara, one of the greatest pitfalls is what she terms excessive environmental regulation—provided the basic environmental structure is maintained. At the moment, she and Councilor Dulac are in the minority, but that will likely change after the next election."

"There are seven councilors, though."

"That's true, but Councilor Steenden is retiring, and Councilor Diforio is likely to be defeated. The Progressives are likely to fill both positions. Don't let the party name deceive you. Progressive stands for progress in development," Aloris concluded wryly.

I nodded. "So whatever I say will be used and reported as an indication that the SoMods in Smithsen wish to stifle development and keep Stittara grossly underdeveloped and poor?"

"That's almost a certainty."

"And if I avoid that?"

"Then Morghan will say something along the lines of your presence should be a reminder that, without councilors committed to the best future for Stittara, the planet is only one ley-liner away from another excessive environmental mandate from the Unity, and that the Unity doesn't want Stittara strong and independent."

"And the Unity understands nothing about the difficulties and realities facing the people of Stittara."

"You could obviously write his speech."

"I've heard most of the rhetoric on both sides," I said dryly.

"I'm sure you have. How was your trip to Rikova?"

"Interesting, since I've never flown a magfield shuttle before, but rather routine besides that. I haven't finished analyzing and comparing the measurements I took with the reports submitted to the Survey Service, but it appears, so far, that there's been no misreporting and no change."

"You didn't expect any, did you?"

"No, but you never know."

"What will you do after you've confirmed the accuracy of all the multi reports?"

"Go on from there. Exactly where . . . well . . . I might have a much better idea after meeting with Morghan and her staff."

"That is possible."

I nodded. "Anyway, I just thought you'd like to know."

"Thank you."

After I returned to my office, I went back to work finishing the comparisons between my measurements and those submitted by RDAEX. Even before I finished, it was clear that there were no discrepancies, or even variations anywhere near being statistically significant.

29

The man and the woman sat at a café table along the arcade. She could see people entering Invireo. He sipped a wine of so dark a shade of red that it was almost black.

"Did he do anything different after he returned?" asked Raasn, his fingers still loosely holding the stem of the wineglass.

"He set up a routine on the console to bypass all the recording and memory, even the keystroke and projection manipulation tracking."

"I told you he was anything but simple," replied Raasn.

"What do you think he discovered at RDAEX?"

"I have the feeling it might not have anything at all to do with his assignment. His official assignment, anyway."

"You're saying he's also—"

"He's either freelancing on the side or he's got another assignment as well. Why else would he be here? The permanent union breakup was real, I'm sure. But why take an assignment with such a loss of time . . . unless it paid a lot more . . . or there were two contracts?"

"We may never know that. What else did he do?"

"Researched two names. Both arrived on the *Persephonya* with him. Rikard Spek was the first. Scientist and engineer specializing in high-energy photonics. The other is a special assistant at the Ministry of Technology."

"Did Vergenya mention either one?"

"No . . . not even indirectly."

Raasn frowned. "RDAEX didn't make a special return trip for Verano. They had five people who went to meet with Dulac and her people."

"That doesn't make sense. Cloras doesn't care about research. All she cares about is whom she can tax more."

"She'd care if RDAEX suggested they might close their facility."

"Why would RDAEX do that?" asked Aloris. "Besides, it would take them years."

"Would it? What if Spek carried instructions from Bachman under seal?"

"I still don't see why they'd do that."

"Cash flow drain. It may be time-discounted, but the RDAEX facility here can't be producing much that's profitable, and they're funding a good share of all Rikova's infrastructure. They're likely under pressure to reduce that drain."

"What about another multi taking over RDAEX?" Aloris glanced down the arcade, then back to Raasn. "Or the local facility?"

"That's highly unlikely. RDAEX has no real competitors."

"That might make it a good target. Can you find out what connection this Spek and a special assistant might have to Verano?"

"I'll see what I can do." Raasn laughed quietly. "Verano may be useful in other ways, as well."

"Officially . . . or unofficially?"

"He's already been useful officially, don't you think? By his very appearance, he's reinforced the position of the Survey Service. Unofficially . . . we'll have to see, but one out of two isn't bad these days." Raasn lifted the goblet and took a sip.

"What about Morghan and Melarez?"

"Let them worry about Verano and the Ministry of Environment in Smithsen for a while. That will keep them looking in the wrong places."

"Melarez has her own agenda. Ministry headquarters seventy-three years away doesn't worry her. She'll just use that as a wedge. She wants Zeglar's position, and Morghan would support her. So would Dulac, just to get Melarez off the Council staff."

Raasn frowned.

"Makes you think, doesn't it?" said Aloris. "Do you really want someone who's that sharp as executive director? Melarez would make Venessa look like a scared tunnel rat."

"I wasn't thinking about that. Melarez had one of her flunkies accompanying a structural inspector the other day. They went through all the Survey spaces, from the vehicle bays to the guest quarters, even the storerooms."

"Taps . . . or worse?"

He shook his head. "I had everything swept."

"If they were inert . . . not activated . . ."

"We're pretty secure, but I upped the security surveillance."

Aloris took a small swallow, then glanced in the direction of Invireo before speaking. "Will Steenden and Willisen oppose Morghan if she pushes Melarez?"

"We'll have to find a way, won't we?"

She nodded. "They're men. They have their weaknesses. Haaran should be here shortly. You can talk that over with him. He's often good at that sort of thing."

"So is Amarios."

"In some circumstances."

They both smiled.

30

On fiveday, once more I had to rise early in order to check out one of the Survey vans and be on my way, because Syntex was close to two hundred kays south and east of Passova. I pulled up the ramp and out into the purple morning at just past seven. It seemed brighter to me than on other mornings, but that might just have been because I was feeling more and more confined in the tunnel cities and installations of Stittara. I also wondered about the rationale behind the subterranean way of life. Since I'd arrived, there had only been one storm anywhere near Passova and, powerful as it had been, it seemed to me that at least some buildings could have been constructed on the surface able to withstand such forces.

As before, there was little traffic on the permacrete strip of highway, but that made sense, given the low population and a reliance on templating for creating most objects used by individuals and synth and tank food technologies. Power was the key, and Stittara had a low enough population that fusactors could handle those requirements.

A little less than two stans later, I entered the down ramp for Syntex. After parking the van, I got out and removed my equipment case, then walked to the pressure door that accessed the underground vehicle bay serving visitors. I did note several other vehicles parked there in spaces clearly designated as for visitors. A wiry woman in a maroon singlesuit with black trim waited for me. I would have known her as a security type even without the stunner at her black equipment belt and the lightning patch on her upper sleeves.

"Dr. Verano?"

"Yes?"

"Please follow me."

As we passed through the pressure doors, I noted the security screening probes, the only ones I'd seen—except at RDAEX. That didn't mean I hadn't been screened, only that I hadn't been aware of it. Once we were past the pressure doors, we entered a tunnel unlike any of the others I'd seen—effectively a circular bore with the bottom filled to create a flat surface, and wider than the oval-topped and narrower tunnels in Passova. The tunnel shape and size and the sense of age suggested that the Syntex facility was likely far older than any other that I'd entered so far. RDAEX might have been close to that old, but because it had been essentially re-built, I couldn't have said for certain.

The old tunnel ended in a domed chamber, from which three other and newer-looking tunnels radiated at right angles to each other. In the center of the chamber was a large console, behind which sat another security guard. My escort led me down the right corridor, past five or six doors, then stopped outside the next on the right side.

"You're expected."

"Thank you." I opened the door and stepped inside, into an anteroom with three consoles, although only one was occupied. The older man behind it glanced up. "Assistant Director Tharon will be with you in a minute, Doctor."

"Thank you."

Since there was nowhere to sit, except behind one of the consoles, I stood. I didn't mind that, not after driving almost two standard hours. I didn't wait long, no more than two or three minutes before the door at the back of the anteroom opened.

A small man stepped out, the top of his head barely to my shoulder. He was wiry, with muddy brown eyes that seemed almost sleepy, especially in contrast to his swift and jerky movements as he stepped forward. "Bryse Tharon. I'm pleased to meet you."

His voice was gravelly, and he sounded anything but pleased.

"I appreciate the time," I replied.

"Do come in."

I did, closing the door behind me. His office was about half the size of the space I had at the Survey Service, and was cramped with a large console, two chairs, and a wall bank of screens, all of them blanked at the moment.

Tharon gestured to the chairs and seated himself behind the console, then began to speak even before I lowered my case and sat down. "I know all this isn't your doing," Tharon went on, "but it's a damned nuisance. We do report after report. We meet all the standards. We hear nothing. Then those SoMod idiots on Bachman send someone so they can claim oversight. What oversight is there, except here, when it takes centuries to exchange communications?" He looked directly at me. "Does what you do even matter?"

I looked straight back at him. "It matters to me."

"Good! Ought to matter to someone. What do you need?"

"Access to all measuring points, especially effluents . . ." I went on with specifics because it was clear that he was the sort who wanted detail, delivered quickly and concisely.

When I finished, he nodded. "Good. No shillyshallying. No vague and open commitments to search everything in sight."

"Unless my measurements reveal something significantly different from what you've submitted to the Survey."

"You won't mind if I match your measurements, Doctor?" asked Tharon.

"Not in the slightest . . . provided we agree on comparative calibration before we begin."

"I would have suggested that if you hadn't."

After that, my investigation and measurements went smoothly, although Syntex was such a sprawling facility that it took until four that afternoon to make about half as many observations as it had in the same time at RDAEX. My legs were aching by the time we returned to what I thought of as the main rotunda, where I set down my equipment case.

"Are you satisfied, Doctor?"

"We'll see when I have the chance to analyze the data." I paused. "Since I'm here, is Aimee Vanslo available?" That was still a guess, but I'd waited until I was ready to leave, just in case I'd guessed wrong.

Tharon frowned. "I don't see what . . ."

"Personal acquaintance. I'd appreciate it if you'd let her know I'm here." I smiled politely.

He walked away, presumably to make an inquiry with his personal link without my overhearing.

I waited, glad that at least my guess had been halfway correct.

When he walked back down the ancient tunnel, he couldn't quite conceal his surprise. "She's in a meeting, but she'll be free in a quarter stan if you wouldn't mind waiting."

"I'd be happy to wait."

"She said you would."

"She knows me too well," I replied. Let him stew over that, given Aimee's preferences.

"I'll take you to her office. Her assistant will be expecting you."

"Thank you."

He turned and headed down the center tunnel. We walked almost half a kay before we turned into another corridor on the left and through another set of open pressure doors. Tharon stopped before recessed double doors on the right and gestured.

"Thank you again."

"You're welcome, Doctor."

I opened the right-hand door and stepped into another anteroom, closing the door behind me as I studied the space. The floor was tiled in large alternating gray and green tiles, while the walls were a slightly grayed off-white faux plaster. The staff assistant was a woman with the thin face and slightly drawn look that suggested anagathics were about to lose their ability to keep her appearance from showing definite age.

She smiled, more than politely and less than effusively. "Executive Director Vanslo will be here in about ten minutes. If you would care to take a seat . . ."

"I would, thank you. I think I've walked a good share of the tunnels today." I took the chair on the end of the three placed against the side wall. That gave me the best view of her. "I take it you've been with Syntex for a while."

"A few years."

I just nodded, understanding the meaning behind the polite response, and sat back to wait for Aimee.

Something like seven minutes after I'd seated myself, the door through which I'd entered opened, and Aimee stepped through. I immediately stood.

"Paulo . . . it's good to see you. Do come in." The smile that went with the words was certainly genuine, or she was an accomplished actress . . . and both were probably true, although her dark eyes smiled as well as her face. She wore a deep green singlesuit, the only touch to fashion being a light green and gray scarf.

"Thank you." I returned the smile and followed her past the staff assistant through another door into an office of comparatively modest dimensions. I did close the door behind me.

What struck me immediately was the pair of wide screens at each end of the space, one behind her console, and the other on the wall she faced while sitting at the console. Each screen was a good two meters wide and one and a half high. Both displayed what appeared to be real-time views of Stittara. Rather than seat myself in one of the green upholstered synthwood chairs before the console—where she remained standing—I gestured to the screen on the wall she faced. "Recently installed, I presume."

"You usually don't presume," she replied with another smile. "But . . . yes."

"You like the view . . . and the screens are . . . useful."

"They are." She paused. "We could sit."

I grinned. "Yes, we could, but I'm attempting to be courteous."

"I'll accept that. Now sit down, Paulo."

There was just the slightest edge of command in her voice. Rather than be difficult, I sat first, and she followed suit.

"I wondered how long it would take for you to come calling."

"You knew I'd figure it out, sooner or later, didn't you?"

"I thought you would. You're the type that worries through everything to the end."

"You figured that out from a few conversations?"

"And from observing you talk with others."

"All that management expertise."

"You're here. What do you want?"

"You've already supplied much of that. I was just curious to see if you were who I thought you might be. And, of course, to ask whether pending research will change Syntex's environmental profile."

"Research always does, one way or another."

"Can you tell me what you hope to discover?"

"Better anagathics." She smiled. "Now . . . my question. Am I who you thought I was?"

"I don't know, except that it's apparent you're part of the family that owns and operates Syntex and other organizations under the VLE imprimatur."

"Do you have any other requests?"

"Is it possible to visit the forerunner site?"

"For curiosity . . . or is it related to your assignment?"

"I couldn't prove it, but I have to wonder if there are any indications of a similar ecology at that time."

"You could tell?"

"That depends on what's left there."

She frowned, if but for a moment, then nodded. "Next threeday I'm scheduled to see the site. Be here at seven hundred and you can come with me. Clearance for you won't be a problem since you're already cleared by your assignment with Systems Survey Service."

"You checked that as well?"

"The things you don't check are the ones that get you in trouble. That's something . . ." She shook her head.

I knew that was no slip, but wondered why. "That you're here to fix."

"Something like that."

"Is there anything I can do to help?"

"Just give me advance notice if you intend to set the Survey Service on Syntex," she said dryly, adding, after the briefest pause, "I know you can't and wouldn't do that, but that's the way I feel."

"Antiquities Commission on your back?"

"Among others."

I nodded, although I did have an idea . . . of sorts.

"You have a most thoughtful expression, Paulo."

"That's because I'm thinking." I kept my tone light. "By the way, is the lady who called herself Constantia Dewers your mother?"

For an instant Aimee stiffened. Then she laughed. "Yes. How did you guess?"

"Intuition . . . and the fact that the only way you could avoid her for three weeks was to travel standard class. I assume she is the principal shareholder in VLE and the trip was taken as much to prevent family infighting that might likely occur in the event of her death."

"Do you have another mission here?" Her voice was definitely colder.

"Hardly . . . those were guesses based on the only rationale I could come up with that made sense . . . and your earlier comments about your children. Oh . . . and on my own daughter's reactions to certain things."

Aimee offered another pause, as well as a look as if her attention happened to be elsewhere, which I suspected it was.

"Do the scanners show I'm telling the truth . . . or not obviously lying?" She focused on me. "Who are you?"

"I'm exactly who I say I am. Paulo Verano, ecologist, doctorate from Reagan University, former head of Verano Associates, financially disadvantaged by a vindictive former spouse, here to determine the need for continued, increased, or decreased Survey Service activity in dealing with the ecological situation here on Stittara."

At that moment everything went black.

31

Questions swirled through my brain, even as my body went from hot to chill and back to fevered. Strange questions . . . some that I'd answered time and time again over my life.

When did you get your undergraduate degree?

Who was your thesis advisor, and on what subject was your thesis?

Who was Exton Land, and why is he important?

Who was your advocate in the dissolution proceedings?

Where were you born?

The questions seemed endless, except they ended, and then I began to shiver.

When my eyes opened, I was still sitting in Aimee Vanslo's office, except she was seated in the chair across from me, and a female medtech in the traditional pale green was watching the portable console in her lap. My head throbbed, and I could feel prickling spots on my forehead and elsewhere on my scalp and neck.

Aimee extended a mug of something. "It's tea, fortified slightly."

"With what?" I meant my tone to be skeptically ironic, but the words just came out hoarsely.

"Various things to ease your headache and reaction to truscope."

"You truscoped me?" I couldn't keep the anger out of my voice.

"It was necessary. I apologize. I'll even offer a significant consulting fee for the inconvenience." She looked to the medtech. "How is he?"

"He's fine, except for a headache."

"Can you remove the monitors and leave us?"

"Yes, ma'am."

I was a bit surprised that Aimee allowed such an anachronistic address, but said nothing while the medtech removed the tabs from my head and neck, slid the console into an equipment bag, and then slipped out of the office. I slowly swallowed some tea and waited for the door to close.

"You have a much bigger problem than mere corporate succession," I finally offered, then took another sip of the tea to soothe my throat.

"When you're dealing with one of the largest family owned and controlled multis in the entire Arm, nothing dealing with succession is 'mere' or minor."

"I take it that you struck up conversations with every single person on *Persephonya* who might have been an assassin or the equivalent?"

"Your phrase 'or the equivalent' suggests you're more than you are. So does your physical condition."

I shook my head. "That's my personal vanity, one of the few remnants of self-esteem remaining."

"That's hard to believe."

"If you're good at what I do, and I'd like to think that I am, you learn as much about people and politics, greed and governance, and just plain hate as you do about the environment. That's because the environment touches everything and is part of everything. What comprises the environment ranges from the direct and brutal to the five steps removed and equally lethal, yet almost untraceable."

"I must say I'd never thought of that."

"Most people don't." When she didn't volunteer more, I went on. "I don't want compensation. I'd still like to see the forerunner site, and I'd like to have the opportunity to ask for a favor at some time in the future."

"What sort of favor?" Her words were even, neither sardonic nor skeptical, the words of a powerful person inquiring directly.

"If I knew, I'd tell you."

She smiled, faintly. "You're not the person I feared you might be, but you're a dangerous man in a different way."

"I scarcely feel dangerous. Just stupid." And I did. I'd blithely speculated and guessed myself into nearly getting killed without realizing the implications of my speculations.

"I don't think so. You just weren't expecting what you ran into."

I couldn't help but laugh, almost helplessly. When I finally stopped, I shook my head, then took another sip of the tea. It did help. "That's the first rule of consulting. Don't expect anything. Consider everything. Expectations can be deadly." *And nearly had been.*

"I have no right to ask it, but I would like a small favor of you."

"To keep my eyes open, and to think over what I've observed as to how it might affect you, your mother, Syntex, and VLE?"

She nodded.

"I can do that." I offered a smile. "I'll see you next threeday morning at seven, then?"

"We'll be expecting you. Wear something you don't care about or something that cleans easily."

"Most of my singlesuits do."

"I can't imagine they wouldn't." Aimee looked at me. "Are you sure you're up to driving back?"

"Something to eat on the way back, in case I get hungry, wouldn't hurt."

"We can take care of that." She stood. "And I am sorry, but it is a matter of life and death."

I rose, realizing that my left arm felt a bit sore. So did my right, and I massaged one and then the other.

"One injection was for the truscope. The other was something to help you recover from any otherwise unexpected aftereffects."

"The way things are going, that might be useful."

"One way or another, they'll be beneficial."

By the time she had walked me to the Survey van, and she did so, another Syntex worker was waiting with a small case, but one large enough for a full meal, I suspected.

"It's all finger food," Aimee assured me as I loaded my equipment case into the van.

As I pulled up the ramp and out into the already dimming twilight, I wondered what Aimee's mother's real name was . . . and who was handling the multi with Aimee and "Constantia" off Bachman. But then, whoever was acting as chief operating officer didn't have to be family . . . but I would have bet it was, and that it was likely Aimee's sister, simply because . . . well, I didn't have more than a feel for that. But why had they picked Stittara? Because Syntex was the most loyal subsidiary . . . or for some other reason?

It had to be the other reason, whatever it was.

I thought I'd have plenty of time to think on the drive back, but it didn't work that way.

The drive back was tiring, and for the last forty-odd kays, a strong wind, with individual gusts of a velocity of close to fifty klicks, blew out of the southwest, buffeting the van and requiring my complete attention, especially after the deep purple darkness settled over the highway and the land. Thankfully, there were no skytubes nearby, but I couldn't help but worry. With all that, I didn't even have a chance to eat the sandwich and other items Aimee had sent with me.

32

The spring's night storms remain unseen, thought four,
Sky swirls come to seek me out once more.

As the sky darkened, Clyann closed the blinds to the armaglass window. "You should sleep below."

"Not tonight. I want the dark in sight," replied Ilsabet.

"As you wish. I'll see you in the morning."

Ilsabet waited until the door to the lower level closed before walking to the window and raising the blinds.

"Close the blinds or I'll tell," announced Alsabet, her screen image nearly identical to that of Ilsabet, save that her hair was blond.

"Tell if you want or will, but I'll open them till Matron's ill."

"You're talking nonsense again," replied the screen image.

"I'll close them before deep night, close them very tight."

"You promise?"

"I'll do what I must, so as to keep their trust." Ilsabet looked into the darkness, as the purple darkened until it was almost indistinguishable from black.

"You said you'd close the blinds," prompted Alsabet.

"I will; I will. Not yet. Keep still."

The image in the screen did not reply.

"Winds in the sky, you'll be coming nigh."

"Is a storm coming?" asked Alsabet, her voice altered.

"No more than now, as if I could say how."

"Ilsabet!"

"When the winds come in the night black, I almost can feel myself come back."

"Come back from where?"

"From where I was so long ago, from the when was not the no."

For a time longer, Ilsabet looked into the dark, then lowered the blinds without speaking. She avoided looking at the wallscreen as she walked to the couch where she would sleep.

33

By the time I returned to Passova and checked the Survey van back in, I was more than a little tired, especially after everything I'd been through, and it was well after nine. Rather than make a separate trip to the office, I just lugged my equipment case to my quarters and left it on the lower level. Then, rather than make anything to eat, I just sat in the small lower-level kitchen and munched on the sandwich and chips I'd carried all the way back from Syntex.

Once I reached the main upper-level bedroom and climbed out of my singlesuit, I stretched out on the bed, my thoughts still going back to what had happened. Aimee had been worried enough to break just about every law about the use of truscope . . . just to make sure I was who I said I was. That meant she was convinced that someone on the *Persephonya* was out to kill her mother, and possibly her. It was also most likely the reason why she had traveled standard class, in an attempt to learn more about the passengers and who might be a possible assassin. While I could have lodged a complaint, I didn't see that doing so would benefit either me or her . . . and I might need her help and goodwill later. She had doubtless calculated that as well.

Given the time differential created by interstellar travel, the only reason I could figure for both Aimee and her mother to travel to Stittara was to effectively keep control from other family members for as long as possible. But why hadn't that been possible under some sort of trust agreement? That was one reason why family trusts were used in the rare instances when multis with interstellar reach were involved—and why controlling family members *didn't* take interstellar journeys. But then, maybe the trust was the problem?

I was still trying to figure that out when I drifted off to sleep, my mind still wrestling with what seemed to be pieces of a half-dozen separate puzzles, pieces that swirled into discordant dreams.

Somewhere in the darkness, I thought I heard someone talking about a pressure door, and warnings, and the darkness got even darker, and then there was a breeze from somewhere. Then I heard the faintest whistling.

"Structural damage! Structural damage! Evacuate this level! Evacuate this level. The pressure door will be closing in one minute!"

At that . . . I woke . . . except the air felt so heavy, and my legs didn't want to obey, as if they had become totally uncoordinated. Somehow . . . I managed to grab my link and personal case and get through the pressure door and onto the ramp to the lower level of the guest quarters before the pressure door closed. I couldn't see anything in the darkness for a moment, until a faint glow appeared along the ceiling, and I stumbled down the ramp to the lower level.

I couldn't hear anything. The air was still, and I began to cough. That lasted forever, or so it seemed, but it was probably only for a few minutes. When I straightened up, I realized that there wasn't anywhere else to go. So I made my way, still unsteadily, into the lower bedroom and sat on the edge of the narrow bed.

For some reason, I was exhausted. How had my quarters been damaged? It had to have been a storm, but why hadn't I awakened earlier? Had there been some pressure loss that had created partial anoxia? I couldn't believe that Stittaran storms were that fierce, but even if I had been able to access the study console, all systems would have been shut down until the storm passed.

Finally, I lay down on the bed . . . and a lesser darkness crept over me.

When the lights came back on, I woke up again. How had I managed to sleep after everything that had happened? I checked the time. It was half past six, and that meant there was no way I was going to sleep longer anyway. So I struggled into a sitting position, and realized I was in my undershorts and nothing more . . . and all my clothes were on the upper level of the quarters. So I went back up the ramp to the pressure door. It was closed, but I could open it, although it shut behind me.

A quick look around confirmed that there wasn't much left in the upper level. Almost everything small had vanished, and the armaglass window to the outside that had dominated the study was gone . . . or rather the armaglass was, except for a few sections around the frame, from what I could see, given that the couch had been wedged partway into the opening.

The small bureau that had held my underwear and sundries had smashed against the wall beside the broken armaglass window, and wedged itself against what was left of the couch. The console in the study had fragmented. Not much else there had been left intact. So I headed into the bedroom . . . initially blocked by what was left of the bed. For some reason, the clothes on one end of the closet were there, but not those on the other end. That left me with two singlesuits and one pair of boots, no underwear except the shorts I was wearing and no toiletries.

I grabbed one of the singlesuits and the boots and went to the lower-level facilities and washed up as best I could and dressed. I'd barely finished when the door opened.

"Dr. Verano! Dr. Verano!"

I recognized Dermotte's voice. "I'm here."

"Are you all right, ser?"

"I'm fine. Most of my stuff and the upper level isn't."

"I came as soon as I checked the boards. I'm so sorry. I just didn't think about the guest quarters. I didn't hurry because I knew it was sixday, and no one was in the offices and laboratories . . ."

"You couldn't have done anything," I pointed out.

"You're sure you're all right, ser?"

"I'm fine, but I'll need to do a lot of shopping."

"Do you mind if I see what happened? I've never heard of an armaglass portal shattering . . . it was the armaglass, wasn't it?"

"I have no idea if that's what caused the problem, but it's definitely shattered. So are most of the furnishings as well." I turned and let Dermotte lead the way up the ramp. He stopped at the pressure door and did something so that it stayed open after we passed through it.

"Oh . . . you really got hit, ser."

"I didn't stay to find out."

"Good thing you didn't." He walked over to the window.

I helped him move the couch away from the opening that had held the armaglass. I did note that the outside wall was almost half a meter thick.

He leaned forward and began to study the sections of the frame where the armaglass had been sealed in place. Finally, he stepped back. "I don't see anything in the frame. It just must have been old, or weakened in some way that wasn't obvious."

"Is it my imagination, Dermotte, or did the outer layer break first?"

"It'd have to be the outer layer, ser. But . . ." He shook his head.

What he wasn't saying was that both layers had to be old enough or weakened enough for something as tough as armaglass to fragment, even in a huge storm. But I didn't see a single fragment inside the quarters, and armaglass was heavy.

I kept looking at the composite window frame or bracket, but it showed no sign of bending or stress. Then I squinted, trying to make out something, a protuberance, under the study window, and I was certain it hadn't been there when I'd first looked over the quarters.

We both looked up as a chime rang.

"What's that?" I asked.

"Someone's at the door. Might be Director Raasn. I left a link for her when the alarms rang."

"Wouldn't she have back-linked?"

"She told me to make sure everything was right for you, ser."

The chime sounded again. I turned and walked back down the ramp and to the door on the lower level. I eased it open, only to find two men and three women with linkcams, all aimed at me.

"Dr. Verano! Dr. Verano . . ."

For a moment I didn't know what to say. How did they know my name?

"Are you Dr. Paulo Verano?"

"Yes, I am." I couldn't very well deny that.

"The city monitors showed a storm breach . . ."

"Are you the Survey investigator from Bachman?"

"Tell us what happened . . ."

I decided to ignore the "investigator" question, although I wondered who had planted that idea and who had set them on me. Instead, I answered the last question, possibly because the woman who had posed it had asked it in a factual way. "I went to sleep. The alarms on the upper level went off, and I grabbed a few things and hurried through the pressure doors. I don't know whether the storm hurled something into the armaglass window or whether it failed, but the upper level of the quarters is a mess. I waited out the storm on the lower level." I offered what I thought was a rueful smile. "I'm happy to be in one piece, but I am going to need to replace most of my wardrobe and a few other items."

"How did it happen?"

"I have no idea. I'm sure the maintenance people will be able to tell me after they look things over."

"Are you really an investigator?"

"No. I'm an ecologist here on contract from the Systems Survey Service on Bachman. I'm doing a periodic environmental study."

"Isn't that an investigation?"

"No. Studies deal with the environment. Investigations deal with the people who oversee environmental matters. I'm here to study the environment."

"You've been meeting with multis. That sounds like an investigation."

"It's not. I meet with environmental professionals to take measurements and review data. I'll be doing field studies before long."

I must have deflected some variety of "investigator" questions a good dozen times before I finally held up a hand. "If you'll excuse me . . . it has been a long night." Then I eased back and closed the door.

"You were real patient, ser," said Dermotte, who'd obviously followed me back down to the lower level.

"I didn't feel patient, but doing anything else would make them think I was hiding something." I shook my head. "What do we do now?"

"We'll have to move you to the guest tech quarters, until we can have the damage repaired and the seals retested," Dermotte said. "They're not as spacious."

"I'm certain that they'll be adequate."

"I'll see what I can do," he said.

"I'll gather my stuff and wait." *And look into a few things in your absence.*

After Dermotte left to make those arrangements, I gathered myself together and headed back up the ramp. I wanted another good look at the bottom edge of the window and the frame.

What I'd thought was a protuberance turned out to be a long and narrow canister-like tube with a narrow nozzle at one end. Half the nozzle had been ripped away, presumably by the wind, but I could see embedded printed circuitry. I would have bet that the canister had been linked to a pressure switch . . . of some sort, and that device had been rigged only to release the sleep gas, or whatever it was, with a pressure drop, and that the window had been weakened so that the pressure drop would be gradual for a time.

I heard voices . . . from outside.

". . . whole portal's smashed . . ."

"Looks like it blew out from inside . . . all the armaglass fragments out here . . . those that are left . . ."

"Lucky bastard . . ."

". . . still say he's an investigator. Why else would the Unity send someone here?"

"Because they like to waste duhlars, Lukan . . . that's why. Just like the Planetary Council . . ."

I flattened myself against the wall and eased out of the study so that the linksters didn't see me, then crept into the bedchamber to gather the few personal belongings that remained at the one end of the closet. Then I retreated to the lower level, thinking.

The blowout of the widow hadn't been an accident, but I wasn't certain that it had been only a deliberate attempt to kill me, either, because no one could predict when a storm would hit. What it did suggest was that whoever had set it up knew I'd be in the quarters for a long time, and it didn't matter whether I was killed or even in the quarters.

In a way, that impersonality chilled me more than a verifiable attempt on my life might have, because it signified that I was a pawn, if not less than that, in some sort of power play.

Yet . . . what could I say? All that was left was an empty canister or case. Hell! It could have held air freshener, for all I could prove. But I didn't think so. I also thought that whoever had set it up would have been happier if I had died . . . but that my death wasn't necessary for them to gain something. That also suggested that there might be other "accidents" waiting, and that definitely worried me.

I waited almost an hour for Dermotte to return, and it turned out that the tech guest quarters were one door down the outside tunnel.

"Adequate" was the right word to describe them. The tech quarters consisted of a small study, a single bedchamber with a bath/fresher, and a kitchen with eating space—all on the same lower level as the bottom floor of my previous guest quarters. And not one of the rooms was really large enough for even my restricted Juchai workouts.

Once I was resettled, with my equipment case, and Dermotte had left to arrange for the repair of the main guest quarters, I readied myself to go shopping, not that I really had much choice.

34

The rest of sixday was a blur of boring necessities. Even before I got out of my temporary quarters, the local patrol arrived, and I had to take them through what had happened. Then I ended up spending most of sixday going from shop to shop because Passova didn't really have a unified link-shopping net. I just hadn't thought about that, but such an infrastructure was anything but cost-effective for a low population consisting of isolated pockets of high density where everything was either in walking distance or within a short tunneltram ride.

Then . . . the kind of singlesuits I liked weren't exactly in style in Passova, and that meant special fabrication and more duhlars, not to mention waiting and going back to pick them up late on sixday. Pretty much every aspect of replacing personal goods involved some degree of waiting and frustration. Given that it had been a long night on fiveday, and a longer day on sixday, I wasn't surprised that I was ready to collapse early . . . although I did sleep fairly well.

First thing on sevenday, after the normal morning routine, I checked on what might be happening, or not, on my former quarters. All the debris had been removed, and a temporary barrier placed where the armaglass had been. The quarters were otherwise empty, and it appeared no work was scheduled for the day. That wasn't totally surprising, given that it was indeed sevenday.

So I went to my space in the Survey office and immediately accessed all the measurements and reports on the storm that had savaged my quarters and belongings. In terms of wind velocity it had been below average, and it hadn't lasted all that long.

Then why hadn't the lights come back on until so much later?

Looking into that took another half hour, but the records were clear. The lights had been out for a little more than an hour. I'd only thought they came on at half past six.

Because you'd been gassed and your body was trying to recover?

Next I tried to find recordings of any linknews clips that concerned me. Short stories had run on every scheduled broadcast in the last day and a longer story was on the continuous news feed. Every single one mentioned that I was a Survey Service consultant sent from Bachman, and that I'd denied being an investigator. Every one of them also mentioned I was scheduled to brief at least one member of the Planetary Council, and most mentioned that the accident seemed freakish, since the storm hadn't been that severe.

The news implications were that someone didn't want me talking to the Council, and the only question was who benefited from such a story. My initial thought was that Melarez or her boss did. But why would they try anything that obvious? Obviously, there was something going on that I didn't understand.

But . . . there wasn't too much more I could do about that, and in the end I spent much of the day looking over the records and reports filed by Syntex and checking them against what I'd seen and measured at the installation. Not exactly to my surprise, by midafternoon I determined that there were no discrepancies.

The next item on my agenda, given the lack of space in my temporary temporary quarters, was to look into the possibility of finding some place where I could work out, preferably privately, or largely privately.

When I searched the linknet, I found that there were more than a few "personal trainers" listed, but only a comparative handful of exercise facilities and one private gymnasium. I linked with the gym and immediately got the image of a pleasant figure, as androgynous as Amarios, who immediately delivered what was a set message.

"Clyantos is presently not accepting applications for membership. If you are interested in applying for the waiting list, please say so to begin the application process."

That wasn't going to help me in the slightest, not when I really—hopefully—only needed to use such a facility for a short period. So I broke that link, and kept looking through the information on each "exercise facility." Most of them were located well away from my quarters and the Survey offices, and in the end, I decided to visit the nearest one, Shriver's Fitness, since I wasn't about to make any decisions based on just linknet information. From what I could determine, it was less than three blocks from my quarters, if seven levels down. One thing I did discover immediately was that while there were ramps and lifts for the upper levels of Passova, access to the lowest four levels—levels six through ten—was by staircase or tunnelcar ramp only. Since I didn't have a tunnelcar and didn't want to rent one or hire one, even if I'd known how or wanted to link the information, I decided to walk.

Going down wasn't difficult, but as I descended, I wondered about climbing back up. Still, when I left the stairs on level seven, the pedestrian tunnel looked the same as other pedestrian ways—well, the same as the narrow tunnels near the arboretum. The light seemed the same, but there was a sense of griminess, a feel rather than a smell, though, and I couldn't place it.

I checked my link directions, but they assured me I was on the right level and headed in the right direction.

"Interested in some fun?" asked a professionally sultry voice from nowhere.

I glanced around before I realized it was projected sound without the holo, except a woman stepped, or more like leaned out of a doorway several yards ahead. She was fully clothed, after a fashion, but in a single flowing gown that turned transparent intermittently. Whether that transparency revealed what was beneath the gown or another fantasy was largely immaterial to me. I wasn't interested in that kind of fun. Even the legal kind of fun had been too expensive for me.

"No."

"You play for the other team? We got guys, you know?"

"No," I repeated.

The sound vanished, as did the apparition posing as a woman.

I neared the next cross tunnel with some trepidation, despite the fact that two scrawny girls were playing some sort of dance game on a projected light grid on the side walkway. That they paid no attention to me and moved in a jerkily rhythmic way suggested they were intensity linked to something that passed for music.

Two clearly older women crossed in front of me, coming down the other tunnel way. Whether they were truly old or old before their time, I couldn't tell. From their near-indifference and their weary walk, I had the feeling that the distinction was immaterial.

Shriver's was in the next block, past a bistro that bore the unlikely name of Malarky's, with only a handful of men with faces ranging from angry to tired seated at the cheaply templated black chairs irregularly gathered around equally cheap circular black tables.

Standing outside an archway with the name Fitness Center in squarish block letters above it, I wondered exactly what lay beyond the doors. There was only one way to find out. I stepped through the projected screen in the archway and into another long corridor that stretched a good fifteen meters straight ahead.

From the seemingly solid wall to my right came a man with a baton, and I reacted, if more slowly than I should have, moving into a Juchai switch-and-reverse. The man vanished, and I realized that it had been a holo projection.

"Not bad! Not bad!" The speaker who stepped out of an alcove was a wizened figure of a man, if trim and still with muscles visible under the formfitting garment that resembled a leotard and was likely a holo projection suit. "You here to try out for the remote fight completion?"

"No," I admitted, deciding not to offer my real reason. "I saw the sign outside, and I was curious."

"Too bad. You're in shape, and you got good technique and reactions. Haven't seen many trained in Juchai in years. You might get good ratings just for that."

Ratings? "The competitions are linkcast?"

"Not the regular way. Can't do that. Private subscription. Payment's delayed a day or so. No more, I promise."

I shook my head. "Not right now. If other things don't turn out, I might be back."

"You do, and you ask for Gregorio. That's me. We pay better than the other fitness centers, too."

"If I do, I will."

"Still think you'd make a lot as a Juchai . . ."

I just smiled before I left, trying to move deliberately.

Once I was back in the tunnel way, I almost shook my head. I had no idea whether the "competition" was full or partial contact, or totally remote, and I didn't care. I was practiced, but not trained, and the last thing I wanted to be involved with was some form of semilegal or illegal fight club.

After visiting Shriver's and knowing that the other fitness/exercise centers were on even lower levels, not to mention that, from Gregorio's off-hand comments, they were also likely disguised versions of remote fight clubs, I trudged back up all seven levels, deciding that, at least for the day, that would have to substitute for exercise. I still couldn't believe that there weren't exercise facilities in an underground city like Stittara, and I had to ask myself what exactly I was missing.

35

Oneday morning found me up early, readying myself for the eight hundred meeting or briefing of someone on the Planetary Council. While staff assistant Melarez had intimated that Councilor Morghan had wanted the briefing, I had my doubts about whether the good councilor would actually be present.

I allowed myself plenty of extra time, and it was a good thing I did, because the tunneltram to the Planetary Council center was jammed, most likely because many support types who worked there were supposed to be at their consoles at eight. Then I discovered that I'd gone the wrong way on level three and that I had to retrace my steps back to the tunneltram stop and head east, instead of west. I should have checked my link, but . . . I'd *thought* I knew exactly where I was headed. Even so, I arrived at the anteroom inside the archway labeled 471 with eight minutes to spare.

No one was there.

I waited several minutes, wondering whether to open the door behind the vacant console, or to go to an adjoining chamber or office. Just as I was about to open the door, a tall, gawky, and very young man stepped out. He looked at me and blinked, as if asking what I happened to be doing there.

"Dr. Paulo Verano," I offered. "I was asked to do a briefing this morning by Paem Melarez."

"Oh . . . just a moment." He waved his hands before the console. "Ms. Melarez . . . Dr. Verano is here." He looked up. "She'll be here in a few minutes, sir."

A few minutes mounted to almost fifteen, most likely a form of punishment because I'd been so inconsiderate as to be unavailable the previous fiveday. Then the door behind the nervous young man opened, and Paem Melarez stepped out, closing it behind her.

"Dr. Verano . . . we'll be walking over to the councilor's office."

"Where is that?"

"About three doors east," Melarez replied.

As I walked beside her, I decided not to bring up the storm or the media interest until she and the councilor or whoever else might be there were all in the same chamber. Just after Melarez opened an unmarked door and before she stepped into it, she brushed back a short lock of heavy black hair.

The space into which we walked was definitely not a briefing room, but the very private personal office of the councilor. Morghan was a big woman, slightly taller than I, with a well-toned physique and not a gram of fat. Muscular as she was, she wasn't slender. Her hair was jet-black, as were her eyes, and her skin held just a touch of amber honey. She didn't rise from behind her console, but gestured brusquely to the chairs facing her.

As soon as I sat down, the councilor looked at me. Her eyes were actually warm, almost amused. "Before you begin, I'd like to inform you that everything you say will be recorded and documented. Is that clear?"

"It is."

"Why are you really here on Stittara? Try to avoid all the meaningless rhetoric."

"My former spouse got the court to seize ninety percent of my assets for her and our daughter. The court said that they might take more in a year. Our daughter hadn't talked to me in two years, and my ex-spouse was screwing the father of my daughter's boyfriend. My advocate turned out to have friends in the Ministry of Environment, and the Ministry had received word from an oversight committee that the Deniers felt the Survey Service was far too hard on the multis on Stittara. The Ministry decided that I was impartial enough that none of the parties in the government, or the opposition, could complain. I needed a lot of money. They provided it. Here I am, a consultant with a good reputation for hire."

Morghan laughed, not totally humorously.

Melarez looked surprised, if only momentarily.

"You're more than that, I think," said Morghan. "We'll leave it at that . . . for now. What is your official mission and how do you see it?"

"My official mission is to assess the overall environmental situation on Stittara, and to report on whether the Survey Service is too aggressively applying the Unity standards, applying them judiciously, or failing to apply them as necessary."

"That gives you a great deal of latitude."

"Theoretically, but I have to back up any recommendation or observation with data, an overwhelming amount of data, and that data has to support it."

"What have you discovered so far? Please don't give me platitudes about the sanctity of data or the need to reserve judgment until you've finished."

"I can tell you what I've discovered so far. But I'm less than a tenth of the way through what's required, and when ninety percent of the job is still undone . . . I'm sorry, but I will withhold judgment."

"Go ahead."

"Every multi I've studied so far is complying with existing standards, and the standards have been applied fairly. There's been no sign of excessive enforcement pressures, and none of the environment directors I've met, or any of the executives, have complained about standards being excessive or unfair."

"What is your opinion of the Stittaran Systems Survey Service?"

"I've so far dealt with only a small percentage of the Service."

"But you've dealt with and met most of the key headquarters people."

"That means little until I've met with the field people and determine whether the view and the facts are the same in both places."

Both Morghan and Melarez nodded at that.

I had the feeling I'd just made a tactical error, if not an out-and-out mistake.

"Have you had a chance to evaluate how the local Survey handles the outies and their impact on the environment?"

"No. I've made preliminary inquiries and found that there's insufficient data in the environmental files." I didn't want to mention enforcement files, because I hadn't had a chance to get beyond a quick survey.

"Why do you think that is?"

"My initial feeling is that no one in enforcement has consolidated the information developed in individual cases into an integrated database. That's generally not an enforcement function."

"Is this true elsewhere?"

"Unfortunately. I've had to deal with that problem more than once."

"Has the Service been cooperative?"

"They've provided everything that I've asked for without hesitation or reservation." *Even if I've had to request additional information a few times.*

"Do you think that the destruction at the guest quarters was an accident?"

"I don't know enough to answer that. It seems unlikely, but until I actually measured Stittaran storms, I would have said that they were not only unlikely, but physically and environmentally impossible."

The questions went on for another half stan, but I had the feeling that the later questions were a cross between formality, the need to provide a documented broad range of inquiry on the part of the councilor, and an attempt to move my attention from some of the initial questions.

As I could tell the questions were heading toward the end, I made a comment of my own. "This has been, shall we say, rather puzzling." I went on before either Morghan or Melarez could interrupt me. "I've done any number of ecological surveys, a few times after devastating storms, but this is the first time I've had half a dozen newslinkers at my door. Most surprisingly, they all knew who I was and what I've been doing."

"Why would that be surprising, Dr. Verano?" replied Morghan, her voice as cool and smooth as ever. "According to the reports we receive from Bachman, the linkers there report everything, and Bachman is far larger. We don't receive ecologists from Bachman that often. Is it surprising that they are interested in you, especially when you are involved in one of the few cases of storm damage in years?"

"Oh . . . I can understand the interest. What I found interesting is that they knew not only who I was, but where I was and what I was doing. So far as I know, there's been no public knowledge of that. Most interesting of all was that they knew I'd be briefing you this morning." I smiled.

I had to give the two credit. Neither of them looked at each other.

"Doctor," said Morghan slowly and distinctly, "nothing can be kept secret on Stittara unless it is known to one person and one person only. Sometimes not even then."

"So there's essentially no security on any comm channel?"

"Only the dubious security of being buried in a welter of comm traffic," answered Melarez.

Abruptly Morghan rose. "Thank you very much, Dr. Verano. I look forward to seeing your final report."

And that was that. Melarez thanked me and said good-bye in the main corridor, leaving me to find my way back to the tunneltram.

I was in the Survey Service offices just after ten. I didn't bother with even stopping in my spaces but made my way to see Aloris.

She was waiting, but said nothing as I took a seat across from her. So I waited.

Finally, she asked, "How did it go?"

"I met with Councilor Morghan and her assistant Melarez. Just the two of them. The councilor asked questions for almost a stan. Then she thanked me and said she looked forward to my final report."

"Will you provide it?"

I nodded, then grinned. "It might be after it's been dispatched to the Ministry."

"What did she ask about, if I might ask?"

I told Aloris . . . mostly.

After I was done, she frowned. "That doesn't sound like her. Usually, she browbeats people more."

"She tried. I don't browbeat easily." Before she could say more, I asked, "Do you know how the repairs on the quarters are coming?"

"They should be done by this evening, but they'll have to wait a day and then test the seals on the window before they'll renew the occupancy certification. How are things coming otherwise?"

"I still need to visit GenArt, Valior, and ABP, before I start visiting the Survey field sites." I didn't mention that I intended to do some more digging into the enforcement files. "And I have to go back to Syntex on threeday for a bit. We ran out of time on fiveday."

"Are there any problems there?"

"Nothing besides it being an older and sprawling facility."

"It is one of the oldest." Aloris didn't sound convinced.

I just smiled, then stood and went back to my office.

Before I started reminding the three laggard multis that they did need to meet with me, I wanted to follow up on something else that had been nagging at me all along. So I began to scan through the Systems Survey personnel records. Before long, I began to see that there had been very few new hires, no more than a handful every year, for the past several years. That seemed low, for an organization that had close to a thousand people in all categories. I skipped farther back, but the pattern was still the same. The number of new hires generally matched the number of deaths and resignations. That was as it should have been. But what I didn't find was many retirements, less than one or two a year.

At that point, a young woman whose name I didn't catch and the screen didn't identify, except for originating from Valior, called me to inform me that Kimon Tibou would be happy to meet with me at ten on twoday morning. I assured her that I would be there, and then went back to searching, looking for specific people. Almost two stans later I still hadn't found out when Systems Survey had hired Aloris Raasn. Either that record was missing, or she'd been hired more than a century and a half earlier.

Anagathics or not, she didn't look that old, and Haaran certainly wasn't very old, either.

I was leaning back in my swivel, puzzling through that, when Zerlyna peered in.

"Do you want to join me for lunch? I'm going to Bellisimo."

"Oh . . . the narrow hole in the wall."

"I'm not a high-paid consultant."

"Neither am I," I quipped back, standing, "but I'd love to join you."

We walked to Bellisimo and snared one of the last two empty tables, near the back of the narrow space. Since the lager I'd ordered before had been passable, I ordered another along with the ravioli, and a cup of potato truffle soup Zerlyna recommended. She ordered a white wine and a large soup.

Once I had a sip of the lager, I pointed to the wall above us. "I've wondered this ever since the last time we were here. Why do they have pictures of ruins on the walls?"

She laughed. "They're a hangover from the previous place. It was called Ruination. Karsen liked the pictures and kept them. He says they're bellisimo ruins."

"How long has he had it?"

"Twenty years, or thereabouts."

That brought me up short. Twenty years, and he hadn't changed the wall decor? "Did you ever go to Ruination?"

"Only once. The food was as bad as the name. I never understood how it lasted as long as it did."

"How long was that?"

"Not quite ten years. That's what I remember anyway." Zerlyna smiled brightly, almost as if challenging me.

Then I swallowed. *Of course . . . you idiot.* Still . . . I wanted to press things just a bit. "You mentioned before that Aloris had a partner. Was she actually married?"

"She was. Technically, she still is, although she could petition for a time/distance dissolution, and the justiciary would grant it automatically."

"How long was her former husband here on Stittara?'

Zerlyna frowned. "Two years. It might have been less."

I thought carefully before I asked the next question. "Is it my imagination or do outsiders either come and leave quickly or stay forever?"

"If they don't leave within a few years, they're here forever," said Zerlyna blandly. "There are some exceptions, usually high-level multi executives."

I glanced around, noting that most of the tables, all eighteen of them, from what I'd counted, were filled. That was to be expected during lunchtime, but I had the feeling that everyone was looking at me, although it was clear that no one was looking at me, except Zerlyna.

"How are you coming on your work? Have you had a chance to visit any of the outland settlements?"

"Not yet. I'd thought to begin later this week."

"That would be good. It will give you a much better feel for Stittara. You can't get that, you know, just from the cities and installations."

"I'm sure you're right. It's just that there's so much to cover."

After that, the conversation was technical and routine. The ravioli were as I remembered them, and the soup was better than either the lager or the ravioli.

When we finished, I paid, saying, "Since I am a high-paid consultant," and Zerlyna didn't complain.

Then we walked back to the Survey offices, and I settled back into my swivel.

The question facing me as I stared blankly at the muted console screen wasn't how I was going to complete getting my contract assignment done, but how I was going to survive getting it done. Or did I just bail out?

For whatever reason, I had the feeling that wasn't going to work, and that meant I needed to pick up the pace of my study. A lot.

I made more contacts on oneday afternoon, finally managing to get a meeting to see the environmental director at GenArt early on fourday. I could sense that no one at ABP wanted to meet with me because I ended up with another promise that someone from environmental services would be contacting me shortly. Then, belatedly, I remembered to arrange for a Survey van on threeday to drive back to Syntex for my trip to the forerunner site, although I only listed the destination as Syntex on the reservation form.

I was in early on twoday, and managed to contact Field Two, looking for Benart Albrot, only to discover that he was "on site" and would return my comm. Reeki Liam at Field One was on vacation visiting her daughter and not available. How could anyone be out of comm range with sat-links? Then I decided to follow up on one of Zerlyna's earlier suggestions and went to find Geneil Paak down in GeoSurv. She was "in the depths," as Zerlyna had said, and that was certainly true, I reflected, as I trudged down ramp after ramp.

Geneil looked at me with a quizzical expression when I appeared in her doorway.

"I'm Paulo Verano, and I'm here from Bachman to conduct an ecological survey. I thought you might be able to help me."

She was a slender and wiry woman with eyes of a hazel shade that seemed similar to the stem color of the native grass/lichen, and her space was about one-third the size of mine, filled with racks, cases, and a row of screens of a type I'd never seen before.

"I'd be happy to help you, Doctor," she replied in a soft voice, "but I'm a geologist. I'm one of the few in the Survey Service who doesn't deal with the living environment. I look at the dead environment, or the record of past environments."

"That's not exactly why I came to see you."

She looked even more puzzled.

"I need to look at outland settlements, and I understand you might have some idea where some of those that are better managed are located."

Immediately a wariness infused her face. "I don't see what this has to do with me."

"I'm here to study the environment of Stittara. Just as the multis impact it, so do the outies, but I haven't been able to find much in the way of data. The enforcement records deal with specific environmental problems discovered at individual settlements. There's no unified data on even one settlement . . . and yet the outies comprise at least half the population of Stittara."

For some reason, her expression, while still wary, was fractionally less tense, but she frowned and said, "I don't know why you would think . . ."

"Zerlyna Eblion said you might be able to help me."

"She would."

"Why do you say that?"

"You don't know?" Geneil shook her head. "There's no way you would know."

I was still confused. So I just waited.

"I come from an outland family. I wanted to do more than just be one with the land. Some of us did . . . do."

"Why geology?"

"I wanted to know how things came to be here on Stittara. Not about how people did things . . ." She smiled shyly. "I guess in some ways we never escape our parents and our history."

"I suspect you're right." I wondered if Leysa felt that way . . . or ever would. "Could you at least give me some suggestions?"

"I'll send you a list of a number of settlements that aren't too far away. That's all I'd feel comfortable doing."

"Could you include basic directions? I can't even find those in the Survey records."

Her gentle laugh held just the hint of an ironic bitterness. "I can do that. You'll have something later today, unless I get buried. Then it will be in the morning."

"Thank you. I do appreciate it."

"Just try to see more than one or two. Each one is different."

"I'll see as many as I reasonably can." Because I had to get to Valior, I excused myself and made my way back up ramp after ramp . . . or so it seemed.

It had taken longer to find Geneil than I'd anticipated, but I'd had the feeling that trying to get what I needed was better accomplished in person . . . and I'd been right. That left me hurrying back to my spaces to grab my equipment bag and head out. Because Valior was the only multi located in Passova proper, I could take a tunneltram.

I hurried too much, because, as I stepped into the tunneltram at the stop closest to the Survey offices, just before the doors closed, I brushed someone.

"You! What the frig are you doing? Think you're special or something?"

As the tram pulled away, I turned to face a man who looked younger than I . . . and ready to fight. "I'm sorry. I didn't mean to bump you. I was just hurrying to make the tram."

"That's no excuse. You got all the time in the world."

That was one thing I didn't have, but I really didn't need a fight. "It was an accident, and I am sorry."

"You offworlders . . ." He snorted and turned away.

For a moment I just stood there, hanging on to the grab bar. One moment he'd been ready to fight, and the next he'd been truly disgusted . . . and not interested. Somehow . . . I didn't think it had been what I'd said, but it might have been how I'd said it. Still . . . I'd had other locals want to attack me because I was from out-system, and this one wanted nothing to do with me.

I did get to Valior just before ten, and the same young woman who hadn't introduced herself before failed to do so again, but led me politely into an office about the size of mine at the Survey Service. She was definitely young, definitely from Stittara, and definitely not interested in an older consultant.

At first glance, Kimon Tibou looked to be older than I was, how much I couldn't say, because on Stittara, perhaps because of the somewhat physically protected lifestyle, at least among city and facility dwellers, or perhaps because of the availability of anagathics. He didn't bother to ask me to have a seat, but immediately spoke. "I really don't understand why you need to see us. The Survey Service has our reports. We're not located away from a city. We're tied into the full environmental services of Passova, and our discharges are minimal . . ."

I'd wondered about the very things Tibou was saying, but Valior was listed as a multi, and I'd wanted to be thorough.

". . . We're barely a multi. We're an equipment designer and manufacturer for all the other multis. We provide special tools. Sometimes, we only design and test a template for them. They all can do their own standard templating." Tibou shrugged boyishly, but some men are boys their entire life, even if they live for close to two centuries. "It's just easier and cheaper for them to have us do it."

"What kind of tools do you provide?"

"Anything they want."

"But . . . for a multi like RDAEX . . . ?"

"We did something special for them . . . it's always special . . ."

"What? A device for cleaning laser photonics used at high pressure?"

"Oh . . . you can't clean those. We made special brackets that simplified replacing focusing heads under high ambient pressures." He paused. "I really shouldn't . . ."

"I understand." I nodded. "Was Valior around way back when Pentura was operating here . . . before they lost the one facility?"

"Oh . . . yes. We've been here almost since the first multis began to operate here."

"What did you do for Pentura?"

"I'm sure it was whatever they wanted, but I couldn't tell you what it was."

"Confidentiality?"

Tibou shook his head. "The storms that destroyed Pentura were so bad that we lost all our records—magnetic fluxes and surges, and then power outages, and then more fluxes. I think everyone did. That was what prompted the Council to insist on power isolation during storms."

"Everyone? Did storms ravage the entire planet?"

"I don't know. I just heard that the storms were bad then." He offered a boyish grin. "That was well before my time, Doctor." The grin vanished. "What do you need from us?"

I told him.

Even though Valior was small as multis went, going through the facility and making and checking measurements and asking questions still took the rest of the morning and half the afternoon. It was almost four when I returned to my office at the Survey Service.

I hadn't checked messages while I'd been at Valior, and I didn't want to check them on the tunneltram. That meant more than a few were waiting by the time I reached my Survey console. One was from Aloris, informing

me that the repairs on the guest quarters had been completed, that testing
was under way, and that it was likely I'd be able to return by fourday or
fiveday. A second was from Erik Engola at ABP, suggesting a meeting
fiveday morning. Another was from Paem Meralez, requesting a return
call, and the last was an outie settlement listing from Geneil Paak.

I confirmed the time and appointment with ABP, sent a quick message
of thanks to Geneil, and then settled behind the console and made the
call to Meralez, wondering exactly what she wanted.

She was in, and she smiled one of those warm political smiles that
meant nothing. "Dr. Verano . . . I was just linking to thank you for briefing Councilor Morghan. She was pleased with both the detail of your
answers to her questions and your candor."

"I did my best." And that was true.

"She did have one more question. How long do you anticipate that
your study will take?"

"The short answer is that I don't know. The longer answer is that I've
never done a study of this scope"—*Ever*—"that didn't require at least
months of work. It might take less because there initially appear to be
fewer points of human impact on the ecology and because air pollutants
and greenhouse gases have been tightly controlled from the first days of
colonization. But . . . the study won't be done until it's done."

"I'll let the councilor know. I'm sure she'll think that you've outlined
a fair estimation."

Perhaps not helpful to you both, but fair. I didn't say that, just nodded.

"Thank you again, Doctor. As always, you've been most helpful."

When she blanked the screen, I thought there was far more to her call
than a mere thank-you, but I couldn't figure out what. I also didn't like
the idea of having been most helpful, because it suggested my words
would be used out of context and in ways not necessarily to my benefit.
There wasn't much I could do about either.

Something that Tibou had said piqued my curiosity, and that was
about the number and ferocity of storms in the past. Was the number
consistent? Or were they truly random?

In the end, as often seemed to be the case for me, I ended up looking
into all the storm data, as far back as they had been charted, which was
three and a half centuries. That was consistent, in terms of timing, with
what Tibou had said about the destruction of records, but there was no

way of telling if there had once been older records that had survived and been removed later. According to the historical records, pretty much every square kay of Stittara was scoured clean every five to ten years—with the exception of the mountains and a few rocky areas. There were a number of studies and hypotheses about why the higher areas were exempt, but none of the studies could support with data any of the hypotheses . . . and there had been no new attempts—or studies—in the last eighty years.

I did come across references to several attempted sampling missions, conducted first with RPVs. All had failed to penetrate the opaque storm wall, and all had been destroyed in the process. The last mission, conducted by the same Service researcher, Jaesyn Wilms, had involved both two RPVs and an armored flitter, with which Wilms had attempted to obtain more precise data. From the loss of signal data, all three vehicles had vanished at the same time. No traces had ever been found of any of them.

And no one ever tried another sampling mission?

To me, that seemed to indicate a definite possibility of low-grade intelligence, perhaps some sort of aerial jellyfish organization . . . or maybe something as basic as lashing out at aerial objects that might be dangerous. Yet there was nothing in the Survey records that even hinted at looking into intelligence. Yet I'd heard the argument before . . . on Bachman.

Had all references to potential skytube intelligence vanished with the older records? Or had they "disappeared" later? Perhaps because far too many duhlars rested on Stittaran anagathics?

By the time I finished the Wilms reports and my speculations, I had even more questions. I was also tired and hungry. I closed down my console and decided to leave for the evening.

36

Getting up reasonably early has never been that much of a problem for me. Getting up at four on threeday felt anything but reasonable, especially since I knew I'd have to hurry, but the thought of struggling up at three-thirty . . . well . . . I didn't even want to consider it. In any case, I was in the Survey van and well away from Passova by just a shade past four-thirty, looking down the tunnel of light that the van's headlamps drilled through the purpled blackness that was Stittaran night . . . or early morning

I saw all of three vehicles on the drive to Syntex, each an unmarked lorry, and each reminded me of the outie vehicles I'd seen earlier. When I reached the entrance to Syntex, I noted a small flitter parked on a permacrete square. One of the pilots was walking around the craft, conducting a preflight, no doubt. I should have realized that, given the early hour and the need for prearrangement, the forerunner site wasn't that close.

No sooner had I parked the van and extracted my equipment case than Aimee herself appeared from the nearest pressure door and walked toward me. She wore another tailored singlesuit, this one two-colored, with black trousers and a white top, over which she wore a short black jacket. "Good morning, Paulo."

"It is morning," I agreed.

"You did want to see the site." She looked at the case. "You can't take samples, you know."

"I didn't think I could, but will anyone protest measurements and ob-servations?"

"Not if you'll agree not to publish them for profit or in any forum where they could be copied and used in such a way."

"I can do that."

"We need to get to the flitter." She turned.

I followed. She moved so quickly toward a small door beside the main pressure door that I nearly had to run to catch up. The door opened onto a narrow set of steps, one of the few I'd seen since I'd been on Stittara, and the heavy door at the top, both armored and a pressure door, opened on the side of the structure with the vehicle door. Aimee strode along a walkway to the permacrete square where the flitter waited. Since she was in a hurry, and we'd likely have time to talk on the flight, I just walked beside her without saying a word.

The man who waited beside the flitter was slender with black hair gray-ing at the temples, the first time I'd seen that on Stittara. The winged in-signia on the chest of his black-trimmed maroon flight suit suggested he was the pilot. The fact that he wore a flight suit also suggested that he was either former military somewhere, or that Syntex's security types included the pilots. I couldn't tell if the flitter held concealed armaments.

"Executive Vanslo . . ." The pilot inclined his head. "Will it just be the two of you?"

"Yes, Josef."

Aimee gestured for me to climb into the flitter, the smallest in which I'd flown in years. While stepping in front of women went against my anachronistic grain, she was the boss, and it was her flitter in more ways than one, I suspected. I stepped up the two rungs of the extended ladder and into the cabin.

The interior of the flitter reflected what I would have called a mixed configuration. Just behind the bulkhead that separated the pilots from the cabin were two upholstered seats with padded restraints, each one set next to a window with a space between. Aft of the two seats was the entry door on the starboard side with a cargo bin on the right. I put my equip-ment case there and made sure that it was securely fastened. Behind the entry space and bin, against the fuselage on each side, were padded bench seats, with three sets of harnesses on each side, and cargo stowage under-neath with net restrainers.

"Take the left seat," suggested Aimee. "The view is better on that side going south."

"You've taken the flight on a previous trip."

She smiled, but only said, "It is the best view."

I strapped in and waited for her to do the same before I asked, "How far away is the site?"

"Not all that far," replied Aimee. "About a hundred kays. It's in the far southeast corner of our lands."

"Do all the multis control tracts that large?"

"It varies. We do. RDAEX does. Eterna's lands are perhaps thirty kays on a side. The others are much smaller."

"The lands dating to the older multis are larger, then."

"That was carefully phrased, Paulo." Her tone was almost bantering.

"I try to be careful. I'm not always successful." I let some irony creep into my last words.

The cabin door closed, and after less than a minute I could hear the turbines start. Then the flitter lifted off the permacrete, nosed down just slightly, and began to accelerate. In moments we were airborne, and I was looking out at an endless, or seemingly endless, expanse of lichen/grass that covered everything. Here and there, I could see patches of darker gray-green, the bushes that seldom grew more than knee-high, except in the mountains or high rocky areas. A thin ribbon of silver-gray wound between two ridges, angling roughly to the southwest. I didn't see any sign of human habitation, but wouldn't have expected to on Syntex lands. Farther to the south, I could see skytubes, slowly moving westward, it appeared.

"Very open . . . and very humbling, don't you think?" asked Aimee.

"Any time I think about worlds with advanced ecosystems I feel humbled."

"What do you think about the skytubes?"

"Officially . . . or unofficially?"

"Both," she replied with a smile.

"Officially, I have no position until the study is complete. Unofficially, I'd have to say that however they're organized . . . structured . . . whatever . . . there has to be some level of intelligence."

"But . . . why . . . why haven't we discovered what that might be?"

"If they are any sort of organism, the penalties for interfering with them are rather stringent. If Syntex, for example, tried to capture a sky-tube, although I don't know how you'd do that, without the express permission of the Ministry of Environment, you could lose all holdings and all rights to anything obtained from Stittara."

She nodded, and I had the feeling she knew that. "But surely . . . there are other ways . . ."

"I've looked into those. Anyone who's gotten too close to one hasn't survived. Neither have any remote RPVs or samplers." I shrugged, or attempted a shrug under the restraints. "What's come from Stittara has proved too valuable to jeopardize by trying military-level force on a sky-tube, and anything less ends up with whoever or whatever tried it destroyed."

"I can't believe that . . ."

Although I had the feeling she was testing me, I gave the straight, and accurate, answer. "The anagathics Syntex and the other multis have developed here have doubled life expectancies in the Arm, at least for those who can afford them. Those who can afford them are powerful. They don't like the idea of messing with something that allows them to keep power longer. That's one reason why the Unity even has a deep-space fleet, and why there are regular patrols and posts on the approaches from the Cloud Combine." I didn't give the rest of the answer, which was that trying to protect a planet was essentially impossible, and that those patrols were there to wreak destruction on Cloud worlds if a Cloud warship came anywhere close to the Stittaran system.

"Do you believe all that?"

I laughed. "Not all of it. But the patrols and ships are real, and so are the profits and the motives of the powerful on Bachman, Randtwo, and a few other worlds. Do you doubt that?"

She shook her head.

"Will you tell me what problem you're here to solve? Besides the difficulties with what—and I'm just guessing—appears to be a family trust issue . . . in both senses of the word."

"No."

Her answer was matter-of-fact, but confirmed, in my mind, my surmises about the family trust.

"How is your mother?"

"She's feeling much better now that she's here, but she does miss her old friends, those who were still left. How is your study coming?"

"I only have two more multis to visit, and then I'll have to start doing fieldwork."

"Why the multis first?"

"It's easier to deal with the possibility of direct emissions first, before anyone who might be skirting the compliance requirements would have a chance to retool or upgrade effluent and emission controls. I doubted that would be a problem, but it's something I have to rule out."

"Do you really think you can learn something from the site?"

I was honest. "I do. I can't justify it logically, but I think it will tell me something." I glanced out the window, catching sight of a narrow road. "You also have a road to the site?"

"It's used mostly for equipment and for the staff. Except for security personnel, no one overnights there."

"That keeps down contamination."

"As much as we can."

"What have you learned?"

"I'll let the archaeologists tell you. They're better at it."

"How many do you have?"

"Three, plus some assistants, and the university supplies some student interns."

"How long have they been actively working?"

"Something like three centuries . . . on and off. Mostly off, until recently."

"Because the Antiquities Commission threatened appropriation?"

"Largely. Also because Mother became interested." Aimee smiled, then asked, "How did you find Councilor Morghan?"

"Very competent. So is her assistant, it appears."

I didn't learn anything else I didn't already know over the course of the rest of the flight. Aimee was effective at letting me know what she wanted me to know. I was less effective in return.

From the air, the site was unprepossessing—just the road leading to a long and low stone structure barely protruding above the lichen/grass on the top of what once might have been a mesa, millions of years before, but now was a wide flat area slightly higher than the rolling grasslands on each side. To one side of the structure was a short permacrete landing strip, toward which the flitter made a smooth but steep descent . . . and a gentle landing.

We unstrapped ourselves; the cabin door opened; and I reclaimed my equipment case and followed Aimee out. The site structure protruded less than a meter from the surrounding grass, although it was far longer than I'd guessed from the air—a good hundred meters—and there were no portals or windows—just featureless gray stone, old enough that I couldn't tell if it happened to be modified native stone or an older formulation of synthstone. The walk led to the north end of the structure ending in an outside ramp that dropped some two meters in the last twenty. The entrance to the building was an armored pressure door.

Once inside the first door, we faced a security type in the maroon uniform of Syntex. Behind him were a stone wall and another armored pressure door. The security type looked suspiciously at me.

"Dr. Verano has been cleared. He's here on assignment for an oversight committee of the Unity government."

I almost protested that I hadn't told her that—except I probably had when she'd put me under truscope.

"I'd feel happier if you'd allow me to scan him, ma'am."

"I don't have a problem with that." I stepped forward, and he ran the scanner over me, then over the equipment case.

He nodded politely to Aimee, then looked back to me. "Thank you, ser."

We'd only gone through the second pressure door and walked a few meters more when Aimee said, "You're most accommodating. Don't you have any awful secrets?"

"I do . . . but they're all in my mind these days."

At that point, another security type emerged from a doorway on the right side of the corridor ahead of us and walked swiftly toward us . . . or toward Aimee.

"Executive Vanslo . . ."

"What is it, Manwel?"

"We've detained an intruder. I thought you ought to know."

"Let's see what he's like." Aimee gestured.

Once more, I followed, this time into what was the station room or the equivalent for site security. I waited there, watched by an older, but junior female security type. Her eyes were very intent on me, so intent that I was feeling very uneasy by the time Aimee returned almost half an hour later. When I stood to leave, the smile bestowed on me by the woman who studied me was warm, inviting, and unsettling.

"I'll have to check back later," Aimee explained as we left the station room.

"Was it serious?" I asked once we were out in the long corridor that angled downward toward the south end of the building.

Aimee shrugged. "It's hard to tell. You tell me. It was one of your fellow passengers."

"Rob Gybyl?"

"How did you know?"

For all that she'd asked a question, she scarcely sounded surprised.

"He made no secret about wanting to do a docu-drama on the site. He said that he'd document the site if you'd let him, and do a documentary on the denial if you didn't."

"He was carrying linkcams and relays, and no weapons, but those could be used to record things that would compromise our security."

"What did you decide?"

"To detain him a bit longer while security makes a few more inquiries. Do you have any thoughts?"

"Just one. Why today?"

"Actually, they found him late last night."

"Still . . . the coincidence between his timing and yours . . ."

"And yours, perhaps?" Her tone was bantering, but I had the feeling she was serious.

"I didn't know him before I bordered the *Persephonya*, and I've not seen him nor contacted him since. And he certainly hasn't contacted me."

"He tried, apparently."

"He did?"

"He was in the crowd of linksters who besieged you after the . . . storm incident at your guest quarters."

"He was?" The fact that Aimee knew more about what was happening around me than I did was disconcerting. "Have you been tracking every passenger who disembarked from the *Persephonya*?"

"Of course."

"What have you discovered?"

"That you're who you say you are, as are some junior employees of various outfits, and almost no one else is."

"Such as you."

"Correct."

"So . . . who *are* you?" I looked directly at her.

"Guess," she said, without breaking stride. Her black eyes almost sparkled in amusement. "You seem to be good at it."

"You're Aimee Vanslo. At least, that's the name you're known by at Syntex and most likely VLE. You went by another name outside of the multi. You were the chief operating officer, or the CEO, under your mother, who controls the family trust that has the majority interest in VLE. She remains as the chair of the board, and your younger sister is the acting CEO in your absence. You were upset over the death of your partner, and someone tried to use that to oust you. That someone is likely a male cousin, or the male spouse of one of your daughters . . ." I shrugged. "That's the best I can do with what I know."

A faint smile crossed her lips and vanished. "You're not bad."

"Are you going to tell me how close I am?"

"No. Not now, anyway."

"How do we reach the site? I can't believe it's anywhere near the surface."

"I could make you walk down the stairs . . ."

I groaned, if only for effect.

". . . but the elevator is easier."

"And if I don't behave, you'll make me walk back up."

"Exactly."

We walked down the inclined corridor, past closed doors, and I finally asked, "All the doors . . . laboratories, research spaces?"

"Largely. Some of them hold security systems. The level below this is all devoted to the site, in one way or another . . . except for the vehicle spaces at the north end."

The corridor ended at two elevator bays. One elevator door was open. The interior was spotless, with shimmering steel walls, and large enough to hold fifteen people without crowding. Since no one else was around, we had it to ourselves.

"Upper site level," Aimee ordered.

The wide elevator doors closed silently, and we headed downward.

"The site's never been uncovered?"

"No. We . . . Syntex was doing seismic mapping and what was below looked just like a city, except flattened. With all the storms, it seemed counterproductive and dangerous to conduct an open dig. Doing it all underground takes time."

"And far more money."

"In a way, but there are cost-savings in other areas."

When the elevator stopped, the rear wall split, and we stepped out into an open space facing yet another armored door. Aimee walked over to it and murmured something. It opened. Beyond was a cavernous space, with an arched roof over it. The roofed area had to extend another half kay to the south, although only one portion was lit, on what I judged to be the west side. The air was cool and dry, about fifteen degrees above freezing.

Aimee pointed. "That's where they're working now."

A woman in a white singlesuit stepped forward out of the dimness to our left. Her red hair was cut short. "Executive Vanslo?"

"Yes. This is Dr. Verano. He'll be accompanying us."

"I'm Elaysan Civer, Dr. Barro's assistant." She looked to me. "Doctor . . . are you an archaeologist?"

"An ecologist."

"I'm afraid we haven't done much along those lines, although we have preserved and stored all past organic remnants, fossilized, of course. After a hundred and twenty million years, it's fossilized or gone."

"I thought the site was some two hundred million years old," I offered.

"No, ser. We've done multiple datings."

A hundred twenty million years was long enough, I supposed, even as I wondered about the discrepancy in the Survey geologic records.

"How much is here?" asked Aimee.

"If the seismic maps are correct, the entire city—or town—was slightly more than a kay on a side. It was laid out as a square, but the vertices of the square were aligned, we think, to geographic cardinal points."

"To us, it would have looked like a diamond?" I asked.

"Yes. We would have seen it that way from above, if we oriented on due geographic north. Follow me, if you would. Please keep your feet on the walkway." Elaysan did something, and the lights in the roof above us went on.

I almost froze where I was. Somehow, I'd expected a rough brick wall, or something dilapidated, but I felt as though an immense seagoing vessel was pointed at me, if such a vessel had a hull of bright violet. The part of the walls that showed above the grayish brown stone out of which they rose extended less than five meters and continued to the southeast and southwest some hundred meters before reaching the cavern walls. *And they go on for another kay on each side?*

"Dr. Barro said we could go inside," Aimee said pleasantly.

"You can. So far, we've found nothing except the structure itself. Not a single artifact, unless there are some hidden in the walls."

"Is this typical of Builder (A) structures?" I asked.

"It is similar, but only in a general sense. Dr. Barro is reluctant to classify it firmly."

"I was under the impression that each of the forerunner cultures differed greatly from each other. If this one is similar . . ."

"You'd have to talk to the doctor about that." She paused, then said, "We've excavated down around the north corner, but we'll have to take the ramp to enter."

"No entrances in the side walls?" I asked.

Elaysan shook her head, continuing to walk toward the ramp ahead.

I didn't press the matter about the forerunner cultures, but continued to study the walls as we walked up the ramp, solid enough that it didn't shake under our steps, not in the slightest. When we passed over the wall, the lines were clean, and sharp. I'd been expecting something beyond the wall, but there wasn't, except that the bright violet extended smoothly from the walls as far as I could see. Apparently, this part of the city had been roofed.

"They covered everything?"

"Not exactly, Doctor." There was a hint of maliciousness in Elaysan's voice. "Please look ahead."

I did. There was an oval structure rising out of the violet. I couldn't tell how far back it was, but it was roughly twenty meters across the short dimension of the oval, and it wasn't colored violet, but a shade of green I couldn't determine.

I thought I understood, then, but I let Elaysan explain.

"The first archaeologists who excavated here didn't immediately understand how the city was designed. Except for the periodic oval entrance areas, it was entirely underground, just as our cities are today."

"That makes sense," offered Aimee.

I tried not to swallow. It made sense, and it didn't, and I wasn't about to say a word.

"You look surprised, Doctor," observed Elaysan.

"I am indeed." I didn't explain.

She looked satisfied.

As we neared the dark oval, I could see that every edge was gracefully rounded, in a way very similar to the way those buildings on the surface of Stittara were now. The green coloration of the synthetic stone—and it had to be a high-tech synthetic to have lasted so long—was close to the shade of the lichen/grass although it was hard to tell in the underground lighting. That made me even less happy.

The opening to the ancient city was only some two and a half meters high but almost ten wide, suggesting that the inhabitants had been differently sized and shaped from humans.

"Was there any form of door or gateway here?" I asked.

"There are suggestions that they may have used some organic-based material, perhaps similar to composite, but whatever it was vanished long before it was rediscovered." Elaysan handed each of us a headband with a lamp on it. "Inside, most passages are unlit. There are open shafts in places. So please stay away from the sides of the corridors. We will be taking the right-hand ramp once we go inside."

Once inside the entry building, I immediately felt more claustrophobic. The overhead was only a few decimeters above my head. The fact that the ramp and the corridor below into which we walked were almost a decameter wide didn't help. Nor did the fact that the rust-colored walls and the violet floor and overhead seemed to soak up light. I wondered why, but then realized that, despite their shiny-looking surfaces, they reflected very little light.

After less than a hundred meters, I suspected I'd seen enough. All that was left were empty chambers with low ceilings and overwide dimensions. As in Passova, the ancient forerunners had largely used ramps, but as Elaysan had warned, there were shafts in many places that might once have held the equivalent of elevators.

"I'm afraid that it's not nearly as interesting as it sounds to someone who hasn't seen it," our guide continued, "but so far it's all been like this."

"How many levels down are there?" I asked.

"In this part of the city, there are thirty. It appears as though it's the same elsewhere, but we haven't explored the southern part as much. It's tricky there, because there's an ancient fault that ran through or under the southern third."

"Is any of the city left there?"

"Oh . . . yes. It's as though it had been cracked into two sections."

"What is it made of?"

"It's a particularly good form of synthetic stone. The Unity Space Forces use something like it, but it's frightfully expensive."

Great. So when we're as extinct as the forerunners, when someone else comes along, all that will be left is the remnants of out-system fortifications and bases.

We plodded on and, a good hour later, emerged through another ramp and oval exit.

There a worn-looking graying man in another white singlesuit stood, waiting for us. He inclined his head to Aimee.

She returned the nod. "Dr. Barro, this is Dr. Verano. He's an ecologist."

"I'm pleased to meet you." Barro nodded brusquely to me, then turned back to Aimee. "What do you think, Executive Vanslo?"

"It's impressive . . . in a depressing way. Are there any indications of technology or materials we might use?"

"There are indications, but outside of the synthstone . . ." He shook his head. "It was stripped, I fear, one way or another, and then abandoned."

"Unless they used biologic technology," I suggested. "That theory has been advanced."

Barro nodded. "It's very possible. We've found some microscopic cellular fossils that are like nothing anyone has seen." He shook his head. "But those fragmentary fossils won't get you technology, biologic or otherwise."

"What about the local ecology around the building at that time? How did it get buried?"

"It's hard to say, but the mud that buried the site did preserve some vegetation that looks very much like the current lichen/grass. The color . . . I can't say, but the structure . . ."

"Was the site buried all at once?"

"No. There was an initial layer of mud close to ten meters thick, like a flash flood deposit, but after that . . . it was just accretion over time."

I didn't have much else to ask, and I listened as he and Aimee talked about the future of his work and what was necessary to keep the Antiquities Service from declaring it insufficient and claiming the site for the "good of the Unity."

More than a half stan later, we reentered the elevator.

"You were rather quiet, Paulo. At one point, you looked like you'd been hit by a skytube," said Aimee.

"I think I was . . ." I broke off my words. I hadn't meant to say that . . . or anything close.

"What do you mean?"

"It's not at all what I expected."

"I'd seen private linkshots, but it's not the same as being there."

"You're right about that. I couldn't have imagined what it was like."

"Did you learn anything that will help with your assignment?"

"I think so, but I'll need to check some historical records to be sure." *To provide documentary backup for what you already suspect is more like it.*

The front elevator doors opened, and we stepped out into the vacant area below the ramp.

"What now?" I asked.

"I need to see what security has discovered about our friend Gybl—and if he's who and what he claims he is. I definitely have my doubts." Her tone was sardonic. "You'll have to wait. I'm sorry, but . . ."

"I understand. You've been more than accommodating, and I can certainly change my schedule to fit what you need to do." *Not that I have any choice.* But I still meant it.

We were about halfway back to the security office, when a security type, wearing the Syntex maroon, naturally, walked toward us from the side corridor. "Executive Vanslo . . ."

I frowned. Had I heard . . . I turned and looked to see a face that shouldn't have been familiar, but almost was . . . not quite, but it was enough.

I literally threw myself at him, just as he raised the black weapon in his right hand.

Something jolted across the edge of my shoulder, just the edge, but the pain was so excruciating that my entire body stiffened and I crashed into him . . . and then . . . there was nothing.

37

I woke up looking at a very gray ceiling . . . and I instantly knew who'd shot me. Nothing like being jolted into awareness.

A medtech was watching me. "Don't move. You'll hurt yourself." She stood and touched a small console beside the bed on which I discovered I was lying.

I also discovered I'd been stripped to my undershorts and covered with a sheet up to my chest . . . and my entire body throbbed. My entire right arm burned and tingled simultaneously, from the top of my right shoulder all the way down to my fingertips. I tried to move them. They did move, but that intensified the burning so much that it became almost unbearable.

"Even little movements of that arm will hurt horribly," the medtech informed me.

"I just discovered that, but I wanted to see if my fingers worked."

"That's good. It would have been better if you had waited."

In moments, Aimee stepped into the room and walked over to the bed, a bit stiffly, I thought. She also looked a shade less . . . crisp. She turned to the medtech. "If you'd give us some time." Her words weren't a request.

The medtech inclined her head, then stepped out of the room.

Aimee waited, then said, "I might owe you my life."

"I don't think so. I might have given you time."

"You moved faster than I could have believed. If I didn't know better . . ."

"You already know that I'm who I am." I never would have believed that just keeping in shape and practicing Juchai would get me mistaken for something I wasn't and had never been. I hadn't planned on paying these sorts of prices for male vanity. "You finished him off, didn't you? Preconditioned defense responses?"

"Sometimes . . . you're really good, even when you can't move. How did you know what he was so quickly?"

"I realized that I recognized his face, and I shouldn't have. There was no way he could have been a Syntex security guard. Where am I?"

"In the main Syntex medical facility. Josef redlined the flitter. It was touch and go for a bit. If that nerver had been three centimeters closer to your heart . . . or if you weren't in such good physical condition . . . the Survey Service would have needed another consultant."

"It was Sinjon Reksba, wasn't it?"

"Yes and no. We don't know who he was. He has to be a replacement for the original Sinjon, a professional who's been given a full makeover to match the original, including complete skin grafts in all the areas where DNA sampling takes place . . . or where the Stittaran samplers are programmed."

"Is he still alive?"

"Yes, but it won't help, not in the short term. He's been programmed into amnesia. Being captured triggered it."

"All that's almost prohibitively expensive. You're playing for enormous stakes."

"I'm afraid so. That's why I won't tell you more."

"How long will I be laid up?"

"Until tomorrow at the earliest."

"Are you considering turning the site over to the Antiquities Commission on your terms?"

"We've considered it." Aimee's voice was neutral.

"But you're not about to consider anything like that until you're certain that it contains nothing of commercial possibilities and that your other difficulties are resolved . . . or you have to in order to preclude a larger area of condemnation."

"That's close enough."

"I don't think you're going to find anything commercial down there."

"It doesn't look that way."

"But you can't make a decision until everything's been explored . . . or you'll face an internal battle that will claim you gave something away."

Aimee smiled. "I did tell you that you were good already."

I got the message. "Thank you."

"You're to stay here. You're not to move until you're told. You'll have guest quarters here. You can leave tomorrow, if the doctor approves." She paused. "Thank you. I mean it."

"You're welcome."

She smiled once more, a friendly warm expression, then turned and left.

The medtech returned immediately. "You still aren't supposed to move much."

"I understand." And I really didn't want to.

Another hour passed before she let me sit up.

I'd hoped to see Aimee again, just to see if I could find out more, but I didn't. I received very kind treatment, a small but very well-prepared evening meal, and well-appointed guest quarters. And I did have to sign a standard confidentiality agreement, but only regarding the forerunner site, which I found interesting.

Before I left on fourday, the Syntex doctor was very clear.

"You'll feel like you're on edge for a few days, maybe a week. You'll be tired, and you may have trouble sleeping. Stay away from stimulants or depressants. Try not to take another jolt, even from a standard stunner. Your system won't recover fully for a good month. Another nerve jolt of any kind in the next week or so might trigger partial paralysis . . . or worse."

I knew exactly what he meant, but the fact that he even considered I might be in a position to be stunned was anything but reassuring.

"That's right. It's unlikely, but it could be fatal."

That was all I needed to know. I could be stunned . . . and die. That left me feeling even more on edge when I left Syntex behind the antiquated steering wheel of the Survey Service van.

I'd already contacted Aloris late the day before telling her that matters at Syntex had taken longer than I had expected. I'd also rescheduled my meeting with GenArt to the following oneday, and leaving Syntex at just after midday meant that I wouldn't get much done when I returned to Passova.

As I drove northward on the permacrete highway, I couldn't help but think over what I'd learned at the forerunner site and what had happened afterward. The fact that the ecology was similar enough to the present, and the fact that what had been exposed to the elements had been shaped to deal with winds—120 million years earlier—offered some unsettling possibilities. I needed to see if the historical records—and Geneil Paak—could either support or reject my tentative thesis.

38

Although I'd hoped to do some work when I got back from Syntex, the doctor had been right. I was tired, and I just checked the van in and went to my temporary guest quarters, where I used the inadequate synthesizer for a small dinner, and then went to bed. I did sleep, if periods of unconsciousness punctuated by the same nightmare of being nerved by a faceless security type in maroon qualified as sleep, and woke up early on fiveday, somewhat less exhausted.

I was in my Survey office early, even before Aloris or Raasn, because I wanted to link to Belk Edo at RDAEX. He didn't take my call immediately, but returned it less than fifteen minutes later.

"Dr. Verano, what can I do for you?"

"I had some general questions about aerial and upper atmospheric sampling."

"Yes." His tone was absolutely neutral, as was his facial expression.

"I've gone over the sampling reports filed with the Survey, and it appears as though there has never been a successful sampling anywhere close to a skytube, at least in the atmosphere. How successful have you been in sampling above them?"

He didn't answer me, just looked pleasantly at me from the screen.

I waited.

He said nothing.

"I could go to the Planetary Council and ask for orbit station records of extra-atmospheric flights."

"You could."

"How many magfield shuttles did you lose?" I had him with that question, because somewhere there had to be a record of that. All aerial or orbital craft accidents had to be reported, and with satellite links, there was no way to avoid it, but I was angling for the follow-up question.

"Two."

"With all data lost?"

"That's a matter of multi privacy, Doctor."

"Thank you."

"You're most welcome. Is there anything else?"

"For the moment, no."

Edo smiled, pleasantly, but he couldn't quite make his eyes match the rest of his face. "Then . . . until we talk again."

The screen blanked.

By his response, he was willing to let me know, very much off the record, and in a way that could never be used in any proceeding, that they had collected some data, and that it had cost them two magfield shuttles—two very expensive magfield shuttles. He wasn't happy about letting me know, but he'd judged that totally stonewalling me would likely cause more problems. His nonadmission admission told me that RDAEX thought obtaining such data was extremely important . . . and potentially extraordinarily profitable. The other implications worried me even more, though.

I was about to put a link through to Geneil Paak when Aloris appeared in my doorway.

"Yes."

"You've been very busy . . ."

"I have been . . . and everything at Syntex took so much longer than I'd ever expected." That was certainly true, and I hoped that she took it the way I tried to convey. "And then there was the business with the fitness centers. I was trying to look for somewhere to work out . . . and all the fitness centers . . . well . . . they weren't what I'd have called fitness centers . . ."

Aloris laughed. "You should have tried looking up Physical Enhancement

Centers. There are a number of quite pleasant ones. All with individual private facilities, of course."

Physical enhancement centers? "Private mini-exercise facilities?" For a moment that didn't seem to make sense. Then I nodded. "Anything public becomes too competitive for men?"

"And for some women."

"And fitness centers are covert fight clubs?"

"So it's said."

I shook my head.

"How did things go at Syntex?"

"Long. I went to see their forerunner site. I was hoping to see if their excavations revealed anything unusual about the ecological history of Stittara. All that took longer than I planned. They were kind enough to give me quarters the night before last, but I didn't leave there until early midafternoon yesterday." Some of that she already knew, but I was trying to see her reactions.

"Were you successful in finding anything?"

"More than I expected, but less than I'd hoped." I managed a rueful smile. "Isn't it always that way?"

"You were in early this morning, Dermotte said."

"I was trying to catch up before I go to ABP."

"Oh . . . the repairs on your quarters are done. You can return any time."

"I just might do that."

"If you need anything . . . we're here to help."

"Thank you."

Then I put a link through to Geneil Paak. Since I'd met her in person, I didn't need to go down there, and I really didn't want to walk that far down . . . and especially back up, not when I'd likely be walking around ABP before long. She wasn't there.

So I made sure I had transport to ABP, and then tried to search out the geologic records I wanted. I couldn't find them, and I was getting frustrated, and more than edgy, when the console screen told me Geneil was returning my call.

I accepted.

She looked concerned. "Was there a problem with my list?"

"No. Not in the slightest. Believe it or not, I have some geology questions for you that relate to my assignment."

Her face registered mild surprise.

"I just got back from visiting the Syntex forerunner site and talking to the archaeologists there . . ." I went on to explain what Barro had told me, then asked, "Is there any way to determine if that sudden mud flood was local, regional, continental . . ."

She almost laughed. "We'd have to drill to that depth all over the planet . . . and probably deeper."

"I was afraid of that. What about seismic studies?"

"For single layer of ten meters down about a hundred meters . . . that would require an environmental impact that the Survey would find unacceptable . . . and costs no one would want to fund. We don't get much help from the planet, either, because Stittara has comparatively few large shifts in tectonic plates or that much volcanism."

"I've wondered about that. How can that be? The core is larger and warmer than normal for a T-type world and plate shifts and volcanism are far lower?"

"It just could be that we're living in a stable period. We've only been here a thousand years. There have definitely been large movements and great volcanism in the past. The other forerunner sites—and there are probably a lot more we know nothing about . . . The old scans are suggestive, but we don't have the money, and neither does the Antiquities Commission." She frowned, then shook her head ruefully. "Just a moment."

I wondered what I'd said, but I sat and waited while she did something at the side of the screen.

After several minutes, she looked up. "I totally forgot. I tend to focus on the question people ask. You asked about planet or continent-wide data. We do have geologic data on the four sites controlled by the Antiquities Commission. I've sent you what we have. It's not very detailed, except in a few places, but it might help."

"Thank you."

"If you have any questions about it, let me know."

"I will."

I made sure that I'd received the data, but didn't look at it, and hurried off to the Survey vehicle bays. I had to check out a tunnel runabout to get to ABP, because it was a good five kays out west of Passova along a feeder tunnel, and that took longer than I'd thought, even though I'd reserved it earlier. I suppose I could have taken a tunneltram, but after the two previous days, I thought I deserved a little less hassle—except that I merely traded one form for another.

In the end, I was five minutes late when I walked through the main pressure door at ABP. It didn't matter, because I had to wait fifteen minutes for Erik Engola to show up.

Erik was short, with a deep honey-colored skin. When he said, "Dr. Verano," his voice was deep enough that it actually rumbled. "How can I help you?"

I explained.

When I finished, he smiled politely. "You're welcome to look at anything, measure anything, ask any questions. We're an infotech multi, the only one on Stittara. The only emissions we have are standard air-filtration emission systems and a fair amount of offgassing from the reformulation of unrepairable equipment into component materials and elements. All the water used for cooling is completely closed cycle through horizontal subsurface piping with a complete monitoring system . . ."

When he finished, I smiled, and we headed off.

Four hours later I was done, and he was right.

We shook hands, and I drove the runabout, or monitored it as it largely drove itself, back to the Survey Service bay. I did make one stop, to get something to eat from a place that was the worst of all the eateries I'd sampled. I should have known from the name—Home Cookery. Once I parked the runabout, I blanked the authorization, and then walked back to my office.

There, I sat down in the swivel and took a deep breath.

I was shivering a bit and exhausted. So I just closed my eyes for several minutes.

"Paulo . . . are you all right?"

I must have dozed, but Aloris's voice jolted me awake. "I'm more tired than I thought. The past few days have been long."

"You don't have to do it all at once, you know. You have a year to finish the assignment. For practical purposes, I mean." She remained standing just inside the office door.

"That's true, if I want a direct ley-liner back to Bachman. Though there must be a few others that go directly elsewhere."

"There are three or four scheduled every year, and another few that aren't."

I nodded.

"You could go to your quarters and rest."

"If I get that tired, I will." I smiled.

Once she left, I called up the data that Geneil had sent.

There were four known forerunner sites on Stittara in addition to the Syntex site, but there were more than fifty other suspected sites based on rough early geoscanning. I nodded. I'd already known that. The four known sites were closed to outside investigation and were under study by the Antiquities Commission. That translated into the fact that they were guarded and minimal work was occurring because initial exploration had revealed little of potential technological interest and because, as Geneil had said, money was tight, especially for sites that likely held only structural ruins.

The limited geological data did indicate that at each of the known sites, the "covered wall structure" had been buried under a mud flow or the equivalent. The depth of those ancient mud flows was not given. There was no data on the other sites, except more notations that exploration of the sites appeared unfeasible at any time soon.

Mud flows or something like them at the five sites with some excavation, located well away from each other, three on Conuno, and two on Contrio, and all of the same approximate age. That was more than coincidence, but not necessarily conclusive. I did find it disturbing.

There was something else at the back of my mind, something that ought to tie into it, but I couldn't quite grasp it. That might have been because I was having trouble concentrating, and my eyes were blurring. And the little shakes that came and went were getting stronger.

Like it or not, I'd have to call it a day.

As I got up to return to my quarters, and to move my even more limited personal clothes and effects from the temporary quarters, I wondered how long I'd be suffering the aftereffects of "Reksba's" nerve tangler.

39

Aloris, Haaran, and Raasn sat around a corner table at Invireo.

"You said something interesting happened today. What was it?" asked Haaran.

"Something unusual happened at Syntex. Verano was there two days, when he only planned on one. He didn't want to talk about it. He just said that his visit to the forerunner site took longer than he'd anticipated and that he'd had to stay over. Then he talked about having trouble finding a gym."

"I said he worked out," Raasn commented.

"And what do you think all that means?" asked Haaran.

"Since when has any multi, especially Syntex, been that solicitous to an outsider when they weren't invited?"

"Maybe he was invited and didn't tell you."

"That doesn't make sense. He said that he'd hoped what he saw there would help with his ecological assignment. I don't see Syntex inviting a consultant to dig up something that could cause them trouble. Then . . . there was the other thing. He looks exhausted, as if he hadn't slept much, and he was shivering . . . or trembling . . . all over. Just little shakes. You almost couldn't see them."

"You obviously did," said Raasn dryly.

Haaran grinned.

Aloris's eyes hardened as she looked at her son.

"I didn't say a word."

"You didn't have to."

"Little shakes. That sounds like a heavy stunner hit," offered Haaran.

"You would know," said Raasn.

"That was years ago."

"How would Verano take a stunner hit at Syntex?" questioned Aloris.

"Maybe he wasn't at Syntex."

"I checked the van logs. He drove straight there. No one touched the van until he got back in on the early afternoon of the next day."

"But . . . if they stunned him . . . why wouldn't they just turn him over to the Council patrollers? And if they didn't . . . who did? And how could that happen at a multi as tightly guarded as Syntex?" asked Haaran.

"Exactly," said Raasn. "Perhaps you and Amarios might make a few . . . quiet inquiries."

"We can see." Haaran frowned, checking the time. "She should be coming on in a few minutes."

"Then we'll enjoy the set," said Aloris. "We can talk about what you two might be able to do later."

Haaran nodded.

40

I woke early on sixday, rested enough that my body was no longer shaking or trembling. I was also glad to be back in the regular guest quarters with the view of outside, but I did skip my exercises . . . and felt guilty for doing so, even though I told myself two days off wouldn't matter. The entire interior smelled . . . well . . . new . . . or newly templated, but I had to admit that the bed had been most comfortable, and the color scheme of the rooms was now largely unified.

I made some breakfast and ate it, then made another mug of tea and trundled—that was the way it felt—up to the study, where I looked out on what passed for the dawn. Then I used the projection screen to check the local news . . . since I hadn't been checking much of anything for the past several days. I didn't see or hear anything of world-shaking importance . . . or interest, especially not the korfball semifinals. The one glance I had before switching views showed something that looked like noncontact roundball in a circle.

Sitting in the comfortable swivel, I might have dozed off for a bit, but it was sixday.

When I came out of my daze . . . or doze, I rose and walked over to the armaglass portal, and for the first time in over a week, perhaps two, I saw Ilsabet walking along the grass on the top of the low ridge. In moments, she had vanished from sight, followed by her guard/guardian.

Could she shed any light on any possible environmental changes? *How would you know unless you ask her?* Getting permission to ask her . . . I smiled. Certainly, either Zerlyna or Aloris would know. My initial impulse was to ask Zerlyna, but I set that aside and let my subconscious work on that. There was no point in worrying about it until oneday, because there was likely little way to get to Ilsabet on the weekend—except unofficially, and I was in no shape to try any unofficial means. Besides, there was no reason to do so.

Although I had yet to meet with GenArt, it was likely the smallest of the multis, and from everything I'd seen and measured so far, none of the multis were creating violations of environmental standards. Next, I needed to determine if any were altering the environment in a way that made significant changes. Then I'd have to determine whether the outies had a negative effect, and there was the remaining question of whether the skytubes were an organic entity or entities and threatened by humans. Looked at in that way, I still had a lot to accomplish, although I already had the definite feeling that the skytubes had some sort of organic organizing principle. I had a strong hunch that RDAEX believed that as well, although RDAEX hadn't, to my knowledge, or to the Survey's, done anything that would have harmed the skytubes. More importantly, I didn't have any evidence, so far, only a feeling, that the skytubes were an organic entity and a living part of the ecosystem, and I had doubts that I would be able to obtain any. The only evidence along those lines was that no one had been able to sample a skytube, but the violence of a storm didn't necessarily prove that it was alive, only that it was violent.

Then, I recalled that somewhere in my sleep or dreaming I'd glimpsed something, but I couldn't remember it . . . only that it made sense. I could have done without just the conclusion. I didn't need to remember a conclusion without recalling what I'd discovered that had made sense. If I'd remembered the insight, I could analyze it and decide, while I was fully awake, that it didn't. Or I could determine that it did and get on with seeing if, sensible or not, it was relevant to something.

When I finally walked away from the window, I realized I was still sore and a bit tired. So I sat down in the swivel and considered what I'd learned, and not learned at Syntex. The multi was thinking about turning the forerunner site over to the Antiquities Commission . . . or at least making noises about it. Why? For a multi that size, the expenditure on maintaining the site and the archaeologists wasn't that significant. It couldn't be. So what did Aimee and her mother have to gain? Or was I too jaded? Might it actually be for altruistic reasons?

I shook my head. I had definite doubts about that. But that aspect of matters had very little, if anything, to do with my assignment. Nor did the fact that Aimee Vanslo and her family were dealing with a particularly deadly form of multi politics. I didn't see any direct connection with my assignment, but I'd still have to keep my eyes open.

41

I spent the rest of the weekend resting, thinking, and doing a few hours more research at my Survey office . . . and slowly working back into exercising, glad that I had enough space that I didn't have to search out a gym or "physical enhancement facility." Then on oneday morning I launched into the official workweek with my rescheduled appointment at GenArt. The meeting and subsequent tour of GenArt, with the measurements I took, were largely perfunctory, and almost a waste, except for allowing me to state that I'd toured all the multis listed as "significant" on the Survey Service's database. Aloris had been right about GenArt not doing much beyond fiddling with a nail additive. At least, it seemed that way to me. I was back in my Survey spaces by a little after one in the afternoon, and that included a quick lunch.

My next step was to review all the data on the various municipalities. That wasn't spelled out in the contract, but I wanted to make certain that they hadn't been cited for violations or for environmental discharges or adverse impacts. After another two hours, it was clear I wasn't going to find any violations. If something else came up, I could always go back and dig deeper.

In an attempt to tie up yet another loose end, I walked over to Zerlyna's cramped office. She looked up as I entered.

"You must have a special need," she said.

"Why? Because I'm here, rather than linking you?"

"It's a good guess, I'd say."

"Better than good. Do you remember when I told you about seeing someone outside . . . and you told me about Ilsabet?"

Zerlyna frowned. "Both Aloris and I told you about her."

"That's right. How would I arrange to be able to talk to her? You did say that she could be interviewed."

"Hmmm . . . I don't know, but I can find out. What reason should I give?"

"I'd like her impressions of the environment. So far as you told me, she's one of the oldest people on Stittara, for whatever reason. Part of my assignment is to see if there have been changes. It couldn't hurt her to see if she recalls anything."

"No . . . probably not."

"You don't sound convinced."

"How will that help with the factual side of your report? Hearsay doesn't count for much in official documents."

"It won't, but it could point me to where I might look. Or it might not tell me anything."

She nodded. "I'll see what I can do."

When I got back to my office, I took out the listing of outie settlements that Geneil had provided—with their directions—and began to plot their locations on the continental maps. That took almost an hour. Then I added the topographic maps. Then I overlaid the official town, city, and settlement maps. More than three-quarters of the outie settlements from Geneil's listing weren't on the "official maps." That was definitely a cause for worry. I did print out a hard copy of the combined and overlaid maps.

From there I selected the outie settlements within three hours ground travel that looked promising. All that map work, and my eyes began to blur. So I sat back for a moment and tried to think about what I might have missed. With all that flooded into my mind, I decided that wasn't a good idea.

At that moment Aloris walked into my office. "You're looking a lot more rested today," she observed. "How are the refurbished quarters?"

"Quite nice, and the new bed is very comfortable. The color scheme is . . . more unified. Did you have something to do with that?"

She gave a short laugh. "My talents don't lie in that area. I asked Amarios to help. She has good taste."

"It's a great improvement. Give her my thanks."

"You can yourself, if you'd like. I'm having a little get-together at my place on sevenday evening. Would you like to join us?"

"I would indeed." *If not necessarily for the normal reasons.* But then, I doubted that she was asking for the normal reasons, either, skeptical man that I was.

"Around half past six. I'll link you the address." She paused. "You'd mentioned that you might be traveling to some of the outie settlements . . ."

"I did."

"You might want to check with Jorl about which ones might be . . . suitable."

"You mean safe?"

"Some are not."

"I haven't seen any news stories suggesting that."

"It's difficult to cover places that officially don't exist."

"I've noticed that more than a few settlements aren't on the official maps. How does the Planetary Council justify that?"

"They're patrolled, and Survey enforcement assures that they don't have negative impacts, but the government doesn't provide any services, and the outies have to provide the links infrastructure there."

"Not legal ones?"

"They're legal. The Council's comm enforcers are effective, but the addresses aren't in the databases."

"They're almost off the map, then?"

"Off the official maps." She paused. "The Planetary Council might not be terribly pleased about references to settlements that aren't supposed to be there."

I couldn't help but frown. "Is there anything in the Planetary Charter that forbids such settlements?" I hadn't seen anything, but there might have been an amendment or a later requirement.

"No."

I thought for a moment. "They're concerned about the representation provisions."

"Wouldn't you be?"

If I were the Council, I'd definitely have been concerned. "How do the outlanders feel?"

"To date, they haven't insisted on representation beyond voting for the Council."

"But the only outlanders voting are those in the recognized settlements?"

"As of the last election."

From the various news reports, and from what I'd overheard, I knew there was an election scheduled at the end of the current planetary year. "You seem to know a great deal about this."

"Amarios is half outlander. She has an interest. That means Haaran does."

And that means you do. "Given all that, I think I need to visit the outie settlements sooner rather than later."

Aloris nodded.

"Thank you."

When she left, I linked Jorl Algeld. He wasn't available, and I left a request that he return my call. Then I went to work on trying to determine what other outland communities from Geneil's list might provide more geographic and ecological diversity.

I was still working on that when Algeld returned my link, and I accepted the call.

"What can I do for you, Doctor?" On the link screen, Algeld looked even more like an ancient Terran bulldog, his round face intent and joined to his body by a neck so short his head and torso seemed almost one piece.

"The next phase of my assignment requires evaluating outland settlements to determine what impact they may have on the ecology. Director Raasn suggested I contact you before firming up my itineraries."

"I'm glad you did. Some of them . . . Well, I'd be happier if some of my people accompanied you to those particular places."

I didn't ask which ones those were, instead saying, "The first three I'd planned to visit were Doones, Hobbes, and Thoreau." They had good classical names for what I suspected were rather rustic outposts, but I saw no point in mentioning that.

"Doones shouldn't be a problem." Algeld paused, as if uncertain how to phrase his next words. "Hobbes and Thoreau . . . they're a bit different."

"That may be, but I'll need a large sample of outland communities, and they need to include the good, the bad, and the indifferent, so to speak."

"You should be safe enough in those three communities. I would appreciate it if you'd check with me before going into any others not listed officially."

Again . . . not listed officially. "I'll still need to visit some of those that might not be as accessible."

"I understand, Doctor. We'll work something out." He paused. "I would caution you against traveling any of the unpaved ways after dark. There are places that can be treacherous in less than full light."

"I'll keep that in mind."

"Good." Then he was gone.

I'd received a link from Zerlyna while I'd been talking to Algeld, and I immediately returned it.

"You linked?"

"You're in luck." Zerlyna smiled, an expression of success. "Ilsabet— she's officially Elisabetta Vonacht—is a ward of the Stittaran Ministry of Health. At first, they weren't pleased about granting an interview. When I explained the purpose, they agreed that a short interview would be acceptable, subject to conditions. I've sent the conditions to your console. You'll have to certify compliance. You have a maximum of one standard hour on threeday at ten in the morning. Oh . . . the address is with the other material."

"Thank you. I do appreciate it."

By then, people were beginning to leave for the day, but I wanted to finish up some things I hadn't had a chance to do because I'd been effectively laid up for part of the weekend.

I did another search on the new special assistant to the Ministry of Technology and Transport, and nothing came up on Torgan Brad, except his name and position. For comparison, I did a search on me. I was listed as a "special consultant" to the Systems Survey Service, but there was also a bio—and a publications listing. That was interesting, because the bio was longer and more inclusive than the one I'd provided Aloris, and I'd never provided a pubs listing.

I also did a search on patroller reports, to see if arrests and detentions by the patrollers of the Planetary Council were listed. They were. Then I searched for Sinjon Reksba, but found only two mentions, one in a legal matter, naming him as the heir-apparent to a land holding on Conuno. I couldn't tell where from the description, although I could have searched it out, I supposed. The second was the landing list from the *Persephonya*. I did a search for the name of a man arrested for assault . . . and his name came up on the patroller report. That was highly suggestive, but not conclusive.

I knew that there were several connections that I was missing, and that was one of the most frustrating results of my run-in with "Reksba" and his nerver. I knew I knew things, or had known them, and I couldn't recall what I was missing. I could only hope that as my body and nerves healed I'd remember.

For some reason, I was in the mood for meat, and I finally closed down the console and decided to have dinner at Rancho Rustico.

42

On twoday morning, I was just finishing my tea while preparing to shower and then dress when something on the local news caught both my ears and eyes.

> *"Late yesterday afternoon, after reviewing satscans of a vehicle apparently stalled or damaged in an uninhabited grassland area over three hundred kays southeast of Passova, authorities sent a team to investigate. When the outland patrol team arrived, they found a body near an abandoned personal landcrawler . . . Initial identification found on the body, and the vehicle registration, suggested the dead man was Sinjon Reksba, an heir to a Stittaran land trust who had recently returned to Stittara. Authorities have determined that skin DNA matches that on file for Reksba, but tissue DNA does not. There is no record on Stittara of the dead man's genetic profile."*

I kept watching and listening.

> *". . . the dead man had been caught trespassing on the private lands of the Syntex forerunner archaeological reserve and briefly detained before being released . . . StittaranNews has verified that more than a dozen Syntex employees and a freelance documentarian all saw the man escorted to his landcrawler and watched him*

*drive away . . . preliminary cause of death is thought to be extreme
dehydration . . . Trust authorities in Passova are now reviewing
the inheritance claimed by the apparently false heir . . ."*

I winced as I considered what had obviously happened while I had
been unconscious. Since "Sinjon's" capture had triggered amnesia, I suspected that Aimee and someone had essentially programmed a series of
compulsions into the would-be killer, enough to have him drive well out
of sight . . . and then paralyze him or something else . . . and let him die
of natural causes. Even if he'd been found while alive, there would have
been no way to refute what had been staged.

I couldn't help but smile, if ironically, at how Aimee had used Rob Gybl.
She'd likely denied him access, but allowed him to see, but doubtless not to
record, the incident with "Sinjon," so that he could have a story on how the
ruthless bureaucrats at Syntex were denying all access to the forerunner site.

At the same time, it was just a bit too coincidental that they both
arrived almost simultaneously, and I could see that my arrival—even
though that had been Aimee's doing—also dovetailed, yet I didn't see
how she could have forecast or maneuvered that. Still, if Gybl had been
part of a team, he'd certainly been given a rather stiff warning. I certainly
wasn't involved in whatever plot involved Aimee, her mother, and Syntex
or VLE, and considering how coldly and effectively Aimee had operated,
I had no desire to go back. None at all.

Once I got to my office, I immediately made arrangements for use of a
Survey van for threeday—after I had my interview with Ilsabet—and then
went to work on setting up a matrix format suitable for use with my link,
and one from which I could upload or download field data as necessary.

I did get a link from Geneil Paak wanting to know if the geologic data she
sent had been helpful, and I assured her that it had been. She even apolo-
gized for not being able to be more helpful. I did my best to reassure her.

While I waited for a time, after doing more work on refining the parameters for my outland field studies, I eventually did a news search on
Sinjon Reksba, but while there were a number of stories, and a great deal
of speculation, none of them revealed anything new, except that the
"original" Sinjon had left Stittara under what might have been called dubious circumstances . . . something to do with having promised to marry
two women, each from a different and rival outland family. His departure

had resulted in heavy damages being required of his family . . . but that had been two centuries earlier, and his brother had died young, leaving the lands in trust.

In midafternoon, my screen registered "Incoming—Unknown."

I jabbed the accept stud, rather than say it, wondering who was linking me.

The image that came up was that of Kali Artema—exactly the same as it had been the first time we'd met, black security suit, black hair, and dark gray eyes.

"Hello, Paulo. I'm here in Passova for the evening. I know it's short notice. Could I interest you in joining me for dinner?"

I didn't have to think twice. "I would. Where and when . . . or am I supposed to decide?"

"I hope you don't mind, but since you took me out the last time, I thought I'd return the favor. Boudica, at seven? It's in the northeast."

"I'll be there."

She smiled. "Good." Then she was gone.

Since I didn't have the faintest idea exactly what Boudica was or where, I did a search and discovered that the name referred to a warrior queen of the distant past and a very upscale restaurant not all that far from Ojolian's, which meant a moderate tunneltram ride, not that I minded.

Then I went back to finishing off what I started with the outland parameters.

After work I did clean up and changed into one of my new singlesuits, black with gray trim, since that color combination seemed to be her preference.

I arrived at Boudica at ten before seven. As soon as I set foot inside, I discovered that while the name might have been ancient, the decor was not. The walls were draped in folds of an ivory fabric, with tasteful abstract designs in silver, edged in thin black lines. The chairs and presumably the tables were wood, dark cherry synthwood, but expensive synthetic, upholstered in black. Table linens matched the ivory of the walls, and the carpet was ivory, with swirling black loops.

"May I help you?" asked the hostess, who wore a short black jacket over an ivory ankle-length dress.

"I'm expecting someone. I don't know if the reservations are under Verano or Artema."

"They're under both, sir. Do you wish to wait here or at your table?"

"Here . . . I think."

After looking around, just to make sure, I didn't see Kali. So I stepped back, then saw her enter, by herself. For a moment I thought she'd changed to a black outfit similar to the one she'd worn at our last dinner, but then I realized she'd simply added a tailored black jacket over the security singlesuit, but on her, the black on black looked dressy.

"Kali, I'm here." Although my words sounded banal to me, I stepped forward.

"I'm flattered," were the first words that followed her smile.

I shrugged in confusion. "I don't know why."

"I said I was flattered because you obviously changed into a singlesuit that I said I liked."

Of course. She'd seen me in the gray when she linked that afternoon.

"Are you ready?" asked the hostess.

I nodded.

As we followed the hostess, I noted that the music came from an actual live string quartet, not that I recognized what they performed, only that it was what I'd have called classical semiromantic, just loud enough to mute and obscure conversations other than one's own.

We ended up at a table for two in a nook along the wall, but all the tables were in isolated nooks. Once the hostess had seated us, I looked across the table at Kali. I thought she looked a little tired, but I was glad she was there. I only asked, "How did you find this place?"

"I cheated. One of the pilots on the ley-liner out from Teppera told me about it. Her cousin owns it."

"That sounds like a story. A restaurant named after a warrior queen owned by a Tepperan on Stittara. And I've been invited by a warrior queen . . . or the current equivalent."

"Not a queen."

"Close enough."

She almost blushed, I thought. Instead, she said, "Life is strange, and at its strangest, stranger than fiction."

"Such as an ecologist from Bachman sitting with a Tepperan officer on detached duty to a Unity multilateral on Stittara? You're what, a light colonel, senior major?"

"Senior major, but I'm not combat services."

"Don't you all get combat training and rotation into combat billets?"

"Just as junior officers. I also took basic flight training, both space and atmospheric."

Before I could pursue that, the server arrived. I deferred to Kali and followed her recommendations, settling on a mushroom bisque, and a mango curried fowl pasta, except I ordered a Zantos, rather than wine. Her wine and my lager arrived immediately.

I lifted my beaker. "To a good dinner and better company."

She nodded and lifted her goblet.

We didn't touch glass. That would have been too familiar, but we both smiled before we sipped our drinks.

"So . . . security is your specialty."

"Security, with logistics as a secondary. They go hand in hand."

"I can see that." I could sense someone looking at me and took a quick glance to the side. The woman at the nearest table kept looking at me, staring in fact. She was blond, and attractive, and probably within a few years of my age. I looked back at Kali.

"Most people don't. They see logistics as supply."

"In a conflict, if you know the enemy's logistics, you know what they can do, and what they can't. The same is true in planning security, I'd imagine." I tried to ignore the stares of the blonde.

I tried to concentrate on Kali, but I could feel the blonde's eyes, and it made me uncomfortable. I couldn't help wondering if women felt that way when I'd looked at them, except I didn't think I'd stared the way the blonde was.

Abruptly Kali turned her head and looked at the blonde. I don't know what was in that look, but the blonde immediately rose and moved away, catching a server, clearly protesting. The server looked at Kali, then back at the blonde, and said something. The blonde walked away, clearly upset . . . and shaken. I had my suspicions about what had happened, but I was glad it had.

"Thank you," I said. "I didn't know what to say without being really rude."

"You were actually squirming." She offered a friendly and sympathetic smile. "I've seen it here and there on Stittara before between local women and offworlders, but you handle it better, I think."

"It's happened to me before," I admitted. "What is it? Do you know?"

She shook her head. "You're the ecologist."

"Can you tell me why you're in Passova this time? Not that I'm not happy to see you."

"The official reason was to order some special templates."

"From Valior?"

"Who else?"

"You had another reason?" I managed to keep my face as guileless as I could.

"Paulo." That was all she said.

"Yes . . . I did read some intriguing information that came my way. Fragmentary information about a research project that appears to be more than it has been represented as . . ."

"And?"

"I couldn't say why, but it scares me to hell, screaming the entire way, so to speak."

"Theoretically, why might that be?"

"The way I interpret it . . . the intersection of high-energy penetration tools with a high-energy barrier field suggests the possibility of an even higher energy reaction. I'm no physicist, but . . ." I shrugged. "There's also another matter that might bear on it as well. There was one person I never met and barely saw onboard the *Persephonya*. I don't know if he has anything to do with your concerns, but when RDAEX hires one of the top scientists in high-energy photonics and sends him to Stittara—"

"How did you know that?"

"The fact that he was hired is public knowledge. All disembarkations are available. Some of his older publications showed up in the Unity data dump . . . and RDAEX wouldn't hire any but the best . . . and they certainly wouldn't send them here unless it was vital."

"Go on. I'm sorry I interrupted."

"As I was saying . . ." I offered what I hoped was an embarrassed grin. "When the Ministry of Technology then sends a special assistant on the same ship . . . and when there's absolutely no information about him, except his name . . . well . . . what do you think?"

"The same as you do, I'm afraid."

For a moment, looking at the chill in Kali's eyes, I wondered if I were about to follow "Sinjon."

"It's not you," she said quickly, then stopped talking as our server and two tureens of mushroom bisque arrived.

We both tried the soup. Then we more than tried it.

"What do you think?" asked Kali, after setting aside her spoon.

"Excellent." I did notice the faintest hint of the heathery scent or flavor I'd experienced now and again. "What were you thinking a moment ago . . . when you looked ready to do battle?"

"About the Ministry of Technology."

"Has RDAEX experienced trouble there?"

"Belk told me to expect it when he learned Dr. Spek was arriving."

"Did he say why?"

She shook her head.

I didn't press her.

After several minutes, and several sips of her wine, Kali went on. "I'd like to ask a favor of you."

"If I can," I replied cautiously.

"If . . . if you find out anything about the skytubes that's not known, would it be possible to let me know?"

"For your benefit . . . or for the benefit of Belk or Haans?"

"Call it . . . my benefit . . . and possibly yours. I won't pass on anything you tell me unless you agree."

"Would you like to tell me why?"

"It would be far better for both of us if I didn't. I think you can guess." She straightened and lifted her goblet again as the server removed the tureens, then replaced them with our entrees.

I had to admit that the curried mango fowl pasta was excellent, even if my appetite had been considerably dulled by the implications of Kali's words. I ate several bites, small bites, before speaking. "I was wondering if the RDAEX purchase of the Pentura lands and facilities included any equipment and data. Would you happen to know that?"

"I do. It did, but there wasn't much, I was told, because the Rikova site was strictly secondary, and not even a full backup. Actually, it was the older facility, and Pentura built a newer and larger facility for their project, whatever it was."

"That's interesting." I nodded. "I imagine forensic engineering has as many challenges as forensic ecology. Isn't that one of the RDAEX specialties? I mean engineering."

"All engineering requires something along that line, I understand. Executive Edo is reputed to be quite good at reverse engineering and associated skills. Don't you apply a similar approach in determining how an ecology came to be?"

"Whenever possible."

She smiled, warmly, but I wasn't so sure that there wasn't steel beneath her mouth and eyes. "We've talked about work, but there's so much I don't know about you."

"I think you have my complete dossier."

"Dossiers contain only the facts. They conceal as much as they reveal. Tell me about how it was to grow up on Bachman."

"If you'll tell me the same about growing up on Teppera . . ."

"We'd better start with the short version, then," Kali said. "I'm the middle of three. My older sister left when I was barely eight. My younger brother is a doctor in Sheritown, but from the time I was little I was interested in being a deep-space pilot. I'd look at the stars at night and think about what it would be like to travel between them. I wondered if the stars moved when you looked at them in trans-space . . ."

In the end, we talked for almost two hours. After dessert and more talk about matters unassociated with either of our work projects, Kali paid for dinner. I did walk her to the Passova quarters maintained by RDAEX, not all that far from Boudica, and not that she needed my protection. If anything, I probably needed hers, especially after the events at Syntex. She kissed me chastely on the cheek, and no objects passed between us. I was more than a little wary on my return to my quarters, but no one even came physically close to me.

What she'd revealed . . . or hinted, assuming I understood what she had intimated, was frightening. Yet I had not a single shred of anything remotely resembling proof, just scattered pieces of information, and the only thing constructive I could do was to push on with my own assignment and hope that certain aspects of it might lead me to proof from another angle . . . and quickly, before RDAEX fully employed Rikard Spek's expertise to launch their full-scale implementation of their deep-drilling project.

I wasn't that hopeful, but I didn't see any other options for me.

43

On threeday morning I thought about not going in to the Survey before my interview with Ilsabet, but the habit of duty dies hard, and I went. Once there, I checked to make sure I still had a Survey van reserved for later. I did.

Then I did a Stittaran-limited search on Pentura . . . and found almost nothing. There were historical mentions, and a few references to the fact that Rikova had originally been created by Pentura and later purchased and expanded greatly by RDAEX. That was it. A Unity-wide info search, obviously based on the periodic information transfers from Bachman and other worlds, was extensive enough that it would have taken a full day, if not longer, to read it. Interestingly enough, when I tried to limit it to "research," there were only a hundred or so entries, and all of them were so general as to be useless, largely with such phrases as "research has always been one of the highest priorities" or "continuing research is the key to success." There wasn't a single technical article or one that revealed anything about any line of research, even in the most general terms.

By the time I finished a quick scan of those, it was time to leave for my interview.

It took less than fifteen minutes to reach the interview address, which, had I been able to walk from my quarters window to it, would have taken perhaps three minutes. A dark-haired young man wearing a medtech singlesuit greeted me.

"Dr. Verano?"

"That's me."

"I'm Clement Ideo. If you'd provide a handprint . . ."

I did, and it verified that I was indeed me and that I was firmly in the planetary ID bank.

Ideo then asked, "What do you know about Elisabetta?"

"Only the basics . . . that she is thought to have been the only survivor of the Pentura disaster, that she's believed to be Elisabetta Vonacht, that she's shown no sign of aging, and that she has the emotional age of an eight-year-old, but access to what amounts to a savant mentality for anything that can be expressed in formulaic terms."

He nodded. "From here on, everything you say will be recorded and archived. So will Elisabetta's responses. Clyann will be observing the interview, and so will I, if from a slightly remote location. Why do you wish to interview her?"

"I'm here on Stittara at the behest of the Ministry of Environment to do a periodic ecological assessment. Elisabetta has been alive longer than most, if not all, inhabitants of Stittara. She visits the outside regularly. I would like to ask her about what she has observed over the time she has been alive. I won't be cross-examining her or anything like that, just asking her about plants, grasses, the sky, anything that she's seen that fascinated her or seemed to have changed . . ."

When I finished, he nodded. "She may not be as much help as you think, but you're welcome to try. Please read the conditions." He motioned to a screen.

I moved over and read them. They were identical to those Zerlyna had already provided, largely standard, except for the provision that forbid questions involving the destruction of Pentura or what had happened to make her the way she was. "I accept."

"Good. You have one hour . . . unless she becomes agitated, or says that she is done, in which case Clyann will notify you. Oh . . . and she only answers to Ilsabet." He stood. "This way."

He gestured toward a pressure door, which opened as we approached. I stepped through it and up the ramp beyond. He followed. The pressure door at the top of the ramp was open, and I stepped into a small chamber. A muscular woman in a dark gray security singlesuit with a wide belt sat in a chair just beyond the door. I recognized her as the guard/guardian who had always accompanied Ilsabet outside.

"Dr. Verano, this is Clyann. Clyann, Dr. Verano. He is to have an hour with Elisabetta. Under the usual conditions."

Clyann nodded.

"I'll introduce you to Ilsabet," said Ideo, "then I'll leave. She prefers to talk to one person at a time." He walked through the archway into a long room.

Ilsabet was looking out the wide armaglass window, her back to us.

"Ilsabet, this is Paulo," said Ideo gently. "He'd like to talk to you for a while." He nodded and then slipped back through the archway.

Ilsabet turned. She was taller than I'd realized, only a few centimeters shorter than me, slender, but muscular rather than willowy. Outside of her hair and eyebrows, both a solid purpled gray, she could have been in her early twenties, with the clear skin of someone barely out of childhood. Yet her hair had the luster of a young person's. Then I saw her eyes, also purpled gray with overlarge pupils, or perhaps a black ring on the rim of the iris around the pupil.

"I'll talk, and you'll speak. The words are hide and seek."

Her voice was that of a young adult, the intonation that of a child, but the words suggested a vocabulary wider than that of someone with a mental age of eight. Then I corrected myself. An emotional age of eight didn't mean a mental age that young.

"I was hoping you could tell me about the plants and the grass. You've been watching them for a long time." I gestured toward the chairs.

She ignored the gesture. "The grass is grass. It's not-green. There are no plants to be seen."

"You've seen the grass for a long, long time. Has it always been the same color?"

"Green is green. Grass is down. Always purple-green-brown." Suddenly she dropped into the chair nearest to her, in the thoughtless way children sometimes have.

I took the chair facing her. "Were there more plants when you first came here?"

"No plants, no place. Flowers have a face."

"There aren't any flowers outside, are there? I haven't seen any."

"I love daisies, daisies in the spring. They're like everything."

"Does Clyann bring you daisies from the public garden?"

"Daisies are the perkiest flowers, don't you think?" Ilsabet looked past me to the blank wallscreen, her face open and guileless. "Petals of sun and light, centers of ink."

That brought me up short. Ilsabet hadn't actually seen a sun in hundreds of years, if ever. But I wasn't supposed to ask about that period. "What about the sun?"

"Stars like sun, their courses run."

I was getting a very uncomfortable feeling, but I managed a smile. "Do you like to run on the grass?"

"The grass is there. The grass is fair."

"What about the sky? What color is it?"

"Purple like the night, brightened by light."

That was a fair description, but it also chilled me. I wanted to look to Clyann, but dared not, besides she was out of sight range.

"Has the sky changed since you first saw it here?"

"North was south then, south north again."

"The sky or the skytubes?"

"All turning around, with blare and sound." Her face momentarily twisted into terror, but the expression vanished so quickly I almost missed it.

"Do you like to watch the skytubes? What do you think they do?"

The guileless look vanished, and she spoke clearly, like an adult. "What is life? What is art? Is greatness strife? Are fingers smart?"

Then the childlike expression reappeared, and she looked past me. "Can I go out and play? I haven't been out today."

"In just a moment." Clyann moved out past the archway and looked at me. "I think she's done. She talked to you much longer than most, Dr. Verano. I think she likes you."

"She's quite something," I replied. *More than something . . .* "Thank you very much, Ilsabet. Have a good time outside." I stood.

So did she, her eyes on me. "I'd like to play, but I'd have to go away." Her face was serious, in the way that children's faces often are.

"How far would you have to go?"

"Very, very high, up beyond the sky." She paused. "Good-bye." Then she turned and walked to the pressure door that led to the grass beyond.

I watched as she stepped out, then turned to leave.

Ideo was standing there. "I listened to what you were trying to do, Doctor. Did you get any hints that might prove helpful?"

"Given her way of answering, it's hard to tell, but she did seem to indicate that there haven't been any plants in the grassland in her life. She also seemed to indicate that the grass hasn't changed, and that skytubes were more prevalent in the north for a time, and then switched. Twice, possibly. No one's mentioned that in any of the meteorological data, but that's something I can check. There might be an environmental link. It's worth looking into." I inclined my head. "Thank you for letting me talk to her."

"Thank you for your kindness to her. She's always happier after she chats with someone new. It doesn't happen often these days."

I tried not to shiver after I left and walked back to the Survey to recover my measuring gear before heading to the Survey vehicle bay. One of Ilsabet's phrases echoed in my mind. "What is life? What is art? Is greatness strife? Are fingers smart?" The look with which she had delivered the words had said as much as the words themselves.

I was all too worried that it meant what I thought it did . . . but, again, it didn't constitute proof.

Once in my office, I did a quick check of messages, but there weren't any. It was a bit of a pain to have to be in the Survey to get official messages, but I could live with it while I was on Stittara.

Zerlyna met me as I was leaving my office. "Where are you off to now?"

"To take some measurements at nearby outie communities."

"Did you talk to Jorl about it?"

"I did. Aloris recommended that."

Zerlyna nodded. "How did your interview with Ilsabet go?"

"Rather strangely. She talks in rhyme. She did suggest that there's a regular shifting in the positioning of the skytubes. At least, I think that's what she meant."

"I recall something about the rhyming, but not the details. I don't know about the skytubes."

"When I get back, I'll see if Raasn can look into that for me. If it's a regular meteorological event, there should be records, even if no one noticed the pattern . . . assuming there is one."

"If there's a pattern, once you've alerted him to the possibility, he'll find it." She looked at my equipment case and then back to me. "Have a productive trip."

"Let's hope so." I offered a pleasant smile and headed out.

I'd decided to begin with Thoreau, the outie community on my list of three that was the farthest from Passova, not for any other reason than it seemed slightly contrary. Thoreau wasn't all that far away, just some sixty kays north-northwest, although it took an hour and a half to get there. Geneil's directions helped, given the essentially featureless terrain of low rises and rolling hills covered with lichen/grass intermittently sprinkled with the low domed bushes that were seldom more than knee-high, especially the one directive that told me to take the road after the one recommended by the SPS, even though it was a dirt track. When I got to the top of a low rise and looked back south, I saw why. The paved road ran into a pond . . . and out of it as well. The dirt road did rejoin the paved one a kay later.

I kept driving through grasslands that looked untouched, except for the road itself, until I found myself in what I presumed was Thoreau. At first glance, Thoreau didn't exactly pop into view. I saw several tan stone ovals rising no more than a meter or so above the lichen/grass, ovals no more than three meters across. Farther down the hillside, off to the side of the road I was traveling, I saw a low and longer building, built from the same tannish stone. Then I saw the croplands, alternating rows of grass and leafy green plants that stretched at least a kay on a stretch of flatter ground. The strips of grass were roughly two meters wide, while the plant strips looked to be three meters wide. As usual, there wasn't a tree in sight.

I kept driving until I reached the long building. While set into the ground, it rose a good two meters above the surrounding grass. There was actually an inscription carved into the stone over what looked to be the main entrance—Thoreau Community Center. I ended up parking the van on a stone-paved square beside the walk leading into the community center.

Then I got out. Standing by the van, I looked around.

A short man in a rough brown singlesuit approached me. "Can I help you?"

"I suspect you can. I'm Paulo Verano. I'm an ecologist, and I'm visiting a number of outland communities to see how they fit into the environment."

"Dannel Craik. I'm the local patroller and coordinator. I thought you might be something of the sort with the Survey van there. What do you intend to do?"

"Look around. Take measurements. Talk to people."

"You're welcome to do all that. If you don't mind, I'll keep you company."

"That would be helpful." Whether it would or not, he intended to do that, and there was no sense in protesting. Besides, I could always learn something, one way or another. "Let me get a few things from my case."

While Craik watched, I took a series of ambient air readings, then took what I needed from the case and put the instruments in the small carrying bag I also extracted. "I'd like to walk down to the fields or crops there."

"It's farther than it looks."

"I'm sure it is, but you can tell me about Thoreau as we walk. How big is it?"

"You see what you see." When I didn't respond, he added, "A little over a thousand folks, eleven hundred twenty last count."

"What else?"

"What is there to say? We're an outie community. We like to be closer to the land and the sky."

"I notice there aren't any surface dwellings."

"There's being close to land and sky and being a damned fool."

"What sort of crops are those?"

"The closer ones are beans."

"They must be irrigated."

"Capillary drip system off tubes on both sides."

"Where does the water come from? Groundwater?"

Craik looked scandalized, if momentarily. "Skies, no. We don't believe in mining groundwater. That's why we locate settlements where we do. We look for places where springs flow naturally, where we can take a small fraction of the water from the springs, or a stream or river. Aren't many rivers on Stittara, mostly streams. That's another reason why most communities aren't that big . . ."

While he talked, I took more readings. When we reached the first row of crops, I bent down and took a reading close to the ground. From a quick look, the monitors weren't picking up anything untoward, but I'd have to check later for concentrations lower than parts per million. Then I looked at the lichen/grass. The blades looked healthy enough. "What's over there?"

"The little patches are herbs and spices. We grow stuff like that special for the eateries in Passova. Next row over is miniature plums. Bred to stay close to the ground."

I kept walking on the narrow path at the end of the rows, from crop row to crop row, passing what would be potatoes, Craik said. I saw a handful of people, mostly checking the irrigation systems or calibration, I suspected. There was also a small machine tilling one row, looking the size of an anemic landcrawler.

"How does the diffused light affect the growing season?"

"It takes longer," Craik replied, "but the seasons are longer, and there's almost no winter. Get two crops a year. Except in the years we lose one."

"Skytubes?"

"Storms around them mostly."

In time, I started back up toward what I thought was the center of Thoreau.

Since I didn't see much sign of building or excavating taking place, I ventured, "Thoreau seems fairly settled, a long-established community."

"One of the older outland holds on Conuno."

"Is there much change in population over time?"

"No. We're pretty stable, no matter what the Council thinks."

"Thoreau . . . or all the outland holds?"

"All those that I know. Wouldn't be that much sense in having more children than we have food or jobs for, would there?"

"Are there any new holds around here?"

"Hasn't been a new hold on Conuno in a hundred years."

I nodded, but that certainly didn't square with what I'd heard in Passova. "How do you support all the agriculture? You've got a sophisticated system here."

"Ingenious application of minimal high tech for simple systems . . . mostly. Don't believe it for a moment that we're some sort of land grubbers or peasants." Craik chuckled. "I'm afraid we'll be disappointing you. Come with me."

I followed him up the gently sloping path past the community center to another stone oval, although this one had a stone-paved ramp leading up from a reinforced composite vehicle door. Beside that door was a solid personal entrance door that Craik opened. The door was solid, but not a pressure door.

He looked back at me scrutinizing the door frame. "It's solid. We use indirect diffuse venting to deal with storm pressure changes. It's worked fine for centuries."

I closed the door, a solid but simple hinged affair, with what looked to be a metal double-bar storm brace on the back side, and followed the patroller down a corridor into a well-lit chamber filled with various sorts of equipment. I didn't immediately see the light sources, then realized that the entire ceiling had point sources of light—simple optic fiber lightpipes most likely running from hidden surface receptors designed to concentrate the diffuse ambient light. I would have guessed that at night, the lightpipes ran off some other powered illumination system.

"Kearyl! Are you here?" called Craik.

"Coming!" called a voice from a side corridor.

"I thought you'd like to meet Kearyl Laine. She's the head engineer for Thoreau." Craik gestured to the fresh-faced muscular woman who entered the main chamber. She could have passed for a security type, except for the wide smile she offered.

"This is Paulo Verano. He's a Survey Service ecologist."

"I'm doing an ecological study of Stittara for the Unity government."

"They sent you here from Bachman?" Her eyebrows lifted. "Does someone think something's wrong?"

"More like the SoMods want proof that nothing is, or if it is, an assessment of what's wrong and how to fix it." I wanted to see how she responded.

"Nothing's wrong in the outland communities. We balance everything."

"Do you see Survey enforcement people here often?" I couldn't help but ask.

"Only from their flitters. You're the first Survey person we've seen in years."

I certainly didn't think of myself as a Survey person, but I let that pass. "You mind if I take a few readings?"

"Go ahead. You'll get a slight spike on volatiles. I was repairing a crawler/tiller, and the filters likely haven't cleaned the air."

They watched as I took out the atmospheric monitor, then fed the data to my link. "A tiny spike," I said.

"The city folk think we grub in the land. We work in it and with it, but here in the community, we use fusactors, the same as the cities and facilities do," explained Laine. "We just use them more efficiently. We have one templating center here . . ." She gestured.

I recognized the equipment . . . and its clearly well-maintained status.

". . . but we can do anything that needs to be done. We can even model our own templates for things like the crawler/tiller."

"Where did you get your training?" I asked, again out of curiosity.

"We've got our own edulink," said Craik. "Some of our people do go to the university."

That sounded defensive, but I just nodded.

"Thanks, Kearyl. I imagine the ecologist has a few more measurements to take."

I took the hint and said, "It's likely to be a long day, even so."

For the next five hours I walked in and through Thoreau—from the spotless community center to a produce processing center, to the main lorry bay, through part of a small school, and through an underground arcade that smelled like the outdoors but held a modest range of shops and craft stalls. While several people initially stared at me, the stares were brief, and they all went back to what they had been doing.

I hadn't known exactly what to expect at Thoreau, and I hadn't found what I expected. The question was whether the other outie settlements would be similar, radically different, or somewhere in between . . . and I wasn't about to guess.

By the time I returned to Passova, it was well past seven. While I parked the van in the Survey vehicle bay, I didn't check it in, since I'd be taking it out again in the morning.

44

Fourday was my day to visit Doones, and I was in the van early, this time heading east and then turning north roughly halfway between Passova and the dropport. Since Jorl Algeld had said that Doones wouldn't be a problem, I was eager to see what the difference might be.

Just before eight, I drove over a low ridge, not that there appeared to be any other kind in the areas of Conuno around Passova, and into a wide valley that stretched to the northern horizon, or so it seemed. Unlike Thoreau, there were at least twenty low buildings, all protruding from the lichen/grass that grew right up to the stone and all showing less than two meters above ground level. They were clustered in general groups of two or three, each grouping separated from the others by roughly a kay. The roads were narrow, but paved. In the end, I followed the road into what looked to be the center of the community and pulled up on the stone-paved square in the middle of three low buildings. Although I saw people walking along the street to the north, and two men working on the top of the end of the building farthest from me, I didn't see anyone immediately nearby as I stepped out of the Survey van. I walked to the rear to get to my equipment case.

"Mykail! What are you—"

I turned to see a woman, wearing the same kind of brown singlesuit as Dannel Craik had the day before, come up a ramp from the entrance to the nearest building.

She broke off her words as she neared, then said, "I'm sorry. I thought you were someone else."

"Mykail of Survey Service enforcement?" I asked in as friendly a tone as I could.

She grinned sheepishly. "As a matter of fact . . . yes. He was only here last week."

"I'm Paulo Verano. I'm doing an ecological assessment of Stittara, and that includes a sampling of outland communities and activities."

The grin vanished. "Poulina Maruka."

"You're the local patroller and coordinator?"

"Yes. Why didn't Mykail come with you?"

"Because I'm not part of enforcement. I was sent from Bachman to do a periodic assessment at the behest of the Unity government."

"Now what?" There was a certain exasperation in her voice.

"Would you like to see my ID and authorization?"

"No. That's not necessary. Could you tell me why you're bothering us, though? We create less of a footprint on the environment than the multis or the cities do."

"I don't intend to bother anyone. I just intend to walk around, talk to people, take some measurements, and depart. Yesterday, I was at Thoreau. Tomorrow, I plan to be at Hobbes. Next week, I'll visit more outland communities."

"How many of the multis have you visited?"

"So far as I can tell, all of the large ones."

"They let you in?"

"They didn't really have a choice. They're multis. If the oversight committee of the Unity government heard they'd refused . . ." I shrugged.

An amused smile replaced the polite hostility. "What did you find?"

"Not all the analyses are done, but . . . they're abiding by all the rules."

"What do you think of the rules?"

"I have the feeling that the rules don't cover everything. That's one of the reasons why I'm here."

For a moment she was silent. Then she said, "Tell me a little about yourself, if you would."

While the whole situation was getting a trace bizarre, I didn't see that telling Poulina Maruka my background, which was known to the Planetary Council and all the multis, could hurt. "I'm Paulo Verano. I've a doctorate in environmental studies from the Reagan Institute on Bachman . . ." From there, I gave her the entire spiel, just the facts, though, and nothing personal. When I finished, I just waited.

She shook her head. "What does the Planetary Council think about your study?"

"Councilor Morghan asked for a briefing. They're following what I'm doing, I suspect."

At that, Maruka smiled again. "What did you do in Thoreau?"

I told her, including Craik's comment about accompanying me.

"I've heard about him. He's very protective."

"Quietly so, I got the impression."

"It's better that way." She paused. "Do you want to start with the crops or the shops? Or the sanitary systems?"

"How about crops, then sanitary systems, templating centers, and then shops and public places?"

"You've got a long day ahead, Doctor."

"So do you, if you're coming with me."

Maruka laughed. "I'd cover most of those places anyway." She pointed. "The oldest crop strips are this way."

We headed out.

Obviously, I couldn't walk every field or even every different kind of crop, but we covered enough that I could point to a broad sample of both crops and locales. We did visit all the sanitary central locations, not that there were many or that they were large, because each dwelling unit recycled and reused the majority of goods, except for the compacted and dehydrated waste organics, which each dwelling owner had to deliver to the central recycling synthesizer.

When we'd finished going through the last arcade of shops, and that was after five in the evening, Maruka walked back to the van with me. She watched as I loaded my gear back into the equipment case.

"You're going to Hobbes tomorrow?"

"That's the plan. Unless a storm comes up or I get into an accident."

"I'll let them know to expect you. You won't get quite as much hassle."

"You're not all that fond of Survey enforcement, I can see."

"The good ones do what they're supposed to do. The others . . . they usually don't come back. I've linked with our Council liaison. The Council doesn't have a problem with what you're doing so long as you do the same sorts of things you did here and in Thoreau."

"There's an Outland Council? I've never heard mention of it."

"The Planetary Council doesn't recognize it. Officially, we call it a coordinating body, and they can't do anything about that."

I nodded. "Tell me, if you don't mind, what you think about the skytubes."

"You tell me first. Then we'll see."

Once again, I'd triggered something, but I just nodded. "Fair enough." I paused to collect my thoughts. "What I'm going to say . . . well, there's no proof that I know of, and it's based on my own observations and analysis of what the data doesn't show."

"Doesn't show . . . Rather interesting way of putting it."

"For thousands of years, analysis of high-altitude weather patterns on T-type water worlds has indicated that microscopic organic material survives at incredibly high altitudes, and in some cases, actually thrives. But there's never been a case of anyone proving that this . . . material was more than thinly spread and largely disorganized. The only evidence here on Stittara consists of privately held reports that I know of but cannot access, which suggests that airborne organic materials are more prevalent and better organized." I looked at Maruka. Had I seen a hint of a nod? I couldn't tell. So I went on. "I suspect that those materials are far better organized. Whether they're the equivalent of airborne jellyfish whose movements influence the weather and storm patterns, and whether the skytubes are a manifestation of that, or whether I'm seeing things, or whether there's even more there, at this point I can't tell."

Maruka shook her head. "If I were you, I wouldn't be saying that anywhere else."

"You said you'd offer your thoughts."

"I did." The amused smile returned. "Like all science types, you're looking for facts you can replicate in your laboratories, or somewhere. This time, you won't be able to do that. We all know that. So will you. Like I said, someone who doesn't understand might hear what you said. It's not likely to be good for your health."

"Has it been unhealthy for others who said such things?"

She shrugged. "I couldn't say. Not for sure. But I wouldn't air your views. Not if I were you."

"Thank you."

"That's only fair. Good fortune in Hobbes."

I smiled and climbed into the van, trying to keep a pleasant expression on my face as I drove off, leaving Doones and heading back to Passova.

From what Maruka had said, it was obvious that the outlanders believed that the skytubes were living creatures, or at least manifestations of living creatures. And . . . if they were . . . and if the Unity discovered that . . .

I was the one who wanted to shake my head. It wasn't as though I hadn't thought about the possibility, and it wasn't as though others hadn't either. But what was crystal clear was that the local Survey Service had taken the position to monitor the environmental rules and to enforce them in a way to assure that human activities did not change the existing ecological balance without revealing why such an emphasis was necessary—because, if the skytubes were intelligent, the Unity would have to remove the inhabitants—and removing four million inhabitants would be impossible, not to mention economically catastrophic. So, if I reported that, assuming I could even prove that, both the report and I would likely be buried. On the other hand, if my study, and continuing data, revealed nothing new, and the skytubes were merely considered a nonsentient part of the overall ecology, the only requirement was that they not be threatened. Reading between the lines of my assignment, that conclusion was what the Ministry of Environment clearly desired.

The next problem was that one way or another, evidence was required. While Maruka and the outlanders might believe the skytubes were sentient, belief in something did not make it so, one way or another.

And then there was the simple last problem. No one on the Planetary Council or in any of the multis had any desire to see the slightest shred of evidence of skytube sentience emerge anywhere . . . and Maruka had caught me off-guard . . . and then reminded me of my stupidity.

No wonder the Planetary Council wanted to know what I was doing.

45

The stars of summer shine unwatched, thought five,
Bright beacons knowing not where minds do strive.

In the late afternoon Ilsabet walked across the lawn to the top of the low ridge. There she stopped and looked to the south, her eyes on the distant skytubes.

Clyann followed, her eyes alternating between the open pressure door behind them and her charge. She finally took a position from where she could continue to observe both.

"From the south, go and turn," Ilsabet chanted softly. "To the north, not to spurn."

"Who are you talking to?" asked Clyann.

"To the sky, those who fly."

"There aren't any chirpers around."

"Not the little flights. Those who change the sights."

"None of that nonsense, now, girl." Clyann's voice held a trace of amusement.

"Nonsense means words and lies, much like dreams of empty skies."

Clyann sighed. "You haven't been quite the same since your visitor. Did he upset you? You should have told me you wanted him to go sooner."

"Not him. Not to go. He's one who should know."

"Know what? Do you want us to tell him something?"

Ilsabet shook her head, still gazing to the south. "To those who first live noon, all will change soon."

"You're not having a fit, now . . . are you, girl?"

"For me no fit. I liked his visit."

"That's good. We're all happy when you like your visitors."

Ilsabet turned, skipping eastward along the top of the low ridge.

46

By the time I got back to Passova and took care of everything, I pretty much just dropped into bed. My feet and legs ached from all the walking. Exhausted as I was, though, I didn't sleep all that well, because I kept waking up thinking about what I'd blurted out in Doones. I could hope that Maruka didn't pass it on to someone who might, in turn, let someone else know, someone more fearful, more political, or more worried about jobs and profit. Those thoughts raised other questions, such as why Maruka, and presumably other outlanders, simply accepted the skytubes for what they were. I could see why they wouldn't talk to the "city folk," but why had she effectively warned me, rather than having me "disappear," or was that because my disappearance might give the Planetary Council or the Survey enforcement people an excuse to remove some or all of the "unofficial" outland communities?

Still aching and tired, I struggled up on fiveday, consoling myself that I didn't really have to visit outie communities on the weekend, that I could take the time and rest . . . or at least just stay put and review and analyze the data I'd already gathered. The news reported that a fierce storm had swirled past Passova to the west during the night, but that it had not been close enough to cause any damage or to require emergency procedures. I hadn't even heard the winds. Had I been that tired? Although I was slow with my exercises and had to hurry my morning tea, I didn't see Ilsabet outside.

I headed straight from my quarters to the vehicle bay, where I loaded my case. I drove out through the vehicle door at the top of the ramp slightly after eight, heading due west. As was always the case, there were few vehicles on the road. To both the northwest and the southwest, I saw concentrations of skytubes, both larger or closer than I'd seen on either threeday or fourday, and the winds that swirled around the van seemed stronger and gustier than previously.

I kept an eye on the skytubes, but they didn't seem to be moving in my direction. At the same time, I couldn't help but marvel at the openness of the land . . . and wonder why the city dwellers preferred their tunnels and warrens, to the point that they didn't even want to look outside. Somehow, the argument about danger from the skytubes and storms seemed overblown. Craik had observed that they occasionally lost crops, and there had only been one storm in hundreds of years strong enough to devastate a multi facility—that of Pentura—and I'd seen no record of recent damage to a town or city. Except, of course, to my own quarters, and I doubted that the damage had been solely the result of the storm. My own suspicions lay with the Planetary Council, but I didn't have any proof of that . . . or even gossip.

Hobbes looked to be slightly larger than Thoreau and was laid out on a long east-facing slope whose grade was so gradual that I didn't even realize it until I got out of the van. Then I looked into the distance, and realized that where I'd pulled up the van in front of the community center was perhaps fifty meters higher than the crop strips some two kays east of me.

A woman in the brown singlesuit that seemed the standard uniform for outland patrollers walked toward the Survey van. She offered a broad smile that showed a wide mouth and sparkling white teeth against skin the color of light amber honey. Her hair was almost the same color, and her eyes were hazel. "You must be the ecologist doctor that Poulina Maruka linked us about."

I returned her smile with one as open as I could manage. "That's right—Paulo Verano."

"Ngaio Biendi. I'm the assistant patroller for Hobbes."

"Just two of you? Must be a pretty orderly group here."

"If you're not orderly and thorough out here, you don't last long."

"And careful?"

"Being careful doesn't count for much if you're also not orderly and thorough."

She had a point there, one that I hadn't considered, not in that light, anyway. "You know why I'm here, I take it?"

"To take measurements, and generally snoop around to see if we're handling the environment all right or making a mess of it."

"That's pretty much it," I agreed cheerfully.

"How did the Planetary Council agree to a study?" Her question was open and blunt, as I suspected she was.

"They didn't have a choice. I was sent from Bachman."

"You'd best be orderly and thorough then."

"I'm trying," I said with a grin.

"Like as not, the Council will also find you trying."

"We'll attempt to avoid that."

"Where do you want to start?"

"The crops. That will probably take the most walking."

"More than you'd like." She glanced to the south, in the direction of the skytubes.

"Do we have to worry about them?"

"Not at the moment. They're grazing."

"Grazing?"

"That's what we call it. Who knows if that's what they're really doing? They turn darker, meaner-looking, when they start to move. You see that, and you want to go to ground."

That made sense, and I mentally filed the notation that darker skytubes meant trouble. Then I took out the carry bag and put in what I needed, and we started out.

It was well past noon when I finished getting a wide enough sample from the crops, discovering, among other things, that Hobbes also grew dwarf apples of a sort, on trees or bushes no higher than the native plains brush. Those crop rows were actually sunk almost half a meter into the ground. Once more, it appeared that water usage followed what Dannel Craik had said, and my instruments showed nothing out of the ordinary.

My legs were aching, and my feet hurt as we walked back in the direction of the community center.

"Have you ever eaten a true outland meal, Doctor?"

I laughed. "I've never even eaten a false one."

"Then you'll be taking us both to the Heatherage."

"I could use a bite to eat." *And a place to sit down and rest my feet.*

The Heatherage turned out to require walking another half kay uphill until we came to a stone path to the right. It, in turn, led down a stone ramp to a heavy single door, held open with a stone wedge. Again, there was no pressure door, just the metal storm bars.

"I brought you a new fellow, Narlon," Ngaio called out as we stepped inside.

"You owe me more than one, you patrollers do." The man who replied stood in a nook just inside the door, behind a narrow desk. The single-room bistro, or the outland equivalent of the same, held nine tables, four of which were small square ones set against the smooth, but not polished, gray stone walls.

Ngaio led the way to one of the tables set against the wall, if in the front corner. Sitting down felt good. I glanced around the bistro. There weren't any screens on the wall, just large fixed images, like ancient photographs. All were pictures of Stittara, several of skytubes, but many just depicting the rolling hills and vistas. The tables were a light synthwood, as were the chairs, although the seats were padded.

"Are all the furnishings synthwood?" I asked.

"They are here. Wish we could use real wood, but the only places that have that are the upland ones. Even there, they can only harvest a score or so of trees every year."

"What do you use for the synthwood feedstock?"

"Crop residue, mostly. It takes less energy that way."

I didn't see a menu, but my search must have been obvious because Ngaio pointed to a square mounted on the wall, with white letters on it. It took me a moment to realize that the square was slate, or the equivalent, with the menu written in chalk. I'd read or heard of that, in novels or dramas set in ancient times, but never seen it. "What's best?"

"It's all good. That's why I brought you here."

I looked over the handwritten slate. "What's Chicken Parmento?"

"It's real fowl, chicken, in a white sauce, with fried apples on the side."

"You *grow* chickens here?"

"We raise them. They like some of the local grubs and bugs. The young ones herd the flocks through the crops."

"The local proteins are compatible?"

"We did some gene-engineering centuries back. You have fowl at the upscale eateries in Passova, likely you're eating our chickens."

I supposed that made sense, even if I'd not considered it.

"Narlon . . . we're ready."

The proprietor—I assumed he was—walked over and looked at me. "What will you have?"

"The Chicken Parmento . . . do you have a good pale lager?"

"Absolutely." He turned. "And you're having the usual?"

"What else? Limoncello Chicken, with the lager," she added almost in an aside to me.

Narlon headed to the rear archway, presumably to the kitchen.

I was still thinking over the fact that the outies raised chickens when three women hurried through the door and settled at the round table closest to us.

"Ngaio . . ." called one. "Who's your friend?"

"Dr. Paulo Verano. He's an ecologist who came here to see how we're doing."

The woman who had called out the patroller's name looked at me, then smiled. "You look to be doing fine, Doctor. What about us?"

"You're all doing fine," I replied, "and you've all made the day better."

They all laughed, then resumed their conversation.

For a moment there was something that I should have noticed, but . . . I couldn't recall what it was. Abruptly it struck me. All three women were at least pleasantly attractive, and the one who had spoken was close to beautiful, and all were older, somewhere around my age, I'd have guessed . . . and not a single one of them had given me more than a friendly glance.

Ngaio nodded. "You noticed it, didn't you?"

"Noticed what?"

"You're an off-worlder, and a fairly good-looking man, and no one stared at you, like those predatory women in Passova or the other cities . . ."

"I've noticed that."

"Aye, and you would, handsome fellow you are." She shook her head.

"Why is that? What's the difference between here and Passova?"

"Comes from spending too much time in tunnels and not out with the grass and the land. You can't live a long and healthy life if you're not balanced."

"How long do people live here?"

"Who knows? We don't count things like that." She paused. "You live as long as you live. Longer than most places in the Arm, and without all those potions and creams the multis dream up based on the lichen/grass. And it's healthier, definitely. You won't see women here lusting after outworlders. You don't see young fellows picking fights at the drop of an unkind word. Don't hear many unkind words, either, and it's not out of fear like in those rodent warrens they call cities."

That is interesting. I just nodded. "Healthy living is best."

"Don't you feel better out here?" she asked.

"As a matter of fact, I do. I was beginning to feel confined, too, as if the tunnels were pressing in on me."

"I have to go to Passova every year or so for patroller training and refresher work. Just two weeks, but I can't wait to leave." She stopped as Narlon returned with two lagers.

I took a cautious sip of the brew, since it was more amber than I would have expected from a pale lager. Then I took another sip. There was no doubt it was the best lager I'd had on Stittara.

"Good. Isn't it?"

"Very good."

"The Zantos folks try to copy it, but they just can't do it quite right."

"And Zantos is better than the others."

"You can drink it. The others I won't try when I'm there."

The Chicken Parmento was good, very good, and I said so.

"It's not quite so good as mine," replied Ngaio. "We still have to synthesize dairy, likely always will, but we grow the miniature limes and lemons. The natural always tastes better, at least to me."

"I'll have to keep that in mind."

When we left the Heatherage, after I paid for both of us—and paylinks worked just fine—the three women were still enjoying their meal, and not a one looked in my direction.

Once outside, we headed for the templating center. After that came the sanitary processing works, and then two different shopping arcades, and the resource reprocessing center. Not a single one emitted anything even close to violating the required standards.

All in all, I finished slightly after three, packed my equipment, and was about ready to climb into the van when Ngaio cleared her throat. I looked to her.

"Doctor . . . you be careful on the way back. Some of the skytubes headed east, and you don't want to cross paths with them."

"Thank you. I'll be careful . . . and orderly and thorough."

Ngaio laughed.

I smiled in return, then climbed into the van and eased my way out of Hobbes.

Less than a half hour after leaving, taking Ngaio's advice, I eased the van to a stop on the top of a rise, watching as a skytube swept out of the southwest, scouring the land. Yet for all the power, and the accompanying winds that rocked the Survey van, although I was a good five kays north of the skytube, I wasn't certain that the skytube was gathering that much material from the lichen/grass or even disturbing it that much. Was that because I just couldn't see the process closely? Or because the lichen/grass was so tough?

Once the skytube passed over the low rises to the southeast, and the winds subsided, I got out of the van and walked to the side of the road, where the lichen/grass grew right up to the edge of the road surface. None of the blades or shoots or roots quite touched the permacrete. The blades of the grass were more like flattened fat conifer needles, but that shouldn't have been a surprise since all the flora was analogous to gymnosperms. The blades were tough, like needles, and the stalks to which they were attached were colored a brownish heather shade. The stalks were even stronger and tougher than the blades. When I tried to pull the branching stalks up from the ground, they barely moved. I did get a resinous sap on my hands. I also got a much more pungent heather-like odor . . . similar to the flavor I'd tasted in some food. Had that food or the herbs or spices that had seasoned it come from the outie communities rather from city tanks or synthesizers?

More than likely.

The lichen/grass was definitely tough. If the skytubes were an organic part of the ecosystem, did they have to be so powerful to feed off the tough grass? Or was the grass so tough to avoid being destroyed by the skytubes? Another ecological question I hadn't seen discussed. In fact, the more I looked, the fewer real questions there were that had been addressed. Another worrying factor about my assignment . . . and Stittara.

I wiped off the resinous stuff as well as I could with a pocket square that would likely never be the same, then got back in the van and resumed my drive back to Stittara. Once in the vehicle bay, I turned in the van, but confirmed my reservation for oneday, and carried my equipment case back to my office.

Since I got back to the office at half past four, I had some time to consider what I'd learned, and with the healthy lunch I'd had, I wasn't particularly hungry.

Among other things I'd realized was that I'd never heard anyone mention their age. Anywhere . . . at any time. Since that wasn't generally an item of conversation for most people, I hadn't thought much about it . . . until Ngaio had directly avoided the issue.

Again, I was realizing that all too often, sometimes you needed to examine the assumptions and the data you took for granted. So I went looking for vital statistics for the population . . . and discovered there weren't any. Not for Passova, not for Stittara. That is, populations for every city and "official" outland community were listed. Deaths were listed, as were births, but I discovered, even in public obituaries, the ages of the deceased were only listed if they died in an accident or from some medical condition that even modern medicine couldn't handle, not that there were many of those. From what I could tell, at least in the recorded statistics, there were no statistics on life expectancy.

So I began to check on insurance . . . and from what I could tell, life insurance didn't exist, except in relation to accidents or casualties.

How long do these people live?

They couldn't live forever, because I'd heard enough references to people dying and things that happened before people were born, and the death rate was close to standard for a modern world—that I could figure out, assuming the published numbers were correct, by using total deaths and total population. My calculations were rough, but rough was good enough.

When I finished, I was feeling very isolated, and very, very worried. I wasn't certain I even wanted to walk from my office to my quarters. But I girded my loins, so to speak, shut down my console, turned off the lights in my office, and walked out to the door from the Survey Service and out into the pedestrian tunnel. The tunnel seemed to press in on me.

Because you've been outside so much and you're realizing how depressing Passova is?

"Paulo! Paulo!" An unfamiliar voice called my name.

I turned and saw someone hurrying toward me. I immediately stiff-ened, wondering if I should run or look for a patroller. Then as the man drew closer, I recognized Roberto Gybl. I gambled that he didn't mean me any harm, at least not immediately . . . and not in a monitored public place. I waited until he was closer before speaking. "Rob . . . Rob Gybl. What are you doing here?"

"Looking for you. I need someone to talk to. Someone from Bach-man . . . or not from Stittara."

"I qualify on both counts." I tried to make my voice light and amused. "You need money?"

"Deep stars, no. You're levelheaded. I'd like to tell you something over dinner and see what you think."

Deep stars? I hadn't heard that expression in years, and usually those who used it were ex–Alliance Space Forcers. "Well . . . I don't have dinner plans. I've been out in the field for the last few days."

"Good. We can go to Ebony."

"Have you ever been to Ojolian's? We could go there."

"Wherever you want," he replied.

His rapid acquiescence suggested he really wanted to talk . . . or that it didn't much matter to him where we went for whatever he had in mind.

Gybl didn't have much to say on the tunneltram . . . or while we waited for a table at Ojolian's—it was fiveday evening after all, although we were actually there a bit earlier than many diners.

Finally, we were seated and had been served drinks—he had red wine, and I had a Zantos, which wasn't as good as the unnamed lager I'd had in Hobbes.

Then he looked at me and took a deep breath. "Do you remember when I talked to you about the forerunner site here on Stittara?"

"Yes. You said there was one controlled by a multi. You said you were going to try to get access to it and do a documentary about it." I smiled. "Or you were going to do one about being denied access."

"That's what happened . . . sort of." He took a sip of his wine.

"From what you're saying, you were the one mentioned in the news the other day. Not by name, but I figured it had to be you after our conversa-tion on the *Persephonya*."

"That was me, all right. Syntex picked me up as soon as I got close. I figured they'd have some sort of guards, and probably a covered site, but that . . ." He shook his head.

"What do you mean?"

"Oh . . . I guess you wouldn't know. But aren't you investigating the multis?"

"I've been to the Syntex main facility, and I've interviewed the environmental director. I've gone over their reports, and I've made measurements of their emissions and effluents . . . but none of that had anything to do with the forerunner site."

"It's in a separate location. South of the main facility. It's like a fortress. There's nothing open to the air."

"I would have expected that, not being open, I mean," I said. "If it's a forerunner site, it's millions of years old, and it has to be buried well underground. With all the storms and the skytubes, they'd have to have it covered or the Antiquities Commission would have long since applied to seize it."

"You know about all that stuff?"

"There are often environmental issues involved with archaeological sites. But you never said what it was that surprised you. Was it running across Sinjon Reksba? Or I guess we should say the man who was impersonating Sinjon. I heard the news reports. Were you two there together?"

Gybl shook his head. "Not together. Oh . . . he might have been following me . . . but it doesn't make sense. If he came back to Stittara to claim an inheritance, and he had enough money to have all the surgery and modifications to impersonate the real Sinjon, then what was he doing at the Syntex forerunner site?"

"I can't answer that." That was certainly true in a literal sense. "Do you think there's ancient forerunner technology there?"

"There might be. Who could tell . . . but no one's ever found anything at any sites before. Some scientists have speculated that they used biotech rather than mech-tech."

"Did the Syntex people do . . . did they act unprofessional?"

"No. They did detain me for longer than they had to, I think." He offered a rough laugh. "I was trespassing. But they didn't rough me up. They just escorted me into the facility. They asked me a lot of questions about why I was there, and they must have made a lot of inquiries about who I was. That made sense. What didn't make sense was Sinjon."

"What do you mean?"

"Why was he there? Why did they let me see him leave? Why didn't they let me record that?"

"You think that was because they didn't want you to record anything else?"

"I don't know. I know I saw Sinjon drive off. That's true." He shook his head once more. "The more I've thought about it, the more I'm convinced there was something wrong."

He stopped as the server brought our entrees. I'd skipped a salad or an appetizer because I'd had a solid lunch, and Gybl had followed my lead.

Once the server left, Gybl turned to me. "How did they treat you? The people at Syntex, I mean?"

"It took a while to get to see them, but they were polite, and they let me take all the readings and measurements I wanted. They didn't tell me I couldn't go this place or that. I'm not sure they were pleased, but they didn't get in the way. So far as I can determine, they're well within the required standards."

"Hmmm. They were like that, in a way, with me."

I waited, taking a bite of the ravioli, with a cheese sauce that held the tiniest hint of bitterness. Was that in comparison to my lunch, or hadn't I noticed it before? Or was it just the dish before me? How could I tell?

"What are you thinking?" asked Gybl suddenly.

"That it was strange that both you and Sinjon Reksba were on the *Persephonya* and that you both ended up at the forerunner site at the same time. That's a little much to be coincidence."

"I've thought that as well," Gybl admitted.

"Did you tell him what you told me? About the forerunner site?"

"I did. Since he was from Stittara—he said he was—I asked him which multi controlled the site. He told me it was Syntex, but I'd figured that out before. What he also said, that I didn't know, was that Syntex was a division or a subsidiary of VLE."

"VLE, the Bachman multi?"

"The same one. And VLE is angling to take over RDAEX. According to Sinjon, a lot of RDAEX projects in the Arm haven't done that well, and they haven't come up with a new profit stream in years."

"That's rather odd. Why would he know that . . . or care?" I paused. "The real Sinjon wouldn't have, but . . ."

"You see what I mean, Paulo? It's definitely strange."

What it told me was that someone in VLE or Syntex had leaked information to "Sinjon" about when Aimee would be visiting the forerunner site. "It is . . . but why would he be going to the forerunner site? If he had been hired to snoop on Syntex people, he should have targeted the main Syntex site. Even that doesn't make sense, because if someone has a problem with VLE, why would they come to Stittara?"

"Unless there really is old technology at the site. Or . . . if there isn't . . . but VLE is using that as the rationale for taking over RDAEX."

I shook my head. "No matter how I look at it, it doesn't make sense."

"That's what I thought. I'm glad to know you see it the same way."

We talked for a while longer, but I didn't learn anything more, and I hoped he didn't either. In the end, he left Ojolian's going one way, and I went another. I kept my eyes open all the way back to my quarters. I still didn't know what to think of Gybl—except that he was more than he claimed to be.

47

Sixday, I slept a little later than I had been, and then ran through my exercises, and the almost ancient if routine Juchai moves, then went in to the office, where I made sure all my readings were integrated into the data matrices I had created for the outland communities. That took several hours because of various predictable glitches that I had failed to predict. After that I consulted my maps and worked out the next sets of outland communities I planned to visit, alternating between "official" and unofficial locations.

Next came the data sets made available by the Planetary Council. While there were no statistics breaking down the population by age group, with actual births and deaths being a matter of record, if only as individuals, I thought I ought to be able to take the names of those who died and track back to when they were born. If I could track a few hundred, tedious as it might be, it would at least give me an idea of life spans on Stittara. So I started with a woman named Maudl Evians. Before long I ran into trouble. All the birth and death records more than a hundred years in the past were "archived." From what I could tell, that meant they were not available. I'd already discovered that the death notices and obituaries didn't give dates of birth or ages unless someone died young of an accident or some form of mischance. So I started looking back at the notices in previous years. The media notices went back a century as well—before they were archived—and the same practice existed as far back as I could access.

Was mentioning age or life span a cultural taboo? Or was there some regulatory or legal requirement?

I went through the Stittaran Planetary Charter. I tried a global search of the entire Stittaran legal code and came up with nothing. I tried a good twenty variations on that search. That still got no results. Then I began to go through the legal code, the codified listing of public laws, line by line, thinking that such a provision must have been worded indirectly. By seven on sixday night, when I quit for the day, I'd found nothing. Just try reading public laws one by one!

Sevenday morning, I was up early. I didn't see Ilsabet, but that didn't surprise me, since she seemed to walk outside later.

On the one hand, I felt sorry for her, with that eternal childlikeness, but I had the feeling, if only from a few gestures and words, that there was more there. Was I the only one who saw that? Or had it been there so long that everyone just felt that was the way she was?

Once I finished a second mug of tea, I washed and dressed and headed back to my office at the Survey Service. I was the only one there.

This time, I began by trying a search of criminal and civil court cases dealing with legal notices of all kinds. Then I tried cases against the media. Nothing about death notices . . . anywhere. So I went back to the legal code. When I finished scanning at four in the afternoon, my eyes were blurring, and probably bloodshot . . . and I'd found nothing.

Yet . . . the evidence, or lack of it, was right there. No ages in the vast majority of death notices. Period.

It wasn't as though people weren't dying. They obviously were. I'd even heard, in passing on the news, references to the deaths of apparently prominent people. It had to be cultural. That wasn't unheard of. There had been some religious sect in the past, somewhere, I recalled, that had mandated a certain number of offspring for every family. That number appeared nowhere in writing, nowhere in religious pronouncements, and yet for centuries, every family had that number of children . . . until they overpopulated the planet, but that was another story.

Figuratively, I threw up my hands and went back to my quarters to clean up and change to go to Aloris's "get-together." I did take a look out the study window before I showered and saw several skytubes in the distance, but they didn't look dark, nor did they seem to be moving much.

At a little before six I walked out of my guest quarters to make my way to Aloris's when I heard a voice I really didn't want to acknowledge.

"Paulo! I have to talk to you . . ."

I really didn't want to see Rob Gybl again, but I stopped and waited for him to catch up. When he neared, I said, "I'm going to a get-together."

"I'll walk with you. I just had some questions." When I said nothing, he went on. "I've been doing some checking. You were at Syntex at the same time I was. You were even at the forerunner site."

While he could have tracked me to Syntex, through vehicle logs, appointments on calendars, and when Aloris and probably half a dozen Survey people knew where I'd been and when, the only place where I'd mentioned the forerunner site was to Aloris . . . and on the comm system. That suggested Gybl had contacts . . . or a way to tap into my console or the Survey Service comm lines, if not both. "How did you find that out?" There was no reason not to ask, if only to see how he avoided answering.

"I have my ways."

"I'm sure you do."

"What were you doing there?"

"I was looking at the forerunner site. What else?"

"They let *you* see it?"

"See it is about the best way to describe it. I had to sign a confidentiality agreement. I was not allowed to record any data or any visuals, and I'm bound not to talk about it, except insofar as it bears on my consulting assignment for the Ministry of Environment."

"But why you?"

"Because that's the only place where I could get even an idea of what the environment might have been like more than a hundred million years ago."

"Why do you need that?" He brushed back his thick black hair, as if it were an annoyance.

"It's called a baseline, Rob."

"They wouldn't even let me talk to anyone. How did you manage it?"

"I was sent here at the behest of a Unity government oversight committee. If Syntex had refused to see me . . . or let me view something that affected my report . . ." I didn't spell out the implications. I just smiled politely.

"Well . . . is there any technology there?"

"I signed a confidentiality agreement, remember?"

"You're telling me that there is."

"I didn't see anything. I didn't see anything that suggested that."

"What about that confidentiality agreement, now?" His voice turned sarcastic.

"I don't recall that it required me not to reveal what I didn't see."

That kept him quiet—for all of a dozen long strides, almost as if he were marching. "Am I supposed to believe that you're just here for an ecological study . . . and you just turned up at the site when I was there?"

"I turned up at the site when Syntex let me come. They decided when that was. If you have a problem with my timing, take it up with them." I let a certain amount of anger show in my voice, not at all difficult considering that I was getting annoyed by being pestered.

"I'm sorry." He actually sounded that way. "It's just that none of this makes sense."

"You're right. It doesn't." *In fact, the entire planet doesn't make sense.* Except, even as I thought that, I was afraid it all made too much sense. "But you're being here suggests you're more than you claim, and your being able to find out things I mentioned in confidential areas suggests you're trying to involve me in something much bigger than me, and something I want no part of . . . and never did."

"You're involved just by having visited Syntex . . . and by knowing Aimee Vanslo."

"What does she have to do with Syntex?"

"Come now, Paulo."

"What does she have to do with Syntex?" I asked again.

"You don't know? Just who did you meet with at Syntex?"

"A Bryse Tharon, the assistant director for environment. Who else would I be meeting with? On environmental issues, especially?"

"Did Aimee tell you who she worked for?"

"No. I asked her several times on the *Persephonya*. She just said she was in management."

"She is. She's a high-level executive at VLE."

"VLE . . . the big Bachman multi? So why is she here on Stittara? Are they going to open a subsidiary here or something?"

"They already have one." He brushed back his hair again with his left hand.

"You're suggesting that Syntex belongs to VLE and that Aimee is some sort of troubleshooter for VLE, then?"

"I'll leave it to you to figure that out." He smiled, coolly. "I'll be in touch." He strode ahead of me and turned at the next corner.

I just stood there for several moments, as if stunned . . . just in case someone else was watching or recording. Then I ran toward the corner and looked around it. Of course, he was gone.

I'd hoped that Aimee's security was better than that of the Survey Service, and from Gybl's reactions, it appeared to be. Even if he had access to my comms from the Survey, I'd only talked to assistants and to Tharon from my console. And now that I recalled it, like a good security person, Kali had never identified herself when she'd linked me at the Survey, and I'd never mentioned her name, and her link had come across as unknown. She'd never even mentioned anything except where we were to meet and when, and that she was in Passova for the evening. Gybl would have a hard time tracking her down . . . unless he could get inside RDAEX security.

Should I send her a link about Gybl? I'd have to do it through my own link to the planetlink, if I didn't want Gybl to know. I decided to think about that. A few stans shouldn't matter, especially on a sevenday evening. *You hope.*

I almost got lost twice, and had to use my link for directions before I finally located the old and narrower pedestrian tunnel on which Aloris's dwelling was situated. Once at her door, I'd only pressed the chime stud for a moment before she opened the door.

"Paulo! Come in!" She stepped back.

I entered, directly into a sitting or living chamber, large enough that it didn't seem crowded even with nearly a dozen people there.

"I told you he'd be punctual," Aloris said, looking to Raasn. "That's something everyone can always count on from Paulo." She smiled, except the smile wasn't quite a smile.

"Women like men they can count on," said Amarios, looking at Haaran.

"The same holds true for men," he replied.

Across the room I spied Jorl Algeld, talking with Venessa and Zerlyna, a rather odd threesome, I thought.

A woman with short-cut blond hair and watery green eyes approached as if she knew me. It took a moment for me to recall her name. "Darlian . . . how are you?"

"As always. No matter how out of hand matters get for their clients, advocates lead fairly dull and predictable lives. How about you?"

"I've spent a lot of time reading reports and gathering and analyzing environmental statistics. So far, I've discovered absolutely nothing surprising and no one violating environmental regulations."

"That's good for you, but not for advocates in the environmental field. I'd heard you've been visiting some of the outie communities. How have you found them?"

"So far, they've been skeptical but polite. A number of them, I've discovered, don't show up on the official maps approved by the Planetary Council."

"That's because unapproved communities can't vote."

"But wouldn't they want to?"

"I think most of the outland communities think that the Council is largely irrelevant to them. I have the feeling that communities are approved slowly and in a way that doesn't change voting patterns."

"But the Survey Service has to enforce compliance with environmental rules . . ." I broke off as Amarios approached with a beaker of ale.

"Zantos, I believe, is your beverage of choice."

"It is, and thank you."

"You're welcome. I hate to see a man thirsty." She smiled, then slipped away.

I took a sip of the Zantos. Welcome as it was, it wasn't as good as the local lager in Hobbes. When I lowered the beaker, I saw Algeld moving toward us.

"I heard you talking about outland enforcement," he said. "How did your visits go?"

"Quietly and politely, and no one seems to be violating anything."

"No. They won't let their people get anywhere close to the limits. They don't want to give the Council any excuses for removing a settlement."

"Has that happened?"

"Not in . . . a very long time," Algeld replied.

"How long have you been with the Survey?"

"Too long," he replied with a laugh. "Let me know if you need anything."

"I will."

"Good." With that, he slipped back to talk to Venessa.

Zerlyna had moved away and was talking with someone I'd never met.

The rest of the evening was the same, pleasant conversation about su-
perficial pleasantries, with an evasive answer to almost anything that
might have required a direct response beyond a pleasantry. Yet everyone
seemed at ease with that, almost as if it were a social convention that
nothing of import be discussed, and I wondered if that happened to be
the case in any gathering in Passova, large or small.

When I felt it was time to go, I slipped away from a conversation
about the better eateries in Passova and found Aloris. "Thank you for an
evening that allowed me to escape my assignment." I inclined my head
to her.

"You're most welcome. You're leaving punctually as well. I'll bet you'll
even be at the Survey vehicle bay at seven-thirty sharp tomorrow, punctual as you are. You've already gotten a reputation for punctuality . . .
with everyone."

"You checked on when I'm using a vehicle?"

"As administrative director, I have to check on everything that costs
the Survey duhlars," she countered. "That's part of what I do."

"You obviously do it well."

"Thank you."

Once I was out in the pedestrian tunnel, I glanced around, but saw
only a couple rather engrossed in each other, and a patroller in gray who
nodded to me and kept walking. As I made my way back to my quarters,
I kept thinking. Aloris had made two references to being punctual . . .
and that was no accident.

48

Before I went to bed on sevenday evening, I decided to be at the Survey vehicle bay *very* early on oneday, just in case what Aloris had offered was in fact a warning. If she hadn't, or it was a general advisory . . . well, then I'd just leave early. So . . . before seven I was already waiting and had stationed myself in what amounted to a corner from where I could watch anything that might happen. I didn't have a weapon, just my equipment case, but where would I have gotten a weapon?

At seven sharp, a man wearing a light blue maintenance-style singlesuit walked into the vehicle bay. He carried a standard-sized tool kit and walked to the first Survey Service vehicle, a runabout, where he opened the rear and apparently checked the electric motor. He closed the rear, and did the same to the second runabout.

While I wasn't totally certain, I had a feeling that the "tech" wasn't anything of the sort. I could let the false maintenance tech go, but the odds were that someone had already programmed the security scanners, or that the "tech" was wearing a face mask or the like, and would never be found. I'd already discovered how hard it was to find out things on Stittara that people didn't want revealed, and I wanted to find out who was setting up the van for a breakdown.

So when he approached the Survey van I'd been using and had reserved, I put on a pleasant expression and walked hurriedly toward the van, swinging my equipment case, stopping short of the man in the dull blue service singlesuit and saying, "Some last-minute maintenance, I see."

He looked up and said politely, "Yes, ser. Can't be too careful. I'll only be a moment. If you'd please stand back."

"I'm sure you can't. Certainly." As I smiled, I shifted my grip on the heavy equipment case.

"No, ser." He turned toward me, and I could see something in his hand.

I had the heavy case moving fast and straight at his gut.

He tried to dodge, but the case hit with a thud, and I let it go, and took his unweaponed hand and arm and used them to lever him down and drive his head and neck into the side of the van.

The stunner clattered onto the permacrete.

I'd obviously used too much force, because he lay there limply on the ground. He was breathing, though. That was fine with me. I didn't need a dead man on my hands.

I didn't even have to link an alarm.

In moments, Dermotte was running across the bay, followed by a uniformed Survey Service guard and, well behind them, a Passova patroller in gray.

"Are you all right, Doctor?" demanded Dermotte.

"I'm fine, but I'd like to know what he was planting in the van . . ."

Then . . . I heard a *click*. I didn't even wait, but grabbed Dermotte and took two long strides and threw the two of us on the permacrete directly behind the van. We were down flat, and the security guard and the patroller had jumped back.

Moments passed . . . and nothing happened.

I waited, lying there, wondering if I'd overreacted.

Whump!

The front end of the van exploded . . . and debris scattered everywhere.

When the debris stopped falling, I scrambled up. I could see that most of the blast had been directed toward the driver's position. That didn't surprise me, but it did explain why the rest of us hadn't been shredded. I could also see that the patroller and the Survey guard were both down, but both looked to be breathing, and I didn't see great gouts of blood. The false tech didn't move, either.

The next few minutes were a blur, with medtechs arriving, and more patrollers.

The patrollers asked me question after question, and they did the same with Dermotte.

I told almost the entire truth, only shading it to the extent that I said I'd seen the stunner before I threw the equipment case at the imposter tech. I did get the case back, and it was tough enough that it was only gouged. And the guard and the patroller had been stunned and had cuts, but nothing serious.

Dermotte said several times that he'd called the patrollers when he'd seen the man fiddling with vehicles, but that he hadn't expected me until later, and he'd been shocked to see me question the imposter.

In retrospect, it did seem incredibly stupid . . . but I wasn't used to people wanting to blow me up. In fact, I'd never faced a mugger or a thief, and the only other time I'd faced a drawn weapon was facing "Reksba." I'd really thought that he was tampering with the engine so that I would have gotten stuck in the middle of nowhere.

Eventually, I got back to Dermotte and asked for another van.

"Ser? After this?" He gestured toward that section of the vehicle bay where a forensic tech and two patrollers were still examining the wreckage.

"Especially after this." For more than a few reasons, I wasn't about to stay in Passova at the moment.

"I'll see what I can do, ser."

It took more than another hour before I left Passova at a few minutes past eleven on the way to Donniga, the nearest outland settlement on my list for the week—although I'd originally planned to go there later. With all the time I'd lost, heading for the nearest made more sense. I'd also taken time to pack a bag with clothes for several days while Dermotte had arranged for another van.

It was still close to two hours away, and I had plenty of time to think about what had happened, especially since the nearest skytubes were well to the north—a definite change from what I'd seen so far.

The questions had piled up in my mind. Who wanted me dead? Rob Gybl? The Planetary Council? Kali Artema? Belk Edo? It was unlikely to be someone in the Survey Service, not in the way the blast had been set up. Yet it appeared as though Dermotte and Survey security had been alerted, while I'd only been warned "unofficially." But why had they been alerted, and not me? Was that because it would be useful to have me out of the way, the hapless bystander in whatever was going on? The fact that Aloris had "warned" me . . . had it really been a warning, or a ruse to get me to where I could be removed? Or had she thought what I'd thought, that someone was going to create a breakdown—and not a murder? Dermotte had said that he hadn't expected me until later, and that was probably true. He wouldn't have had any reason to know or think otherwise.

The problem was that there were too many possibilities and not enough facts, whereas, with my environmental assignment, I had plenty of facts, but the ones I needed were missing.

I arrived at the community center building in the middle of Donniga at twenty-one minutes to two. The building was located on a gentle hillside overlooking a long and narrow lake that wound between the rolling hills to the southeast. From the link map, the town was some twenty kays southwest of the Syntex main facility and looked to be even smaller than Thoreau.

I'd barely opened the rear of the Survey van to remove the equipment I needed from my battered and gouged equipment case when a man walked toward me. He wore the brown outland patroller singlesuit, but his hair was gray.

"You must be the ecologist from Bachman . . . and, yes, my hair is gray. Harmless mutation, and I'm not old or dying."

"You must get that look or question often from outsiders."

"I do. That's why I address it right off."

"Here's another question. Does everyone in every outland community know about me?"

"I'd be surprised if all our patrollers on Conuno don't. Poulina Maruka is very conscientious."

"From what I've seen," I said dryly, "you're all that way. By the way, officially and unofficially, I'm Paulo Verano."

"Benje Voeryn."

"You're the head patroller here?"

"I suppose so, since I'm the only one." He smiled. "You plan to start with the crops again?"

"I'd thought to."

"It'll take a while. You might not be able to finish today."

"I got an unavoidably slow start." I shrugged. "Would there be any place here I could stay the night?"

"We don't have fancy places, but there are three or four guesthouses. They're mostly for visitors from other outland communities . . ."

"I understand, but I'm not demanding. As an ecologist, I've stayed in less than the best of circumstances, and I expect even the most modest guesthouse would be better than some places I've stayed." *And probably safer.*

Voeryn nodded, but didn't commit himself.

I loaded the monitors I needed into the smaller bag, and then closed the van, glancing toward the north.

"Skytubes won't be heading this way any time soon," said the patroller.

"Because they're not dark enough . . . or for some other reason?"

"I couldn't give you a reason. After a while you just get to know."

"And if you don't, sooner or later it doesn't matter?"

He nodded. "Pretty much . . . unless you've got enough sense to look to someone who does know. The closest crop strips are uphill."

I got the message. He really didn't want to talk. So for the next three hours we didn't, except for his occasional directions or responses to my questions about items or locations. I just took my readings and entered them into my link, but only into the unit I carried. From what I could tell, once again I could find nothing that was even close to any limits. Still . . . four communities were far too small a sample to conclude much beside the point that, so far, those close to Passova seemed not to present an environmental problem.

As we walked back toward the center of Donniga, Voeryn finally volunteered something. "Loreen and Dunuld, that's Loreen Untlor and Dunuld Strem, they've got a room free tonight." He paused momentarily, then added, "Good people."

"That would be wonderful." I didn't know about wonderful, but it was definitely good. "Ah . . . I don't know much about the protocol . . . the recompense . . ."

Voeryn laughed. "They've got posted rates. Paylinks work here as well as in Passova. Better, I'd say. I'll let them know. When will you be done?"

"I still have to cover any templating centers, recycling and sanitary works, plus an arcade, if you have one."

"Two, we have. I'll tell them it's likely to be closer to seven."

He was right. It was half past six before I finished.

Then I had to walk to Loreen and Dunuld's place, a good half kay south of the community center, its entry distinguished from the other stone ovals only by the blue square that Benje had mentioned. I was glad it wasn't farther, because I'd had to park the van in the underground visitors' vehicle bay at the community center and carry the kit bag that held my clothing. I kept looking to the north, but the skytubes hadn't darkened.

When I got to the bottom of the entry ramp, I didn't have to knock on the door because a young-looking woman opened the heavy door as I walked up.

"You look like an ecologist," she said.

"I am." I inclined my head. "I'm Paulo Verano, and you must be Loreen."

"The very same. I hope you'll be wanting supper." She stepped back and gestured for me to enter the small entry hall, then closed the door behind me.

"That would be wonderful. I've not eaten since early this morning."

"I'll have Dunuld show you to your room, and I'll be getting supper on the table . . . if that's all right with you?"

"That's just fine. I'd like to wash my hands."

"He'll show you where."

Dunuld appeared from the corridor to the right. He was a slender young man with short black curly hair and bright blue clear eyes. "This way, if you please."

I followed him to the first door on the left, open and waiting, The guest chamber was modest, but not cramped, roughly four meters by three, with a small closet, a dresser, a writing table, a bed for two, and a bedside table.

"The filter for the lightpipes is right there." Dunuld pointed. "The fresher is right across the hall."

"Thank you." I set my kit bag on the writing table and went to wash up. After that, I walked back down the corridor to find the eating area, a long table at one side of a comparatively spacious kitchen. Dunuld was already seated.

"Just sit down," said Loreen.

I did.

In moments, a platter appeared before me. "Would you like lager, ale, or water?"

"Lager, please."

In moments, each of us had a platter of a meat pie of some sort, as well as a beaker of lager, and a small salad. I had to admit that the aroma was wonderful, but I wasn't certain what rituals might precede eating.

"No ceremony," said Loreen with a smile. "Just eat and drink or drink and eat."

"Thank you." I didn't need any more encouragement. The fowl—or chicken—pie was simple with various vegetables in a thick sauce and a flaky crust. I took several mouthfuls and then a swallow of lager—good but slightly different from what I'd had in Hobbes, and better than Zantos.

"What is Bachman like?" asked Loreen. "In all the years we've had the guesthouse we've never had an offworlder."

"I'll do my best to give you an idea." I paused. "How long have you been running the guesthouse?"

"It must have been, well, five years before Clorena left to go to Hispanoli, and that was when her daughter was fifteen, and . . . now young Sammel—that's Clorena's daughter Chloe's son, well, he must be forty now . . . hard to think of him as that old, since he's still single . . . anyway, it's been a while."

I managed to keep my jaw in place. Loreen looked younger than I was, and Dunuld certainly did. I'd thought they were a young couple running the extra rooms as guest chambers just trying to help make ends meet. That meant, if my quick mental arithmetic happened to be correct, they'd been operating the guesthouse at least sixty years. "You've obviously had a few guests over that time."

"At times, and then not so many at other times," added Dunuld.

"You asked about Bachman. It's much more crowded than Stittara, and, of course, you can see the sun, except when it's cloudy or storming . . ." I must have talked about Bachman for a good ten minutes before I stopped for another bite of the fowl—or chicken—pie.

"What brings you here to Donniga?" asked Dunuld.

I told them, honestly, if without the politics.

"Sounds like the folks on Bachman aren't much different from the city people in Passova," observed Dunuld.

"Probably not," I replied. "What do you think the difference is be-tween you and the city people?"

"They talk about balance and doing the right thing. We just do it."

"Is that because you're closer to the land?"

"It helps." Dunuld grinned. "It also helps when you see skytubes, and you're reminded that you're not all that significant in the scheme of things. In the end, all any of us has is what we are as a result of what we've done."

I couldn't disagree with that.

We talked over dinner, not that much else of great import was said, although I got a better feel of the outland communities, and I had a small piece of a plumapple pie. When I began to try to stifle yawns, Loreen sent me to bed.

I didn't protest. It had been a long, long day.

49

"What really happened there this morning?" asked Raasn.

"You've seen what the security links showed. I don't know any more than that," replied Aloris, her legs crossed under the table at the arcade restaurant.

"You know more than that. You're tapping your toes. You do that—"

"You're so perceptive. You tell me."

"Why did you warn him? We agreed that it was better that the patrollers take care of it and trace it back to the Council."

"That wouldn't have happened, and you know it. Meralez is too good for that."

"Was that why you warned him?"

"I had to know whether he was a brilliant and talented economist or a Unity agent of some sort. Meralez just assumed he was an agent. That's so typical of her. Just eliminate a possible danger before you understand it. We'd never prove it. The minute her tool woke up, every recollection of the last week, if not longer, was gone."

"And your conclusion about Verano?"

"He's an ecologist. No agent would walk into that situation, especially without a weapon."

"Your little test could have gotten him killed, you know?"

"That was a risk, but it wasn't as much of a risk as not knowing who he really is. Meralez didn't understand that."

"You talk about my being unfeeling . . ." Raasn shook his head.

"You don't understand," Aloris said. "He's even more dangerous than an agent. He's determined, and he's dogged, and he's very perceptive. And now, he's out there in the outland communities, and he's visiting the ones where Algeld has almost no contacts and no control."

"Neither does the Council."

"Just what will happen when he reports what the environment is really like here?"

"Do you think we'll be around in a hundred and fifty years? That's how long it would take for anyone to act."

"We might be. Haaran and Amarios will be. And their children."

"You still think we're here on sufferance?"

"Do you want to wager against that?"

Raasn shook his head. "What do you suggest?"

"Wait . . . for now. All we have to do is to make sure Verano doesn't send a preliminary report . . . or get on the shuttle to orbit control . . . and that we can assure. Tadao will take care of that . . . if necessary."

50

Before I'd gone to bed, I'd set the filter on the lightpipes to allow some illumination to filter into the room so that, I hoped, I'd wake gradually on twoday . . . and I did. I lay there enjoying the slight flow of fresh air from the ventilation system of the guesthouse . . . with its slightly heather-ish scent, that scent that I'd discovered came from the lichen/grass . . . and thinking about everything that had happened . . . and about Rob Gybl . . . and the pieces clicked together—"deep stars!"; the annoying gesture with his hair; the precise long strides; the apparent ability to inter-cept or track comms. He had to be Alliance Space Force, or ex–Space Force. They kept their hair short, and he wasn't used to longer hair. Why he was on Stittara was another question, but he had to be working with someone. But whom? Someone on the Planetary Council, like Morghan or Melarez? Another councilor? Or someone at RDAEX?

I doubted, if RDAEX was involved, that it was Kali, not because I liked her, but because she was essentially a hired gun, and I didn't see Belk Edo revealing internal strategy to a hired gun, especially one from Teppera, particularly if Gybl happened to be Space Force. The Tepperans preferred not to fight, but if they did, they had a tendency to leave few survivors and no witnesses, and they detested the kind of bravado for which the Alliance Spacers were known.

Where did Syntex fit in?

Syntex didn't. VLE did . . . and VLE wanted to take over RDAEX. I'd have bet Aimee was behind it, and I'd also have bet that the Alliance Space Force had some sort of quiet hidden arrangement with RDAEX, because most of RDAEX was space-oriented, with a number of deep-space installations. From the fragmentary information Kali had provided, I also had an uneasy feeling that the RDAEX deep drilling project had an objective dealing with the skytubes, most likely with a way either to replicate them or control them because space was filled with extremes of temperature and pressure and the skytubes seemed to operate across a wide range of both. I couldn't prove that, but I didn't think I was all that far off.

I didn't lie in bed all that long, but rose and crossed the hall to shower and get cleaned up for the day. After I dressed, I used my link to pay, according to the instructions on the small card I'd noticed on the dresser the night before.

Just after I'd finished packing, there was a light knock on the door. "Breakfast is ready any time you are."

"I'll be right there."

When I got to the table, Dunuld was already seated and enjoying a mug of something steaming.

"Tea or café? Or something else?" asked Loreen.

"Tea, please." I sat down. "Is there a charge for me to link the planetary comm from here?"

"No. We don't believe in unnecessary charges."

"Thank you. I'll be making several quick links after breakfast, before I get on the road again."

"Where might you be headed?" asked Dunuld.

"What's the most scenic route to a nearby community?"

"You could take the west lake road to the south end of the lake and then take the hill road through the badlands. Sort of stark, but definitely scenic. On the other side, maybe ten kays farther on, you'll be in Docota."

Loreen set a platter of scrambled eggs and some sort of meat strips in front of me, with an enormous hot sweet roll on the side, and a dish of fried apples.

"Badlands?"

"You'll see," said Dunuld laconically.

"What caused them?"

"What do you think? They can do a lot more than blow, if they've a mind to. Might be worth your while to look close."

"I will. Thank you." I took a bite of the fried apples, and then another one. "What's Docota like?"

"Flatter than here. No lake. About as many people."

"Are most outland communities limited to around a thousand people?"

Dunuld frowned for a moment. "The council—our council—has never set a limit, and there are a few that might have five thousand. There are quite a few here in Conuno around two thousand people."

"What about new communities?"

"Every so often there's a new one, but I can't remember, offhand, when we've had a new one around here."

"You just have the one grandchild?"

"Two," replied Loreen. "Sammel and Carisa. No great-grandchildren yet."

"They'll take their time," said Dunuld, with a laugh.

I ended up eating every last crumb of breakfast and having a second mug of tea before I retreated to my chamber and got ready to head out.

Then I tried a link to Kali Artema, but only got a message screen.

So I just said, "If you haven't already, check the news for an explosion in Passova. Apparently, an ecologist was targeted." Should I have said more? I decided against it.

Then I put in a link to Aimee Vanslo, and her aide put me right through.

Aimee looked intently at me. That was how it appeared in the small projected image, anyway. "I saw the news story. You were the ecologist who was the likely target of the explosion, weren't you?"

"They didn't name me?"

"No. They can't give names without consent."

"Yes. I presume I was at least a target."

"Where are you?"

"Somewhere. Here's something I suspect, but can't prove. Rob Gybl, you might remember him, Roberto Gybl . . . might likely be an Alliance Space Force type . . . or ex–Space Force . . . and I don't think he likes your acquisition plans."

"I'd thought something along those lines, but the acquisition was finalized before I left Bachman . . . They can't do anything, regardless."

"RDAEX here doesn't know?"

"There was one condition. It allows them to complete a project. If it works, there's a revision in the compensation and management structure. How did you find out about the acquisition?"

"From Gybl. He claimed that the phony Reksba told him."

"You understand what that means?"

"They were either working together, which Gybl denies, or you've got two parties unhappy with a VLE takeover, regardless of whether it's a fait accompli . . . because they have to know that." I paused. "I just thought you'd like to know. Until later." I broke the link. With what she said, I thought it would be best if I left Donniga expeditiously.

Then I made my last link of the morning—to Aloris at the Survey Service.

She was there. "Paulo . . . where are you?"

"On my inspection tour of outland communities. Is there anything I should know?"

"I imagine your official link is flooded with requests from linksters all over Passova. Something like yesterday has never happened before."

"It's certainly never happened to me before. Has anything been discovered about who the imposter tech actually is?"

"The Council's patrollers have him in custody. There's nothing in the links about who he is."

"I'd like to know, but we'll have to see. I just wanted to let you know I'm fine, and I'll be touring and measuring in outland communities for a while. I'll let you know periodically."

"But . . . what will I tell people?"

"Tell them what I told you. After all, if what I'm doing is upsetting someone, the sooner I get it done, then the less sense it makes for them to try again." That was poor logic, and I knew it, but it was the best I could do without saying things I didn't want to say. "I'll talk to you later." With that, I broke the link.

Loreen was standing by the door as I walked out of the guest chamber.

"I linked the money according to the directions."

"I know. We do check." She smiled. "Have a good trip."

"Thank you."

As I walked down the narrow stone road toward the community center, I considered what might lie ahead. I hadn't told anyone where I was headed but, before talking to Dunuld, had tentatively decided on another unofficial outland community called Greenpax, which was a good hundred kays almost due south of Donniga. I could still go there from Docota . . . unless something else came up.

I also wondered just how much Aimee knew about the RDAEX "project." She either didn't know all that was involved or was very good at revealing nothing. I shook my head. I already knew that she was good at revealing nothing. I wished I knew more, because all I did know was that the RDAEX project involved high-energy photonic deep drilling. I had the uneasy feeling that it was very deep drilling perhaps close to the actual outer planetary core, although I had no idea if that were possible . . . or even what RDAEX might be doing. But . . . if that happened to be the case . . . I certainly didn't want to be nearby.

Stittara had a core more molten than it should be, given what we knew about planetary dynamics, an active and moving molten core that generated a magnetic field far stronger than it had any right to be. Tectonic processes were subdued, and had been for over a hundred million years, and that was inconsistent with the planetary core. A forerunner culture had vanished, and all habitations had apparently become uninhabited at the same time, and the cities so far investigated had been buried in mud floods, suggesting that the entire planetary surface had been affected at close to the same time. Yet, it appeared, from the Syntex site, that the ecology at present was similar, if not identical to that of 120 million years ago. And . . . the construction of the forerunner cities intimated strongly that there had been skytubes then.

All that sent a chill down my spine.

The Survey Service van was where I'd left it. I loaded my bag, then did look the van over thoroughly, even peering into the engine compartment. Everything looked to be normal. So I got in and drove out, following Dunuld's directions and taking the road along the west side of the lake.

I actually saw a bird or ducklike avian, if one that seemed very small, and then a gaggle of four a little farther on, if a good kay south of Donniga. The low hills blocked my view of all but the upper portions of the skytubes in my rear viewer, and I didn't see any to the south.

When I got to the end of the lake, the road split. One branch continued due south, and another headed close to due west, and the middle and slightly narrower way went straight up the gentle hill. With a smile, I turned the van onto the middle road.

The slope was gentle enough that I drove uphill for almost a kay through the lichen/grass, noting clumps of the low bushes here and there, but nothing that could remotely be considered badlands.

That was until I reached the top of the hill.

Beginning less than a hundred meters to the left of the road, the grass stopped, and the terrain dropped into a lower and vast expanse of twisted stone that stretched to the south as far as I could see, and for at least three or four kays westward. I stopped the van and just stared. The stone all appeared to be vitrified, almost glazed, swirled with vaguely earth-toned colors, as well as black, grays, and purples. There were scattered spikes of pointed stone, here and there, but most of the formations, if they could be called that, were just odd misshapen lumps. I'd seen images of the red-rock spires of New Utah, called hoodoos, but those hoodoos appeared to have a sense, almost of order, about them. So far as I could discern, there was nothing resembling a pattern in the wasteland I beheld. It was as if some primeval chaos had solidified, and then been blasted by a solar flare for a nanosecond, with the results frozen in their anarchistic ugliness for eternity.

It wasn't "evil." The badlands, to me, were just . . . anarchistic chaos, almost a reminder, at least to me in my state of mind, that at least part of the universe could be totally meaningless, without pattern, direction, or purpose. The contrast between the orderly, grass-covered rolling hills, open and sparsely beautiful, on one side of the road, and the "badlands" on the other side was stunning . . . and unsettling.

I eased the van to the side of the road, then stopped, and got out, going to the rear and extracting a rock hammer from my equipment case. Then I walked across the grass to the edge of the badlands. There I got another surprise, because the rim of the vitrified area was just that—a smooth curved edge that was a precise line of demarcation between grass and the amorphous masses of the badlands. The surface of the stone, or whatever it was, was as smooth as if it had been finished, but there was no gloss, and I doubted that the surface was particularly reflective, although without anything resembling direct sunlight, it was hard to tell. The colors were even darker and "muddier" than they had appeared from the road.

After a moment I knelt and tapped the stone. The sound was more like a dull thump. I hit harder, and the thump was hardly any louder. There were also no impact markings. I reversed the hammer and swung it as hard as I could. It was like hitting armor, and the shock that went from my hand all the way up my arm hurt like hell or somewhere even worse. I set down the hammer and flexed my hand and fingers for a minute or so, then looked at the stone. There were only the faintest scratches on the stone.

After a moment I stood and surveyed the vitrified wasteland, but I could still discern no sense of pattern. Finally, I began to walk along the rim. Some sixty yards on, I found a place where the slope downward was so gradual it was almost flat, but when I put one boot on the surface I could feel my foot slide. If I tried to explore the place, the surfaces were so smooth, I'd likely be trapped. The only way to be certain to avoid that would be to anchor a line to the van, and I didn't have any rope or cable.

So I settled for walking another hundred yards or so along the rim. In the end, all I could see anywhere was smoothed-over, vitrified amorphous chaos. As I walked back toward the van, I realized something else. There was no dust or dirt collected in the depressions below, as would have been the case on any other world. Was that because it couldn't stick to the smooth stone? It couldn't be just that. The storms and the skytubes had to be scouring it clean at least periodically.

I swallowed and kept walking.

I finally resumed driving, shaking my head at the incredible understatement behind the word "badlands."

51

The northern edge of the badlands that I drove along appeared to be only slightly more than five kays across, although I could see that the frozen chaos of once molten rock was far wider to the south. Another ten kays farther, and just before nine I pulled up and parked the van in front of the community center of Docota, a town that appeared far smaller than any of the other outland communities I'd visited so far.

Once more, about the time I was transferring my monitoring gear into the carry bag, a patroller strolled up the ramp from the entrance to the community center and walked to the rear of the Survey van.

"You're the ecologist, Dr. Verano?"

"I am."

"Pierse Shawn." The patroller nodded slightly. "Dunuld sent word that you might show up here. What do you think of the badlands?"

"Besides the fact that the term 'badlands' is about as understated as you can get?"

"Understatement is an outland trait."

"How long has that badlands been there?"

"Since before Stittara was colonized. The best estimate is over two million years."

"Are there other badlands?"

"A few hundred. I wouldn't know for sure."

"And they're not mapped?"

"They show on the maps as 'rugged terrain' or 'rocky areas.'"

I'd seen those, but hadn't realized that such labeling was also an understatement. "Are there any that postdate colonization?"

Shawn shook his head. "Not that we know of."

"It's rather impressive . . . and unsettling."

"It gives that impression . . . almost as if it had been intended to."

"By the skytubes?"

"Can't say that, Doctor. No one's ever seen that kind of power or destruction from a skytube."

"Something focused a lot of heat or energy there."

"Had to be," he agreed. "You want to monitor the crops first."

I understood. That was all he was about to say, and another question about whether the skytubes created the badlands would only get me another nonanswer . . . and irritate someone there was no point in irritating.

Pierse Shawn was like all the other outland community patrollers I'd met—cordial, helpful, but not effusively friendly. He was also quietly organized, and I finished everything I needed to do, helped by the fact that Docota was indeed a small community, comparatively quickly. By a little before one in the afternoon, I was packing my monitors back into the equipment case, with Shawn standing by.

"Will the south road take me to Greenpax?" I asked.

"It does go there."

"Is there somewhere else that might be better?"

"Well . . . if you take the south road about five kays, and go west for twenty-two kays, then south on the road on the west side of the river for forty, you could likely be in Jaens before dark. That would let you see Jaens, and the next drive to Greenpax would be shorter. I'd not be telling you your travels, though."

"Are there any guesthouses there where I could stay in Jaens?"

"More than a few." Shawn offered an amused smile, suggesting that Jaens was indeed larger than Docota.

I offered my thanks and appreciation, got back in the Survey van, and followed his directions, knowing full well I was being guided or directed. But when one side doesn't want you to see something, following the guidance of the other side can be instructive, both in letting you see what you might not otherwise . . . and by the places from which you're detoured, giving you an idea of where else to look. Or . . . if you end up seeing everything you need to see, you have a better idea of whom to trust about what.

When I got to the last turn mentioned by Shawn, it wasn't so much a turn as an entry onto the largest paved road I'd seen since the one linking Passova and the dropport, and several lorries rumbled by going both north and south. Then, on the flat some five kays short of where Shawn told me to expect the beginning of Jaens, I passed what my link told me was the regional flitter port. It didn't look all that different from the Passova dropport. From there into the center of Jaens, I encountered a scattering of vehicles of various sizes . . . but more than I'd seen in total in all the other outland communities.

The building in the center of Jaens wasn't a community center, either. The entrance—entirely aboveground, something I hadn't seen in any outland community—bore an inscription carved in stone: "Outland Communities Council Center." This time, I didn't even get to the rear of the van before a tall man in a brown dress singlesuit with a tan jacket over it walked quickly from the building to meet me.

"Greetings, Dr. Verano. I'm Merrik Rahle." Rahle was a good head taller than me, with flawless honey-dark skin and short red hair. His voice was a rumbling bass, its sonorous menace only slightly disarmed by the warm smile. "I'm the head of outland security for the Council. You've been very cooperative. We do appreciate it, and we hope that it will be to your benefit as well."

"All the community patrollers report to you, then?"

"Technically, but in reality they report to the regional security coordinators, who report to me." He glanced to the north. "While I don't want to hurry you, it might be best if you moved the Survey van to the security bay."

"Should I be more worried about the multis or the Planetary Council?"

"At the moment, there's likely not much difference so far as you're personally concerned." He walked around to the passenger side of the van, opened the door, and slid in. "I'll give you directions."

I got back into the van and followed his guidance, roughly a block north and a half block east, to an unmarked vehicle door that opened as I drove up. Unlike the other outland vehicle doors, the few I'd seen, this one was not only a pressure door, but there was a second armored pressure door one level down. I parked in a bay down the ramp from the second door, which did close behind us.

"This should shield whatever tracer is in the van and also hide it from satellite surveillance."

"What did you mean about there not being much difference?"

"I think you know exactly what I mean, but I'll spell it out just to be clear. For differing reasons, neither the Planetary Council nor the multis want you to know too much about Stittara. Yet they'd prefer you to complete your report without controversy and in a way that will give the Unity no reason for concern and no reason to make changes in either the governance of Stittara or the operational controls of the existing multis."

"And what does the Outland Council want?"

"Almost the same thing, except we want an end to present and possible future atmospheric and high-energy experimental projects such as the ill-fated Pentura project and the current RDAEX effort."

"And you'd like political parity with the Planetary Council."

"That would be nice, but it's unnecessary, since we believe that will occur in time."

From just my one meeting and briefing—and the explosion directed at me—not to mention the "official" maps of Stittara towns and cities, I had my doubts about the Planetary Council's easy or early acquiescence in sharing power. Yet . . . with Rahle's knowledge of both the Pentura project, and whatever it had been, and of the RDAEX project, it was clear he had more information than I did.

Without saying more, Rahle opened the door and stepped out of the van.

I followed his example and found myself standing in a well-lighted vehicle bay that made the Survey Service bays look slightly grimy.

"You can bring your monitoring gear if you'd like. Take whatever readings please you."

I did take one monitor from the case, just in case, but I was getting the impression that more environmental monitoring outland communities wasn't going to add much to my assessment or improve my chances of surviving to complete the assessment.

"Why is the Outland Council worried about the RDAEX project? Have you brought your concerns before the Planetary Council?"

"We've attempted to suggest that any directed high energy is not particularly wise. The previous two Planetary Councils, in turn, which shared our belief, conveyed their concerns to RDAEX. That resulted in some . . . more active . . . Council elections. The present Council does not believe that it should interfere with the business and research decisions of powerful multis."

"I understand that there will be elections later this year."

"Four members are up for reelection. Most of those are members who share our views . . . although we have heard that some other factors may be in play."

"What other factors?"

"I'm afraid those are only rumors at the moment. The Outland Council is only advisory, and advisory bodies cannot afford to deal in rumors. I trust you understand."

"Has Councilor Morghan come down for or against 'conveying concerns' to RDAEX? That should be factual . . . somewhere."

"The councilor has been greatly concerned in the past. The present Council has held no votes on the matter."

"She's concerned about RDAEX getting into Stittaran politics, then?"

"That has always been a concern of every Council member," replied Rahle smoothly. "Stittara only has a few million people. We must rely on the support of the Unity government in matters dealing with any Arm multi."

"And if a multi has the Arm government behind it?"

"I'm certain you can see where that would leave the Planetary Council, Doctor." Rahle turned and walked toward an archway, beyond which a ramp was visible.

The ramp, in turn, led to a tunnel that brought us into a rotunda. On one side ramps led down from the entry gallery I'd observed from outside. On the other were two sets of double doors, closed. Light poured down from a domed ceiling. It had to be some form of intensified light-piping because I didn't believe the outlanders would use artificial illumination for a rotunda and because the natural illumination of Stittara was too diffuse to provide such intensity.

"Lightpipes?"

Rahle nodded.

"How did you manage to step up the intensity?"

"The use of natural diffusion in reverse, I understand. I have no idea how it works."

"There's a Council chamber here?"

"Through those double doors. They're not meeting this week."

"What do they think of my assignment here? Do they even know?"

Rahle smiled. "They know. They think it could be beneficial or a disaster."

"That's why all the not-so-indirect guidance?"

He nodded.

"Might I ask how you know?"

"I'm on the Council."

"Oh." That was involuntary. I'd figured that Rahle was important, just not as high up as he obviously was. "I see. I think."

"Not yet. This way." Rahle continued across the rotunda to a single door on the far side.

Seeing as I didn't have much real choice, I followed. We entered a wide corridor with regularly spaced doors on the left side.

"I'm assuming that Jaens is the unofficial outland capital, or at least the Conuno continental outland capital."

"Both, in fact."

"Where are we headed?"

"To a short meeting. After that, you'll be free to do what you want in Jaens. Oh . . . you won't need to worry about a place to stay. We're putting you up in one of the Council's guest quarters."

"That's very kind of you."

"Kind . . . and in our self-interest."

We only walked another fifty meters or so before Rahle turned down a side corridor to the left. At the end was a door.

A young-looking patroller stood by the door. Unlike the others I'd seen, he wore both a long-barreled stunner and a truncheon at his waist. He nodded and said, "He's expecting you and the doctor, Councilor."

Rahle opened the door and stepped through. I followed. The patroller closed the door behind us.

The chamber was oval-shaped, with one end of the oval at the entry, except the other end had been cut off by a flat wall perhaps two-thirds of the way from the widest point to where it otherwise would have ended, so that the distance from the entry door to the rear wall was some fifteen meters. Old-fashioned bookshelves, some two meters high, comprised the lower section of the rear wall. About half the shelves held books. The other shelves appeared to hold objects or artifacts. Set before the bookcases was a wide antique console desk, with a semicircle of eight chairs facing it.

The man who stood from behind the desk console was slightly shorter than I, so thin he might not have cast more than a rodlike shadow on any world with direct sunlight, and with short black hair shot with silver, something I hadn't seen before on Stittara . . . suggesting he was ill or quite old, although he appeared to be neither. He did not speak as Rahle and I approached, walking across a light brown oval carpet whose border appeared to represent entwined lichen/grass and purple skytubes.

Rahle stopped short of the chairs. "Dr. Verano, I'd like to present you to Tedor Roosan, the first councilor of the Outland Communities Council."

"I'm honored to meet you, sir." I inclined my head politely.

"As am I to meet such a noted ecologist," replied the first councilor, adding dryly, "and one who has caused so much quiet consternation." He gestured to the chairs. "Please do sit down."

We all sat.

"I noticed you studying the carpet as you entered, Doctor."

"I was. It's quite striking and appears to be of excellent quality."

"It is." Roosan nodded sagely, although I thought I caught a twinkle in his eyes. "The grass/lichen and the skytubes have great similarities, for all their apparent differences, don't you think?"

"I don't know enough about the skytubes to make that kind of analysis."

"Then I will merely observe that there is far more to each than meets the eye, and leave it to you to complete your analysis as you can. I did wish to meet you. It's not often that the Unity sends someone so qualified to assess a planetary ecology as a whole."

"Not often?" I questioned. "Has it ever?"

"No. Not that we know. I do have a question or two for you, Doctor. Do you consider yourself an honest ecologist?"

I laughed. Then I said, "I'd consider myself well educated and well grounded, experienced, careful, as thorough as possible under the situational circumstances, and even-handed in assessing situations. But . . . honest? Probably not, because using honesty as a term of evaluation in dealing with the environment indicates that nonenvironmental considerations are in play, and taking such factors into consideration can't help but bias any environmental assessment."

A look passed between the two councilors.

Roosan nodded once more. "So you would place an accurate assessment above other factors?"

"Begging your pardon, but that's a deceptively dishonest question. Decisions have to be made on some basis. If you don't have an accurate assessment, you're likely to have bad decisions."

"That's true. But what if the decision-maker is incapable of understanding the assessment or unable to act in a way that would not result in what, shall we say, an impartial observer, not that there are any in real life, would consider a disastrous result?"

"That's usually not the role of an ecologist doing an assessment."

"I'm sure you're correct in that," replied Roosan. "I'd like to ask you one more question, but I don't want an answer now. I'd prefer your answer *after* you finish your assessment."

I had a feeling I knew what was coming. I nodded.

"What would you consider the right course in presenting an assessment to an authority where an incorrect policy based on that assessment would result in great ecological and enormous physical harm?"

I was very much afraid I knew exactly what he meant. "You don't pose an easy question there."

"It wasn't meant to be easy." Roosan smiled wryly. "I've captured our discussion. I'd like your permission to share it with other councilors."

"Because they weren't here?"

"They couldn't be. No one knew if you would come here."

That was true enough. "I'd appreciate it if you'd restrict it to councilors . . . and key staffers, if you think necessary." He probably would have included some staff anyway, and I might as well make the gesture.

"Thank you." He stood. "I do appreciate your taking the time to talk with me, and to visit Jaens. I do hope we will see more of you in the future."

"And I you." Again . . . for many reasons. I stood, as did Rahle.

"We'd appreciate it if you'd wander through Jaens and talk to people," added Roosan. "You don't have to, but it might be useful to you."

"And to you," I replied.

"We wouldn't suggest it otherwise. That doesn't mean it's not of value to you."

He was right about that as well. Sometimes, though, I get just a little irritated with people who always seem to be right.

Rahle looked toward the door. So I inclined my head once more, then turned and made my way out.

Outside in the corridor, a youngish-looking black-haired woman waited. She wore a red jacket over a pale gold shirt and black trousers and black boots—scarcely inconspicuous. Rahle looked to her. "Ebby, thank you for coming."

"My pleasure, ser." She offered what I could only have described as a bubbly smile.

"Doctor, this is Ebby Tiensu. She works for me, and she'll accompany you to assure your safety. She won't guide you unless you request it."

"I'd be a fool not to request guidance, especially here." I smiled at her. "Could we begin with the sanitation works?"

"That's a good place to start," she replied. "After that, everything will seem brighter."

"Enjoy your day," said Rahle, stepping back.

Ebby led the way along the tunnel corridor away from the Council chamber.

"The bright colors are to put the focus on you, then?"

"Naturally." Even her voice was bubbly. Somehow, I could see her destroying an attacker without losing that bubbliness. That sent a chill down my spine.

"I'm really not that bad," she said softly, adding in the bubbly tone, "most of the time, anyway."

That she could read me that quickly didn't help my feelings of apprehension, but we walked from the tunnel to a ramp and back outside, then another five blocks to the main sanitation center. I only took a few readings. From there, we visited templating centers, a school, three recycling centers, before she suggested the main shopping arcade, underground, but brightly lit with the same amplified piped light I'd encountered in the Council rotunda.

As we walked down the ramp to the main arcade level, I asked, "Do you know how they manage to amplify the piped light?"

"Not really. I understand that it requires a type of wave management that some of the science types at the university here reverse engineered from some of the airborne microorganisms."

"From the skytubes?"

"Oh, no. You couldn't do that. The upper atmospherics, the ones that diffuse the solar radiation."

"I wasn't aware that they'd even been studied."

Ebby snorted. It wasn't a bubbly sound. "The city types haven't maybe."

"Do you think those microorganisms evolved or were evolved or engineered?"

"Does it matter?"

"I think it does. Very much."

Ebby offered a bubbly laugh. "You should look at the shops and think about that later. Over there—see that shop. Each jacket is totally unique."

"Like yours?"

"I got it there."

"Should I get one?" I wasn't quite teasing.

She stepped back and surveyed me, then shook her head. "You're a classic, not a reb. You know it, and that's good."

In the end, I didn't learn much more—except that Jaens was as environmentally clean as any other outland community and certainly more so than Passova. I also got a decent dinner, but not an outstanding one. Ebby wasn't into cuisine, but that wasn't why she was accompanying me.

After dinner, Ebby escorted me back to the guest quarters, rather lavish for the outland, I thought, with a study and a sleeping chamber, all containing a tasteful if somewhat formal decor of pale blue, dark blue, and cream.

The whole matter of my "safety" was getting more and more interesting. The outlanders clearly wanted me safe. So did, I thought, Aimee and Syntex. I didn't know about Aloris and Algeld, and I doubted that Morghan and Meralez cared at all. Zerlyna wasn't out to get me, but might use me if she could. I got the impression that Kali cared to a degree, but Belk Edo was likely another matter. For Rob Gybl, I was just a means to an end, and clearly I'd been less than that to "Reksba."

That still left a few other matters I needed to look into. I linked into the local net and tried several different searches on the bombing incident, but while speculation still showed up on the main and secondary newslinks, there was nothing on the identity of the bomber. I thought about linking Kali . . . but realized it was the middle of the night, if not later, in Rikova, and it was well after hours at Syntex.

So I went to bed.

52

When I woke on threeday, I knew what I had to do. I could only hope that I had enough time in which to do it . . . and that it would be a few more days before RDAEX stepped up efforts to implement its "project," because at the moment I had no hard proof of what I knew to be true, and lack of hard evidence or proof doesn't work when you're facing the Alliance Space Force and a multibillion-duhlar multi, not to mention an executive wanting to keep the likely resulting Space Force contract worth billions, a possible independent spin-off, under his control, and a multimillion bonus. To make matters worse, even if I could find the hard evidence, revealing it would likely destroy Stittara itself in one way or another, if not several. While I knew I had to act, I still wasn't sure what act would be effective, only that remaining in the outlands wouldn't help in the slightest.

Even before I did anything else, I used my link to search the news. Tapping into the outland network was faster than using the personal link, and Rahle would know what I'd looked for in any case. Of that, I was certain. I found what I was seeking. I watched it twice, concentrating on the critical part.

> *NewsOne has learned that the Planetary Council is investigating the recent bombing of a Survey Services van in Passova. The man alleged to have planted an explosive device in the van being used*

*by an ecologist on a mission from Bachman is thought to have ties
to an Arm multi with operations and facilities on Stittara. Neither the patrol center nor the Council has responded to NewsOne
inquiries. Nor has the identity of the bomber been released.*

After that, there were short interviews with people I didn't know, either
by title or name, all of whom either distrusted ecologists, multis, or the
Council, if not all three.

I fixed a quick breakfast in the Council's guest quarters, cleaned up,
picked up my gear, and headed out.

Rahle joined me as I walked toward the parking bay. "Leaving us,
I see."

"It's time to head back to Passova."

"We also took the liberty of removing all the tracers from your van."
Rahle smiled.

"Except yours?"

"We don't need tracers while you're in the outlands, and we don't need
to know where you are when you're not."

"You know you're in danger?" I asked casually.

"No, we're not. You may be, though."

The way in which he said that told me that he was just as blind, in a
different way, as the Planetary Council, and I was a stumbling, one-eyed
man, indeed, trying to see a way clear of catastrophe. All I could do was
smile because to try to explain might well cause him to decide not to let
me depart . . . or to take some other unwise act, all because he could not
see what was so clearly before him. I did add, "Thank you. I'll be as careful as I can."

Even by beginning early, driving at a speed faster than I was comfortable with, and taking the most direct route back to Passova, I didn't ease
the van to a stop in the Survey parking bay until a shade after eleven.
From there I hurried to my office, nodding to Dermotte in the corridor,
and immediately dropping in front of my console.

The first thing I did was to call up detailed maps of the area between
Donniga and Docota. As I'd suspected, the badlands were shown, but
only labeled as "rough terrain (minimal ecological diversity)." That was
certainly one way of putting it. I did a global search. There were 1311
such areas on Stittara.

I tried not to shudder. That meant I had to find out more about the status of the RDAEX project . . . and soon.

I tried a link to Kali. She wasn't answering.

My second link was to Aimee Vanslo. She wasn't in, either.

Do you want to try Edo now? I didn't. Not yet.

So I walked over to Aloris's spaces.

She looked up in mild surprise, but not in shock. "I thought you were in the outlands."

"I was. I'm back for a while."

"How did it go?"

"I saw a number of outland communities and some interesting sights, officially called something like rough terrain of minimal ecological diversity."

"The badlands?"

"That's more accurate. Who came up with the euphemism?" I had a good idea why, but I wanted to hear what she had to say.

"I don't know. It was well before my time. Jorl might know."

"I'll ask him. I do need to talk to him."

"What else happened?" The hint of a smile crossed her lips.

"Besides taking lots of measurements in more outland communities? Not much. I did meet with the outland head of security and the first councilor of the Outland Communities Council."

"They were willing to meet with you?"

"They seemed to think my assignment was important. They insisted on meeting with me."

"I don't recall who holds those positions . . ."

I understood. She wondered how much I was stretching the truth. "Merrik Rahle, tall, honey-dark skin, and short red hair. Deepest bass voice I've ever heard. He's the head of security and a councilor. Tedor Roosan, the first councilor, small, thin, black hair shot with silver."

"That's . . . quite something. Did they say why they wanted to meet with you?"

"They wanted to impress on me the complete interdependence of all facets of Stittaran ecology . . . and to assure me that they respected that interdependence." That was absolutely true, although I wasn't about to elaborate.

"Kind of them."

"At least, they didn't throw me out." I smiled. "I need to see Jorl." With a nod, I left and headed toward enforcement.

Jorl Algeld was standing outside his doorway. He looked as though he'd been expecting me, and he walked into his office and shut the door behind us before speaking. "Why did you remove the tracers on the van? If anything happened to you, no one would have been able to help you."

"I did nothing of the sort. I wouldn't know a tracer from a neutrino neutralizer." I didn't even know if such a device existed, but I'm not always the best at inventing things on the spur of the moment.

"Someone did."

I shrugged. "They might have been removed before I left Passova. Or someone in the outland communities did."

"They weren't removed here. They vanished once you got to Jaens. It had to be . . ." Algeld shook his head. "Could have been any of them."

"Any of whom? The Outland Council members? Their staff? Or agents of the Planetary Council?"

Algeld sighed. "We'd like you to finish your study. Alive. In one piece."

"It doesn't help much when things are mislabeled or misdescribed . . . such as 'rough terrain of minimal ecological diversity.'"

"All you had to do was ask."

I found I was actually glaring at the idiot. "When you use words to hide meaning, you're lying. When there are no words and no descriptions, when critical facts are simply not there, that's also lying. You can call it deception in the cause of a greater good, or service to a higher ideal, but in the end, it's lying, and it will cost you in ways you can't possibly comprehend because you're perverting the very basis of human communication, and every time in history that's happened on a large scale the result has been disaster. I just hope that doesn't happen here."

He actually stepped back, but his face reddened. "You may be the best ecologist in the galaxy, but you've been on Stittara a month or so . . ."

"—and I have absolutely no understanding of the history or what everyone here has gone through. Nor do I understand the constraints imposed upon the Survey Service and the Planetary Council, or the economic pressures exerted by the presence of powerful multis. Is that it? Or would you like to add more?"

He opened his mouth, then shut it. After a long moment he said, "I hope you know what you're doing. For the sake of everyone."

"I don't. Not exactly, but what I do know is that your planet-wide conspiracy of silence hasn't a chance against the forces already in motion." *Nor does your self-imposed blindness to the implications of what you already know.* But that . . . that I wasn't ready to say.

"What do you plan to do?"

"What needs to be done." *As soon as I can figure out what exactly that is.*

When I got back to my console, I checked for messages, even though my link should have alerted me. Neither Kali nor Aimee had returned my link. So I tried to reach Geneil Paak. She was in.

"What can I do for you, Dr. Verano?"

"Help me with some geologic dating. On my recent tour of outland communities, I drove past something the outlanders called a badlands. They said it was more than a million years old. What can you tell me about the badlands?"

"There's not too much known beyond what you saw. Did you examine the stone at all?"

"As I could. I couldn't even scratch it with a rock hammer."

"It's as tough as any composite, and very resistant to geologic and environmental forces."

"What's it made of?"

"It's effectively a natural composite, call it anomalous stone. It can be cut, but it's scarcely worth the effort."

"How old are the badlands?"

"All of the badlands appear to date to the same time period, a little over three million years ago." She paused, as if that were significant.

Three million years ago? Why would that . . . I swallowed, then said, "The only thing I knew about that period was that it was the time of the first Ansaran Expansion."

"There's nothing in the files, Doctor," she said, her voice precise and careful, "but it is said that there are places where strangely shaped objects are visible through translucent sections of stone."

"Hasn't anyone investigated?"

"In the early years there were dozens of expeditions. Most of those records were lost, but you can check the more recent ones, if you want. There's no record of anyone ever finding anything."

Or if they did, they didn't record it. That all sounded preposterous . . . until I thought it over. Stittara wasn't a small world. The population was only a few million, and there were over a thousand badland areas, ranging in size from fifteen square kays to over 150. If there were only scattered traces . . . it was quite possible that official investigators had found nothing . . . particularly if, over time, they had become less and less motivated. It was also possible that the records of those few traces found earlier had been lost in the storms before shielding and full power backups had been installed.

"Did you ever investigate a badlands?" I asked.

"Most of us did at one time or another," Geneil admitted. "It's work, though. You need ropes and backups because the stone is so smooth. Once in a while someone gets caught there and dies. Mothers warn their children, all the time."

"Did you ever see anything . . . unusual?"

"The whole place was . . . spooky. Outside of that, it was like vitrified geological chaos, as if all sorts of materials had been melted and swirled together, and left to congeal willy-nilly."

"No sign of technology melted inside that stone?"

She smiled, faintly. "I always wondered. Most of the kids I knew did, but we never saw anything like that."

Given how weird Ansaran stuff looks anyway, how would outland children even know?

"Is there anything else you can tell me about the badlands? Radioactivity? Magnetic field distortions?"

She shook her head. "The only strange things are that they all date from the same time, and that they all are composed of the same general type of composite. It's called natural, but it appears nowhere else in nature."

As if those weren't strange enough. "Thank you. If I have other questions, I'll get back to you."

"I'll be here, Doctor."

I sat there in front of a blank console for several moments before I tried to reach Aimee Vanslo again. She was there.

"Paulo. I saw you'd linked. I can't talk long."

"I just wanted to see if my thoughts had been useful . . ."

"Your observations cleared up a number of misconceptions on the part of several parties." She offered the professional smile. "Our friend Gybl has vanished, as well, but I've been led to believe he was trailing the other man, who was the one who opposed the takeover."

"You're convinced of that?"

"As much as is possible under the circumstances. How is your assignment coming?"

"My contract with the Service? I've mostly finished with the multis and the municipalities, and I've been surveying outland communities. So far as I can tell, to date, they're all within Survey regulations and guidelines."

"Then you're essentially finished."

"Hardly. There's a lot of data to crunch and finish, and then I have to write it all up. And, as we've discovered, nothing's over until it's over. Tell me. Does the successful conclusion of the project we discussed result in a partial spin-off?"

For just an instant, her face tightened. "To discuss anything along those lines would be premature."

"I understand. I won't presume again." And I did understand, and I wouldn't presume, because it would either be futile . . . or too late. "Thank you again."

She actually smiled. "As I said before, you're good. It's too bad you're wasted as an ecologist." Then her image vanished.

That confirmed part of what I knew, but, once more, it scarcely constituted proof.

Who else might know something? With a shrug I began to track down Torgan Brad. It wasn't hard, and he was there and agreed to a personal meeting in a stan.

I walked into his small office in an area to the west and south of the Planetary Council area. He didn't stand, but gestured for me to take one of the two chairs before his console. The office was almost square, with no decorations except two images, one on the right wall and one on the left. The image on the right was a stylized image of a ley-liner in trans-space, or what purported to be that, since capturing such an image was not possible. The one on the left was what I thought was a concept tunneltrain— likely based on a magnetic linear accelerator principle, not that I knew of any ever having been built, given the costs and technical obstacles.

Brad offered that world-weary smile I'd noted on the *Persephonya*. While his light brown hair wasn't thinning, it was so fine it gave that impression, and there was a tiredness in his eyes. "I'm happy to meet with you, Dr. Verano, but I have to admit that I still don't understand how the Ministry of Technology and Transportation can be of assistance to you."

"That's why I'm here . . . is it Dr. Brad?"

"Ah . . . well . . . yes."

"You're an engineer by original trade?" That was a guess, but if I didn't happen to be right, I thought he'd correct me.

"Electrical . . . but transport related."

"Fields dealing with deep-space transport, like linear accelerators? You weren't involved in the exploratory effort to determine what might happen when a linear accelerator was used in trans-space were you?"

"No." He shook his head. "I opposed that project from the beginning. That was a fool's quest, and I fear our descendants will see the results."

"I didn't hear that there were any results."

"Oh . . . there were results. That's why I'm here. Indirectly. But you still haven't answered my question."

"I'll try. I may be wrong, but I assume you're here in regard to Dr. Spek's work with RDAEX."

"That's not widely known, but it's not a secret. What does that have to do with the environment?"

I wanted to grin—broadly. I didn't. "From what I can determine, Dr. Spek is involved in a RDAEX project with high-energy photonics. Part of that project involves either drilling or passing a high-energy beam close to or into the outer core of Stittara. The more than normal plasticity, heat, and circulation of the planetary core has created a far more powerful magnetic field for the planet than is customary for a T-type world or, for that matter, virtually any world of its size—"

"There are other worlds with such fields," Brad pointed out.

"There may be, but I'm not aware of any that are habitable or inhabited. And all are larger than T-type worlds."

He frowned, then nodded slowly. "You may be correct in that."

"From an environmental point of view, I worry that such a project might disrupt the magnetic field. Given that Stittara requires that field for life to exist, it does seem to me that the project might have environmental consequences." Even as I said the words, I couldn't believe that any ministry in the Arm government would approve of a project with the potential consequences I'd spelled out in what was essentially my educated guess.

Brad's frown deepened. "The project description does not mention a penetration that deep."

"Given the larger core size, the mantle is correspondingly thinner." That was another concern of mine, because there should have been more tectonic activity under those circumstances. "What exactly is your role here?" I pressed. "To observe to see if the project meets the Ministry's criteria?"

"Why else?"

"Why do you think the technology would be applicable to transport?"

"I have my doubts. My superiors may also, but there is a chance that the technology may allow for multiple trans-light speeds in trans-space."

"Nondestructive acceleration in trans-space?"

He nodded.

That explained another piece of the puzzle. It also made my situation worse. "Do you have any idea when the final trials will be complete?"

"That's entirely up to RDAEX."

"Will you be meeting with them again soon?"

"On . . ." He stopped. "I don't believe that's a matter I should discuss at present."

"I understand. I do hope you understand that my concerns are entirely environmental, and while I have conveyed those concerns to Executive Edo, I would appreciate your conveying the fact that I have expressed those concerns to you as well."

"I can do that, but it seems to me that you're stretching."

I stood. "Thank you for seeing me."

Although I forced myself to leave almost sedately, I wanted to run, or at least walk as fast as I could because it was threeday, and the way in which Brad had started to answer the question suggested he would be meeting with RDAEX within the week.

What else could I do?

I could see what I could find out from Kali—if I could ever reach her. As soon as I reached my office, I tried the link again. This time she was in.

"You've linked several times. I would have gotten back to you. You know, it is rather late here."

"I know. I'm sorry. I've been out, but I have a proposition for you. I understand your shuttle will be coming to Passova tomorrow." That had to be the case if Torgan Brad was going to RDAEX. "And I was wondering if I could persuade you to come with it, perhaps take the day off and spend it with me."

"You're very resourceful, Paulo."

"I'm hoping that I'm persuasive as well." I smiled as cheerfully as I could.

"I'd love to, but I just can't."

"Official escort duty again?"

"You know I can't comment on something like that."

"I can always try. Any chance of your coming for the weekend?"

She shook her head.

"Well . . . I'll keep trying."

"You are persistent, I must say."

"There's a fine line between persistence and annoyance in these matters," I offered. "I hope to be persistent without crossing it."

"Thank you. I do have to go."

"Then go. I hope we'll talk later."

She did smile, but it was sadder and almost pitying.

So much for your charm. But I had learned that my suppositions were likely correct. That still didn't leave me much in the way of options.

I couldn't very well go to the Planetary Council, not with my structure of coincidences and geology and history—not a shred of real technical proof—and beg or demand that they insist RDAEX suspend an experiment or project potentially worth billions because something terrible *might* happen.

I knew that if the RDAEX project worked, the consequences were potentially devastating. But what if it didn't work?

What else could I try?

I tried to link Belk Edo. All I got was his message screen. Given that it was well into late evening in Rikova, that didn't surprise me.

I thought. There was one totally insane possibility. It couldn't hurt, and it might help . . . somehow.

So I left the office and made my way to an upper-level doorway, where I pressed the entry button.

A peephole in the door opened. I hadn't seen one of those before. I thought the face I saw was that of Clyann, Ilsabet's muscular guardian.

"What do you want?"

"I'm Dr. Verano. I spoke with Ilsabet a week or so ago."

"Yes?"

I could sense the unspoken "so what?" but I had to try. "I need to speak with her. Just briefly. It's very important."

Clyann glared at me. "You don't have an appointment."

"Please, it's really important."

"How do I know . . ."

"Look . . . there's no one with me. I'll strip to my underwear and let you hold a stunner to my head."

Abruptly she laughed. "That's the best proposition I've had in years."

"Please."

"Just a moment."

After several moments the door opened. Clyann stepped well back, and the stunner was out. She motioned me in and to one side of the entry foyer. "Close the door."

I did. Then I started to unfasten my singlesuit.

"You don't have to go that far, handsome as you are."

For some reason, the words recalled the way Ilsabet spoke, but I decided not to make that comparison.

"Just stand there while I scan you."

I waited, watching as she played the scanner over me.

"Turn around."

I turned.

"You're clean. Now . . . what's this all about?"

"I think the skytubes are going to get a shock from an experiment. I've tried to talk to people, but I don't have enough proof to convince them to stop. What Ilsabet told me last time was helpful. I'm hoping I can find out something . . ."

"Can it wait?"

"I'm afraid to wait. Even if she can help, then I have to do work to confirm . . ."

"Clement said you were honest. I'll trust you. At a distance. You get within two meters of her, and I'll stun you where you stand. Understand?"

"Yes. Thank you."

Clyann motioned for me to walk toward the pressure door, already open. I walked up the ramp beyond through the open second pressure door, then stopped in the small antechamber.

"Ilsabet . . . the doctor you liked is here to talk to you again." Clyann turned to me. "Go on in, but don't get too close to her."

"I won't," I said in a low voice.

Ilsabet was sitting beside the armaglass window looking out. She didn't turn as I approached and stopped.

I spoke gently. "Ilsabet . . . some scientists are trying to send brilliant light down deep into the ground. It might upset the skytubes. I can't seem to stop them. I don't want anyone else hurt."

She turned her head and just looked at me.

"Light so bright, of such might, could give the skytubes fright." Maybe the verse would help.

Her eyes darkened. The color of her irises actually deepened into a deep dark purple. After several moments, she spoke clearly, again like a dispassionate adult in the way she had so briefly during our first meeting, "Light so bright brings back might."

I had to think. How could I phrase what was needed in verse? I did the best I could. "Few men and not all, on only them should might fall."

Once more there was a long silence before she spoke. "Light that shines so bright rebounds in double might."

I was in no position to negotiate . . . if indeed that was what I was doing, and not merely engaging in an elaborate and meaningless charade. "With your might, take the few, with the right, do what you do."

There was no answer.

"Tell me something new, tell me something true," I asked gently.

"Is one life? Is color art? Is might strife? Are fingers smart?"

She'd said something like that before, but not quite.

"I'm done. That was fun." Her eyes lightened into a pale purple-gray, and she smiled.

As much as anything, that told me that I'd done what I could . . . if I'd done anything at all.

"Thank you, Ilsabet. I hope you have a pleasant evening."

"Purple night, pleasant sight."

I nodded, then turned, making my way back to the small anteroom.

Clyann stood there, holding the stunner aimed squarely at me. "You know, don't you?"

I had no doubts what she meant . . . or that the stunner was likely set on lethal. "I didn't know. I guessed. But what I said was true."

"Why did you come here?"

"Because . . . because going almost anywhere else wouldn't have done much good. I'll try again, tomorrow, but . . ." I shrugged. "Does the medtech know?"

Clyann shook her head. "If they knew . . . they'd torture her, question her to death. She's happy enough in her own way, and it wouldn't make any difference. People don't want to see."

In the land of the blind, no one believes the one-eyed man. My lips curled into a brief ironic smile that faded as quickly as it had inadvertently come. "That's why you've stayed?"

"Someone has to." Clyann's voice was level.

"To save her . . . and Stittara."

"You'd better go, Doctor." She paused. "There won't be any record of your visit. Don't ever mention it."

"I won't." I understood that condition, and just how protective Clyann was, in all senses of the word.

She didn't say another word as I left. Neither did I.

The cryptic nature of the last rhyme preyed on me as I walked back toward the Survey Service, where I needed to arrange for a van for the evening so that I could leave early, very early, in the morning.

Is one life? Is color art? Is might strife? Are fingers smart?

53

No one even questioned my van requisition, and I made sure the van was locked before I headed back to the office. There, I went over a few more facts, such as they were, then finally retreated to my quarters.

The last words Ilsabet had spoken when she had had that different expression kept going through my mind.

Is one life? Is color art? Is might strife? Are fingers smart?

Abruptly I did understand—and it was so damned obvious . . . and frightening, all at once. And . . . like everything else that fit together, it wasn't the kind of proof that would convince anyone who could do anything. And once more I felt very much like the one-eyed man in the land of the blind, crying out, "Can't you see?"

Eventually, I did drop off to sleep, although I didn't feel that rested when I struggled up on fourday morning and hurried through getting ready.

I arrived at the dropport early. As I'd expected—if regretfully—the RDAEX magfield shuttle was already there, waiting on the expansive permacrete square linked to the runway. The passenger ramp was down, but I didn't see anyone outside the craft. I pulled the van over beside the low drop shuttle receiving building, where most of the vehicle wouldn't be visible from the RDAEX shuttle, leaving just enough of the front so that I could see if another vehicle showed up.

I waited almost half an hour, until ten minutes to seven, when a black vehicle the size of a small van—with the Ministry of Technology and

Transport logo on the side—stopped perhaps ten meters short of the ramp. I immediately pulled out with the van and drove over beside the Technology vehicle. I jumped out and headed for the ramp. Torgan Brad was already entering the shuttle, and he hadn't even looked back.

As I expected, Kali met me before I even got to the bottom of the ramp.

"What do you think you're doing here?"

"Would you believe trying to abduct you for dinner?"

"No." Ice was warmer than that single word.

"How about trying to save your life?"

"What . . . are you insane?"

"I may be. But I think that the RDAEX test has a very good chance of destroying at least RDAEX and possibly Rikova."

"What proof do you have?"

"Several hundred forerunner Builder (A) sites buried in mud at the same time a hundred and twenty million years ago. Thirteen hundred and eleven separate badlands, vitrified in exactly the same fashion exactly at the same time three million years ago, with occasional artifacts similar to the first Ansaran wave cultures. A Stittaran ecology that has remained stable all that time, something that's never happened on that wide a scale anywhere else. A planetary core that should produce extreme volcanism and hasn't since a hundred and twenty million years ago. Upper atmospheric life forms that regulate the amount of solar radiation that Stittara receives, and, oh yes, skytubes that just happened to destroy the last research facility on Stittara, which was likely investigating the magnetic containment properties around the planetary outer core." All of that was true, except for the very last bit about what Pentura had been doing, which was speculation on my part.

"You're stretching the facts."

"Not much."

"And I'm supposed to walk off with you?"

"If you won't, do us both a favor. Find a security duty to handle well away from Rikova when the project goes active and they send that energy beam down at the core."

"I appreciate your concern." Her voice wasn't quite as cold, merely at liquid oxygen levels, as opposed to absolute zero. "Now . . . we need to take off. We'll likely be late anyway."

I inclined my head and stepped back.

She looked at me for a moment longer, then turned and headed back up the ramp, while I retreated to the van.

I did watch the magfield shuttle lift off, near silently and gracefully.

Then I drove back to Passova. While I parked the van, I didn't surrender it. Not yet.

Once I was back in my office, I made a link to Syntex. Aimee was actually in, and if the background happened to be real-time, she was actually at Syntex.

"I didn't know whether you were at Syntex proper or the site . . . and if you'd answer."

"I'm here. Where else would I be?"

"As an executive, you could be anywhere on Stittara."

"What other interesting suggestions or hints do you have?" Her smile was somewhere between professional and amused.

"Let's just say that I'm very glad you're where you are. What about interesting tidbits you have that you might be willing to share?"

"Matters here have been quiet."

"Do you know any more about Rob Gybl?"

"Only that it's unlikely that such is his appellation. You suggested that already, though."

"I also think that the other fellow was there on your account, perhaps trying to slow down what was already a fait accompli."

"Constantia thought so. She has some ideas. After everything settles down, we should have dinner. I'll let you know."

"Thank you."

The screen blanked, again suggesting that she'd said all she had to say. I hoped she was indeed at Syntex, but with links you could never be certain. *As with so many things, especially now.*

For several minutes I just sat there. I'd almost run out of options. There was no point in trying to persuade the Planetary Council. They weren't about to go against a major multi, and even if they did protest, they had no power to stop the project. I had no environmental proof that would meet Survey Service standards. Those standards were high because of past abuses by environmental extremists. And that left Belk Edo.

So I tried to link him. I got his aide, the handsome Fabio Marghina.

"Dr. Verano . . . what can I do for you?"

"You could put me through to Executive Edo."

"I'm sorry. He's not available at the moment."

"When will he be?"

"I really couldn't say, ser."

"Then, can you get him a message?"

"I don't know. It's possible."

I sighed. "Tell him that I need to talk to him about a similarity between the deep drilling project and the Pentura project."

"I'll see what I can do, Doctor."

"Thank you."

I waited almost an hour, fretting, stewing, and looking at the time readouts, every few minutes, before the screen announced Edo's return call.

"Verano, what's this nonsense about the similarity between Pentura and us?"

"I'm fairly certain that they were looking at magnetic containment in the upper level of the planetary core. You're going to beam high energy at the core. The result won't be pleasant. It's likely to be far worse than that." I couldn't very well tell him that it might destroy Rikova or all settlements on Contrio near RDAEX. He'd ignore that as hysterical environmentalist rhetoric.

"You may be a first-class ecologist, Doctor, but you're not even a fifth-class engineer. Spek assures us that the test won't create any problems. On what do you base your contentions?"

"That running that high an energy field close to the core will cause major disruptions in the planetary magnetic field, and those will engender tectonic readjustments."

"All of our engineers, and our geologists, have studied the matter, and they've concluded that there is absolutely no danger. Are you a high-energy physicist? Or an engineer? We've had the best people in the Arm working on this for a generation. And you're telling me that because we *might* upset the planetary magnetic field just a bit, we face some sort of danger? Come now. If you've got some evidence beyond that, I'd like to know."

"What about all the Builder (A) forerunner sites buried in mud at the same time one hundred twenty million years back? Or the badlands that date to the same time three million years ago—"

"Mere chance. Besides, what was happening hundreds of millions of years ago was under different conditions."

"What about the fact that no one has yet been able to sample a skytube?"

"Oh . . . now you're suggesting that they're intelligent? Total rubbish. The density of the organic entities in the atmosphere precludes even low-level cognitive organization."

I couldn't help but think of the last line of Ilsabet's rhyme—*Are fingers smart?* But Edo wouldn't have bought that, either.

"Come now, Verano. Isn't it time for you to deliver a meaningless threat? Isn't that what environmentalists do when they've run out of facts and science?"

"No. I won't threaten. I've offered my concerns. You've dismissed them. You'll go ahead with your project, and I'll have to hope I'm wrong."

"Of course you are. I do appreciate your not trying to play politics and your not resorting to hysterics. And once the project proves out, I'll even have you out for a celebratory dinner."

"Thank you. I'll hope for that dinner."

"You actually might." He smiled. "Until then."

I stared at the blank screen for a moment, then shook my head.

Half an hour later, I got a link from Kali.

"Are you satisfied?" she asked coldly.

"With what?"

"Edo thinks I leaked everything to you. You've probably cost me and Teppera more than you could ever repay."

"Is this a secure link?"

"At the moment. Over time, no."

What she meant was that it was encrypted deeply enough that real-time decryption was unlikely, but if anyone recorded it . . . they'd eventually break the encryption.

"Please do what I asked . . . If I'm wrong, I'll turn over all my assets to you. I'll even garnish future earnings to pay damages. Just . . . think about it."

She shrugged. Even that expression was cold.

"Please." I hated begging. I'd sworn to myself that, after Chelesina, I'd never do it again.

The screen went blank.

What could I have done? No one would believe what I'd seen with Ilsabet . . . and if I'd tried to explain that . . .

Why wouldn't anyone see?

54

I woke before what passed for dawn on fiveday—bolting wide awake. I immediately checked the news. There were no reports of anything untoward or even slightly unusual anywhere on Stittara. I still cleaned up and dressed quickly. I skipped my workout and exercises, something I'd been doing too often of late, but I wanted to get to the office and the console there.

I made it early enough that the lights were mostly off, and I was the first one around in my section. I checked the news again. Nothing.

I sat and waited. Aloris walked past, stopped, nodded, and went on. So did Zerlyna. Dermotte waved. Raasn didn't even look in my direction as he hurried past my door and toward Aloris's spaces.

I checked the news again.

Then the screen indicated a link from Meralez, Planetary Council, and I immediately accepted.

"I just received a call from Executive Edo at RDAEX. He intimated that your environmental assessment might be less than unbiased."

"I'm sure that he didn't say that," I replied dryly. "He might have suggested that, in recent conversations with me, I'd revealed a concern for the environment disproportionate to the factual evidence available."

Meralez's laugh was actually warmly humorous. "What did you tell him?"

"That I was concerned about the current RDAEX project, that from what I'd been able to piece together, it resembled the Pentura project in many ways, and that I thought there was some risk of triggering tectonic disturbances."

"Why didn't you contact me or Councilor Morghan?" Her voice was quiet, almost menacing.

"For the same reason I didn't go to Executive Director Zeglar or Director Algeld. I don't have anything in the way of evidence that comes close to meeting Survey Service requirements for environmental endangerment."

"So you expressed your concerns to Edo in a way that made him complain to the councilor." Meralez nodded thoughtfully. "Rather effective way of bringing it to our attention. What do you think will happen if RDAEX proceeds?"

"I don't know. That's another reason why I didn't bring it to you. I hope nothing does. I'm afraid that hope is unfounded."

"You haven't answered my question. Not really."

I shrugged. "Best-case scenario . . . nothing happens. Most likely in my opinion . . . RDAEX and part of Rikova are destroyed. Worst case . . . the same thing that happened to the Ansarans." I mentioned the Ansarans because I wanted to know just how far the selective blindness of Stittarans went.

Her face froze for an instant. "Did you tell Edo that?"

"No . . . I did mention that Stittara wasn't as stable as he thought, not with all the badlands dating to three million years, and all the forerunner sites being buried in mud at the same time a hundred and twenty million years ago."

"It could be worse."

"Worse than what happened to them?"

"No . . . what you said."

"I have the feeling it won't matter," I said glumly.

"There is that." She paused. "I'd appreciate it if you wouldn't mention any of that until . . ."

"Until the results of the RDAEX project are known?"

"Until the results are in . . . and we have another chance to talk."

I nodded. That was an acknowledgment, not an agreement.

The screen blanked.

Zerlyna walked into my office just after I blanked the console. She looked at me. "You've been sitting here, on and off, since yesterday afternoon. You checked out a van and haven't touched it since yesterday morning."

"I'm waiting. I don't wait well."

"What are you waiting for?"

"The results of an experiment, you might say."

She looked as though she might say something, then offered a faint smile. "Let's hope it goes the way you want." Then she slipped out of the office.

What is the way you want? If nothing happened, in all likelihood RDAEX would proceed until something truly terrible happened . . . unless I was totally wrong, in which case, I'd likely have destroyed what remained of my career as an ecologist. If what I thought would happen did in fact occur, thousands if not tens of thousands of people would die, Kali Artema among them, but those across the rest of Stittara would survive, at least until some other idiot tried to probe the mystery of Stittara. And, if the worst occurred, as it had appeared to have happened to the forerunners and the Ansarans . . . well, I wouldn't be around to worry.

In the meantime, I kept going over what I knew and what I'd done.

Less than an hour later, the screen flashed red, burning priority, and my whole body tensed. "Accept."

Meralez appeared. She was pale, and her hair was just slightly disarrayed. There was a hint of wildness in her eyes. "How did you know?"

"Rikova? Or worse?"

"Rikova is gone . . . all of it. There's just a twisted vitrified mass there."

"Can you show me the images?"

"They'll be rough, even with enhancement. The sky makes hash out of even infrared images."

The screen split, with Meralez on the left, and a satellite zoom scan on the right, not in color but in shades of black and white and gray. I'd half expected skytubes cluttering the target area, but there were none near. Then I realized there wouldn't be. There wasn't any smoke, but IR minimized it, so that, even if there had been, most of it wouldn't show on the screen. What the image did show was an oval area that, even from an apparent height of over a thousand meters, looked just like the badlands I'd seen outside Docota, except it appeared larger. The lumps and amorphous masses, and the few bent and twisted spires, were enclosed in a depression, not quite a crater, but with much of the devastation below the level of the surrounding rolling plains. The stone appeared to be solidly vitrified and shinier than the older badlands, but that might have been an affect of the IR imaging. I couldn't make out any pattern to the odd misshapen lumps, not a trace of the underground installation and city that had been there. Once more, it looked as though a solar flare had struck, turning everything into primeval chaos that had solidified instantly.

I just looked. I'd *known* it would happen. I'd even bargained to keep the damage to less than it would have been. At least, I thought I had. And I'd gotten what I'd bargained for . . . and lost the only person on the entire planet I really cared about.

"Verano!"

There was a voice somewhere, but I sat fixated on the image.

"Verano!"

I jolted upright in the swivel. For a moment I couldn't remember to whom I'd been talking.

"Are you there?" demanded Meralez.

"I'm sorry. It . . . it hit me . . ."

"It hit them harder."

I swallowed, trying to clear the lump in my throat. Finally, I said, "Did any of the satellites register a surge in directed solar energy?"

"Hold. I can check that."

Half the screen blanked, and I kept looking at the other half. I didn't see anything moving. I wondered about the fact that I'd felt nothing, but then, Contrio was a third of the planet away, and what had hit Rikova hadn't been a tectonic disturbance.

Meralez's image returned. "There was some sort of energy surge. All the sensors focused anywhere near overloaded. Some blew totally."

I nodded.

"You never answered my question."

"What question?" I stalled.

"How did you know what was going to happen?"

"What *might* happen," I corrected her. "It makes perfect sense. It's much less disruptive than using volcanism to send a message. First came the volcanism, because Stittara didn't know better, but I imagine it took eons to rebuild the planet. When the Ansarans started to change things too much . . . well that was when their cities and towns turned to badlands."

"Why now? Why not before?"

"I imagine that we provide something Stittara needs, amusement, stimulation, whatever. So long as the ecology stays balanced. When that changes . . . then Stittara gets less tolerant."

"You're suggesting that the entire planet . . . is alive?"

"I doubt that, but there's definitely some sort of massive intelligence . . . or grouping of them."

"I have to go." Meralez looked hard at me. "You *will* brief the entire Planetary Council, Dr. Verano."

"Once we know the scope of the damage . . ." I broke off what I was saying because the screen blanked.

I was still sitting there several minutes later, when Aloris, Zerlyna, and Jorl Algeld all filed into my office. That confirmed what I'd already known and expected.

They looked at me. I just looked back at them.

"Is it true?" Aloris finally asked.

"What? That something turned RDAEX and Rikova into an instant badlands? According to the Planetary Council, it is."

"It just came across on News One," added Zerlyna, looking at her link.

"And you *knew* it was going to happen?" asked Algeld.

"No. I thought it was possible if RDAEX went ahead with their deep-drilling project. I told Executive Edo that it was dangerous and that doing it could endanger all Rikova. He told me that I didn't know what I was talking about, and that I was a fifth-rate engineer."

"That's why you've been sitting here, brooding?" asked Zerlyna.

"I told Meralez there was a problem, and I told Edo. I didn't have anything that meets Survey Service standards for proof."

"No one ever does," said Algeld sardonically. That he spoke so was surprising to me.

"Why did you think it was possible?" asked Aloris.

"Because it appeared to have happened before . . ." I explained everything except my last conversation with Ilsabet. No one but Clyann was likely to ever find that out, since I'd never made an appointment or used a link, and there was likely nothing in the tunnelcams to call attention to me. Even if they did, and questioned Clyann, I doubted she'd say anything except I'd asked to speak to Ilsabet and that she'd turned me down.

"Now what?" asked Aloris.

"I still have an assessment to finish." *If only out of pride.* "There's not much I can do about what happened."

None of them said a word.

After they left, I still sat there.

Could you have done anything different to protect Kali?

I didn't know what. I couldn't have kidnapped her. She likely knew more about combat, hand-to-hand, and weapons than anyone on Stittara, except perhaps Rob Gybl, if he still happened to be alive, and that was something we'd likely never know, one way or the other. Kali wasn't the type who wanted or needed protection—unless she was dealing with a planetary intelligence.

55

I spent the remainder of fiveday going over everything I'd learned, as well as all the environmental data . . . and I still didn't have anything that would actually prove in a legal or scientific sense that there was any solid reason for the disaster at RDAEX. I'd tried to convey the problem . . . and certainly Melarez had known in time to have advised Belk Edo, but either she hadn't or he hadn't listened.

Once I returned to my quarters, I watched all the news about the disaster until I finally turned it off and collapsed into more of a stupor than a sleep. Sixday morning, as soon as I awakened, I called up OneNews and watched their commentary summary, listening and sipping tea that had cooled too quickly.

". . . the more we have learned about the horrifying disaster that obliterated the city of Rikova, the more perplexing it appears. There are no satellite or sensor images of the destruction. One moment, the city appears normal. The next all images vanish. When those sensors in working order resume, they show only the destruction. One scientist at Stittara University stated that the ruins look like a giant had stirred up the city and then directed a solar flare at it for an instant. There is no significant radioactivity, and no indication that military weapons of any sort were employed. The orbit control station has confirmed that the few spacecraft in

the area of Stittara have all been accounted for and none possess any weaponry capable of such destruction . . . There are no known survivors in the area of the devastation . . . and no recognizable remaining structures . . . The Planetary Council has sent aid to the one nearby outland community, but . . . it appears that little damage, except to vegetation, occurred much beyond the area of total destruction . . . such an effect corresponds to no known weaponry . . .

". . . the only clue is that the multi RDAEX had planned to conduct tests in a confined deep bore yesterday. The tests were the first step in a project to develop a radical new power application, according to sources. It has also been reported that a Survey Services scientist had contacted RDAEX asking that the tests not be conducted on environmental grounds . . ."

There was more, and it went on and on, but there was essentially nothing new. An entire city gone, so sorry, terrible news . . .

I got tired of sitting there, and finally dressed and cleaned up, and then made my way to my office. I could at least start on putting together my report. I didn't feel like it, but what else was I going to do?

Less than an hour after I'd begun to organize data, the screen announced, "Executive Vanslo."

"Accept." I couldn't say I was surprised.

Aimee's image appeared. She looked as tired and bedraggled as I felt. "I thought I'd find you there."

I forced a rueful smile. "Where else would I be?"

"You were that anonymous scientist who warned Edo not to do the tests, weren't you?"

"Yes." I nodded. There wasn't any point in denying it.

"Did you actually know this . . . would happen?"

"Actually know? No. There were indications that it wasn't a good idea, especially after the Pentura episode . . ."

"What indications?" Her voice was sharp. "And you didn't tell me?"

"Except for Pentura, they were millions of years old . . ." I went on to explain about the forerunners and the "Ansaran badlands" as well as I could, ending up with words that were becoming all too trite, true as they were, ". . . and even with all that, I had absolutely no scientifically verifiable proof, no way to use the Survey's injunction power—and I couldn't do that anyway, because I'm only a consultant. All I could do was link Belk Edo and tell him essentially what I told you. I had the feeling they were pursuing the same lines or lines similar to Pentura. I worried about it. I even asked Edo to reconsider. He laughed and said I was a fifth-rate engineer. He complained to the Planetary Council, and one of the Council's staffers contacted me before the tests, and I told her as well."

"That was why you were relieved that I was at Syntex?"

"Yes. If you had been at RDAEX, I would have suggested you leave."

She didn't say anything for a time.

I waited.

"I could bring you into this, you know?"

"I don't think that would be a very good idea. You pointed out that Edo remained independent until after the project was completed. He kept the details hidden from you. He certainly kept them from me. With nothing remaining of the RDAEX Stittara facility, I doubt that whatever plans Edo had for the spin-off and whatever possible contracts he may have had will ever come up." I wasn't about to mention the possibility of the Alliance Space Force tie-in on a monitored console. While I had hinted at it earlier, I doubted that the Planetary Council, for reasons of its own, would ever raise the issue, either.

"That's true."

"So far as the Stittaran environmental assessment is concerned, there's nothing left to assess of RDAEX, and the initial indications are that the destruction, however accomplished by whatever force, will not have long-term consequences on the environment, except in a small area, and that area will be indistinguishable from other badlands. Syntex is fully in compliance with all environmental requirements." I smiled politely, much as I didn't feel like it.

"You can be quite convincing, Paulo."

"I wish I'd been more convincing to Edo."

She shook her head. "He didn't want to see what you showed him."

Like all too many of the willful blind everywhere, but I didn't say that. "And his unwillingness to listen and look beyond cost thousands their lives."

"It's also going to be expensive for VLE. It could have ruined us, except that the liability rested with RDAEX Stittara and its assets until the project was completed to our satisfaction. That was a requirement for the spin-off, and the Alliance Space Force may have some liability as well. Even so, the ancillary claims on VLE will still be significant . . ."

Trust Aimee not to have VLE exposed any more than necessary, I reflected.

"What are you going to do, Paulo?"

"Finish my contract assignment. What else?"

"And after that?"

"I'll have to consider."

"VLE could use someone like you."

"Thank you, but I won't make any decisions until after I turn in the assessment."

"I'll be in touch."

The screen blanked.

I sat there. Somehow . . . I wasn't that thrilled with the idea of working for VLE or Syntex, or Aimee.

I had to wonder. Was whatever the Stittaran intelligence/entity was or what those entities were . . . did they consider human cities or communities as single intelligent entities? That would make sense . . .

Are fingers smart?

56

Purple is the loneliest color of all
Standing guard alone along the world's wall

Ilsabet skipped along the top of the ridge. Then she stopped and looked to the east, empty of skytubes, seemingly oblivious to her guardian beside her. "The clouds sweep, and the sky will weep."

"Are you talking about what happened after you talked to the doctor the other day?" asked Clyann.

"Too long are the years; too great are the fears."

"I'm sorry, Ilsabet." Clyann paused. "Did you like him?"

"He saw what few will see. That makes him kin to me."

"He won't stay here, not after what he saw in your eyes," replied the guardian softly.

"What's seen is done, even under a hidden sun."

"Isn't it always that way?"

Abruptly Ilsabet laughed, childlike. "Daisies are the perkiest flowers, don't you think? Petals of sun and light, centers of ink."

57

I spent most of sevenday in the office at the Survey Service, working on my assessment. I had enough tables and data to begin setting it up, and it took my mind off Kali . . . for at least part of the time. I also knew I needed to meet with Benart Albrot and probably Reeki Liam, if only to be able to note their input on the final assessment, although I doubted that whatever they said would likely change anything, only provide supplemental support. And supplemental support was always good, especially on an assessment of the kind mine would be.

Beyond that, there were other realizations that ran through my thoughts, too many things that hadn't made sense, or that I knew had made sense, but hadn't figured out why, were now all too clear.

Extreme longevity had its cost, biologically, and one of those costs had to be a far lower fertility level, especially among males. That likely accounted for the attraction of local older women to outworld males, most probably almost a subconscious and biologically triggered recognition of a higher probability of offspring. With a lower probability of offspring, male hostility to offworld males was higher, although that baseline hostility to all other males was already high, but there couldn't be too high a level because population levels were low . . . and those were just a few of the ramifications.

I still didn't know exactly the foundation of the Stittaran intelligence, or intelligences, and I doubted that I ever would . . . or anyone would—not until that intelligence decided on a more direct form of communication. But then . . . were we too different from each other for that to happen? Or did the Stittaran intelligence just prefer it that way?

As for attempting to document what I knew to be true . . . that wasn't going to happen, for two reasons. The first was that if I did so, there would be more Belk Edos . . . and the disasters that would follow. There would be anyway, in time, but I saw no point in speeding that up . . . and condemning four million Stittarans to what had apparently occurred to the forerunners and the Ansarans. There are times when believing the best of human beings is foolishness, if not insanity.

The second reason was that any such attempt to prove what I knew had the same problem as I'd had with the RDAEX project. I had no real evidence, nothing that couldn't be explained away. For all that anybody could determine, what had happened to Rikova might just be an occasional fluke irising and focusing of the microorganisms that shielded the planet. After all, why bother with something that only happened every few million years? Especially when Stittara was the source of the anagathics that kept hundreds of millions of Arm citizens youthful to ages once only dreamed of.

All of that was, of course, going to complicate what I was getting paid to do on Stittara.

Between thoughts and work and regrets, and some quiet mourning, I made it through sevenday, and even managed to get some sleep that night . . . and wake and return to my work on oneday.

The quiet didn't last more than a few moments after I returned to the office.

The screen announced Paem Melarez, and I accepted.

"Good morning, Doctor."

"It is morning," I replied.

"We need to set up your briefing for the Council. Several councilors are still in Contrio. What about fourday at ten in the morning."

Since she wasn't really requesting, I nodded and said, "Ten on fourday. How much detail do you and Councilor Morghan want?"

"I think just your basic concerns and why you were concerned, with as much environmental support as you can provide in a brief statement." She paused. "You might also address what effect the disaster might have on your environmental assessment."

"I doubt it will have much effect. The disaster doesn't appear to have altered the ecology, except in a very limited region. But I can address that."

In my own way . . .

"Since there was a putative takeover by VLE/Syntex, I imagine they aren't pleased," ventured Melarez, clearly wanting a reaction.

"I've already discussed this with Executive Vanslo. She is not totally pleased, but insofar as my assessment mentions the disaster, my report will lay the entire responsibility for the disaster on the secretive practices of Executive Edo and the failure of RDAEX to consult with the environmental specialists of both other multis and of the Survey Service."

"Nothing . . . else?"

I managed a rueful smile. "What else is there? The badlands prove that what happened at Rikova has happened before, tragic as it is. Every world has some natural phenomena that are not entirely predictable and that can prove fatal. It seems to me that the citizens and government of Stittara have, with the regrettable exception of RDAEX, managed to achieve an environmental balance, while providing great benefits to the people of the Unity. I don't see much sense in throwing all that away with unfounded speculations."

"You're not just saying that, are you?"

I shook my head . . . and meant it. "No. You can read what I write after it's done. You can't edit it, though, but you shouldn't have to, not that there won't likely be a few parts that you'd prefer to be otherwise."

She raised her eyebrows.

"You wouldn't want the report of an independent consultant to sound like you wrote it, would you? I will have recommendations for improvements. We consultants always do."

That was the important part of the conversation, although I had to go over a few things several times, and it was almost an hour later before the screen blanked.

Then Aloris was in the office.

"You forgot something."

"What?"

"You never officially returned the Survey van."

I laughed ruefully. "I plead guilty. Do I need to go to the bay?"

"I took care of it. I did want to remind you, though. Did you leave anything in it?"

"Oh . . . yes. My equipment case. I'd thought I'd be going out again."

"I'll have Dermotte make sure someone brings it here, if that's all right."

"That's fine."

Aloris looked at me, intently, but not critically. "The business with Rikova upset you a lot, didn't it?"

I nodded. *Not quite for the reasons you think, I suspect.* I still kept thinking about Kali and wondering what I could have done.

"Some people don't listen, and some don't see." She offered a fleeting smile. "You hear more than people realize, and you see far more. What will you say in your assessment?"

"I'll run it by you, Raasn, and Algeld before I finalize it." I held up a hand. "That's for factual accuracy, not for editorial comments."

"What about grammar?" Her smile held a hint of mischief.

"I'll listen to suggestions on grammar."

When she left I forced myself back to work. I knew the day was going to be long. Most days would be for a while.

58

I'd thought about going out to dinner when I finally shut down my console in the Survey Service office, but I couldn't stand the thought of going out alone, and I certainly didn't want to go out, only to have a Stittaran woman staring at me as if I were some sort of shiny treasure. So I slipped out of the Survey Service and walked quickly the short distance to my guest quarters. I was careful to make sure the door was secure behind me before I headed up the ramp to the study.

I'd just started into the study, when someone spoke.

"It took you long enough. You always work late, don't you?" Standing by the armaglass window was a figure in a black security singlesuit, gray-eyed and black-haired. She offered a tired smile.

I wanted to dash across the room and throw my arms around her. I didn't. I just looked at her, my eyes burning. I swallowed. Finally, I managed to say, "You don't know how . . . how glad . . . I am to see you."

"I hope so."

"I kept looking, praying that you'd listened to me. The days have been long." *Very long.*

"So have our days. We took out the magfield shuttle for a test flight on fiveday, over some of the badlands. We didn't get back . . . until after it happened. Then we were pressed into service—asked, but it amounted to the same thing. By this morning, it was obvious we couldn't do any more. The magfield shuttle now belongs to VLE, I understand, and I'm probably their employee as well . . . No one's pushing." She paused, her eyes still on me. "You look like you need something to drink. There are some Zantos in the cooler. I've already had a few."

"How did you get in?"

"Your security is third-rate. By design, I imagine. We security types know a few things. I let myself in. I hoped you wouldn't mind."

"Not at all."

"Get that Zantos. You need it."

She was probably right. I went to the study cooler and extracted a sealed beaker.

By the time I had it open, Kali had seated herself in one of the two swivels. I took the other, facing her, and looked at her. Even exhausted, she was striking.

Her lips quirked, self-consciously, I thought.

"Why did you listen to me? I thought you wouldn't. You were so cold."

"I've never seen someone so desperate, or who made such an effort. You're not the type for that."

I shook my head. "For some people . . ."

"Stop. You asked. I'm talking."

I stopped.

Abruptly she smiled, but only for an instant. "Marcel—the pilot—thought I was crazy, but I said we needed to take a quick look at the badlands. I had him log it as a test and observation flight. We were barely there when the entire west turned so bright that we couldn't see. The high-res sensors burned out. When we could see . . . RDAEX . . . Rikova . . . they . . . were . . . just . . . just like the badlands."

"I'm sorry. I tried to get Edo not to run the project. He wouldn't listen. He said . . . I was a fifth-rate engineer."

Kali nodded, then took a swallow of the beaker. "He didn't like to listen."

I didn't want to talk about that. "Why were you in my guest quarters at RDAEX? Honestly?"

"Edo ordered me to keep you absolutely safe while you were in Rikova."

"He was worried I'd be killed there, and that would lead to an investigation?"

"He didn't give specifics. He just said that it would be very bad if anything happened to you. I've come to the same conclusion." She looked down for a moment, before she added, "For different reasons. What are you going to do?"

I could sense the tension, and the last thing I wanted to do was to push. So I said, "Finish my assignment. I'll need to be careful, but the report will indicate that Stittara is currently in a very delicate, but balanced position, and that any major change in either its ecological or economic structures would result in very adverse conditions, including the loss of all future anagathic developments and improvements, and that the recent localized disaster is proof of that, and why any new and sustained multi development is unwise.

"There will be a section commending the Planetary Council for its recent action in bifurcating local control and ceding all control of the outland communities to their coordinating council . . ." *Not that they've agreed to that yet, but they will.*

". . . and there will be another section commending the local Survey Service for working with the Planetary Council to ban any future attempts at magnetic field manipulations as a result of the tragedy at Rikova . . ."

"I'm assuming you'll make sure your report is delivered to so many places that it can't be muffled or hidden."

"That was my intent, but I could use your help in that. I'm not terribly versed in such matters."

There was a hint, just a hint, of a smile. "Then what?"

"Well . . . I doubt that I'll be terribly welcome on Bachman." I paused and looked into her gray eyes. "Do you think Teppera could use another ecologist?"

Her smile was the answer I'd hoped for.

I'd like to have felt her arms around me, but that would come. Even a one-eyed man can see some things . . . in any country.

AFTERWORD . . . AND INTRODUCTION

The One-Eyed Man is a novel that was one I never intended to write. Some two years ago, my editor, the esteemed David Hartwell, approached me and several other authors and asked us to write a short story based on a painting by John Jude Palencar. That painting is the one used for the cover of this book. I started writing, and I kept writing, and by the time I got to 15,000 words or so, and was just beginning to get into the story, I realized two things: first, that I was nowhere close to finishing the story, and, that, in fact, it wasn't a story; and second, that I wasn't going to finish the Imager Portfolio book I was also working on by the time I'd promised it to David. So . . . I put aside the story that had become at least the beginning of a novella, if not a novel, and wrote a much shorter story entitled "New World Blues," which was published by Tor.com in February of 2012 as part of the "Palencar Project," consisting of five stories, all based on the painting, by different writers.

But I couldn't get the story I'd started originally out of my mind, and I told David that I was going to take a short break from the Imager Portfolio and write the novel that became *The One-Eyed Man*. He graciously agreed to the project, just hoping, I suspect, that it wouldn't take too long. It didn't, and Tor bought the book and, obviously, published it.

The more I thought about it, however, the more I wanted Tor to include "New World Blues" as an addition to *The One-Eyed Man*, both because both stories came from the same source, and both are very different, even though written by the same person. One features a male protagonist, the other a female. One is written in first person past tense, the other in third person present tense. One takes place in the far future, the other in the near future . . . and there are a few other differences. Thankfully,

Tom Doherty and David Hartwell agreed with me and allowed it to happen, if not without a few glitches along the way.

It all goes to show, in a rather dramatic way, that an author can get more than one inspiration from the same vision . . . and I hope you enjoy, if you haven't already read it, "New World Blues."

L. E. Modesitt, Jr.

NEW WORLD BLUES

She walks into the control center, feeling foolish in the ankle-length purple-gray skirt and the long-sleeved high-collared white blouse.

"Perfect," says Rikard. "You look like all the locals."

His use of the term "locals" bothers her, but, rather than express her irritation, she looks past him toward all the equipment.

Rikard turns to glance at the field projectors, smiles, then looks back at her. "Fantastic, isn't it? Opens the way to new worlds. Maybe parallel realities, or something like it. I leave the details to the techs. We haven't begun to explore all the possibilities. Even I don't know all that it can do."

"You're still having problems, aren't you?" She knows the answer, but has to ask anyway.

"Nothing serious. Like I told you, when we pulled Keisha out, she was a bit freaked. That's all."

A bit freaked? She won't talk to anyone. "I think it was a bit more than that."

"The doctors say nothing's wrong with her. She's always been more emotional than you. That's why I thought you'd be perfect for this. More settled, more mature."

Over the hill is what you mean. She smiles politely, waiting.

He is quiet for a moment before asking, "Look . . . do you want to do this or not?"

What choice is there? She doesn't voice that. "Full benefits for Alora for the next five years, and a year's pay. No matter what." *All that for a liability release.* She has trouble meeting his eyes. She always has, even though he is only a few centimeters taller than she is.

"That's in the contract. Myles witnessed it. There's a lot of money be-hind the project. You don't know how much."

"I can do it."

"You're sure? I don't want to press you."

You already did. Years ago, and I'm still paying for it. "I'm sure." She looks past him once more, rather than into his eyes.

He turns his head and calls, "Stand by for infodump."

"Ready and dropping," comes the reply from one of the techs she doesn't know, not that she knows many of them any longer.

The helmet descends, encasing her head above the ears and above her blond eyebrows, then constricting, not exactly pressuring her, yet she wants to rip it off, push it away. She does not.

"Begin impression," Rikard orders.

She winces as information pours into her, about the inverted structure of Bliss, the evils of the dark sun Dis, the tentacled probes of the sky-dweller that the locals call the Almighty . . . When she is so saturated with the sights, the smells, the understanding of Bliss that she feels she will burst, Rikard looks up from the console and gestures. "That's enough."

The helmet releases its hold and rises away from her. She tosses her head, if briefly, as though the information that has flooded through her has pressed palpable weight upon her, flattening her blond hair, but not disarraying the girl-like pigtails that he'd insisted on.

"Remember. It may look like somewhere on Earth, but it's not."

"I understand that." *And you'd better be ready to pull me out if it goes side-ways or worse.* Again, she does not vocalize that thought. She needs the contract—and the benefits for Alora. As if Rikard ever cared about what his protégé had dumped on her before he'd left TDE . . . and her and Alora.

"Stand by for insertion."

"Insertion"—sounds obscene, but Rikard makes everything sound obscene.

"Hold the feeling . . ."

Hold the feeling of insertion? Even though she knows that is not what even Rikard meant, she wants to laugh.

"You're going to be dealing with something that looks like it could be way beyond you. It could be overpowering if you don't concentrate on what you have to do." Those are Rikard's last words as he and the techs set her on the platform.

The humming from the projectors and the field generators rises until she can hear nothing else. Then . . . the world—everything—twists around her, and she has to swallow to keep the nausea from triumphing.

When she regains her balance and sight, she stands in comparative silence in a world she knows she could not have conceived of, with purple grayness all around her. Stunned and silent—for all the briefings and descriptions that they have provided, for all that the impression helmet has forced into her.

"It's different. It's not that different." Her barely murmured words sound empty against the vastness of the grassy plain before her, an expanse extending to a horizon so far in the distance she can barely discern it.

Not that different? The gloom is overwhelming, a form of hell in purple, even though it is really not that dark. She turns, but finds no sign of the portal through which she had been thrust, no sign of the platform. She takes several steps, but her footsteps only carry her across the browned grass that stretches levelly in all directions. The grass bends under her shoes, but does not crackle or snap, for all its brownness. If anything, her steps release a sighing sound.

The light wind comes from the west. She hadn't expected wind, nor the distant rumbling like thunder.

Finally, she stops. There's no escape, not until she's done what she must . . . but she wonders if that will be enough.

He promised . . . they promised . . .

"We've fixed everything now," Rikard had said.

But had they, really? Yet . . . what else can she do, to keep the benefits? After a long moment, another thought comes to her, not for the first time. *You're too old for this, for being the first with cutting-edge technology, being transported to who knows where.* Despite what Rikard said and promised, she worries about the technology and what it might do to her. She fears the technology that has projected her here, wherever "here" is, close as it is supposed to be, far more than what she knows she will soon face.

She concentrates on the grass, not quite like any she has ever seen, mostly browned, with shoots like Bermuda grass poking up here and there, the brown drowning out the hints of green underneath, and the even fainter hints of purple. She realizes that there is not a tree anywhere in sight, just the endless grass and gray-purple sky, although she *knows* that, somewhere behind her over a low rise, there is a village. That is why she stands where she does, holding the single stem of the flower.

For all the seeming space around her, the purple grayness closes in.

The wind dies away, and for several moments the air barely moves as she stands there, watching, waiting, as the probes in the distance twist in the late afternoon, an afternoon without sun, for the sky-motes diffuse the light of Dis so that only indirect illumination falls across the domain of Bliss.

The sky darkens in the direction she thinks of as west, although she has no way of knowing it is, except that it seems marginally brighter—or did until the intertwined and seething mass of sky-tentacles began to swim through the deep grayness of the atmosphere toward her, seeking the sacrifice she is being sent to prevent . . . if she can . . . with only a single flower.

Who thought of stopping something like that with a flower, a stupid, stupid flower?

But then, apparently, the weapons Keisha had held had had little effect. *But that was what Rikard said, and he isn't the most trustworthy . . .*

Her right hand, the one holding the flower, lifts the long heavy skirt, involuntarily, even as she knows that she can never outrun the onrushing sky-being . . . the Almighty. Still holding the skirt, she half-turns to face the monstrosity that has come to fill the darkening sky. The stillness of the air vanishes, and the wind rises once more. The tentacles near, twisting downward.

She waits, watching . . .

"Say it! Now!"

That command echoes in her ears, as if from a god, and she supposes it amounts to the same thing. She swallows, her eyes taking in the growing roar as the sky-tubes swell, moving toward her, knowing that, despite all Rikard has promised, if she fails, the maid in the village she cannot see, and her daughter, will suffer, though the suffering of her daughter will be longer.

Finally, she speaks, trying to project her voice. "How has it come to this . . . that the dark of the sun reaches out to seize the young and the innocent?"

Her words make no sense, but those are the words necessary to pull the tubes—tentacles, she corrects herself—even more toward her, because they key on sound, especially on the sound of a woman's voice. Her voice. A voice pitched to divert the tentacles of the hell of the sky from one maiden to a woman, young as she feels, who has already seen and experienced too much.

The wind rises even more, and she clutches the long skirt more firmly with the hand that holds the white flower on a single stem. A white flower of youth and purity, not a rose, for a rose promises romantic love, Rikard had said. That died a long time before, before she'd entered the screens, machines, and projection portals that had sent her reeling into a world that she'd never expected to find, so unlike anything she ever experienced, so gray, so purple, so immensely overwhelming.

As the probing tentacles sweep slowly down from the sky, toward her, she stiffens. *The damned thing is real!*

The voice, larger than the sky-tentacle that hovers above her, buffets her with power, so that her very bones feel as though they are instants away from shattering: "YOU WOULD DENY ME MY RIGHT AS YOUR GOD?"

It wasn't supposed to be like this! It wasn't. Her knees shake, and her eyes burn. Why had she ever agreed? *Did you have a choice? Any real options?*

Not after the collapse of TDE.

"Answer him!"

She swallows, then throws her voice at the power beyond the probes. "I deny your right to the innocent. I deny your right to claim divinity if you would take the life of one who has done no evil."

"EVERY WOMAN, EVERY CHILD, HAS DECEIVED. ALL HAVE LIED. NONE ARE INNOCENT, LEAST OF ALL YOU."

She knows that. She does indeed, and her bones are but instants from dissolving under the power that towers over her. *Wasn't that what happened to Keisha?* No . . . she'd just withdrawn into herself, so much that no one could reach her.

She remembers the words, the silly words. "One can be pure, but not innocent."

And innocent, but not pure.

"WORD GAMES, CREATURE OF THE DUST AND DIRT. SHALL WE PLAY OTHER GAMES?"

A tentacle, a thin probing tip snaking out from the solidity of the writhing and entwined sky-tubes, plucks the flower from her hand, and white petals scatter as the tentacle lifts it skyward toward the cloud/sky/monster/god that is so much more than it is supposed to be.

For a moment, she freezes. *That's not supposed to happen.*

"*Keep talking!*" comes the command.

"Games," she improvises. "Are life and death games? Are sacrifices games?"

"*Good. That's good.*"

"YOU WOULD NOT WISH TO DO MORE THAN PLAY GAMES, SMALL CREATURE."

She forces herself to ignore the power that confronts her, on the tingling and the sense of impending action from the sky-being that towers over her. That is not so hard as she thought, because the massive tentacled being is acting like a typical domineering male. "I do not wish to play games. You are the one who called my observations a game. That is merely a way to avoid addressing their validity."

"YOU SPEAK OF TRUTH AND VALIDITY. WHO ARE YOU TO DO SO?"

That question she can answer. Amazingly, she realizes that the answer applies to more than the situation in which she finds herself. "Truth and validity do not depend on who I am, or who you are. They are what they are."

An enormous sound, like a hiccupping rumble, shakes her.

Is that laughter?

"YOU DO NOT BELONG HERE."

"I belong where I belong. You have no right to demand sacrifices. You are powerful enough that you do not need to bully poor women. Or girls." *Young girls especially.*

"WHO ARE YOU TO SAY—"

The wind swirls around her, buffeting her so violently that she can barely keep her feet. She takes two steps back to keep her balance, then forces herself forward, fueled by anger that she did not know she had. "I am who I am! You have no need to prove your power. You're just being sadistic, and sadism doesn't become an Almighty."

After a moment . . . the wind dies away.

"SADISM? SADISM?"

"Don't toy with me. If you want to destroy me, go ahead." As she speaks the words, they are aimed as much at Rikard as at the immense being above her. "But don't pretend that those who are sacrificed are willing. Don't pretend that it's a . . . trade . . . and an exchange . . ."

"TRADE?"

She can sense the puzzlement, but that fades, and the laughter that is like thunder enfolds her.

Shaken though she is, she forces the words out: "Almighty you may be, but no good will ever come from seizing the young and the innocent." She adds, quickly, "Or the pure in heart."

"TRADE? EXCHANGE?" More laughter follows. "YOU AMUSE ME, SMALL CREATURE. I WILL TAKE YOUR TRADE."

Take my trade?

Then the sky collapses into a purple deeper than blackness.

Time passes . . . and she remains suspended . . . somewhere.

From nowhere . . . brilliant light floods around her.

When she can see again, she is standing on the platform.

"She's back! What the hell did you do, Rikard?" The tech's voice contains tones of worry, anger, and relief. "She wasn't supposed to disappear."

Rikard steps toward her, then stops. His mouth opens, then closes, and he frowns, as if something is not quite right. Abruptly, he asks, "Scared you, didn't it, babe?"

"It didn't scare *you* when it pulled the flower from my hand? You said nothing there could touch me."

"You'd be surprised."

"That's bullshit. You still don't know what you're doing. I didn't hear a word from you when that thing was trying to tear me apart with its tornadoes or tentacles or whatever."

"We had a little communication problem—"

"A *little* communication problem?"

"It doesn't matter. I got great shots. We'll have to dub over those last few lines, but the synthesizer will take care of that."

Great shots. That's all you've ever cared about. But there's no sense in saying the obvious. Not anymore.

"Can you believe how real and impressive it all was?" Rikard continues. "Pixar and all the others. They've got nothing compared to this."

"You didn't think it was real?" *It was all too real. You weren't there.*

"Just studio smoke and mirrors, babe."

"The name is Aleisha, Rikard."

"Babe . . ."

She glares at him.

He steps back.

She smiles. "Good-bye, Rikard."

"What? You can't do that. We need more takes."

"You have what you need from me. The contract called for one session. One successful session, with the fee and full health benefits for five years. It was successful. Myles recorded it. Find yourself another insecure former ingénue who's scared to grow up. Or get yourself projected where you sent me."

"I don't believe you're saying this." His eyes turn toward the banks of equipment. "It's just a temporary effect. You'll feel more like yourself tomorrow."

I hope not. "I like feeling the way I do right now."

"You . . ."

"Bitch? No . . . just a woman. A real one, after all these years." She looks at him once more, and their eyes are level. No. Not level. She is actually taller, if only by a few centimeters. *How did that happen?* She pushes the thought away for later examination.

"Your eyes . . ." His words falter. "Your hair . . ."

"Yes?"

"They're purple-gray. That can't happen . . ."

"Good. Other things have changed, too. I'll expect payment tomorrow."

His eyes are the ones that drop before she turns and leaves him amid the welter of screens and projectors that have created a new world in the studio . . . and more. Her steps are no longer tentative as she turns and strides toward the sunshine that lies beyond the door from the studio sensorium, sunshine she'd never really appreciated . . . until now.